THE LONG GOODBYE

Yury Trifonov

The Long Goodbye

Three Novellas

Translated by
  Helen P. Burlingame & Ellendea Proffer

Ardis, Ann Arbor

Yury, Trifonov, *The Long Goodbye*
Introduction, English translations of "Taking Stock"
and "The Long Goodbye" © 1978 by Ardis
English translation of "The Exchange" © 1973 by Ardis
Printed in the United States of America

Third Printing, 1986

Translated from the original Russian

Ardis Publishers
2901 Heatherway
Ann Arbor, Michigan 48104

ISBN 0-88233-282-1

Cover photograph of the Moscow Embankment (1981)
by Sergei Gitman

CONTENTS

INTRODUCTION

Yury Trifonov's early career gave no indication that he would become a controversial writer. Born in Moscow in 1925, he began publishing in 1947, and received a Stalin Prize for his novel *Students* in 1951. He wrote a number of well-received works: a novel, *The Quenching of Thirst* (1963), about the construction of a canal in Turkmenia; four books of short stories; a documentary work, *Reflection of the Fire* (1965); and the scenario for a movie *(The Hockey Players,* 1965). All of this established him as one of the leading Soviet writers. However, a qualitative change in his writing and his career took place when he published "The Exchange" (1969), quickly followed by "Taking Stock" (1970) and "The Long Goodbye" (1971), all in the leading Soviet literary review *Novyi Mir (A New World).* Widely reviewed in the Soviet press, these novellas were seen by some critics as an attack on the intelligentsia as a whole—by one of their own. Other Soviet critics complained that the author was too objective, too alienated from the characters, that he was showing only the ugly side of contemporary life. Maybe this was realism, but it was not, by ordinary definitions, socialist realism.

Trifonov's reputation grew. He continued to write in what readers perceived as a new style—prose which combined relentless and accurate observation with psychological and moral analysis.

In 1973 Trifonov wrote *Impatience*, a historical novel about Andrei Zhelyabov of the revolutionary People's Will party.

In 1975 he published another novella, "Another Life," written in the same key as the trilogy offered here. Trifonov's highly regarded and very controversial novel *The House on the Embankment* appeared in 1976 (the "house" in the title is a Moscow building where many government leaders lived, and the themes of betrayal and careerism are prominent). "The Exchange" was made into a very successful play which is currently enjoying a long run at the Taganka Theater. A new novel entitled

The Old Man is scheduled for publication in 1978.

Like Balzac, Trifonov is interested in the specifics of existence: his characters are so firmly embedded in their social milieu that it is hard to imagine them alone, as individuals, without their relatives, friends and co-workers. What they have for breakfast, where they go on vacations, what they do with their money—all of these things go into the characterization of a Trifonov family. In these novellas the world of the middle-class professional is subjected to the somber, unblinking observation of the moralist. For all his ethnographic description—many readers have been convinced that he knew their families—Trifonov's real interest lies not in excoriating the vices of his class, but rather in examining the precise moment when a man takes a wrong turn in his life, the moment of moral betrayal. This is the real subject of Trifonov's later work, and through all of the catalogue of Moscow life he never loses sight of it for a moment.

"The Exchange," for example, is firmly grounded in Moscow life; and its plot is based on the eternal housing shortage in Russia. What may seem unclear to a non-Russian reader is miserably familiar to Russian readers: due to the chronic shortage of "living space," especially in Moscow, many people try to exchange different rooms for one apartment where an entire family can live together. Otherwise one must wait for years to get into a decent apartment, or spend a great deal of money to buy into a cooperative apartment house as it is being built.

The moral conflict in this novella seems simple at first glance: Dmitriev's aggressive wife Lena sees a chance to get a larger apartment by inviting her mother-in-law, whom she dislikes, to move in with them, exchanging both her old room and theirs for a real apartment. Lena's real motive, of course, is that she knows that her mother-in-law is dying, and will thus leave them with an extra room in the apartment they could not get otherwise—Soviet law allotting space on the basis of how many members there are in the family. From all of this it appears that Dmitriev's wife is the villain of the story. She is indeed unlikable, but in Trifonov's world nothing is quite so black and white.

10

Dmitriev's mother is a cultivated woman who looks down on her daughter-in-law, also an educated person, because she is not of the intelligentsia, that nebulous category of people who find ideas more interesting than money. Lena and her family, the Lukianovs (who in some ways symbolize the crassness of the future, something like the Snopes family in Faulkner), represent those who "know how to live," know which strings to pull to get the things they need and want. Despite his mother's views, Dmitriev himself sees that the Lukianovs have their value: his father-in-law, for example, is the only one able to get the dilapidated Dmitriev dacha fixed, and Lena is aggressive about helping her husband and child, not just herself. Dmitriev sees that his mother is proud of not knowing "how to live"; many of her good deeds are done so that she can think well of herself. Lena's contention that her mother-in-law is something of a hypocrite is not without foundation.

Dmitriev is caught in the middle, torn between the noble ideas of his family and the practical views of his wife, who is ready to do whatever is necessary to help her family—even if it means hurting someone else. Dmitriev's wife is in favor of the exchange because she knows that her daughter and husband will benefit, and is almost blind to the reprehensible aspects of the plan. Dmitriev, however, is aware of everything. Just as he has rationalized so many things in the past, he rationalizes this, even though he knows it to be wrong. Dmitriev wills himself to forget the fact that he will profit from his mother's death, using various arguments to make himself as blind as his wife is by nature.

A less obvious, but equally important theme here is the tension between the intelligentsia and the rising middle class. Dmitriev's mother and sister perceive Lena as coming from a background which we would call bourgeois, and they censure her for her materialism. This conflict is the basis of the funny and terrible fight between Dmitriev's cousin and wife about Picasso, phoniness, and philistinism. The fading of the intelligentsia is also embodied in Dmitriev's relationship with his grandfather, a highly educated former revolutionary whose moral code is

11

uncomfortably rigid. Dmitriev sees this man as irrelevant—to the life he is leading, at any rate. Dmitriev's generation is unheroic, too young for World War II, and too far removed from the events of the Revolution to feel their influence. Like the protagonist of "Taking Stock," Dmitriev is tired; he just wants to live his life comfortably without all the in-fighting between his family and his wife's. In the end he gets what he wants, but at the end we see that he has paid dearly for his decision.

In "Taking Stock" we find another middle-aged man at a moment of crisis. But here there is no decision to be made—they have already been made in the past, and now the protagonist must evaluate the results. The Russian title can also be translated as "Preliminary Conclusions," a title which could also apply to the other novellas in this collection. Gennady's task in this work is to evaluate and come to terms with his life. Again, neither his wife nor his son sees moral problems clearly. Like Dmitriev, he has sinned against himself. A crucial moment for him is when he realizes that he never did what he wanted to in life, but only what was expected. Now, when it is too late, he hears his son refer to his work as rubbish (which it is), he dishonorably reads his son's diary, and the conflict of generations develops into a full-scale war, with his wife on his son's side.

Gennady is suffering both physically and morally from a feeling of suffocation, whose source is indicated early in the story: "Yet if a person doesn't feel the love of those who are close to him, then no matter how intellectually developed he may be, no matter how ideologically sound, spiritually he begins to suffocate. There simply isn't enough air for him to breathe." At the end of the work we return to this theme of suffocation as Gennady has a dream-memory which presages his return to his family.

The spiritual poverty of the entire family is shown most clearly in their treatment of the maid Nyura. This woman's role in their life is that of the good person, who, Gennady says, will "forgive the egotist his faults." When Nyura goes to the hospital the family seems to disintegrate, but they are unwilling to take her back after they learn she is sick—they will not accept the responsibility for a sick woman. Nyura's simple religious faith is contrasted to the faddish way Gennady's wife Rita and her pretentious friend Gartvig talk about old churches, ikons, and the religious philosophers such as Berdiaev. But as Gennady says, neither of them is a true Christian in the way they live their lives. Nyura's ikon, the object of much admiration, plays an important role in the story; but it is also a symbol of something that cannot really be bought and sold—the Christian love she brings to this family of egotists.

Rita, for all her lazy pretensions, does understand her husband, as he himself admits. He rejects her analysis of his character, as a man who is a victim of his environment, who merely adapts and doesn't have the strength to rebel against his way of life; but it strikes the reader as very accurate. When it comes to bribing an examiner to get his son into an institute (a practice which is not at all unusual, since there are so many applicants and so few places), Gennady recognizes that it is wrong, cheating in fact, but the desire to get his son in overrides his conscience. As in "The Exchange," the wife is practical and realistic about what must be done and wastes little time on ethical considerations.

Gennady's justification for his career of hack translation is that it was all for his family. This rings true until one takes a closer look at what this sacrifice has brought his family: his wife is self-indulgent, and his son is a spoiled brat who is unrepentant even when caught in criminal activity.

In Tokhir, where he has gone to get away from this unbearable situation at home, Gennady sees a Turkmenian family that has far less wealth than his, but greater happiness. Atabaly has eleven children, one of them adopted—something Gennady's family, unable to deal with a sick maid, would never have done. Here in this remote village Gennady finds one more good person to forgive his sins—the nurse Valya, Atabaly's adopted child. After this moment of forgiveness he returns, just as he knew he would, to his family.

"The Long Goodbye," the most complex of these works, is

13

ostensibly about a protracted love affair between an actress and a writer, but once again the evaluation of life is central. Here the hero, Rebrov, is a failure, but he is still young; life may give him a chance to be successful—the evaluation is taking place too early.

The moral choices in this story are so tightly bound up with character and psychology that it is impossible to separate them: do these people make the choices they make because of their sense of morality, or because of their essential personalities? —The narrative point of view shifts from the actress to her lover and back again, making easy answers impossible. We can understand both sides.

There are two careers: Lyalya, the actress, becomes a great success during the course of the story; but her lover Rebrov is unable to get anywhere in his career as a script-writer. Lyalya is a woman of instinct, a consoler—not unlike Valya in "Taking Stock," and Dmitriev's mistress Tanya in "The Exchange." But the difference is that she is young and beautiful, and capable of consoling anyone who arouses her sympathy enough. The portrait of a woman who needs to be needed more than she needs to be loved is masterful. For all her living by instinct, Lyalya is capable of decisiveness once things become clear to her—her affair with Smolyanov depends on his being weak, and once she sees that he is actually strong she leaves him, telling him that weak men don't do despicable things or hurt people. Smolyanov tells her that this is not true, something that she will discover herself when her weak lover Rebrov leaves her. Like the heroines of the other works, Lyalya is ready to do almost anything to help those she loves. She goes as far as asking Smolyanov, her lover, to help Rebrov, the lover she lives with.

But it is Rebrov who brings down these things upon himself. He will not commit himself to Lyalya by marrying her, preferring to wonder if she is having affairs. Rebrov takes part in humiliating scenes with Lyalya's lover—to help his career, just as she sleeps with Smolyanov in the first place to help *her* career. By the end a chain of circumstances leads to his decision—she has finally told him about all of her lovers, he is in trouble for not having a certificate of employment, which means he can lose

14

his room and permission to reside in Moscow, and he sees that she will never be free of her mother, whom he hates. But the refrain in "The Long Goodbye" is that life is long, meaning that one cannot judge a life, as Rebrov does so hastily, until all of the evidence is in. The end of the story shows that many of the characters did indeed get the lives they deserved.

All of these novellas share certain submerged themes. One is the changing face of Moscow, Trifonov's main geographical setting. The locations in Trifonov's stories are all real—restaurants, bars, cafes, parks, regions, streets—his work reflects all the physical realia of Moscow life as well as the spiritual atmosphere. In "The Long Goodbye" the lilac bushes on the first page are more than just local color: they foreshadow the theme of the destruction of nature (Lyalya's father and his garden), which is to be supplanted by much needed apartment houses. Beauty, as so often in Trifonov's world, gives way to practicality.

In "The Exchange" this process is exemplified by the new cement embankment which borders Dmitriev's beloved river, and the new buildings which have changed the face of the countryside into something not necessarily worse, but very different.

The novellas are joined by a somber style, deliberately prosaic in its imagery. Trifonov's heroes do not reach for poetic metaphors when they are happy or sad, they use concepts and objects from their everyday life, their ordinariness is emphasized. Which is the point about these people—they are not better or worse than others, they are ordinary, but they have serious problems, enjoy moments of euphoria when they feel that life has promise; in a word they are *human,* a category that comes up several times in the stories, when it is affirmed that whether a man is an intellectual or not is not important—but whether he has humanity is. In these works humanity is often denied, but the characters have their memories of happier times, usually in their childhood, and these memories can be both consoling and saddening.

Trifonov's works give us the texture of everyday life, with the interlocking worlds of family, career and conscience; but he provides no solutions, makes no conclusions that can be used. He is content to state the problem clearly, and show us that there are no heroes, no real villains. This is the gray blur of adult moral compromise, not the black-and-white photograph of childhood conceptions of honor. But Trifonov's characters long for the consoling sharpness and clarity of those early beliefs.

Ellendea Proffer

THE EXCHANGE

In July Dmitriev's mother, Ksenya Fyodorovna, became seriously ill. They took her to Botkin hospital where she spent twelve days suspecting the worst. In September they operated on her and the worst was confirmed, but Ksenya Fyodorovna, thinking that she had ulcers, felt better, began to walk soon after, and in October was sent home weighing more and firmly convinced that things were on the mend. It was at that moment, after Ksenya Fyodorovna came back from the hospital, that Dmitriev's wife began the business about an exchange: she had decided to move in as quickly as possible with her mother-in-law, who lived alone in a nice twenty-by-sixteen room on Profsoyuznaya Street.

Dmitriev himself had raised the idea of moving in with his mother many times. But that had been long ago, at a time when the relationship between Lena and Ksenya Fyodorovna had not yet assumed the form of such hardened and solid enemity that it had now, after the fourteen years of Dmitriev's marriage. He had always run up against Lena's firm opposition, and the idea had come up less and less over the years. And then only in moments of irritation. It had turned into a portable and comfortable *handy object*, a weapon in minor family skirmishes. When Dmitriev wanted to get Lena for something, accuse her of egotism or callousness, he would say: "And that's why you don't want to live with my mother." When Lena felt the need to taunt or to hit a sore spot, she would say: "And that's why I can't live with your mother, and never will, because you are the very image of her, and one of you is enough for me."

At one time all this had bothered and tormented Dmitriev. On account of his mother he had harsh words with his wife, driven to extreme animosity because of some malicious witticisms made by Lena; on account of his wife he let himself in for a painful "clearing of the air" with his mother, after which his mother didn't talk to him for several days. He stubbornly tried to throw them together, reconcile them, settle them together at the dacha; and once he bought them both vouchers for the Riga seashore, but nothing ever really came of it.

Some barrier stood between the two women, and they could not overcome it. Why it was like that he did not understand, although he'd often thought it over in the past. Why two intelligent women, respected by all— Ksenya Fyodorovna was the senior bibliographer of a major academic library; Lena translated English technical texts, she was an excellent translator, everyone said, and she had even taken part in the compilation of some special textbook of translation—why had two good women who dearly loved Dmitriev, also a good person, and his daughter Natashka, stubbornly cultivated mutual hostility which had grown harder with the years?

He was upset, amazed, racked his brains, but then he got used to it. He got used to it because he saw that the same thing had happened to all of them—they had all gotten used to it. And he soothed himself with the truism that there is nothing wiser or more valuable in life than peace, and that one must protect it with all one's strength. Therefore, when Lena suddenly began to talk of an exchange with the Markusheviches—it was late in the evening, supper had long been over, Natashka was sleeping—Dmitriev was frightened. Who were the Markusheviches? Where did she find them? A two-room apartment on Malaya Gruzinskaya. He understood Lena's simple secret thought, and his comprehension made fear pierce his heart and he grew pale, then bent over, unable to raise his eyes to Lena.

Since he was silent Lena continued: they would be sure to like his mother's room on Profsoyuznaya; the location would suit them because Markushevich's wife worked somewhere near Kaluga Gate, and they would probably have to add a premium for their own room. Otherwise you wouldn't get them interested. One could of course try to exchange their room for something more worthwhile, that would be a third exchange, nothing so terrible about that. Must act energetically. Do something every day.The best thing would be to find an agent. Lucy knew an agent, a little old man, very nice. True, he couldn't give anybody his address or telephone number; he would just suddenly appear out of nowhere, such a conspirator, but he was supposed to make an appearance at Lucy's soon, she owed him money. That's the rule: never give them money in advance. . . .

As she was talking, Lena made the bed. There was no way he could look her in the eye: now he wanted to, but Lena stood first sideways, then with her back to him, but when she turned and he glanced straight into her eyes, which were nearsighted, with enlarged pupils from the evening's reading, he saw—resolution. She'd probably been preparing for this conversation for a long time, maybe since the first day she'd found out about his mother's illness. Then it had come to her. And while he, terror-stricken, was running around to the doctors, calling the hospitals, making arrangements, being miserable—she had been considering, mulling it over. And now she'd found some Markusheviches. Strange that he felt neither anger nor pain now. Only something flashed by—about the ruthlessness of life. Lena wasn't the thing, she was a part of this life, a part of the ruthlessness of life. Besides, does one get angry at a person who is deprived, for example, of an ear for music? Lena had always been distinguished by a certain spiritual—no, not deafness, that would be too strong—by a certain spiritual imprecision, and this characteristic was further intensified whenever another even stronger quality of Lena's came into action: the ability to get her own way.

He latched on to what was handy: why did they need the agent if the apartment on Gruzinskaya had already been found? The agent's needed if it's necessary to change rooms. And to speed the whole process in general. She wouldn't pay him a kopek until she had the order in her hand. It doesn't cost so much, a hundred rubles, one hundred fifty maximum. That's how it is! She assessed his gloominess in her own way. Such a refined soul, such a little psychologist. He said that it would be better if she'd waited until he'd started this conversation himself, and if he didn't that meant it wasn't necessary, not at all, that this wasn't the time to think about it.

"Vitya, I understand. Forgive me," said Lena with an effort. "But. . . ." (He saw that it was hard for her, but that she was going to get it all out.) "In the first place, you began this conversation already didn't you? You started it many times. Secondly, this is necessary for all of us, most of all for your mama. Vitka, my dearest, I understand you, I feel for you like no one else does, and I say: it's necessary! Believe me. . . ."

She embraced him. Her arms hugged him tighter
and tighter. He knew: this sudden love was genuine. But
he felt irritated and he moved her away by the elbow.

"You shouldn't have started it now," he repeated
sullenly.

"Well, all right, so I'm sorry. But I'm not worrying
about myself, really, really. . . ."

"Be quiet!" he almost screamed in a whisper.

Lena went over to the turkish mattress and continued making the bed in silence. Out of the chest at the
head of the mattress she took the thick, plaid tablecloth
which usually served as a pad under the sheets, but
which was occasionally used for its proper purpose on
the dinner table; on top of the tablecloth she lay the
sheet which had puffed up and lay not too evenly, so
Lena bent over, stretching her arms out in front, to
reach the far side of the mattress—her face reddened
from it, and her belly hung down very low and seemed
very big to Dmitriev,—she smoothed out the tucked under corners (when Dmitriev made the bed he never
smoothed the corners), then she threw two pillows on
the bed in the direction of the chest, one of which had a
case that was less fresh than the other; that pillow belonged to Dmitriev. Taking the two blankets out of the
chest and putting them on the mattress, Lena said in a
trembling voice:

"It's as if you're blaming me for tactlessness, but
word of honor, Vitya, I was really thinking of all of us. .. .
Of Natashka's future. . . ."

"Oh, how can you!"

"What?"

"How can you talk about it at all right now? How
can your tongue work? That's what amazes me." He felt
that the irritation was going to grow and break out into
the open. "For God's sake, you've got some kind of

spiritual defect in you. A kind of underdevelopment of feelings. Something, forgive me, *subhuman*. How can you? The thing is that *my mother* is sick and not yours, right? And if I were in your place. . . ."

"Talk softer."

"In your place I would never first. . . ."

"Softer!" She waved her hand.

They both listened. No, everything was quiet. Their daughter was sleeping behind the screen in the corner. Behind the screen there stood a little desk at which she did her homework each evening. Dmitriev had played carpenter and had hung a bookshelf over the desk, and put in electricity for the lamp—he had made a special little room behind the screen, the "cell" as it was called in the family. Dmitriev and Lena slept on a wide turkish mattress of Czechoslovakian make, luckily purchased some three years before, which was an object of envy among their acquaintances. The mattress was by the window, separated from the "cell" by a carved oak buffet which had come to Lena from her grandmother, —a ridiculous thing which Dmitriev had many times suggested selling, Lena also not being against the idea, but his mother-in-law had objected. Vera Lazarevna lived not far away, two buildings from them and came to Lena's almost daily on the pretext of "helping Natashenka" and "making things easier for Lenusha," but in actual fact with one sole aim—to unforgivably interfere in someone else's life.

In the evening when they were lying on their Czech bed—which turned out to be not very durable, quickly getting rickety and squeaking with every move—Dmitriev and Lena always listened a long time for sounds from the "cell," trying to figure out whether their daughter had gone to sleep or not. Dmitriev would call, checking, in an undertone: "Natash! Hey, Natash!" Lena would go up on tiptoe and look through the crack in the screen. Some six years earlier they'd gotten a nurse who had slept on a cot here in the room. Their neighbors, the Fandeevs, had objected to her sleeping in the hall. The old lady suffered from insomnia and was possessed of the keenest hearing; all night long she would mutter something, groan, and listen: a mouse was scratching, a cockroach was running, someone had forgotten to turn off the faucet in the kitchen. When the old lady left, something like a honeymoon began for the Dmitrievs.

"She was doing physics till eleven again," said Lena in a whisper. "We'd better get someone. . . . Antonina Alexeevna has a good tutor."

The fact that Lena had shifted the conversation to Natashka's problems and had submitted to all of Dmitriev's insults, let them pass by—which was not like her—signified that she definitely wanted to make up and bring things to an end. But Dmitriev didn't want to make up yet. On the contrary, his irritation grew stronger because he suddenly realized what was Lena's chief tactlessness: she talked as if everything were predetermined, and as if it were also clear to him, Dmitriev, that it was all predetermined, and that they understood each other without words. She talked as if there were no hope. She had no right to talk that way!

It was impossible to explain all that. Dmitriev jumped up from the chair with a jerk, grabbed his pyjamas and towel, and without saying a word practically ran out of the room.

When he returned after a few minutes, the bed was ready. There was a smell of perfume in the room. Lena was combing her hair, in an unbuttoned robe, standing in front of the mirror, and her face expressed indifference, and if you please, even well-screened resentment. But the smell of the perfume gave her away. This was a

25

call, an invitation to a truce. Holding the flap of her robe with one hand at her chin and the other at her stomach, Lena, with a quick businesslike step, and not looking at Dmitriev, walked past him into the hall. He again remembered the lines of poetry he'd been muttering all the time these past days: "O Lord, how perfect are thy deeds. . . ." Closing his eyes, he sat down on the mattress. "He thought, the sick man. . . ." He sat like that for several seconds. He knew that in the depths of her soul Lena was satisfied, the most difficult thing had been done: she'd spoken. Now to lick the wound, it wasn't a wound though, but a small scratch which it had been absolutely necessary to make. Like an internal injection. Hold on to the cotton pad. A little painful, but it's so that later everything will be fine. It's very important that *later everything be fine*. But he didn't shout, didn't stamp his feet, he just blurted out a few irritated words, went into the bathroom, washed up, brushed his teeth, and now he would sleep. He lay down in his place near the wall and turned his face toward the wallpaper.

Lena came back quickly, clicked the lock on the door, swished her robe, rustled a fresh nightshirt and turned out the light. No matter how hard she tried to move lightly and be as weightless as possible, the mattress began to crack under her weight, and Lena, on account of this crackling, started to whisper with something like drollness, even:

"Oh God, what a nightmare. . . ."

Dmitriev was silent, he didn't move. Some time went by and then Lena put her hand on his shoulder. It wasn't a caress, but a friendly gesture, perhaps an honest acknowledgement of her guilt even and a plea to turn over. But Dmitriev didn't stir. He wanted to get to sleep right away. With a vindictive feeling he was enjoying the fact that he was sinking into immobility, into sleep, that he didn't have time to forgive, explain in whispers, turn over, show generosity, he could only punish for insensitivity. Lena's hands began to stroke his shoulder gently. The final surrender! With shy touches she was sorry for him, she begged forgiveness, made excuses for her callousness of soul, for which one could find justification, however, and appealed to him for wisdom, goodness, and that he find in himself the strength to pity her. But he didn't give in. Something unsettled in him kept him from turning and embracing her with his right arm. Through the approaching drowsiness he saw the porch of the wooden house, Ksenya Fyodorovna standing on its highest step, wiping her hands with a crumpled waffle-weave towel, her slow look directly into Dmitriev's eyes, past the light brown head, past the blue silk dress, he heard the muffled voice: "Sonny, have you given it careful thought?" Muffled because it was from far away, from an icy May day when everyone was very young, Valka went to swim, Dmitriev lifted a 70 pound weight, Tolya rushed off on his "Wanderer" for wine, wrecked a fence on the way, police came, and later, on the cold veranda with the light of a lantern wavering in its glass, Lena cried, was miserable, embraced him, whispering that never, no one, it was for life, that it didn't matter at all. In the morning his mama got on the motorbike, hung a little milk can on the wheel and went to the station for milk and bread. Her misfortune: to say exactly whatever came into her head. "Sonny, have you given it careful thought?" What could be more ineffectual than that absurd and pitiful phrase? He couldn't think about anything. May with its icy winds tearing off the tender barely born leaf,—that's what they were breathing then. Mama was studying English, just so, for herself, so she could read novels, and Dmitriev was getting ready for graduate school, so they both

studied with Irina Evgenievna together and suddenly
stopped when Lena appeared. Mama tapped the veranda
glass with the umbrella tip—it wasn't late, about seven in
the evening: "Get up! Irina Evgenievna's waiting!"
Dmitriev and Lena, hiding under a roomy quilt, pretended they were sleeping. The umbrella tapped indeci-
sively two more times, then cones crunched under shoes
—mama left in silence. She didn't want to study English
any more herself, and had lost interest in the detective
novels. Once she heard Lena, laughing, mimic her pro-
nunciation. And from that, from that country veranda
with the small-paned windows, began what it was now
impossible to set right.

Lena's hand displayed persistence. In fourteen
years that hand had also changed—before it had been so
light, so cool. Now, when her arm lay on Dmitriev's
shoulder, it pressed down with no little weight. Dmitriev,
without saying a word, turned over on his left side, embraced Lena with his right arm and moved her closer,
sleepily suggesting to himself that he had the right to,
he'd already been asleep, had had dreams, and maybe he
was even still asleep. At any rate, he said nothing, his
eyes were closed, just like those of a man who was really
sleeping, and during the moments when Lena really
wanted him to say something to her, he continued to be
silent. Only later, when he'd really fallen into a deep
sleep, at about two in the morning, he mumbled something inarticulate in his sleep.

Dmitriev had turned thirty-seven in August. Sometimes it seemed to him that everything was still ahead.

Such surges of optimism came in the mornings
when he suddenly awoke fresh, with inadvertent cheerfulness—the weather had a lot to do with it—and, opening the vent window he would begin to wave his arms in
rhythm and bend and unbend at the waist. Lena and

Natashka got up fifteen minutes earlier. Sometimes Vera Lazarevna would appear early in the morning to walk Natashka to school. Lying with closed eyes he heard how the women shuffled, moved around, exchanging words in a loud whisper, clattering the dishes, and Natashka would grumble: "Kasha again! Don't you have any imagination?" Lena reacted with her usual morning wrath: "I'll show you imagination! Sit as you should!" And his mother-in-law would growl: "If other children had what you have. . . ." That was a deliberate lie. Other children had the same things and a lot more even. But on those mornings when Dmitriev awoke, gripped by that incomprehensible optimism, nothing irritated him. From the height of the fifth floor he looked out onto the square with the fountain, the street, the column holding the trolley schedule, and a dense crowd around it, and further on, the park, the multi-storied building against the horizon and sky. On a balcony of the next building, very close by, twenty meters away, a young unpretty woman in glasses appeared in a short, carelessly tied houserobe. She squatted down and did something with the flowers which stood in pots on the balcony. She touched and stroked them, checked under their leaves, lifted up some of the leaves and sniffed them. Because she was squatting, her robe opened and her large bluish-white knees became visible. The womman's face was the same shade as her knees, bluish-white. Dmitriev watched the woman bending and unbending at the waist. He watched her from behind the curtain. Why was inconceivable—he didn't like the woman at all,—but the secret observation of her inspired him. He thought about how all was not yet lost, thirty-seven—that's not forty-seven or fifty-seven and that he still could achieve something.

Pattering down the hall in turmoil, accompanied

by Lena's cries: "Did you take the bags? Don't run across the street! Attention, children, attention! . . ."— Natashka and the Fandeevs' Valya, a sixth-grader, left the house at 8:30. The staircase shook under their jumps. Dmitriev slipped into the bathroom, locked himself in, and in three minutes a light knock interrupted his meditations: "Viktor Georgievich, today's Friday, I've got to do laundry, I implore you—hurry up!" This was the voice of their neighbor Iraida Vasilievna, whom Dmitriev's mother-in-law didn't speak to, and with whom Lena maintained chilly relations, but Dmitriev tried to be proper, protecting his objectivity and independence. "All right!" he answered through the noise of the water. "It will be done!" He shaved quickly, turning on the water heater and rinsing the brush under the hot stream, then washed his face over the old yellowed washstand with the broken corner—it was supposed to have been replaced a long time ago, but the Fandeevs didn't give a damn what kind of washstand they washed up over, and Iraida Vasilievna begrudged the money— and soon, gently whistling, with the papers in his hand which he had had time to get from the box on his way to the bathroom, he returned to his room. The table was still loaded down with the dishes after Natashka's and Lena's recent meal. Now Lena was hurrying: she left ten minutes after Natashka, and his mother-in-law took upon herself the morning service of Dmitriev. Dmitriev didn't especially like it, and his mother-in-law waited on him with little enthusiasm—it was her little matutinal sacrifice, one of those inconspicuous feats which make up the entire life of the toilers who have the self-abnegating nature of Vera Lazarevna.

Sometimes, Dmitriev noticed, Lena just tried to act like she didn't have any time, but in fact she would have had plenty of time to make his breakfast, but she

purposely relinquished this mission to her mother: as if
in order that Dmitriev be in some way, if only for a min-
ite, obliged to his mother-in-law. She was even capable
of whispering in his ear in passing: "Don't forget to
thank Mama!" He thanked. He saw through all these
subterfuges in the regulation of family ties and, depend-
ing on his mood, would either pay no attention to them
or quietly get irritated. Vera Lazarevna always responded
in her usual way to quiet irritation—with the tenderest
malice. "My, how quickly Viktor Georgievich freed the
bathroom! What a hero!" she said smiling, and wiped a
place on the oilcloth for Dmitriev with a damp kitchen
towel. "Which means our neighbor asked you to. . . ."
Lena cut her off decisively: "What does our neighbor
have to do with it? Vitya always washed up fast." "That's
what I say, a hero, a military style hero. . . ."

On that early October morning there was dark blue
beyond the window, the room filled with the light reflected by the yellow bricks of the building opposite,
and the voice of Vera Lazarevna was not audible. At
first glance, having barely unglued his eyes, Dmitriev unconsciously—because of the sun and the light—felt joy,
but in the succeeding second remembered everything,
the blue darkened, and beyond the window a relentless-
ly clear and cold autumn day had set in. Before breakfast neither he nor Lena said anything to each other.
But after Dmitriev had called up Ksenya Fydorovna—
he called his sister Lora's at Pavlinovo, where his mother
now lived, and Ksenya Fyodorovna related in a cheerful
voice that late yesterday Isidor Markovich had come by,
found her condition fine, pressure normal, suggested
that she go into some Moscow area sanitorium by the
first snow, and then followed questions about Natashka's affairs, how were her eyes, had she improved on her
C in physics, were they giving her raw ground carrots,

the most effective food for eyes, and what was happening about Dmitriev's business trip,—he experienced sudden relief, just like an ebbing of pain from his head. All at once it seemed like maybe everything would come out all right. Mistakes can happen, the most incredible mistakes. And with this insignificant joy and the minute of hope, he returned to the room after the telephone conversation—Natashka had already run off, and Lena was hurriedly sewing something, half dressed in a skirt and a black slip with naked shoulders—and passing Lena he lightly slapped her on the bottom and asked amiably:

"Well, how's your mood?"

Lena abruptly answered drily that she was in a bad mood.

"What's the matter with you?" said Dmitriev, affected by the fact that his amiability was answered so drily. "What's it from?"

"As far as I'm concerned, I've got more than enough reason. Mama's sick."

"Your mother?"

"You think only yours can get sick?"

"And what does Vera Lazarevna have?"

"Something very serious with her head. She's been on her back for two days, I didn't tell you yesterday, but this morning she called. . . . Some kind of brain spasms."

Lena finished the sewing, put on the blouse and went over to the mirror, looking at herself superciliously. The blouse was short-sleeved, which wasn't attractive— Lena's arms were heavy at the top, her summer tan had gone, her skin had little white bumps showing through. She should only wear long sleeves, but it would be imprudent to tell her that. Such restraint—not a sound about her proposal of yesterday! Maybe she was ashamed, but more likely there was a certain arrogance in it: she had been accused of tactlessness, of a lack of delicacy, those very traits, as it happened, which she found most unpleasant in other people, and she had swallowed this injustice, had even asked forgiveness and somehow abased herself. But now she'd be silent. Why always be in the wrong? No, now you're already asking—you won't get anything out of me. Besides that, her mind's not on that, she's worried about her mother's illness (Dmitriev was ready to bet a hundred rubles to one that his mother-in-law had her usual migraine. Lord, he'd learned to read that book till he was blind!). But Dmitriev didn't have enough time to enjoy that last thought full of smugness before Lena stunned him. Completely prosaically, peacefully, she said:

"Vitka, I'm asking you—talk with Ksenya Fydorovna today. Just warn her that the Markusheviches may look at her room, and the key has to be gotten."

After a silence he asked:

"When do they want to look at it?"

"Tomorrow or the day after, I don't know exactly. They'll call. And if you go to Pavlinovo today, don't forget, get the key from Ksenya Fyodorovna. Put the kefir in the refrigerator please, and the bread in the bag. Or else it'll dry out from you leaving it out all the time. Bye!"

Waving in a friendly way, she went out into the hall. She slammed the entrance door. The elevator buzzed. Dmitriev wanted to say something, some vaguely anxious thought had dawned on the threshold of his consciousness, but didn't quite dawn, and he, having made two steps after Lena, stood in the hall and then returned to his room.

There was not a trace left of the early dark blue. When Dmitriev went out to the trolley stop there was a fine drizzling rain, and it was cold. The last few days

had been rainy. Isidor Markovich was right, of course—
he's an experienced surgeon, an old hand, they invite
him for consultations in other cities—his mother must
be taken out of the city, but not during such influenza
dampness. But if he advises a Moscow area sanatorium
that means he doesn't see any immediate threats—that's
it! And for the second time this morning Dmitriev
timidly thought that maybe everything might turn out
all right. They would make the exchange, receive a good
separate apartment, would live together. And the sooner
the exchange was made the better. For his mother's well-
being. Her dream would be realized. It would be psycho-
therapy, the healing of the soul! No, Lena was sometimes very wise, intuitively, womanlike—suddenly it
dawns on her. Really, that's possibly the only brilliant
means of saving a life. When the surgeons are powerless
other forces come into play. . . . And that's what not
one professor could do, no one, no one, no one!

Dmitriev could think of nothing else standing at
the trolley stop in the drizzling rain, and after, making
his way inside the car, among the wet raincoats, briefcases which knocked against the knees, the coats smell-
ing of damp cloth, and he thought about it running
down the dirty subway steps, slippery from the rainy
slop brought in by thousands of feet, and standing in
the short line for the cashier to change a fifteen-kopek
piece into five kopek pieces, and again running down
even further along the steps, and throwing the five into
the slot of the turnstile, and walking along the platform
ahead with quick steps so as to get a seat in the fourth
car, which would stop exactly opposite the archway
leading to the stairway to the connecting passage. And
he was still thinking about it when the shuffling crowd
carried him along the long hall where the air was stifling,
and it always smelled of damp alabaster, and when he

stood on the escalator, squeezed himself into the car, looked over the passengers, the hats, the briefcases, bits of newspapers, plastic envelopes, the flabby morning faces, the old man with the household bags on his knees, going to shop in the city center—any one of these people might be the saving variant. Dmitriev was ready to shout at the whole car: "Who wants a good room, twenty by sixteen? . . ."

At a quarter of nine he got out of the cave and onto the square, at five of he crossed the alley and, overtaking the cars standing by the entrance, entered a door beside which hung, under glass, the black plaque "IOGA."

On this day they were deciding the question of the business trip to Golishmanovo in the Tumenskaya district. The trip had already been confirmed back in July, and none other than Dmitriev was supposed to go. Pumps were his domain. He alone was responsible for this business, and he alone really understood it, unless you counted Snitkin. Dmitriev had started a conversation with him the week before, but Pasha Snitkin, a cunningly wise operator (in the office they called him "Pasha Snitkin-with-the-world-on-a-string," because he had never done one single job on his own, but was always able to fix it so that everybody helped him), said that unfortunately he absolutely could not go—also due to family reasons. He was probably lying. But it was his right. Who wanted to go in bad weather, in the cold, to Siberia? It was awkward for Snitkin to refuse, and he burst out with irritation: "Didn't you say that your mother had gotten better?"

Dmitriev didn't start to explain, he just waved his hand: "How, better. . . ." And Pasha had always inquired about Ksenya Fyodorovna's health so attentively, gave the phone numbers of doctors, in general expressed his sympathy, and Dmitriev was for some reason completely sure of his agreeing. But why? Why should he be? Now it was clear that this sureness had been stupidity. No, they're not pretending when they express sympathy and ask with moving carefulness: "Well, how are things at home?"—it's just that that sympathy and carefulness have sizes, like shoes or hats do. You should never stretch them too much. Pasha Snitkin was transferring his daughter to a music school, and the only one who could deal with this troublesome business was he himself—not the mother or the grandmother. And if he went away in October on a business trip, the music school would definitely fall through for this year, which would cause a deep trauma in the girl and the moral destruction of the whole Snitkin family. But my God, can one really compare them—a person is dying and a girl is entering music school? Yes, yes. One can. They are hats of approximately the same size—if a stranger is dying and your very own daughter is entering music school.

The director was waiting for Dmitriev at 10:30. Cocking his head to one side and looking Dmitriev in the eye with a sort of shy wonder, the director said:

"So what are we going to do?"

Dmitriev answered:

"I don't know. I can't go."

The director was silent, touched the skin of his cheeks and chin with his wide white fingers, as if checking to see whether he'd shaved well. His glance became thoughtful. He was really thinking very hard about something and even began to hum a tune unconsciously.

"Mm yes. . . . What to do, Viktor Georgievich? Um? And if it's for about ten days?"

"No!" said Dmitriev abruptly.

He understood that he could stand like a rock and they couldn't budge him. Only he shouldn't explain anything. And the director, after thinking it over, said the name of Tyagusov, a young fellow who'd finished the institute a year ago, and who, it seemed to Dmitriev, was a complete booby.

Not long ago Dmitriev would have started to protest, but now he suddenly felt that all this had no significance. So why not Tyagusov?

"Of course," he said. "I'll spend two days with him and explain everything to him. He'll manage. Bright guy."

After he got back to his room on the first floor, Dmitriev worked an hour and a half without unbending, preparing   the documentation for Golishmanovo. Even though earlier he had not believed that they'd make him go, the thought of the trip had weighed upon him, had been just one more little weight added to all his other burdens, and now when they'd removed the weight he experienced a relief. And he thought hopefully that today, maybe, would be a lucky day. Like all people who are oppressed by fate, Dmitriev cultivated superstition: he noticed that there were lucky days when success followed success, and on those days you had to try to deal with as many things as possible, and there were bad luck days when not a damn thing went right no matter what you did. It looked like a lucky day had begun. Now to borrow money. Lora had asked that he bring at least fifty rubles. On Isidor Markovich alone they'd spent—four times fifteen—sixty rubles this month. But where to get it? Such a crummy thing—borrowing money. But he had to do it today, since today was already a lucky day.

Dmitriev began to think of who he could hit for it. Almost everyone, he remembered, had complained that they had no money, that they'd used it up over the summer. Sashka Prutyov had gotten a cooperative apartment, and was totally in debt himself. Vasily Gerasimovich, the colonel, partner in games of preference and fishing trips, Dmitriev's constant rescuer, had suffered a tragedy —he'd left his wife, and it was awkward to ask him. Dmitriev's friends at the CSM (Club of the Semi-Married), to whom Dmitriev turned in moments of despair when he fought with Lena, were people of little resources—their fortune consisted of someone with a car, with a motorboat, a camping tent, bottles of French cognac or White Horse whiskey, bought by chance in Stoleshnikov and kept for any special occasions of the house on the bookcase—and they could lend you no more than twenty-five rubles, forty at the most, but he had to get no less than 150. Of course there was the ultimate possibility, the limit of torment: to ask his mother-in-law. But that would mean going downhill. Dmitriev could have forced himself to take it, but Lena took such things very badly. She knew her mother better. All at once it came to Dmitriev—it was the same thought which had vaguely come before and which now suddenly cut through—how was he going to tell his mother about the exchange? After all, she knew perfectly well how Lena had felt about the idea and now for some reason she had suggested moving in together. Why?

Just considering all this made Dmitriev sweat. He went out into the hall where there was a telephone on a stand, and called Lena at work. Usually it was not easy to get through to her. But he was lucky (a lucky day!); Lena happened to be in the office and she picked up the phone. Dmitriev hurriedly got out his doubts in one long confused sentence. Lena was silent, then asked:

"That means what, that you don't want to tell her?"

"I don't know how. Couldn't I suggest it to her— you understand?"

After another silence Lena told him to call her again

in five minutes on another phone where she could speak more freely. He called. Now Lena talked loudly and energetically:

"Say it like this: say that you really want it, but I'm against it. But you insisted. That is despite me, clear? Then it'll be natural and your Mama won't think anything of it. Put it all on me. Only don't overdo it—just some hints. . . ." Unexpectedly she began to talk in a changed, flattering voice: "Excuse me please, just a minute, I'm leaving now! So everything's clear? Yes, Vitya, Vitya! Talk to somebody there in your office who's accomplished an exchange successfully, you hear? Bye!"

What Lena said was, of course, correct and cunning, but anguish gripped Dmitriev's heart. He was incapable of going back into the room right away, and he wandered along the empty hall for a few minutes.

He didn't go find anyone or find anything out before lunch, but after lunch he went up to the third floor to the economists. As soon as he opened the door, Tanya saw him and came out. Not asking anything, she looked at him fearfully.

"No, nothing bad," he said. "Maybe even a bit better. Tan, do you know, has anyone here made an exchange? Exchange apartments?"

"I don't know. I think Zherekhov. Why?"

"I need some advice. We have to make an exchange, urgently, you understand?"

"You?"

"Yes."

"You want . . ." her face reddened, "to move in with Ksenya Fyodorovna?"

"Yes, yes! It's very important. It'd take a long time to explain, but it's absolutely essential now."

Tanya was silent, hanging her head. There was a lot of gray in the hair which had fallen over her face. She was thirty-four, still a young woman, but in the last year she'd gotten to look a lot older. Maybe she was sick? She'd gotten very thin: the slender neck stuck out of the collar, in the thin face only the eyes—good ones— shone out of the millet-colored freckled pallor in their habitual fright. This fright was over him, for him. Tanya would have been a better wife for him, probably. It had begun three years ago, had lasted one summer and had ended itself when Lena and Natashka came back from Odessa. No, it hadn't ended, it had dragged out in a thin thread, it broke for months, for half a year. He knew that if one were reasoning sensibly, she would have been a better wife for him, probably. But you know, sensibly, sensibly. . . . Tanya had a son, Alec, and a husband with the strange last name of Toft. He had never seen him. He knew the husband loved Tanya very much, had for-given her everything, but after that summer three years ago, she could no longer live with him, and they separated. He was very sorry that it turned out that way, that the husband became unhappy, quit his job, left Moscow, and Tanya also became an unhappy person, but there was nothing to be done about it. Tanya wanted to leave IOGA, so that she wouldn't have to see Dmitriev every day, but getting away turned out to be very difficult. Then she gradually became reconciled to it all, and learned how to meet Dmitriev calmly and talk with him as an old friend.

Dmitriev suddenly perceived what she was now thinking: this means—that's all, never.

"Well, what can I do?" he said. "You see, this would be a kind of a chance, a hope. It was my mother's dream to live with me."

"What are you talking about? She probably wasn't dreaming about this."

"I know."

"Oy, Vitya. . . . Well, have a talk with your Zhere-khov. I'll call him now. Only he's a big mouth, keep it in mind." Suddenly she asked: "Do you need any money?"

"Money? No."

"Vitya, take it. I know what being sick means. My aunt was sick for eight months. I set aside 200 rubles for a summer coat, but as you see, the summer's over and I didn't buy anything. So I can give it to you till spring with absolutely no trouble."

"No, I don't need money. I have some."—He frowned. What else: borrow from Tanya! Suddenly he laughed. "Really, what a strange sort of day! One after another. . . ."

"We'll go to my place after work, and I'll give it to you, all right?"

After a silence he said:

"I'm lying, I haven't got any money. But I don't want to take it from you."

"Fool!" She lightly slapped him on the cheek.

Dmitriev saw that she was glad. As they walked to the doors of the room Zherekhov was in she even took him by the hand.

"Leonid Grigorievich!" called Tanya. "Can I see you for a minute?"

Zherekhov, a small, affable old man, completely bald, with white, even false teeth, very kindly and willingly began to recount how he'd made an exchange. Dmitriev didn't know Zherekhov very well, but he'd noticed that the latter was kindly and affable with everyone—probably because, finding himself at pitiful retirement age, the old man was fighting for his place and wanted to have the best relations with everyone. Because of this, he told the story at unbearable length and detail. Someone went abroad, someone was in a desperate situation. Someone had to pay. None of this was right. But then Zherekhov exclaimed suddenly, and his light blue old man's eyes widened from the flood of benevolence:

"Yes. That's who you should see—Neviadomsky! You know Alexei Kirillovich? From KB-3? It was the same story with him, he also made an exchange because . . ." Zherekhov lowered his voice, "the mother-in-law was hopelessly sick. She had an excellent room, almost twenty-five meters, somewhere in the city center. But Alexei Kirillovich lived at Usachevka. Everything had to be done very fast. And he succeeded, succeeded terrifically! He'll tell you. True, he had connections at the local Housing Commission. So in a word, like this: he succeeded in making the exchange, made repairs in the apartment—he was forced to do it by ZHEK* —he moved his mother-in-law, got the personal account, and the old lady died three days later. Can you imagine? The poor guy, he went through a lot that winter, I remember. Almost took to his bed. But now he's got an exceptional apartment, like a general's, deluxe. Loggias, two balconies, lots of all kinds of secondary cubic capacity. He's even growing tomatoes on one balcony. You drop by, drop by, he'll tell you. Wish you success!"

Zherekhov benevolently nodded, moving back, backed into the room with his seat. While he talked, Tanya stood beside Dmitriev and inconspicuously held onto the end of his little finger.

"Go downstairs at 6:00, and we'll go immediately," she said in a whisper.

"You understand I've got to go to Lora's in Pavlinovo. My mother's expecting me. She's at Lora's now."

He knew he was dealing a blow to certain hopes of Tanya's, but it was better to say it right away.

"Well, all right. Do what you have to." Everything immediately left an impression on her face: it darkened.

"No, and besides that. . . ."

"I understand! You really think I do not understand! I won't hold you for a second. You'll get the money and then—be off."

Nodding, she walked quickly away from down the hall. Not long ago, a year back, her tall figure was something exciting for Dmitriev. Especially at those times when she was walking away from him, and he looked after her. But now there was nothing left. It had all disappeared somewhere. Now she was just a tall, thin, very long-legged woman with hennaed hair in a bun on a slender neck. And still, every time he looked at her, he thought that she would have been the best wife for him.

Dmitriev returned to the office and sat over the papers for half an hour—his thoughts turned around the same thing: mother, Lora, Tanya, Lena, money, the exchange—and he saw that he'd have to leave work earlier, or else he'd get to Pavlinovo much too late. Tanya lived in an out-of-the-way place, a worse one you couldn't imagine—Nagatina. Dmitriev went to the little office of Varvara Alexeevna, his superior, and said that if it was possible, he'd like to leave today at five. Varvara Alexeevna agreed. Everyone in the office knew what was going on in Dmitriev's life and acted with understanding: every week, once or twice he could leave work early. Once even, it was such a sin, he ran to the Moskva department store under this pretext and bought a uniform for Natashka. Dmitriev went up to the third floor again and told Tanya to ask to leave at five. Then he went in to see Neviadomsky, also on the third floor.

Dmitriev decided to go to Neviadomsky after hesitation. Relations between them were cool—through the fault of a friend of Dmitriev's who, it's true, hadn't worked at IOGA for half a year. Neviadomsky had had some kind of scandal with this friend at the local trade union committee. And they stopped speaking to each other. And when Neviadomsky met Dmitriev in the company of this friend, he—at the same time—didn't say hello to Dmitriev either, and out of solidarity with his friend Dmitriev acted exactly the same way. However, when Dmitriev and Neviadomsky met alone, they greeted each other totally correctly, although a little coolly, and even exchanged two or three phrases. All this was utter nonsense, and Dmitriev decided to ignore it and go. And if Neviadomsky really has connections, will he share them?

Neviadomsky, a lean dark-haired man with a blackish-reddish curly little beard, raised his eyebrows in surprise when Dmitriev, stopping by the office, asked him for "a brief audience." At a small table in the corner there were two smashing away at chess, moving the figures about very quickly. Neviadomsky was standing by them, watching. The favorite occupation of the "Kabetrishniki" [project researchers] was chess, they played blitzes, five-minute ones, but among the "Kabedvashniki" ["projdevelopers"] ping pong flourished. The battles took place during the lunch hour, but sometimes they borrowed from work time, especially towards the end of the day. Neviadomsky, after saying: "Just a minute! I'll come!"—continued to observe the players. The latter were slamming the figures around the board with the speed of automatons, until one cried, "Oh damn!"—and with a blow of the hand tipped over his king. Neviadomsky began to laugh maliciously and said:

"At that Balda said by way of reproach: if only you hadn't been so interested, priest, in the cheap price!"*

After this, he moved toward the door with the expression of the malicious smile on his face, but, meeting Dmitriev with a glance, he wiped off his smile and again his brows rose in surprise. Dmitriev began to clumsily put forward his request, or more precisely, to hint at his request, cloaked in hurried and inconsequential mumblings. Neviadomsky had to guess it: he was being requested to share his advice on how to behave in circumstances familiar to him. But Neviadomsky didn't guess. His blackish-red curly beard rose higher, his eyes looked more and more coldly, and it seemed to Dmitriev, more haughtily.

"Excuse me, I don't exactly understand. . . ."

"I'll explain right now. The problem is that the causes prompting you and me. . . . In a word, we're in the same situation. . . ."

"What have you got in mind?"

"What do I have in mind?" Dmitriev felt how his neck and cheeks were flooding with color. "This is what I've got in mind: I've got to make an exchange as quick as possible too. So I wanted to consult you about how it's done, generally? What do you start with?"

"What do you start with? What do you mean—what do you start with? With the exchange bureau, of course. You pay three rubles and make an announcement in the bulletin."

"But you understand, that if a person is seriously ill, very seriously, and every hour is dear. . . ."

"But you can't start any other way. With the exchange bureau, I don't know any other routes,"—Neviadomsky stuck a thumb into his nostril and began with concentration to extricate something from there. Obviously he was tensely trying to figure out whether it was worth it or not to let Dmitriev in on his connections. He decided: not worth it. "I didn't have any other ways." —Suddenly Neviadomsky chuckled. "You know, you've reminded me of the stupidest story! When I was a student, my father died. Two or three months went by. . . ." —While he related this, he continued to extract something from his nose with his thumb.—"And a neighbor unexpectedly dropped by, an unknown man from another building entrance, and he says, 'My father died and I heard yours died not long ago too. So I've come to make your acquaintance and to ask you to share your experience.' What kind of experience? What? How? I, of course, courteously got rid of him."

"And I've got to take this too," thought Dmitriev, feeling numb. Turn around, leave, but he continued to stand there looking at the blackish-red beard. "There are tomatoes on the mother-in-law's grave. It's all the same. And this too. And there will be more of it."

"If you want it, I've got the number of one Adam Vikentievich, an agent. I could look for it. . . ."

Overcoming his numbness, Dmitriev turned and walked away down the hall. At five he and Tanya went out onto the square and there—rare occurrence!—an empty taxi turned up. Dmitriev whistled, they jumped in and drove off. The alleyway was filled with a crowd moving in one direction toward the subway. The factory shift had just ended. The taxi moved slowly. People glanced into the cab, someone knocked on the roof with their palms. When they passed the subway and escaped onto the avenue, Dmitriev began to talk about Neviadomsky with malice.

Tanya took him by the hand.

"Why are you being so malicious? Don't do it. Stop it. . . ."

He felt how her calm and joy poured into him. Tanya, smiling, said:

"We are all very different. We are people. . . . My cousin's little son died. This was incredible grief, of course, suffering, and along with it a kind of passionate love for children, especially sick ones. She was sorry for them all, tried to help as much as she could. And I have an acquaintance whose son also died, of leukemia. That woman hated everyone so much, she wished everyone dead. She gets happy when she reads in the paper that someone's died. . . ."

Tanya moved closer. She put her head on his shoulder and asked:

"Is it all right? It doesn't bother you?"

"It's all right," he said.

They traveled by way of the outskirts, through the new areas. Dmitriev told about Ksenya Fyodorovna. Tanya asked about her with compassion—this was sincere, Dmitriev knew, she felt sympathy for this mother. And Ksenya liked Tanya; they'd seen each other once or twice in summer, in Pavlinovo. . . . Tanya held his hand in hers, sometimes she softly tickled his palm with her finger. Tanya's caresses were always somehow school-girlish.

Without taking his hand away, he gave the details about his mother: what Zurin said, what Isidor Markovich said. Tanya began to laugh:

"Oh, what a rotten dame! She lends money and pesters with tendernesses, right?" She suddenly knocked against his cheek with her nose, snuggled. "Forgive me, Vitya. . . . I can't. . . ."

He stroked her head. For a long time they rode in silence. They went past the Varshavka.

"Well, what's the matter?" he asked.

"Nothing. I can't. . . ."

"What? . . ."

"I'm sorry for you, for your mother. . . . And for myself at the same time."

Dmitriev didn't know what to say. He simply stroked her head and nothing more. She began to sniffle, he felt dampness on his cheek. Then she moved away from him, turned and began to look out the window.

Finally the embankment flashed by, they took the bus route past some factories, along a solitary, long stone fence. Near a beer stand there was a dense black crowd of men. Some of them, singly and in pairs, with mugs in their hands, stood at some distance. Dmitriev felt like his throat was dry—he wanted to have a drop of something, to get his spirits up. "I should ask," he thought, "Tanyushka used to have stuff around. Anything would do."

The new sixteen-story building stood on the edge of a field. The road went in a detour, around the field.

"Right here," said Tanya.

Dmitriev remembered quite well that it was here. The last time he'd been here was about a year ago.

"Will you have the car wait?" asked Tanya.

Of course he would have it wait. But his usual timidity—he saw that Tanya passionately didn't want that—made him answer:

"Yes, O.K., let it go. I'll find one there."

"Of course, you will!" said Tanya.

They went up to the eleventh floor. Tanya lived alone with her son in a large three-room apartment. That poor devil Toft had constructed this ship in the coop building, and had just enough time to move into it when everything happened. At that time Alec was at camp, Toft was somewhere in Dagestan—he was a mining engineer—and Tanya lived alone in empty unfurnished rooms which smelled of paint. There were newspapers on the floors. In one room there stood a huge couch, and nothing more. And Dmitriev's love was inseparable from the smell of paint and fresh oak floors, as yet not polished once. Barefoot, he slapped over the newspapers into the kitchen and drank water from the tap. Tanya knew a lot of poetry and liked to recite it in a soft voice, almost whispering it. He was astonished at her memory. He himself didn't remember, if you please, even one poem by heart—just occasional quatrains. "You are still alive, my old one, and so am I, greetings to you by and by." But Tanya could whisper for hours. She had something like twenty notebooks, from her student days, where in the large clear handwriting of the A student was copied the poetry of Marina Tsvetaeva, Pasternak, Mandelstam, Blok. And so in moments of rest, or when there was nothing to talk about and it got sad, she would begin to whisper: "O Lord, how perfect are thy deeds, thought the sick man. . . ." Or: "Take your palm from my breast, we are wires under current."

Sometimes when he got tired of the monotonous murmuring of her lips he would say: "All right my love, take a rest. Why is it that your Khizhnyak doesn't say hello to Alexeevna Varvara?" After a pause she answered sadly: "I don't know." All of her resentments were momentary. Even when she could have taken offense for good reason. For some reason he was convinced that she would never fall out of love with him. That summer he lived in a state he had never experienced before: love toward himself. An incredible state! One could have defined it as the condition of usual bliss, for its strength consisted in its constancy, in the fact that it lasted weeks, months, and continued to exist even when everything was already over.

But Dmitriev didn't think about why: why did he have this bliss? Why him exactly—a not very young, heavy man with an unhealthy color in his face, with the eternal smell of tobacco in his mouth? It seemed to him that there was nothing puzzling about it. That was how it should be. Generally, it seemed to him that he had just joined in that normal, truly human condition, which people should—and would in time—always be in. Tanya, the opposite, lived in constant fear and a kind of passionate bewilderment. Embracing, she would whisper, like she did the poetry: "Lord, for what? For what?"

She didn't ask for anything or about anything and he didn't promise anything. No, not once did he promise. Why should he promise if he definitely knew that no matter what she would never fall out of love with him. It simply came into his head that she would have been the best wife for him.

New furniture had appeared in the rooms—in one room there was a breakfront and a round polished table, in the other—a half-empty bookcase. But as before, the parquet hadn't been polished and it looked sort of dirty. Alec came out of the room, noticeably taller, a pale freckled creature of about eleven, with glasses on his thin little nose. He held his head slightly tilted back and to the side, perhaps because he wasn't well, or perhaps he could see through his glasses better. This set of the head and his small compressed mouth gave the boy an expression of superciliousness.

"Mom, I'm going to Andrusha's. We're going to trade stamps," he announced in a squeaky voice, and rushed through the hall to the door.

"Wait! Why didn't you say hello to Viktor Georgievich?"

"Hi," Alec threw over his shoulder, not looking.

Hurrying, he unlocked the lock and jumped out, slamming the door.

"Be back no later than eight!" Tanya yelled to the closed door. "The young man doesn't shine in the manners department."

"He's probably forgotten me. I haven't been here for a long time, after all."

"And even if a stranger came? Doesn't one have to say hello?" Tanya went into the big room, opened the side door of the breakfront and said: "He didn't forget you."

She took a rolled newspaper from under a pile of clean linen, unrolled it and gave Dmitriev a bundle of money. He stuck it in his pocket.

"Well go," said Tanya. "You haven't got any time."

He suddenly pulled out a chair and sat down at the polished table.

"I'll sit a bit. I'm sort of tired." He took off his hat, touched his head with his palm. "My head aches."

"Do you want to eat? Could I get you anything?"

"Is there anything to drink?"

"No. . . . Wait!" Her eyes shone with happiness— "It seems to me that there's a bottle of cognac left some-place, which we didn't finish drinking. Remember, when you were here last time? I'll take a look right now!"

She ran into the kitchen and brought in the bottle a minute later. There were about a hundred grams left at the bottom.

"Now we'll have some hors d'oeuvres. One minute!"

"What do we need hors d'oeuvres for?"

"Just a second, just a second!" Again she rushed headlong into the kitchen.

Dmitriev got up and went to the balcony doors. There was a wonderful view from the eleventh floor of the stretching field, the river, and the village of Kolomensk, visible by the cupolas of its cathedral. Dmitriev thought of how he could move into this three-room apartment tomorrow, see the river and the village in the morning and evening, breathe in the field, go to work on the bus to Serpukhovka, from there on the subway, it wouldn't take so long. Tanya carried in sprats, two tomatoes, bread and butter on a crystal dish, and wine glasses. He poured half a glass for himself, and the rest for Tanya. She always drank very little, she got drunk quickly.

"What are we drinking to?" asked Tanya.

"To everything going well with you."

"Well, all right! No. Not to that. Everything will go well with me anyway. Let it be to everything going well for you. All right?"

"O.K." It was all the same to him. He'd already drunk up, and was chewing on a tomato. He grunted, "The tomatoes are from the grave of Neviadomsky's mother-in-law, aren't they?"

"Because, Vitya," she said, "it's not likely that things are ever going to go well with you. But suppose, all of a sudden, they do? To that then."

He didn't think to ask what she had in mind. Superfluous conversations. After the cognac it got warm and he ate the tomato with pleasure and looked at Tanya, who was hunched over in a reverie, leaning on the table with her elbows, and gazing at the corner of the room.

"Don't slouch!" he said, paternally slapping her lightly on the shoulder blades.

Tanya straightened up, continuing to gaze at the corner of the room. On her stupefied face, with the red spots due to the cognac on her cheekbones, suffering was distinctly visible. For one moment he pitied her very sharply, but then he remembered that somewhere far and near, through all of Moscow, on the shore of this same river, his mother was waiting for him, his mother who was experiencing the sufferings of death, but Tanya's sufferings belonged to life, so—what was there to pity her for? There is nothing in the world except life and death. And everything that is dependent on the first is happiness, and everything dependent on the second is the destruction of happiness. And there is nothing else in this world. Dmitriev got up with a jerk, with sudden haste, exactly as if someone strong had grabbed him and pulled him by the arms, and saying, "Bye! I've got to run!"—bolting with quick steps down the hall to the door. Tanya didn't have time to say anything to him. Maybe she didn't want to say anything to him.

Dmitriev went by bus to the subway—there was of course no taxi around at all—transferred twice and came out on the last station of the new line. A fine snow was drizzling down. Moscow was far away, its large buildings were white against the horizon, but here was a field torn up by foundation pits, pipes lay on the damp earth, and a line of people waiting for the trolley stood by a pillar on the highway. The sky was full of clouds, arranged in layers—on the top something motionless and dark-violet was thickening, lower light, crumbly clouds were moving, and lower still there flew on the wind a kind of white cloudy rag, like wisps of steam.

About forty years earlier, when Dmitriev's father, Georgy Alexeevich, had built a house in the settlement of Red Partisan, this place, Pavlinovo, was considered a dacha-resort area. It was a resort, and until the revolution they came here by horse train from the point. In the 30s the boy Vitya, a mediocre student, but diligent bike-rider, fisherman, and player of "501," devourer of Sienkiewicz, and Gustav Emar, came here on summer days, on the squeaky old bus which left at hourly intervals from the cobblestoned Zvenigorodskaya Square. It was always stuffy in the bus, the windows didn't open, it smelled of sackcloth. Waste lands flashed by, orchards, little villages, an ice-house, a radar field, a school with a white brick fence, a church on a knoll, and suddenly the arc of the mill-pond opened and the heart of the boy Vitya tightened. The road from the bus-stop went through pines, past unpainted fences black from rain, past dachas hidden by lilac bushes, sweetbriar, and elder with their small-paned verandas showing through the green. You had to walk for a long time along this road, the tar ended, then there was the dusty high road, to the right there was a pine grove on a little hill with a spacious clearing—in the 1920s a plane crashed there and the grove had burned down—and to the left the fences continued to stretch out. Behind one of the fences, in no way camouflaged by young bushes, there stuck up a log building of two stories and a basement, not at all similar to a resort house, but more to a trading post somewhere in the forests of Canada, or to a hacienda in the Argentine savannah.

The building had been built by a cooperative, with the resounding name of "Red Partisan."* Georgy Alexeevich wasn't a red partisan; his brother Vasily Alexeevich, who was a red partisan and an OGPU* worker, and the owner of a two-seater sports Opel, had invited him into the co-op. The third brother, Nikolai Aleexevich lived in a little dacha nearby. Also a red partisan, he'd worked for Vneshtorg* and had lived for months at a time in both Japan and China. From China he'd brought the game of mah-jongg—a mahogany box containing 144 stones (bamboo on one side, ivory on the other) placed on four little pull-out shelves. At first the grownups gambled for money at mah-jongg, then when the grownups got bored or couldn't take it anymore, the game passed into the possession of Nikolai Alexeevich's children, and the whole crowd of the Pavlinovo children's commune. Nothing was left of those evenings with the phonograph music ("The weary sun tenderly said farewell to the sea"), with the loud conversation of the two deaf red partisans who were always arguing about something on the second floor, the clack of the Chinese stones on Nikolai Alexeevich's veranda. It's not just people who disappear in this world, it turns out, but whole nests, tribes with their environment, conversation, games and music. They disappear completely, so that it's impossible to find their traces. Although Lora was still left there in Pavlinovo. But besides Lora there was no one—not one single person. Of the brothers, the eldest, Georgy Alexeevich, died first. Instantaneous death from a stroke—they called it apoplectic stroke then—occurred right on the street one sweltering day.

Dmitriev remembered his father poorly, in fragments. He remembered a dark mustache and beard, gold-rimmed glasses and a very thin, yellowish tussore shirt, soft to the touch, with flakes of tobacco, a fat belly under it, and constant chuckling at all people and things. Georgy Alexeevich was a railway engineer, but his whole life he'd dreamed of leaving that job and taking up writing humorous stories. It seemed to him that this was his calling. He always went walking with a notebook in his pocket. Dmitriev recalled how quickly and easily his father composed funny stories—they went walking in the evening to the garden to water the cucumbers and saw how Marya Petrovna, the aunt of one of the red partisans, was trying to knock down her nephew Petka's ball from a pine tree. First she threw a stick, the stick got stuck; then she began throwing her shoe, and the shoe got stuck too. While they were walking to the garden, his father told Dmitriev a killingly funny fairy tale about how Marya Petrovna hurled her other shoe at the pine, then her blouse, belt, skirt; all this hung on the pine, and Marya Petrovna, naked, sat beneath, and then Uncle Matvei came running and started to throw his shoes and pants. A few days later his father came from town and brought with him a journal in which his story "The Ball" was printed. Georgy Alexeevich made fun of his brothers, whom he considered none too bright, and as a joke called them "woodchoppers."

He himself had graduated from the university, but his brothers hadn't even managed to finish high school: the civil war was raging, tossing one to the Caucasus, the other to the Far East. Sometimes talking with his mother he marvelled: "And how is it they send such woodchoppers abroad when they can't say two words in any other language?" He further reproached his brothers for greed, for the fat life, mocked their Chinese stones, their eternal fussing with the car on days off—he always added a "Zh" when referring to his brother's Opel.* And in Kozlov, aunts related to them went hungry, dying one after another; their nephews had no means of getting to Moscow. Only Georgy Alexeevich helped as much as he could.

Sometimes the brothers would have quarrels —for months at a time he didn't visit them, or they him. His mother considered that Marianka and Raika were to blame for the quarrels and all the brothers' subsequent misfortunes, since they were contaminated by the petty-bourgeois mentality, but things didn't come out so sweet for them later on either, the poor things.

Generally, his father had been the best one, more intelligent than his brothers, a rather good man. But unlucky. He died early, didn't have time for anything. What was preserved of his notebooks, in which there had been so much that was funny, wonderful? They had gone, just like all the rest. Also gone was Raika, Nikolai Alexeevich's wife, who'd been a beauty at one time, and the main fashion plate of the Red Partisan settlement. Gone too was the sandy slope on the river bank where in the mornings, very early, there used to be excellent fishing. After eight o'clock the fish left here—the river passenger boat began to rumble between its moorage and the village, and the motorboats came out. You had to cross over to the other bank, there were quiet inlets

there where fish hid, but sitting in the hot sun was unbearable—there was neither tree nor bush, just a naked
meadow with stiff weeds.

Dmitriev jumped off the bus one stop before he
should have. He wanted to walk to the place where his
favorite slope had once been. He knew that now there
was a concrete embankment there, but the fishermen
still came anyway. New fishermen, from five-story
buildings that were beyond the bridge. It was very convenient for them—they came by trolley.

He went down the stone steps—everything was
done solidly, as in an real city park—at the bottom he
walked along the concrete slabs which rose about six
feet above the water level. You could walk along the
river like that almost to the house itself. There was no
crawling along the shore now. Every spring chunks of
the bank crumbled down, sometimes along with the
benches and pines.

The sky sparkled on the wet slabs, and not one
fool was around. But no, there was somebody sitting
there, off in the distance, and Dmitriev slowly walked
up to him. The water seemed very clean, undirtied, but
dark—autumn water. Dmitriev stopped behind the fisherman's back and began to watch the float. He watched
for about five minutes, with increasing anxiety and a
kind of sudden weakening of the spirit, thinking of how
hard it was going to be to say it. Impossibly hard. With
Lora too. What could he do? They would all understand, of course. However, it was possible his mother
wouldn't—if one were to present the matter exactly as
Lena had suggested, his mother was very unsophisti-
cated—but Lora would understand it all right away.
Lora was sharp, perspicacious, and didn't like Lena at
all. If his mother, despite all of Lena's unfriendliness,
had all the same made peace with her, had learned to

Yury Trifonov

pay no attention to this, forgive that, Lora's dislike had grown stronger over the years—on their mother's account. She once said: "I don't know what kind of person one would have to be to treat our mother without respect." True, friends loved Ksenya Fyodorovna, her colleagues respected her, her apartment neighbors and Pavlinovo dacha neighbors esteemed her because she was benevolent, compliant, ready to come to your aid and sympathize. But Lora didn't understand. . . . Oh, she didn't understand, she didn't! Lora hadn't learned to look beyond what lay on the surface. Her thoughts never bent. They always stuck out and pricked like horsehair from a poorly sewn jacket. How could one not understand that you don't dislike people just because of their vices and you don't love them on account of their virtues!

It was all the truth, the real truth: his mother was constantly surrounded by people in whose fates she constantly *took part.* For months some elderly people she barely knew had been living in her room, friends of Georgy Alexeevich's, and some old ladies who were even more decrepit, his grandfather's friends, and some casual acquaintances from vacation houses who wanted to get to the Moscow doctors, or provincial boys and girls, children of distant relatives who had come to Moscow to enter institutes. His mother tried to help all of them absolutely disinterestedly. But why should she help? All ties had been lost long ago, and she was worn out. But still—with shelter, advice, sympathy. She liked to help unselfishly. But to put it more exactly: she liked to help in such a way that God forbid any profit should come out of it. But the profit was this: in doing good deeds to be always conscious of being a good person. And Lena, sensing his mother's slightest weakness, said about her in moments of irritation: the hypocrite. And

58

he would fly into a rage. He would yell: "Who's a hypocrite? My mother's a hypocrite? How dare you say that. . . ." And—it would begin, get rolling. . . . Neither his mother nor Lora knew how he got violent on their account. Of course they guessed about a little of it, they'd been witnesses to some of it, but in full strength —with the whole battery of insults, Natashka's crying, the no talking for days on end, and at times even a little physical violence—this was unknown to them. They considered, Lora with especial firmness, that he'd quietly betrayed them. His sister one day said: "Vitka, how Lukanized you've gotten." Lukianov was the last name of Lena's family.

Dmitriev suddenly decided that he had to think through something important, definitive. He didn't have the strength to walk to the house, so he delayed it a minute.

He sat down not far from the fisherman, on a wooden box—also someone's fishing gear—which had lain there a long time, getting brown and damp all the way through. As soon as Dmitriev sat down, the box began to list slightly, and he had to lean very firmly on his legs to maintain balance. On the opposite bank, where there had been a meadow at one time, they were now making a huge beach, with cabanas, reclining chairs, and refreshment stands. The recliners were piled into two stacks, but for some reason two recliners still stood right by the water, making a spot of dim blue on the dark gray sand. Everything on that shore was dark gray, the color of cement. Beyond the beach a young grove of birches curled, planed some ten years before, and beyond the grove towered the mountains of housing in foggy white blocks, along which stood two especially tall towers. Everything on that shore had changed. Everything had "gotten Lukanized." Every year something changed in its details, but when fourteen years passed, it turned out that everything got Lukanized,—finally and hopelessly. But perhaps that wasn't so bad? And if it happens to everything—even the shore, the river and the grass—does that mean maybe that it's natural and that's how it should be?

The first year Dmitriev and Lena had to live in Pavlinovo. Lora, then still without Felix, was living in Moscow with Ksenya Fyodorovna, the dacha was empty and Dmitriev and Lena wanted to be alone. But they didn't succeed even so. The dacha apartment at Pavlinovo had been unoccupied for a long time. The roof was leaking, the porch was rotting. The cesspool gave the most trouble—from time to time it overflowed, especially when it rained, and an unbearable stench spread throughout the entire area, blending with the smells of the lilac, linden and phlox. The inhabitants had come to terms with this blending of smells long ago, and it had become an inevitable characteristic of dacha life for them, and with it the thought that it was pointless to repair the cesspool, that it cost incredible money, which none of them had. The village had grown poor, the inhabitants were not what they had been,—the former owners had died off, they'd all faded from sight, and their heirs, widows and children, lived a rather hard and not at all dacha-like life. Petka, for example, Marya Petrovna's nephew and the son of a Red professor,* worked as a simple truck driver at the lumber center. And Valerka, Vasily Alexeevich's son, Dmitriev's cousin, got mixed up with trash and became a thief and landed somewhere in the camps. Some of the heirs, wearied by the dacha extortions and looking ahead—the city was coming—sold their shares, and totally strange people appeared in the village, who had no relation at all to red partisans. And only the birches and lindens, planted forty years ago by Dmitriev's father, a passionate gardener, grew into a mighty forest, choked with foliage, and proudly gave notice to the passersby who looked through the fence that everything in the village was bubbling, flowering, thriving as it should.

And then suddenly Ivan Vasilievich Lukianov, Lena's father, who came by to call on the youngsters and to be a guest for a day, said that Kalugin, the master plumber who had fixed the pipes in the settlement for thirty years, was a swindler and a no-good, and that he, along with the sewer man, who was invited regularly to come pump out the pool, was robbing the red partisans and that it was possible to make the repair of the pool quickly and cheaply. Everyone was stunned. They collected the money. Ivan Vasilievich brought the workers, and in a week the repair was finished. The heirs of the red partisans were very afraid that Kalugin, offended, would quit the settlement, leaving them at the mercy of fate, but Ivan Vasilievich managed it so that the old sot didn't get offended by anyone, but was even filled with respect for Ivan Vasilievich and began to call him "Vasilich."*

Lora, with her way of speaking right out, remarked that this was probably because Kalugin had sensed a kindred spirit in Ivan Vasilievich. Where had he gotten the workers? Where had he gotten the bricks? The cement? Obviously underhanded. Through not exactly noble means. His mother was indignant: "How do you know? What right have you to so rudely slander someone without proof?"

"Well, I don't know, I don't know, Mama. Maybe I'm mistaken." Lora smiled mysteriously. "It was just a supposition. We'll see."

And Ivan Vasilievich really was a powerful man.

His main strength was his connections, old acquaintances. In six months he had put in a phone at the Pavlinovo dacha. Ivan Vasilievich was a tanner by profession, he had begun with a master in the town of Kirsanov, but already by 1926, when they made him director of a factory—a crummy little factory requisitioned from a Nepman* in Marian Grove,—he was moving along the administrative line. When Dmitriev first met him, Ivan Vasilievich was already quite old and heavy. He suffered from short breath, had had a stroke and all kinds of misfortunes, such as being fired, party penalties, reinstatement, appointment with a raise, the slanders and libels of various rats who aimed to ruin him, but as he himself admitted, "As far as those moments were concerned, I was saved by only one thing: I was on the alert."

The habit of constant distrust and unremitting vigilance had insinuated itself so much into his nature that Ivan Vasilievich displayed it about the slightest trifles. For example, he'd ask Dmitriev before going to bed at night: "Viktor, did you put the hook on the door?"— "Yes," replies Dmitriev, and listens as his father-in-law slips down the hall to the door to check. (This was later, when they lived in the Lukianov's apartment in the city.) Sometimes Dmitriev got so fed up that he'd yell: "Ivan Vasilievich, why are you asking, for God's sake?"— "Don't you get insulted, precious man, I do it automatically, with no evil intention." It was amusing that the same distrust for each and every one—first of all for the people living side by side—infected Vera Lazarevna too. Sometimes she'd telephone from somewhere and ask for Lena. Dmitriev would say that Lena wasn't home. In a little while there'd be another call, and Vera Lazarevna, changing her voice, would ask for Lena. And what comic scenes would occur sometimes in the evening when his mother and father-in-law would feed each other medicine!

"What did you give me, Ivan?" "I gave you what you asked for."–"But what, what exactly? Say it!"–"You asked for diabasol, it seems to me."–"You gave me diabasol?"–"Yes."–"Sure?"–"Why are you bringing up this question?"–"Tell you what: please bring me the container you got it out of,–for some reason it seems to me that this isn't diabasol. . . ."

There was a time when such conversations heard in passing soothed Dmitriev, as did his father-in-law's manner of expressing himself: "In this respect, Ksenya Fyodorovna, I'll give you the following axiom." Or like this: "I was never my father's technical executor, and I demanded the analogical from Lena." They laughed silently about it. His mother called her new relative "The learned neighbor"–behind his back of course–and considered that he was not a bad man, in some ways nice even, although of course not at all of the intelligentsia, unfortunately. Both he and Vera Lazarevna were of a different breed–those "who know how to live." Well, it wasn't so bad to get related to people of a different breed. Inject fresh blood. Profit from someone else's abilities. Those who don't know how to live begin to oppress each other after living together–by their noble inability itself, which they are secretly proud of.

After all, could Dmitriev or Ksenya Fyodorovna, or anyone else of the Dmitriev relatives, have organized and carried through the repair of the dacha as dashingly as Ivan Vasilievich? He'd lent the money for all that music too. Dmitriev and Lena went away their first summer, to the south. When they returned in August the old little rooms were unrecognizable–the floors shone, the frames and the doors sparkled with white, the wallpapers in all of the rooms were expensive, with embossed patterns, green in one room, blue in another, brick-red in the third. True, the old furniture, which was wretched, and had been bought by Georgy Alexeevich a long time ago, was still there. It hadn't been noticeable before, but now it struck the eye: what shabbiness! Some iron bedsprings on a sawhorse instead of a bed, tables and cupboards of painted plywood, a wicker trestle bed, another wicker object, impossibly dilapidated. Lena of course took all of the junk out of the large room with the green wallpaper where the young couple was installed, and bought a few very simple but new things: a mattress with legs, a student desk, two chairs, a lamp, some curtains, and brought in two rugs from the other rooms—old rugs, but very good ones, Bokharas, one for the wall, the other for the floor. Dmitriev was amazed: how wonderfully things had changed! Even his mother said: "See what taste Lena has! We lived here so long and not once did we think of hanging that rug on the wall. No, she's got very fine taste!"

Vera Lazarevna and Ivan Vasilievich settled into the middle room temporarily, the blue one, for August and September, to help Lenochka, who was already expecting a child. Ksenya Fyodorovna lived in the small brick-red room and now and then Lora stayed over. It was then that Lora's tedious romance with Felix began, and she wasn't interested in the dacha. Their grandfather, Ksenya Fyodorovna's father, was still alive, and he also was a guest sometimes—he slept in the connecting room on the trestle bed. Strange to remember it. Could it have really been like that: everyone sitting together on the veranda at the big table, drinking tea, Ksenya Fyodorovna pouring, Vera Lazarevna cutting the pie? And she called Lora *Lorochka* at one time, and arranged for her to have her best dressmakers. It had been like that, for sure. It had been, it had been. Only it didn't stay in his memory, it rushed past, vanished, because he couldn't live for anything, or see anyone but

Lena. There was the south, sultriness, hot Batum, old
lady Vlastopulo, from whom they rented a room next
to the bazaar, an Abkhazian he'd fought with over
Lena, on the embankment at night, the Abkhazian had
tried to pass a note to Lena in a restaurant. they sat
there with no money and only cucumbers to live on,
they telegraphed to Moscow, Lena lay naked and black
on the sheet with no strength, and he ran to sell the
camera. And then all of it continued on, although it was
different, Moscow, he was already working—one wild
summer flew with momentum—again Lena lay like a
mulatto on the sheet, again there was bathing at night,
races to the shore, a cooling meadow, conversations,
discoveries, tirelessness, suppleness, fingers ashamed of
nothing, lips always ready for love. And besides that her
devilish powers of observation! Oho, how she could pick
up the weak or the funny things. And everything
pleased him, he was struck by everything, astonished,
registered it.

He liked the facility with which she made friends
and became intimate with people. This was exactly what
he lacked, as it happened. Especially remarkable was the
way she succeeded in making *necessary* acquaintances.
She'd hardly settled in Pavlinovo when she already knew
all the neighbors, the police chief, the watchmen at the
wharf, and was on familiar terms with the young dir-
ectress of the sanatorium and the latter gave Lena permission to have dinner in the sanatorium dining room,
which was considered the height of comfort in Pavlinovo, and a success almost unattainable by mere mortals. And how she scratched Downstairs Dusya, who
lived in the semibasement, when the latter appeared
with her usual arrogance, to demand that they clean
their own, the Dmitrievs', shed, which it was true Downstairs Dusya had used as her own for the past ten years!

Yury Trifoñov

Downstairs Dusya flew from the porch as if the wind had knocked her down. Dmitriev was delighted, and whispered to his mother: "So, how do you like it? This isn't how it was with us milksops, is it?" But all his secret delight quickly passed because he knew that there wasn't and couldn't be a woman more beautiful, intelligent, and energetic than Lena, therefore—why be delighted? It was all natural, in the order of things. No one had such soft skin as Lena. No one could read Agatha Christie so entertainingly, at the same time translating from English into Russian. No one could love him like Lena. And Dmitriev himself—that remote thin one with the absurd curly forelock—lived stunned and stupefied, as during heat, when a man can't think well, doesn't want to eat or drink, and just dozes off, lying in bed half asleep in a room with draped windows.

But once in the evening, at the end of the summer, Lora said: "Vitka, can we talk?" They went off the porch, down to the road, and while they were in the square of light which fell from the veranda, they walked in silence until they were in the shadow of the lindens. Lora, laughing unsurely, said: "Vitya, I wanted to talk about Lena, all right? It's nothing really, don't worry, just little things.You know I'm in favor of her,I like her, but the main thing for me is that you love her." This introduction offended him right away, because the *main thing* was not at all that he loved her. She was wonderful by herself, unrelated to him. And already on guard, he prepared to listen further.

"I'm just surprised by certain things. Our mother would never say it herself, but I see it. . . . Vitka, you won't take offense?"—"No, no, what do you mean! Go on."—"Well, this is really nonsense, trivial—that Lena took all our best cups, for example, and that she puts the bucket by Mama's door. . . ." ("Lord!" he thought.

"And Lorka's saying this!") "I didn't notice it," he said aloud. "But I'll tell her."–"You don't have to! And I shouldn't have pointed it out to you." –Lora again laughed somehow abashedly. "That's all you needed, to be told every bit of nonsense! But I scolded Mama. Why not simply say: 'Lenochka, we need the cups, and please don't put the pail here, put it there.' I said that today, and I don't think she got offended at all. Although it's very unpleasant to talk about such trivial things, believe me. But something else jarred me–for some reason she took Father's portrait from the middle room and put it in the connecting room. Mama was very surprised. You should know about this because it's not some domestic trifle, but something else. In my opinion it's just tactlessness." Lora was silent and for a while they walked, not saying anything. Dmitriev ran his open palm over the lilac bushes, feeling how the little sharp twigs were pricking him. "Well, all right!" he said finally. "As far as the portrait goes, I'll tell her. Only listen: what if you happened to come into a strange house, Lora? Wouldn't you commit some involuntary tactlessnesses, slips?" –"It's possible. But not that kind. Generally we shouldn't be silent, but should speak out–I think that's correct– and then everything'll turn out right."

He told Lena about the portrait, not that night but the next morning. Lena was amazed. She'd taken down the portrait only because she needed the nail for the wall clock, and there had been absolutely no other meaning in her action. It seemed odd to her that Ksenya Fyodorovna didn't tell her about such a trivial matter herself, but sent Viktor as an ambassador, which gave the trivial matter exaggerated significance. He remarked that Ksenya Fyodorovna hadn't talked to him about this at all. But who had said it? At this point he blurted out from stupidity–how much would be "blurted out" from stupidity later on!—that Lora had spoken. Lena, reddening, said that his sister had apparently taken upon herself the role of rebuking her: sometimes independently, sometimes through a third person.

When Dmitriev returned from town that day it was unusually quiet in the apartment. Lena didn't come out to meet him right away, but appeared a few minutes later and asked the unnecessary question: "Shall I warm your dinner?" Lora had gone to Moscow. His mother didn't come out of her room. Then Vera Lazarevna appeared, dressed in town clothes, powdered, with beads on her powerfully jutting chest, and said, smiling, that she and Ivan Vasilievich thanked them for the hospitality, and were waiting for him to say goodbye. Ivan Vasilievich would arrive soon with the car. Through the door, which was opened for a second, Dmitriev saw that his father's portrait was hanging in its former place. He wondered: why so suddenly? They had wanted to live there all of September. Yes, but some business had come up—with Ivan Vasilievich at work, and she had household chores, had to make jam, and in general— haven't your dear guests tired you out. . . . Ksenya Fyodorovna came out to say goodbye to the relatives—she had a dispirited look—and invited them to come again. Vera Lazarevna didn't promise to, "I'm afraid we won't manage it, dear Ksenya Fyodorovna. Really, there are so many concerns of all possible sorts. So many friends want to see us, they're also inviting us to their dachas. . . ."

They left, and Dmitriev and Lena went to the dacha next door to play poker. Late that night, when Dmitriev returned, Ksenya Fyodorovna called him into her room with the brick-red wallpaper, and said that she was in a rotten mood and that she couldn't get to sleep because of this business. He didn't understand: "What business?"—"Well, because they left."

Dmitriev had drunk two glasses of cognac at the neighbors', was slightly excited, wasn't thinking clearly. Waving his hand, he said with annoyance: "Oh, nonsense, mother! Is it worth talking about?"—"No, but Lora is uncontrolled. Why did she start all this? And you passed it on to Lena for some reason, she—to her mother, there was the stupidest conversation. . . . Complete absurdity!" "And because you don't go around moving portraits!" said Dmitriev, hardening his voice and shaking his finger with severity. Suddenly he felt himself to be in the role of family arbitrator, which was sort of pleasant even.—"Well they left, so fine. Lenka said absolutely nothing to me, she's a smart lady. So don't get upset and sleep quietly." He gave his mother a smack on the cheek and left.

But when he went to Lena and lay down beside her, she moved away to the wall, and asked why he'd stopped in at Ksenya Fyodorovna's room. Sensing danger of some sort, he began to make excuses, said that he was tired of conversations and wanted something else entirely, but Lena, alternating between severity and caresses, got what she wanted to know out of him anyway. Then she said her parents were very proud people. Vera Lazarevna was especially proud and touchy. The problem was that she'd never been dependent on anyone in her whole life, therefore the slightest hint at dependency was taken badly by her. Dmitriev thought: "How is it she's not dependent, since she never worked and lives as a dependent of Ivan Vasilievich?"—but he didn't say it out loud, but just asked how they'd infringed on Vera Lazarevna's independence. It turned out that when Lena related the conversation about the portrait to Vera Lazarevna, the latter simply oohed: Lord, did they really think they'd had any pretensions to that room? Dmitriev didn't understand something here at all:

"Have pretensions? Why have pretensions?" Besides that, he wanted something else. It ended with Lena making him promise that he'd call Vera Lazarevna from work the next day, and gently, delicately, not mentioning the portrait or insults, invite them to Pavlinovo. Of course, they wouldn't come, because they were very proud people. But he should call. To clear his conscience.

He called. They arrived the next day. Why had he remembered this ancient business? Later there was a lot that was worse, blacker. Well, probably because the first was engraved forever. He even remembered what dress Vera Lazarevna was wearing when she arrived the next day, and with a look of unshakable worth—proudly and vainly looking before her—ascended to the porch, carrying a boxed torte in her right hand.

Then there was the matter of his grandfather. The same autumn that Lena was expecting Natashka. Oh, grandfather! Dmitriev hadn't seen his grandfather for many years, but there had smoldered in his heart for an incalculably long time the splinter of childhood devotion. The old man was so alien to any kind of *Lukianovableness*—he simply didn't comprehend a lot of things,—that it was of course crazy to invite him to the dacha when those people were living there. But then no one understood that, or could foresee it. It was impossible not to invite their grandfather, he'd recently come back to Moscow, was very sick, and needed a rest. In a year he got a room in the Southwest.

His grandfather said to Dmitriev, marvelling: "Some worker came today to move the couch, and your marvellous Elena, and no less marvellous mother-in-law, used the familiar "you" with him in a friendly way. What does it mean? Is it accepted now? To the father of a family, a man of forty?" Another time he started a funny and unbearably tiresome conversation with

Dmitriev and Lena because they'd given the salesman in
the electronics store—and made merry when they told
about it—fifty rubles so he'd put aside a radio for them.
And Dmitriev couldn't explain any of it to his grandfather. Lena, laughing, said: "Fyodor Nikolaich, you're a
monster!" His grandfather wasn't a monster, he was just
very old—seventy-nine—there were very few such old
men left in Russia, and of jurists who'd graduated from
Petersburg University still less, and of those who'd been
involved in revolutionary activities, had been in prison,
exiles, fled abroad, worked in Switzerland and Belgium,
been acquainted with Vera Zasulich—there were no
more than one or two in all. Perhaps his grandfather, in
a sense, was a monster after all.

And what kind of conversations could he have with
Ivan Vasilievich and Vera Lazarevna? No matter how
they exerted themselves, both sides found nothing in
common. Ivan Vasilievich and Vera Lazarevna were absolutely disinterested in his grandfather's past, and his
grandfather understood so little of modern life that he
couldn't report anything useful, and so they acted with
indifference: just an old man. He shuffled along the veranda, smoked cheap, stinking cigarettes. Vera Lazarevna
usually talked with his grandfather about his smoking.

His grandfather was small in height, dried up,
with bluish-copper tanned skin on his face, and stiff
hands rough and disfigured by hard work. He always
dressed neatly and wore a shirt and tie. He polished his
boyish little shoes, size eight, to a shine and liked to take
walks along the shore. There was one Sunday, the last
hot one in September, when everyone got together for a
walk—a strain had already appeared in their conversations, no one needed this excursion, but somehow it was
agreed: they gathered at the same time and strolled
along together.

Yury Trifonov

There were loads of people around that day. They bumped against each other in the woods, on the shore, they sat all over the benches: some in sports clothes, some in pyjamas, with children, dogs, guitars, and fifths on newspaper. And Dmitriev began to get ironical about the contemporary dacha residents: the deuce knows, he said, what kind of public this is. But before the war, he remembered, others with beards, in pince-nez, strolled here. . . . Vera Lazarevna unexpectedly supported him, saying that before the revolution Pavlinovo was also a marvellous resort area, she'd been a little girl here at her uncle's. There had been a restaurant with gypsies, called "The Riverside," they'd burned it down. Generally solid people had lived here: stock market speculators, businessmen, lawyers, artists. Over there in the clearing, Chaliapin's dacha had stood.

Ksenya Fyodorovna was interested: who was her uncle? To which Vera Lazarevna answered: "My papa was a simple worker, a furrier, but a very good, qualified furrier, they ordered expensive things from him. . . ." —"Mamochka!"—laughed Lena. "They ask you about your uncle, and you tell about your father." The uncle, it turned out, had a leather goods shop: purses, suitcases, briefcases. On Kuznetsky, on the second floor, where there is a woman's dress shop now. During NEP there had been a leather goods store there, but no longer her uncle's, because uncle had disappeared in 1919, during the famine time. No, he hadn't run away, hadn't died, he'd just disappeared somewhere. Ivan Vasilievich interrupted his spouse, remarking that these autobiographical facts weren't too interesting to anyone anyway.

And at that point, grandfather, till then silent, suddenly began to speak. "So, dear Vitya, just imagine, if your mother-in-law's uncle had lived to the time when the beards and pince-nez strolled here, what would he

have said? Probably: what kind of public, he'd say, is in
Pavlinovo now! Some riffraff in Tolstoi blouses and
pince-nez. . . . Ah? Wouldn't he? And even earlier there
used to be an estate there, the landowner ruined himself, sold his house, sold his land and fifty years later
some heir would drop by here in passing, out of a sad interest, would look at the merchant's wife, the bureau-
crat's wife, at the gentlemen in bowlers, at your uncle,"
—grandfather bowed to Vera Lazarevna, "who rolled up
in a cab and thought: 'Foo, filth! Well, this bunch of
people are just trash!' Ah?" he laughed. "Wouldn't he?"
    Vera Lazarevna remarked with a certain astonish-
ment: "I don't understand, why trash? Why talk like
that?" Then grandfather explained: contempt is stupidity. One doesn't have to be contemptuous of anyone.
He said this for Dmitriev, and Dmitriev suddenly saw
that his grandfather was in some degree right. . . . In
some way which touched close to him, Dmitriev. Everyone grew thoughtful, then Ksenya Fyodorovna said no,
that she couldn't agree with her father. If we refuse to
be contemptuous, we deprive ourselves of our last
weapon. Let this feeling be inside us, absolutely invisible
from the outside, but it should be there. Then Lena, gig-
gling, said: "I agree completely with Fyodor Nikolaich.
How many people are conceited about who knows what,
myths, chimeras. It's so funny."—"Who exactly, and
what are they conceited about?" asked Dmitriev in a
half-joking tone, although the direction of the conversation had begun to disturb him slightly. "Who knows,"
said Lena, "you want to know everything, don't you?"
—"Conceit and quiet contempt are two different things,"
pronounced Ksenya Fyodorovna, smiling. "That depends on who's looking," answered Lena. "I hate honor
in general. In my opinion there's nothing more repulsive."—"You take a tone—as if I were proving that honor

is something beautiful. I don't love honor either."—
"Especially when there's no basis for it. Built on
empty space. . . ."

And so from this, from an innocent altercation, developed the conversation which concluded with Lena's
heart attack that night, the call for the ambulance, cries
from Vera Lazarevna about egotism and cruel-hearted-
ness, with their hurried departure by taxi the next
morning, and then Ksenya Fyodorovna's departure and
the silence which came over the dacha when two were
left: Dmitriev and the old man. They walked by the
lake, talked for a long time. Dmitriev wanted to have a
conversation about Lena with his grandfather—her departure worried him—to curse her for her nonsensicality,
her parents for idiocy, and maybe damn himself, or
somehow pick at the wound; but his grandfather didn't
utter a word either about Lena or her parents. He talked
about death, and how he wasn't afraid of it. He'd carried out what he'd been appointed to do in this life, and
that was all. "My God, I wonder how she is there? What
if something serious happens suddenly, to her heart?"

His grandfather talked about how the past and his
whole endlessly long life didn't interest him at all. There
was nothing stupider than looking for ideals in the past.
He only looked ahead with interest, but unfortunately
saw little.

"Should I call or not?"—thought Dmitriev.—"Anyway, no matter what her condition is, that doesn't give
her the right. . . ."

He called in the evening.

His grandfather died three years later.

Dmitriev came to the crematorium straight from
work, and looked stupid with his thick yellow briefcase
in which there were several cans of "Saira" [a popular
fish from the eastern USSR], bought by chance on the

street. Lena loved Saira. When they entered into the crematorium's premises from the street, Dmitriev quickly went to the right and put his briefcase on the floor in a corner, behind a column, so no one would see it. And repeated mentally, "Don't forget the briefcase." During the funeral ceremony he remembered about the briefcase several times, looked at the column, and at the same time thought that his grandfather's death had turned out to be not as awful an experience as he had supposed it would. He was very sorry for his mother. Supporting her under her arms was Aunt Zhenya on one side, Lora on the other, and his mother's face, white from tears, was new somehow: simultaneously very old and childish.

Lena came too, sniffled, wiped her eyes with a handkerchief, and when the moment of farewell came she suddenly began to sob in a loud low voice, seized Dmitriev's arm and began to whisper that his grandfather had been a good man, the best of all the Dmitriev relatives, and how she loved him. That was news. But Lena sobbed so sincerely; real tears were in her eyes, and Dmitriev believed. Her parents also appeared at the last minute, in black coats with black umbrellas; Vera Lazarevna even had a black veil on her hat and they managed to throw a bouquet of flowers into the coffin, as it was lowered into the cellar. Then Vera Lazarevna said in amazement: "How many people there were!" That's why they came, out of old people's curiosity: to see whether there were a lot there to see him off. To Dmitriev's amazement a lot came. And the main thing was that there had come creeping from somewhere, in no small number, those who had seemed to disappear; but no, those strange old men were still alive, old lady smokers with angry dry eyes, a few of whom Dmitriev remembered from childhood. One hunchbacked old lady with a myopic ancient face, who his mother said had been a desperate revolutionary, a terrorist, and had thrown a bomb at someone, came. This hunchbacked lady gave the speech over the casket. In the courtyard, when everyone came out and stood in bunches, not dispersing, Lora came up and asked if Lena and he were going to Aunt Zhenya's, where the friends and relatives were gathering. Until that minute, Dmitriev had considered that they were going to Aunt Zhenya's without fail, but now he wavered: there was the possibility of choice in Lora's question itself. That meant that both Lora and his mother supposed that he, if he so desired, could not go, i.e., that it wasn't necessary for him to go because—suddenly he understood it—in their eyes he no longer existed as a part of the Dmitriev family, but as a different thing, connected with Lena, and maybe even with those in the black coats with the black umbrellas; and they had to ask him like an outsider.

"Are you going to Aunt Zhenya's?" The question was casually asked, but how much it signified! Among other things: "If you were alone, we wouldn't have asked. We always want to see you, you know. But when we have grief, why have strange people around? If it's possible, it'd be better to do without them. If it's possible, but—whatever you want. . . ." Dmitriev said that most likely they would not go to Aunt Zhenya's. "Why? You go!" said Lena. "I don't feel so well, but you go. Of course, go!" No, he wouldn't go, Lena had a bad headache. Lora nodded understandingly, and even smiled at Lena with sympathy and asked whether she should give her some aspirin. "Yes!" said Dmitriev. "I forgot my briefcase!" He went back to the crematorium's premises, where a new deceased was already lying in a coffin on a pedestal, around which a thin group of people were huddling, and on tiptoe he walked behind the column. After getting his briefcase he stopped, to be alone for a minute. The feeling of irrevocability, of being cut off, which comes at funerals—one thing had irrevocably gone, cut off forever, and now continues the other, but not that, something new, in other combinations—was the most tormenting pain, even stronger than the sadness about his grandfather. His grandfather had been old after all, he was due to die, but along with him disappeared something not directly connected with him, existing separately: threads of some kind among Dmitriev and his mother and sister. And this disappearance was revealed so implacably and right away, a few moments after they came out of the heavy floral smell into the air. Lora calmly agreed to his not going to Aunt Zhenya's, and he came to terms with her calmness easily. And only his mother, turning halfway around, made a weak farewell gesture with her hand, and he suddenly felt that he'd added a pain to her, so he rushed to catch up—rushed internally for a moment,—but it was already too late, irrevocable, it had been cut off; Lena pulled him to the taxi to go home.

Along with his mother, Lora, Felix, Aunt Zhenya and other relatives, there was also Lyovka Bubrik. Maybe he'd been there earlier, but Dmitriev noticed him only when they came outside. Lyovka was hatless, dark, tousled, and his glasses were blindingly bright. He didn't come up to Dmitriev, but nodded from a distance. Lena asked in a whisper: "Why's Bubrik here?" Dmitriev, stifling a feeling of unpleasant surprise, said: "Well, so? He's related somehow. Second cousin twice removed."

This was the first time Dmitriev had seen Lyovka Bubrik for several months after that tedious story with the Institute. And he immediately remembered that his deceased grandfather had censured him on account of Lyovka. There had been a conversation in which his grandfather had said: "Ksenya and I expected you to become something else. Of course nothing terrible happened. You're not a bad man. But not wonderful."

He'd known Lyovka since childhood, they'd gone to school at the same institute. Not friends "you couldn't separate with water," but friends connected by the ties of home and family. Lyovka's father, Dr. Bubrik, who'd taken care of Dmitriev even in infancy, was the brother of Aunt Zhenya's husband, who died during the war. So Lyovka was an unrelated nephew of Aunt Zhenya's. Right after the Institute Lyovka went to Bashkiria and worked there for three years in industrial surveying, while at the same time Dmitriev, who was older, and had gotten his diploma a year earlier, stayed to work in Moscow at the gas factory, in the laboratory. They'd offered him various enticing odysseys, but it had been difficult to accept them. His mother wanted him very much to go to Turkmenia, to Dargan-Tepe, because it wasn't far from Lora's native Kunia-Urgench—some 600 kilometers, a trifle!—and the brother and sister could have met over a cup of kok-chai tea and have been homesick together. Natashka was born weak, she was sick, Lena was sick too, she had no milk so they found the wet-nurse, Frosya, the school cleaning lady who lived in the barracks near Tarakanovka, Dmitriev went there in the evenings for the bottles. Sure, Dargan-Tepe! Yes, and there was to be no Dargan-Tepe. There were dreams in the morning, in the silence when he awoke with the unexpected cheerfulness and thought: "It would be nice if. . . ." And it all rose up before him, so transparent, clearcut as if he'd gone up a mountain on a clear day and looked down from it. "Vitya," said Lena (or "Vitenka," if it was a period of serenity and love),— "Why are you fooling yourself? You can't go away anywhere from us. I don't know whether you love us, but

you can't, you can't! It's over! You're late. It should
have been earlier. . . ." And embracing him, she looked
into his eyes with the dark blue caressing eyes of a witch.
He was silent because these were his own thoughts,
which he was afraid of. Yes, yes, he was too late, the
train had left. Four years had gone by since he'd finished the Institute, then five, seven, ten went by. Natashka became a schoolgirl. The English Special School
on Utiny Lane, the object of lust, envy, the measure of
parental love and *putting yourself out to get it.* Another
school district, almost unthinkable. And no one but
Lena would've had the strength. For: she gnawed on her
desires like a bulldog. Such a nice-looking lady-bulldog
with short straw-colored hair, and an always pleas-
antly tanned, slightly dark face. She didn't let up until
her wishes—right in her teeth—turned into flesh. A great
trait! Wonderful, amazingly decisive in life. The trait of
real men.

"No expeditions. Not for longer than a week"—
that was her wish. A poor simple-hearted wish with
dents in it from iron teeth. Lena's other wish, which occupied her during the course of several years, was: to get
into IICI. Oh, IICI, unattainable, beyond the clouds,
like Everest! Conversations about IICI, telephone calls
in connection with IICI, tearful despair, flashes of hope.

"Papa, did you talk with Grigory Grigorievich
about IICI?"—"Lenochka, they called you from IICI!"—
"From where?"—"From IICI!"—"Oh, my God, from
the personnel section or just Zoika?" Two friends,
ideally situated in this life, worked in IICI—the Institute
of International Coordination of Information. Finally
she succeeded. IICI became flesh and crunched in her
teeth like a well-cooked chicken wing. Convenient, it
was piece work, beautifully located,—a minute's walk
from GUM*, and her own boss was one of the friends

she had studied with at the Institute. Her friend gave
Lena as much to translate as she asked for. Later on, they
had a fight, but for about three years everything was
"okay." During their lunch break they ran to GUM to
see if they'd put out some blouses. On Thursdays they
showed foreign films in the original language. But unfortunately Lena couldn't get Dmitriev's dissertation done
for him. At that time Dmitriev was getting 130 at the
laboratory, but an acquaintance of his from the Institute, from the same class—a little gray guy, but a big
worker, clever Mitri, who'd denied himself everything
and didn't even get married ahead of time—received
twice that because he'd sat through his dissertation on
his lead rear. Lena wanted Dmitriev to become a Ph.D.
terribly. Everyone wanted it. Lena helped him with English, his mother approved, Natashka spoke in a whisper
at night, and his mother-in-law grew quiet, but after half
a year he gave up. Probably because of that: the train
had left. He didn't have the energy, every night he came
home with a headache, and with one desire—to tumble
into bed. And he did tumble in if there wasn't anything
worthwhile on television—football, or an old comedy.
And after giving in, he began to hate all that dissertation
junk, he said it was better to receive the honest 130
rubles than to torture himself and overtax his health and
humble himself before the necessary people. And now
Lena looked at it the same way and contemptuously referred to the Ph.D.'s of their acquaintance as smart
operators and sly foxes. At this time, as never more op-
portunely—but perhaps inopportunely—Lyovka Bubrik
showed up with his request about the Institute of Oil
and Gas Apparatus, abbreviated IOGA.

Lyovka couldn't find work for a long time after he
returned from Bashkiria. Then he found IOGA. But he
had to find a way to get in. Neither he nor anyone else
would've gotten into IOGA if Ivan Vasilievich hadn't
called Prusakov. Then he went to see Prusakov himself,

in an official car. Prusakov was holding the job for someone else, but Ivan Vasilievich pressed and Prusakov agreed. In the end it wasn't Lyovka's father-in-law who went, but Dmitriev's! True, on Lyovka's behalf. That was true. Because Lena had asked her father, she was sorry for Lyovka and his wife, that fat hen Innochka. Then Innochka made a big mess when they were all guests at mutual friends', and cried: "You're an awful person!" But Lena had been ready for all of this and held on staunchly and coolly. Their friends said that Lena held on magnificently. She took everything on herself and said that Dmitriev hadn't wanted it, but she'd insisted. "I'm guilty, only me, don't blame Vitka! You'd have wanted us to live on 130 and Vitka to kill three hours on the road?"

Of course, that's how it was. The thought first came to her when Ivan Vasilievich came and told what kind of job it was. And Dmitriev really didn't want to do it. He didn't sleep for three nights, he wavered and worried but gradually that which it was impossible to think of, which was not the thing to do, turned into something inconsequential, diminutive, well-packed like a capsule you had to—it was necessary even, for your health—swallow, despite the nastiness it contained inside. There is no one who doesn't notice the nastiness after all. But everyone swallows the capsules. "I respect Lev," said Lena, "and I even love him, but for some reason I love my husband more. And if papa, an old man who can't bear to be obliged, got ready and went. . . ."

They should have told them right away, but they didn't have the nerve—they dragged it out, kept quiet. They found out from someone else. And how they cut them off: they didn't come, they didn't call. The devil knows, maybe they were right, but it isn't done that way either: you come, you talk nicely, you find out

why and how. And when they met at friends', Bubrik
turned up his nose, but Innochka yelled like a fishwife.
So the hell with it, forget it. And it was only after about
four or five years—it was Ksenya Fyodorovna's birthday, winter, the end of February—that the whole story
was stirred up again. His mother and grandfather had
pestered Dmitriev about it before, but not very spitefully, because they correctly considered that Lena had
started everything. And what kind of demand is there
on Lena? You had to reconcile yourself to Lena as with
bad weather. But then, on his mother's birthday. . . .

It was as clear as if it were now. They go up the
stairs, stop at the door. Natashka holds the presents, a
box of candy and a book in English, Thackeray's *Vanity
Fair*, and Lena is leaning with her shoulder against the
door and with closed eyes whispers as if to herself, but
of course to Dmitriev: "Oh, my God, my God, my God.
God. . . ." Look, she says, what ordeals I go through for
your sake. And he begins to seethe as usual. Lena
doesn't like to go to her mother-in-law's. Each year she
has to force herself more. What was there to do? Well,
she doesn't like to, she can't, can't stand it. Everything
irritates her. No matter how nicely they fed them, no
matter how kindly they conversed, it was useless: like
heating the street. Dmitriev talks tenderly to his daughter, purposely, hugging her: "So, little monkey, are you
happy that we've come to grandma's?"—"Uh-hunh!"—
"You like to come here?"—"I like to!" But Lena, smiling, adds: "I like to, say, but I've got to go to bed early.
And little papa, say, don't stay too long so that we've
got to drag you from the table by force. Say, we should
get up and go at 9:30."

Everything would have been avoided then if it
hadn't been for that fool Marina, his cousin. As soon as
he glimpsed her red physiognomy at the table over the

pies and wafers, he immediately understood: it's going to be bad. Lena was much smarter than she was, but in some ways they were similar. And whenever they met at family gatherings, there was always some sort of cock-fight started between them. Sometimes they fought out in the open, other times they pricked slyly, so that you wouldn't notice it from the sidelines. Like water polo players, who hit each other with their legs under water, which the spectators don't see. At night Dmitriev would suddenly be stunned: "Why did your cousin taunt me all evening?"—"What do you mean, taunt?"—"Didn't you hear it?"—"What exactly?"—"Well, even what she was saying about women of the East? About their behinds and legs?"—"But after all, you're obviously not a woman of the East, are you?"—"Oh! What point is there in talking to you. . . ."

And then in February,—he remembered every last word for some reason—it all started with the most innocent underwater bumps. He remembered it because it was the last time Lena was ever a guest at his mother's. Since that time, never. It had been five years, and not once. Ksenya Fyodorovna would come to visit her niece, but Lena never went to her. "How are you, Marina? Everything the same with you?"—"Of course! And you? Still working at the same place?" These phrases, said with a smile and within the boundaries of the rules, in actuality meant: "So, Marina, as before, no one's bit? I'm sure no one's bit, and never will bite, my dear old maid."—"But that doesn't upset me because I live the creative life. Not what you do. After all, you work, but I create, I live by creation." At that time Marina was working as an editor in a publishing house. Now somewhere in television. "Have you published anything good lately?"—"We've published a few things. What kind of fabric is that you've got? Did you get it at GUM?" Here were resilient kicks underwater: "What creative work are you babbling about? Have you personally edited even one good book, put it out?"—"Yes, of course. But there's no sense in talking about it with you, it couldn't interest you. Mass production's what interests you." There were some arguments about poetry, about world-wide philistinism. Marina liked this subject a lot and didn't let a chance slip to trample on philistinism. Oh, the philistines! When she was boiling on account of those who didn't recognize Picasso or the sculptor Erzu, something curled up in her mouth and even seemed to sparkle.

Everything hateful that for Marina was connected to the word "philistinism" was contained for Lena in the word "phoniness." And she declared that "All that's phoniness." Marina was amazed: "Phoniness?"—"Yes, yes, phony."—"Loving Picasso is phony?"—"Of course, because those who say they love Picasso usually don't understand him, and that's phoniness."—"My God! Hold me back!" laughed Marina. "It's phony to love Picasso! Oy-oy-oy!" Both of their faces were burning, their eyes blazed with an unjoking brilliance. Picasso! Van Gogh! Sublimation! Acceleration! Paul Jackson! What Paul Jackson? It doesn't matter, because it's phony! Phony? Phony, phony. No, you explain then: what do you call phony? Well, everything that's done not from the heart, but with an ulterior motive, with the desire to show oneself in the best light. "Aha! That means you are being phony when you visit Aunt Ksenya on her birthday and you bring her candy?"

Lena, after glancing at Viktor with a smile in which there was almost triumph (I predicted it, but you insisted, so take it, enjoy it!), said that her relations with Ksenya Fyodorovna weren't the best but she'd come to wish her well not out of phoniness, but because Vitya had requested it. Something along those lines. Then there was a gap. The guests said goodbye. His mother stumbled along. Aunt Zhenya began to talk about Lyovka Bubrik, why—no one knew. She always wanted to do things right, but it always came out the opposite. His mother said: a disgraceful story, and she couldn't believe for a long time that Vitya could behave like that. "Ah, you consider me guilty for everything? And your Viktor had nothing to do with it?"—"I'm not justifying Viktor."—"But still,—me?!"— Lena's cheeks were covered with a stormy flush and Ksenya Fyodorovna's face showed granite features.

"Yes, sure, I'm capable of everything. Your Viktor's a good boy, I corrupted him." Aunt Zhenya spoke, shaking her benevolent gray head: "Dear Lena, you yourself explained it that way to Lyovochka, I remember it very well."—"What I explained doesn't matter! I was worried about my husband. And you don't have, you don't have. . . ."—"Stop yelling!"—"And you're a traitor! I don't want to talk with you." Grabbing Natashka, she walked away from the table. "Why do you always keep quiet when I'm being insulted?" And—onto the stairs, out into the frost, forever. He ran downstairs and slipped on the frozen puddle. Lena and Natashka were stupidly bounding away from him to the bus, the door closed, and he didn't know where else to go, what would be. He couldn't go anywhere. When his home was destroyed he couldn't go anywhere, to anyone. No, she had gone to his mother's one more time after that February—there had been no way out of it, Ivan Vasilievich was laid up with a stroke and his mother-in-law was spending her days and nights with him; but Dmitriev and Lena were hot for a trip to Golden Sands—and there was no one to leave Natashka with. In Bulgaria they took walks in sweaters, and loved each other very strongly. In the daytime the room got very hot even though they opened the curtain, the shower water was warm. And they had never loved each other so strongly.

Dmitriev stood in front of the house and looked at the single lighted window—the kitchen. The second floor and the left side of the building were dark. At this time of the year no one lived around here. Lora was doing something in the kitchen. Dmitriev saw her head lowered over the table, the black hair with the gray streaks, which shone under the electric bulb, the tanned forehead—the yearly five months in Central Asia had made her almost an Uzbek. From the darkness of the garden he viewed Lora just as if on a luminous screen, as a strange woman—he saw her lack of youth, the diseases earned through years of life in the tents, saw the rough anguish of her heart, now gripped by one anxiety.

What was she doing there? Ironing or something? He felt that he couldn't say anything to her. At any rate today, now. The hell with all that! Nobody needed it, it wouldn't save anyone, it would just bring sufferings and new pain.

Because there is nothing dearer than a kindred soul.

When he went up the steps of the porch his heart was thumping. Lora was cutting the newspaper on the table into long strips with the scissors. Felix came in with a basin which contained paste. Dmitriev began to help them. First they sealed the window in the kitchen, then they moved to the middle room. His mother had gone to sleep at six o'clock, but she would probably wake up soon. At about four thirty it had gotten bad, the pains had started, Lora had been very frightened and wanted to call an ambulance, but his mother said it was useless, that she should call Isidor Markovich, or the doctor from the hospital. She took papavirin and the pains went away. What was the matter? Their mother

was very depressed. Such a sudden worsening. The first
since the hospital. She says it's just exactly like it was in
May: pains exactly as strong and in the same place.

They conversed in an undertone.

"I called you at four!"

"Yes, and everything was all right. But an hour
later. . . ."

Felix, humming something, was stuffing an old nylon stocking into a crack between the folds of the
frames with a kitchen knife; Lora spread strips of newspapers with paste and Dmitriev pasted them. Then they
sat down to tea. They listened for sounds from their
mother's room the whole time. Lora's eyes were pitiful,
she answered irrelevantly, and when Felix went out of
the room she whispered quickly:

"I'm begging you: he's going to start about Kunia-
Urgench, so say you're definitely against it. . . . That
you can't. . . ."

Felix came back with a black packet in which there
were photographs. Still humming, he began to show
them. They were color pictures of the Kunia-Urgench
excavations: crocks, camels, bearded men, Lora in
trousers, a quilted jacket, Felix squatting, with some old
men, also squatting. Felix said that they had to leave at
the end of November. At the very latest—the beginning
of December. They had to be there by the fifteenth, like
a bayonet. Lora said he'd be there, be there, just not to
get worried. She'd let him go. Of course he must go,
eighteen people were waiting. Collecting the photos and
sticking them into the back packet—his fingers trembled
slightly,—Felix said that Lora, unfortunately, had to go
too. Because eighteen people were waiting for her as
well.

"We agreed: first you go. . . ."

"How can you conceive of that?"

Yury Trifonov

The glasses were bouncing on Felix's big nose, and
he raised them up with a special sort of movement of his
cheeks and brows.

"And how do you conceive of it all?"

"But there's Vitya, I believe, her son. . . ."

"Well, that's enough! Vitya, Vitya. It doesn't matter about Vitya. . . . We can't talk about this today."

Felix stuck the packet into the pocket of his bike
jacket, headed for the door into the other room, but
stopped at the doorway.

"And when do you plan to discuss it? We have to
send a telegram to Mamedov."

Lora waved her hand again, more energetically, and
Felix disappeared, closing the door. Lora said that Felix
was very good, loved mama, mama loved him, but sometimes he was dense. Sometimes it seems pathological to
Lora. There are things it's impossible to explain to him,
and then one simply had to say categorically: such and
such, you say, and nothing else! And then he's resigned
himself. He can't argue. Dmitriev should have said that
he can't stay with mama, and then he'd stop being so
tiresome. And how could Dmitriev stay, really? Take
mama to his place? Move to Profsoyuznaya? Lena
would never agree to either of these choices. It was important to Felix to go to Kunia of course, to her as well,
all very true, but what could they do?

In Ksenya Fyodorovna's room it was still quiet as
before. Felix took the coal bucket and stamped across
the veranda and down the stairs to the shed. He made a
clatter with the shovel, getting the coal. Dmitriev said
that he could of course try to exchange the two rooms
for a two-room apartment—which he'd tried to do before—so as to live with his mother, but that was a whole
story. Not so simple. Although there was at the moment
such a possibility right now.

He didn't want to say it, but it somehow said itself, comfortably and appropriately. Lora looked at Dmitriev slightly surprised. Then she asked:

"Is this idea Lena's or something?"

"No, mine. My old idea."

"Only don't report *your idea* to Felix, all right?" said Lora. "Because he'll grab it. And mama doesn't need this at all. When she's in such bad shape, to go through something else. . . . I know: everything'll be fine at first, noble, and then the irritation will start. No, it's an awful idea. A nightmare. Brr, I can imagine!" And Lora convulsed her shoulders with an expression of momentary fear and aversion. "No, I'll be with mama, I don't go anywhere, and Felix will manage somehow."

Felix returned with the bucket of coal. You could hear how quiet he was being so as not to awaken Ksenya Fyodorovna, scrabbling with his hands in the bucket, taking out the coal pieces and with care putting the pieces on an iron leaf in front of the stove. A slight clanging of the iron damper. Lora grinned, wanting to say something, but she remained silent.

"What is it?" asked Dmitriev.

"No, nothing. I often wondered, by the way: why don't you get yourself a co-op apartment? It's not so expensive. The relatives would help. They love their granddaughter so much. . . ." Her face was smiling, but there was spite in her eyes. This was the old familiar Lora face from years ago. They'd often fought in childhood, and Lora, enraged, was capable of hitting with anything that came to hand—a fork, a teapot.

"What are you talking about in there?"—asked Felix from the kitchen. He had sensed something in Lora's voice.

"I'm saying: why don't Vitya and Lena build a co-op apartment? A little one, two rooms. Right?"

"We don't need any apartment at all," said Dmitriev in a choked voice. "We don't need it, you understand? In any case *I* don't need it. I, me! I don't need a damn thing, absolutely not a damn thing. Other than our mother to be well. She's always wanted to live with me anyway, you know that, and if it could help her now. . . ."

Lora covered her face with her palms. Only her lips remained visible: they were worrying, compressing. Dmitriev thought in despair: "Idiot! Why am I saying this? I really don't need anything. . . ." He wanted to throw himself at his sister, embrace her. But he continued to sit there, chained to the chair. Felix, standing in the doorway, with a distracted look, looked now at his wife, now at his wife's brother. He walked like a master among these rooms—an unfamiliar squab in a bike jacket with slant pockets, something jackdawish, round, alien, in squeaky house slippers with inner soles—among the rooms in which Dmitriev's childhood had passed. He looked upon the crying sister in bewilderment, as upon disorder in the house, like a buffet door left open for some reason. Dmitriev muttered:

"Felix, get out for a minute!"

The man in the bike jacket got out. Dmitriev went up to Lora and with awkwardness tapped her on the shoulder:

"Come on, stop. . . ."

She shook her head, she didn't have the strength to raise it. . . .

"As you wish, as you wish. . . . If she wants it—all right. . . ."

In precisely a minute Felix's voice was behind the door: "Can I come in, friends?"

He came in with an envelope.

"Today, see here, came a message from Ashirik

Mamedov. The poor guy's asking if he should buy sleeping bags on our share. This is at Chardzhu, at the base of the Guber. He's got the money, but we have to answer fast: to have him get them or not. By telegraph."

He hummed and squeaked his inner soles, standing near Lora's chair with the envelope in his hand. They heard a sound from Ksenya Fydorovna's room. Dmitriev rushed to the door on tiptoe; he immediately saw his mother's face was different.

"Well, you see this ugliness?" said Ksenya Fyodorovna in a weak voice, trying to get up.

A book that had been lying on the blanket slipped to the floor. Dmitriev bent over: it was the same *Doctor Faustus*, with the bookmark after a hundred pages.

"I talked to you this morning!" said Dmitriev in a kind of fervent reproach, as if this fact were extremely important for his mother's condition and the whole course of the illness.

"How is it now, Mama?" asked Lora. "Here's the medicine. And put in the thermometer."

Ksenya Fyodorovna sat a moment on the bed, not moving, with an expression of deep concentration—she penetrated into herself with all her feelings. Then she said:

"But now it's as if. . . ."—she carefully extended her hand and took the cup of water from Lora. She bent a little forward.—"It's as if there's nothing there. Foo, such nonsense!" She smiled and made a sign to Dmitriev so that he'd sit on the chair next to the bed. "Still, it's an awful filthy thing, this ulcerous disease. I'm indignant, I want to write a protest. To demand the complaint book. Only from whom? From Lord God or something?"

"Is it comfortable for you lying like that?" asked Lora. "Move over a little closer here. Now hold the

91

thermometer, and then I'll bring tea. Give me the hot water bottle."

Lora went out. Dmitriev sat down on the chair.

"Yes, Vitya! It's good that you came," said Ksenya Fyodorovna. "Lora and I were arguing today. On that chocolate bar. See the drawing from your childhood? Over there on the windowsill. Lorochka found it in the green cupboard. I think you drew it in the summer of '39 or '40, but Lorochka says it was after the war. When that one was living there, what was his name? Well? Such an unpleasant guy, with the eastern name. I forget, tell me yourself."

Dmitriev didn't remember. He also didn't remember the drawing. All which had to do with his art work was cut out forever. But his mother cherished these memories, and for that reason he said: yes, '39 or '40. After the war the figured fence was no longer in existence because they'd burned it. Ksenya Fyodorovna asked about Dmitriev's business trip, and he said that as it happened, today it had been decided that he wasn't going.

Ksenya Fyodorovna stopped smiling.

"I hope it wasn't because of my illness?"

"No, they just put it off. What does your illness have to do with it?"

"Vitya, I don't want the most minor of your affairs to be upset. Because business before everything. For what? All old ladies are sick, that's their profession. We lie around a bit, groan a bit, get up on our legs, but you lose precious time and wreck your job. No, that's not the way. For example, what's tormenting me now ..." —she lowered her voice,—"is Lorochka. She lies to me without compunction, says that it's not necessary to go this year; Felix hems and haws, answers evasively. And I know what's going on with them! Why do they do that?

Am I really a helpless old lady that can't be left alone? Nothing of the sort! Of course there may be relapses like today, even strong pain, I'll admit, because the process works slowly, but in principle I'm getting better. And I'll get better alone beautifully. Aunt Pasha will come. You're near, there's a telephone—Lord, what problems are there? There is Marinka, of course, there is Valeriya Kuzminichna, who with pleasure. . . ."—she became silent because Lora came into the room with the tea.

"Mama, don't get excited," said Lora. "Let Vitka talk and you listen. Why are you so excited?"

"Certain people make me indignant when they tell falsehoods."

"Ah! Well. Give me the thermometer. . . ."—Lora took the thermometer. "Normal. Vitka, don't make mother get excited, you hear? Or I'll chase you out. And come have supper in ten minutes."

When Lora left, Ksenya Fyodorovna began to whisper about the same thing again: how to fix it so that old people could be sick quietly, and then nothing would get disturbed with the children. As always, his mother spoke half-jokingly, half-seriously. Dmitriev began to get a little annoyed. Why talk about it so much? These were pointless conversations. You couldn't change anything anyway. Then Dmitriev was called to the phone. Lena was asking if he was coming home, or if he was going to spend the night at Pavlinovo. It was already after eleven. Dmitriev said he'd stay there. Lena istructed him to give warm greetings to Ksenya Fyodorovna, and asked if he'd taken the key. He answered "Good night,"—and hung up the receiver.

This applied only to him. He alone could decide: to ask for the key or not to. About an hour and a half before bedtime, he seized a minute when Ksenya

Fyodorovna was alone and said:

"There's still one other possibility: we could make an exchange, settle with you all in one apartment—then Lora would also be independent. . . ."

"Make an exchange with you?"

"No, not with me, but with someone else, so you could live with me."

"Ach, that? Well, of course I understand. I wanted to live with you and Natashenka very much. . . ." Ksenya Fydorovna became silent. "But now—no."

"Why?"

"I don't know. I haven't had the desire to for a long time."

He was silent, stunned.

Ksenya Fyodorovna looked at him calmly, and closed her eyes. It looked as if she were going to sleep. Then she said:

"You already made an exchange, Vitya. The exchange has occurred. . . ." Again silence fell. With eyes closed, she whispered some gibberish: "It was a long time ago. And it always happens, every day, so don't be surprised, Vitya. And don't be angry. Just like that, unnoticeably. . . ."

After sitting there a while he got up and left on tiptoe.

Dmitriev went to be in the room in which he'd lived with Lena at one time, that first summer. As before, the carpet hung there on the wall, nailed up by Lena. But the beautiful green wallpaper with the embossed drawing had noticeably faded and grown worn. Falling asleep, Dmitriev thought about his old watercolor: a bit of garden, a fence, the porch of the dacha and the dog Nelda on the porch. The dog had looked like a sheep. How could Lora have forgotten that after the war there was no Nelda? After the war he'd drawn like mad. Was never separated from his sketch pad. The pen and ink things came out especially well. If only he hadn't failed the exam, and hadn't thrown himself in misery into the first thing that came along, no matter what—chemical, oil, the food industry. . . . Then he began to think about Golishmanovo. He saw the room in the barracks where he'd lived last year for a month and a half. And he thought of how Tanya would have been the best wife for him. Once in the middle of the night he awoke and heard Felix and Lora talking in undertones.

In the morning Dmitriev left early while Ksenya Fyodorovna was still sleeping. He gave Lora the hundred rubles. Lora said it was very handy. They had breakfast in a hurry and he ran to the trolley. It was a dark dawn. The night rain ran off the trees in the garden. At the stop there were two men standing slightly apart, and a big German shepherd sitting on the ground. Who he belonged to was unclear. The empty trolley stopped, they all got in, and after everyone else the shepherd unexpectedly jumped in. The dog was big-bellied, it jumped heavily and sat down on the floor near the ticket dispenser. Two people, frightened, went up ahead, but Dmitriev stayed there in indecision. The shepherd looked out the window. It needed something in the trolley. Dmitriev thought that the driver perhaps might take it far away and it would get lost. After all, no one would understand what it was doing and why it was on the trolley. At the next stop, when people were dashing from the door, Dmitriev got out and called: "Come out, come out!"—and the dog jumped down obediently and sat on the ground. And Dmitriev managed to jump back on. Through the glass of the departing trolley he saw the dog, who was looking at him.

Ksenya Fyodorovna called Dmitriev at work two days later and said that she agreed to move in together, but that all she asked was that it be fast.

The whole drag started. The Markusheviches, of course, passed it up, many others did too, and then there appeared an expert on the sport of biking and everything was accomplished with him in the middle of April. Ksenya Fyodorovna wasn't so bad. They even had a housewarming, relatives came, the only ones that weren't there were Lora and Felix, who hadn't returned yet from their Kunia, where as usual, they were sticking around until the big summer heat started. But their troubles didn't end there: they still had to transfer both personal accounts to the name of Dmitriev, which turned out to be no less burdensome than the exchange. First the executive committe refused because the claim hadn't been correctly composed and some papers were lacking. The old geezer, Spiridon Samoilovich, the agent, who'd always boasted that the jurist of the regional housing section was his close acquaintance, turned out to be a plain liar. The jurist didn't even say hello to him when they ran into each other face to face. But this jurist was the major screw in the matter, because the claimants aren't called to the meeting, and the decision is only carried out on the basis of the jurist's conclusions and the presented documents. At the end of July, Ksenya Fyodorovna became sharply worse, and they took her to that same hospital which she'd been in almost a year before. Lena managed to get a second hearing of the claim. This time the jurist was inclined properly and all the documents were in order: a) the document affirming family relations, i.e., witness about Dmitriev's birth; b) a copy of the orders given out at one time for the right to occupy floor space; c) extracts from the building records; d) copies of the financial

personal accounts given to ZHEK in which the OZHK*
requested that the executive committee satisfy the request that the personal accounts be united. Well, this
time the decision was favorable.

After Ksenya Fyodorovna's death, Dmitriev had a
high blood pressure crisis, and he spent three weeks in
the hospital strictly confined to his bed.

What could I say to Dmitriev when we once met at
mutual friends' and he related all this to me? He didn't
look too well. He'd somehow gotten older all at once,
had turned gray. Not yet an old man, but already middle-aged, with the flabby cheeks of an old uncle. I can
remember him still a boy at the Pavlinovo dachas. Then
he'd been a fat boy. We called him "Vituchni." He's
three years younger than I and in those days I was closer
to Lora than to him. Not long ago they took away the
Dmitriev dacha as well as all the surrounding dachas,
and built the "Stormy Petrel Stadium," and Lora and
her Felix moved to Zyuzino, into a nine-story building.

1969   *Translated by Ellendea Proffer*

TAKING STOCK

I

At the beginning of May the city was struck by a tropical heat wave and life became unbearable. From eleven in the morning until sunset the hotel room was as hot as an oven and I would begin to feel dizzy and short of breath. One night was particularly bad, and tormented by sleeplessness, pains in my chest, and the fear of death, I lost heart. The next morning I put in a call to Moscow. It was almost nine o'clock here, so in Moscow it would be almost seven. I heard Rita's frightened voice at the other end of the line: "What's the matter?" But a second later, remembering how *I had behaved*, she began to speak more calmly and coolly, even with a faint note of displeasure. Why did I have to call at such an ungodly hour if there was no emergency? But it was almost seven! But after two months of silence? This must mean something. It could mean a lot of things: a catastrophe, a desire for reconciliation, repentance, loneliness—any one of these or all of them together. But she calmed down right away when I told her, "There's nothing to be frightened about, it's simply the heat. It's ninety-three in the shade here, and I want to fly home today or tomorrow, as soon as I can get a ticket." She replied, "Well, come on home then. What's wrong, has your blood pressure gone up?" I told her that I hadn't

101

Yury Trifonov

checked it, but it probably had gone up. I had been advised to take my hypertension pills and to stop and see
the doctor before picking up my plane ticket. It was
sensible advice, and I had agreed to follow it.

All in all, I had behaved very foolishly. If I was
planning to return I should have done so without any
phone calls. It was all a result of my late-night panic.
Something old-mannish in that. And it was this that
bothered me more than anything else. Nonetheless, I
was determined to leave this place right away.

Mansur arrived later that morning and dissuaded
me. My benefactor told me that he would set me up in
Tokhir, a wonderful cool place where I would be able to
work in peace and to relax as if I were in an Islamic
paradise. Mansur winked as he spoke, his broad, pock-
marked face hinting at something or other, and he
wagged his right thumb provocatively. He was trying to
excite my curiosity, but I was quite aware that his main
goal was to see that I didn't return home until the job
was finished. And what sort of paradise could there be
in Tokhir! The running water would be restricted to certain hours, there would be an outhouse in the courtyard,
and instead of voluptuous houris there would be a few
retired ladies from some trade union health resort.

But I didn't have enough money for a plane ticket
—nor enough to live on, for that matter—so I was stuck.

I rode to Tokhir in an open jeep, an antedeluvian
rattletrap that was as rickety as a bicycle. Mansur had
acquired this hearse for his organization after it had already been retired from somewhere else. And I think I
can guess why. Not least among its attractions were its
dusty but extremely broad seat, on which three or four
people could have lain abreast or spread out a tablecloth
and even covered it with the carcass of a gazelle. I sat on
one of these lordly seats, breathing in their dusty scent

and a lingering trace of perfume which the hot wind beating against my face was unable to erase.

As my hearse sped southward along the highway, I pictured to myself how Rita would at this moment be rushing around Moscow, not knowing what to do next. My call would naturally have unsettled her. She wouldn't say anything about it to her mother, but she might mention it to Kirill with a slightly triumphant air, "Your father called. He seems to be putting out feelers." To which my know-it-all son, who couldn't care less, would say, "What did I tell you? I told you he wouldn't hold out for more than two months." Then she would go running off to one of her friends for advice, probably to Larisa. I had always felt there was something shameful about her friendship with Larisa, and several times I had tried to open Rita's eyes to the fact. I had remonstrated, insisted, and had purposely been rude to Larisa over the phone and even when she visited our apartment—but without the slightest success. Rita didn't want to face the truth and, in her usual way, acted to spite me. Larisa, for her part, forgave my insulting manner and responded with jokes and flattery. In the early days of their friendship—the ladies had met in Essentuki some seven years ago—Rita would speak of Larisa with unfeigned enthusiasm. What a fantastic woman—she really knows how to live! She has an ideal relationship with her husband, an ideal relationship with her mother-in-law, and an ideal relationship with everyone at work. In actual fact, however, she deceived her husband shamelessly, absolutely despised her mother-in-law, and managed to get away without doing a damn thing at work: either she had some sort of compensatory time off, or she was off somewhere on a business trip. Larisa had already been working for ten years in some sort of complex as some sort of sales manager. Initially Rita's enthusiasm for her friend's endearing qualities was tempered by a certain detachment—as if she were viewing something distant and alien. Sometimes she even responded to Larisa's exploits with humor and not without a certain inner satisfaction: I wouldn't be up to that sort of thing! And she would say, "Larisa's not a friend but an insititution. The Larisa Bureau. There's nothing she can't arrange." And in fact, her range of competence was enormous: she could obtain woolen tights, tickets to Raikin,* tourist accommodations, maps of resort areas, access to important officials to whom mere mortals simply couldn't get through. Gradually, however, the institution turned into a friend. Somehow I failed to see what was happening or didn't pay any attention. And now, when it really didn't matter anymore, they were bosom companions. Just made for each other. At the moment, for example, they were probably discussing what was to be done about me.

They'd be sitting in Larisa's one-room apartment in the tower-shaped building next to Sokol subway station, drinking coffee from Larisa's Bulgarian demitasses and discussing my health. Both of them are up-to-date on the situation. Two years ago I had a heart attack. It was summer, and we were in a train, headed for a dacha we had rented in Khotkovo. Suddenly I felt as if I were going to faint and began gasping for air. We got off at the next stop and rushed to the nearest first-aid station. Rita held up very bravely on this occasion, and after we returned to Moscow Larisa arranged for me to see a certain A.E. Pecheneg, a top specialist. Normally you have to wait in line for some two months just to register for his clinic, but she managed to drag him straight to our apartment. She served him tea, played my French records for him, and did her best to charm him. I'm not sure exactly what her charms are, but she does have something. She has a round, pretty face, and her eyes are always bright and sparkling. Such a rosy-cheeked, sly little creature—you'd never guess that she's forty years old. As a woman though, I find her unappealing—short, stout, and low-slung. But, good Lord, why do I keep going on about Larisa? What's Larisa got to do with all of this? I must be losing my mind. It's all a result of this heat, and my high blood pressure, and—well, of course!—the fact that I'm falling apart at the seams, just like this purple hearse I'm riding in. No, it's not Larisa who's to blame for what happened on the nineteenth of March.

But right now I was sure that Larisa was giving advice, and that Rita was listening to her. "Alexander Efimovich told me, *entre nous*, as they say, that with a heart like Gennady's one could live to be a hundred. That's what he said. I just wanted you to know." "I do know already. He told me the same thing. But if Gennady phoned me. . . . You can imagine, with his pride?" "Rita, my dear, how naive you are!" "I know, but still. . . ." "Don't give in to him now, for heaven's sake. You're coming home, Gennady? Fine. You're sick? We'll take care of you and see that you get the necessary medicines. We'll find you a good hospital if necessary. But your illness, unfortunately, cannot erase what you've done or the suffering you've caused. Everything in this life has its price, my dear, and until you realize that. . . . That, I think, is the only line you should take." "You really think so?" Rita would say. "Of course I do!" Larisa would reply, simultaneously amazed and indignant that the matter could be open to doubt.

From the next room would come the whir of an electric floor polisher. On Sundays Larisa's husband Tsebrikov was a splendid husband and a great helper around the house. Whenever he had a free moment, he would immediately reach for the dustpan and broom and begin to sweep the rug. Sometimes he would rinse out the coffee cups, vacuum the sofa, or even do a bit of laundry. Larisa would now take a slightly frosty bottle of Armenian cognac from the refrigerator and two liqueur glasses from the cupboard. "Vitasik!" She would pound against the wall. "Would you like a glass of cognac?" "No, thanks!" His cheerful shout would be heard above the whir of the floor polisher. "But add a piece of lemon, I bought one this morning. Just be sure to scald it first!"

On the nineteenth of March, when I left the apartment at midnight and walked out into the snow, I thought: if I don't have the right to act in my own home, if I can't be independent here, in my own little nest, where no outsider has any business interfering, then I'm a nobody, a mere insect.

II

Well, what sort of place is Tokhir? It's located sixty kilometers outside the city, to the south, where the desert ends and the mountains begin. At one time this small village belonged to the Persians. According to Atabaly there was a certain khan who had a daughter Tokhira, and it was in her honor that he named the spot Tokhir.

I hear on the radio that it's ninety in the city, but here it really is like being in another country. The air is cool, there's always a breeze, and you can even hear the rustle of leaves. When you walk along the village's only street, which is long, gently sloping, and shaded by ancient poplars and plane trees, you can hear the loud, incessant roar of water running through an irrigation

ditch. At first, whenever I heard this roar, I would involuntarily look around, trying to locate the waterfall
which I imagined must be somewhere nearby.

There are no Persian remains in Tokhir except for
two wretched huts made of clay and dung. One of them
is falling apart, and the other has been converted into a
shed; Atabaly keeps his hoes and rakes in it. From the
window of my room I look out at these former posses-
sions of the Shah and think to myself: *Also sprach Zarathustra*. I have a passion for quotations and am always
plucking them from books. *Also*, I think with satisfaction, *sprach Zarathustra*. A wonderfully concise quota-
tion, and one that has accompanied me my whole life. It
suggests a philosophical attitude toward life, erudition,
intellect, a knowledge of foreign languages, and at the
same time, nonsense and deception. For most of my
knowledge is superficial, my intellectuality is only for
show, and I've never seriously read Nietzsche. I don't
really know anything about either Persia or Zarathustra,
and I know only enough German and French to be able,
when travelling abroad, to ask a waiter for more bread.

Once I managed to turn a certain girl's head. She
was thirteen and I was fourteen. This happened in the
center of Moscow, on a street which today no longer
exists. Needless to say, the apartment building is gone
too. It was a solid five-story building in the pretentious
style of the turn of the century. I remember that the
stairway smelled of cats and garbage, but the thin iron
grillwork on the bay windows at each landing was as
delicately refined as the drawings of Aubrey Beardsley.
Her apartment, I remember, was as tortuous to pass
through as an aquarium full of plants. There were several
corridors which one had to slip through sideways, as
they were crammed from floor to ceiling with cupboards and wardrobes. The girl sat on the sofa—the scent

of iodine emanating from her hands—and recited her own poems, which struck me as beautiful. I in turn asked her, "Have you ever read *Also sprach Zarathustra?*" And afterwards, on the basis of this petty deception, she responded to my boyish advances.

Also I'm now living in a wooden cottage located on the grounds of a resort for cultural workers. The resort has five such cottages, but right now they're all empty. The season doesn't start until June. Tired of working and of sitting in one spot, I walk out into the garden and start up a conversation with Atabaly Kulmamedov, the resort manager, who also serves as its gardener and caretaker. He is about fifty-five and is tall and thin like most Turkmen of the Tekke tribe. His face is swarthy and unshaven, with gaunt, sunken cheeks, and he wears a constantly harried look which is perhaps to be expected of a man with a horde of children. He's very industrious and yet so kind and good-natured that if he sees that I feel like talking, he'll drop whatever he's doing and chat with me for an hour or two. He serves me tea with damson preserves, buys cigarettes for me if I request them, and performs other small services. Atabaly's wife, whose name is Yazgul, is also a Tekke. She is plump and stately, and moves slowly in her long, plum-colored dress, which in Turkmen is called a *kuynak*. Yazgul's worn, dusty-brown face is somewhat squarish, like that of a lioness, and is covered with wrinkles from her constant childbearing. Her arms, however, which are usually bared to the elbow, look young and strong. And probably her body too, with its big stomach and heavy-hanging breasts just barely outlined under the folds of her *kuynak*, is still young and full of life. She is about forty-six or seven, and the older children have long since married and left home. Right now only five of their children remain here in Tokhir—three daughters and two sons. The youngest is called Durdkuli. He is a grave and sober little person of five, from whom you have to coax every word. Once I happened to ask him, "Durdkuli, how old are you?" Rather than reply, he turned with a dignified air and ran off. But he held one hand behind him, with outstretched fingers, indicating the number five. He's always disappearing somewhere, and as his mother searches for him, her cry reverberates throughout the garden: "Durdkuli-i!"

Although Yazgul is illiterate and speaks Russian very badly, she has none of that wearisome Oriental timidity which characterizes so many Turkmen women. She is quite talkative with me, and though she has trouble finding the right words, she looks me calmly in the face with her yellow, unblinking eyes.

"Yazgul," I ask, "do you have any scissors?"

"Just a minute," she nods majestically, and turning toward the interior of the house, she shouts something in Turkmen.

One of her daughters comes out of the house, and glancing past me and somewhere off to the side, she hands me the scissors. At other times I may ask for a bar of soap, or a lightbulb, or a needle and thread, or a clean notebook, or some glue, and all of these things are to be found in Yazgul's house. Of course, I try to pay her for them, but she will never take any money.

"Ay," she says, with a scornful sweep of her hand.

Once, thinking about Yazgul, I had trouble falling asleep. It even frightened me a bit—though what did I have to be frightened about at this point? Actually, what I felt was a momentary flash of bitterness. A man becomes aware of his age only belatedly. It's the same way with a wife's infidelity: you don't suspect a thing, and everyone else already knows all about it. But there is something that exists beyond the realm of consciousness, some mysterious, clocklike mechanism, which suddenly gives a signal. I remember once as an adolescent, riding in a streetcar and seeing a young woman seated opposite me. There was nothing remarkable about her. She was tanned, big-bosomed, with a pocketbook on her knees and bare legs which were carelessly crossed. But *the way* in which I saw this woman—that was something new and startling, and just as now, it frightened me a bit. Right after thinking about Yazgul that night, I shifted to thoughts of myself. There's an inevitable connection here. Whenever I start thinking about time, I immediately make a mental leap to my own precious person. Who am I, what am I, and so forth. Sometimes you think to yourself: everything's okay, my life is as it should be. But at other times you feel sad and depressed. No, you think, my life has made no sense. I've never done what I wanted to do, but only what was expected of me, what was needed to get by. And most likely I could have done what I wanted to. If only back then, right after the institute, in the late forties. . . . Well, and so forth and so on.

I'm already forty-eight, but I look about ten years older. From my sedentary life and excessive smoking my face has taken on a yellowish cast. It's become flabby and I have circles under my eyes, which expand and grow darker after a night of "dilating the arteries." I used to drink a good deal—I called it "dilating the arteries"—but now the doctor has forbidden it, and I myself can feel how after the third drink, or sometimes even after the second, my heart starts pounding wildly and I have trouble catching my breath. I've also had to stop smoking. But this is beside the point, completely beside the point! For a person can get sick, a person can spend his whole life working at something he doesn't really care for, but what is important is to feel himself a human being. And for this, only one thing is necessary: an atmosphere of simply humanity—as simple as arithmetic. No one can generate this feeling autonomously, on his own; it arises from others, from those one loves. Sometimes we fail to notice the loss of this age-old essential—the need to feel loved by those one loves. But what sort of old wine in new bottles is this—love thy neighbor as thyself? Biblical nonsense and idealism? Yet if a person doesn't feel the love of those who are close to him, then no matter how intellectually developed he may be, no matter how ideologically sound, spiritually he begins to suffocate. There simply isn't enough air for him to breathe.

When Kirill said to me, "And how are you, any better? You keep turning out rubbish, and that doesn't seem to bother your conscience," I felt a constriction in my chest, and my heart momentarily stopped beating. I opened my mouth but couldn't utter a word, and now he looked at me, not as before, but with fright. Finally I said, "You bastard! I've fed and clothed you for seventeen years and gotten you through school on this rubbish, as you call it! And thanks to this rubbish you're able to buy yourself jeans, records, and other such trash! In fact, you're nothing but trash yourself!" And here, I struck him. He recoiled and ran off to his room. I knew that I had hurt him, but I felt no pity—and this despite the fact that I had rarely hit him, perhaps only two or three times in his whole life. All I felt was a certain emptiness, which soon gave way to despair. The words with which he had taunted me had not been thought up on the spur of the moment. The hatred and contempt which lay behind them must have been stored up for months, perhaps even years. And in these words I felt not only Kirill, but Rita as well. This was the way they talked about me when they were by themselves.

Even worse, I recognized myself in these words. Yes, myself! It was my own phrase he had used: "turning out rubbish." Contempt is a contagious thing, and I would never have flared up so violently if I hadn't felt myself in this phrase. For lodged deep inside me, like some hidden, evil disease, is a secret contempt for any sort of rubbish, my own included.

But the boy, after all, was unaware of all this. He had received a slap in the face and had run off to his room, half-stunned and choking back tears.

The day had begun with my finding a small leather-bound book with a lock in Kirill's room. I had felt an urge to smoke and had gone in there looking for cigarettes. The little book had intrigued me and I had opened it, since the key lay right beside it. It turned out to be a diary which Kirill had started keeping several months before. I skimmed some twenty pages written in his large, faint, adolescent hand. I felt a bit awkward, but told myself that as a parent I had an absolute right to read it. A lot of it was trivia: a description of a soccer match with another school; his thoughts on some science-fiction work by a contemporary author which was apparently pretty trashy; a description of his relationship with some fellow with the initial "A" and some girl with the initial "O"—this written in a long-winded, elliptical style. Then came a description of his own birthday celebration. On the day before his birthday he had written a detailed forecast of what he would get, and from whom. This passion for gifts which Kirill had exhibited with such remarkable directness and candor from infancy on had always grated on me, though by now I was used to it. It was nothing new, and Rita was the same way. "Let's see what Dad will come up with. Last summer he promised me a tape recorder—well, not a Grundig of course (he wouldn't go that far)—but perhaps a Comet. Sery's Comet works pretty well, so I'm going to be very *satisfied* [this last word written in English and misspelled]." I was somewhat stung by his cavalier tone, but I swallowed my hurt feelings and kept reading. In actual fact I had given the boy a Comet, and I remember anticipating the impression that the tape recorder would make on him. I, for one, had been sure that it would come as a complete surprise. That summer's promise had completely skipped my mind, but not his. And as a result I had been somewhat taken aback by his reaction. He had thanked me, of course, but rather calmly, without any great enthusiasm.

What made me boil was another notation: "The scarecrow came and brought me some sort of sorry postcard album and a paint set. About three rubles all told. No wonder Mama says that old maids are known for being stingy and suspicious. . . ." This he was saying about my sister and his own Aunt Natasha. If Natasha were to read this—brrr! I shuddered. I felt like ripping out the page so that this horrible eventuality could never occur. But I stopped myself. The page might be needed later on. Poor Natasha had undoubtedly been thinking back to our own birthdays, when a postcard album and paint set would have been considered a treasure. Yet it wasn't so much his mercenary appraisal of her gift that disgusted me, as his coldblooded hypocrisy. After all, the scoundrel had thanked his aunt, he'd even kissed her on the cheek, given her a welcoming smile, and inquired like an affectionate nephew, "How are things at work? And when are you going on vacation?" And then on that very same evening: "the scarecrow"!

I gazed absentmindedly at the diary, its leather binding, its little lock and key (hadn't Natasha given it to him on his previous birthday?), and debated whether to confront him with it or to say nothing. I decided to say nothing and to keep this in mind for some future occasion. I had a feeling, though, that I wouldn't be able to restrain myself. And sure enough, that very evening he began whining about tickets for an American jazz concert. First he pestered his mother, and then me. Rita said she was flatly against it. In the first place, he had an important exam the next day. In the second place, it was too expensive. He was planning to go with his girl-friend and the two tickets would come to five rubles. And thirdly, Rita didn't like the girl. In Rita's opinion she had no manners and didn't show sufficient respect when she came to visit. Well, the girl didn't concern me, and in any case I hadn't noticed her lack of manners. My objections were on other grounds. Kirill continued to whine with his usual persistence. "Da-ad . . ." he kept repeating in a hurt, whimpering voice, just like a little boy. "There aren't any tickets left, and there's no way to get them. And that's that! Period!" I said. "Now go to your room and study!" "Maybe I should ask Aunt Natasha?" I glanced at him with curiosity, but his blue eyes were serene and respectful. Natasha works in one of the ministries and is sometimes able to obtain hard-to-get tickets. "Aunt Natasha?" "Well, yes, don't you remember, she was the one who got the tickets to Dean Reed?" "But won't you find it unpleasant," I asked, carefully enunciating every word, "to take tickets from a scarecrow?"

He gazed at me with stunned eyes. "What scare-crow?" "Well, you do call Aunt Natasha a scarecrow, don't you?" And now I saw a dark flush spread from my son's ears and instantly cover his whole face, as if it were some sort of infra-red print developing right before my eyes. "You've been reading my diary!" he screamed. "How could you?" His features grew distorted, his eyes narrowed, and he looked at me with furious contempt. I explained to him, of course, that it was not a question of "how could I" but "how could he" write in such a nasty way about his aunt, a relative who sincerely loved him. I spoke with great agitation. Rita came out of her room and stood there without a word. Although our relations were strained at this point, she did not try to defend Kirill, who wasn't listening to anything I was saying, but merely kept repeating as he shook his head, "Oh, how could you? How could you?" Undoubtedly this was unpleasant for Rita, but Kirill didn't understand a thing. What killed him, apparently, was the fact that I had read the foolish stuff he had written about A. and O. Finally Rita opened her mouth and said reproachfully, "Really, Kirka, how could you have written such a thing?"

It shouldn't surprise you," I said to Rita. "He only wrote down what you say aloud." Naturally this provoked a cry of protest, a look of righteous indignation, and a smug and pedantic response: "I'm certainly not defending Kirill, but your way to talking to the boy is most offensive!" And she left the room. This was all Kirill needed. He said that I had offended everyone, both him and his mother, and that I myself had no conscience if I went around reading other people's diaries. I began shouting in reply that it was my right as a father to do so; that until he turned eighteen, the little squirt, I was responsible for him, and it was my duty to know what he was doing and thinking, and that included all the ins and outs of his personal life. I was, I shouted, responsible for him for one more year. But after that, he could take off wherever he pleased, I certainly wouldn't object. "I won't object either," he mumbled insolently. "But right now, when I see something vile," I thundered, "I'm not going to stand by and let you get away with it!" "But what about when I see something vile? . . ."

Thus we continued to wrangle in scandalous fashion, like a couple of fishwives—I feeling more and more powerless with each passing moment—until finally he uttered the words "turning out rubbish," after which I struck him on the mouth with the palm of my hand and he ran off—initially to his room, and later out of the house.

He disappeared for a whole day. These were probably the worst twenty-four hours of my life, since I felt to blame for what had happened and couldn't stop tormenting myself. And of course Rita did not keep quiet either, but her ravings didn't affect me. I was simply numb with horror, with my own imaginings, and with what I saw as my own guilt, my guilt alone—neurotic idiot that I was. To think that I had let loose with my hands because someone had called my sister a scarecrow! Well, so what? Was it really necessary to slap the boy, to drag him over the coals, to insult and humiliate him? Sometime after two a.m. a policeman informed us that the body of a seventeen-year-old youth who had been stabbed to death had been found in Koptevo. Had our boy perhaps been wearing a fur cap—he had! But not a fur-trimmed leather vest. On the other hand, he could have borrowed the vest from a friend. And for some reason or other he might have gone to Koptevo. We grabbed a taxi and rushed off to Koptevo, at the other end of the city. Rita fainted in the taxi. We stopped, and I massaged her heart while the driver ran off to get some medicine in the first-aid room of the Belorussky railroad station. Upon arrival at the Koptevo Hospital I entered the morgue by myself, while Rita remained in the taxi. Although I was absolutely convinced that our son couldn't be here, my legs seemed to give way beneath me as I descended the stairs from the narrow stone passageway. The youth in question had black hair.

One eye was open, the other was obscured by a black, bloody scab. We arrived home around five a.m.

At seven he called and told us not to be upset. He was at his girlfriend's dacha, and there wasn't any telephone there, which was why he hadn't called earlier. He was sorry, "excuse me" (this in English). Right now he was calling from the railroad station. "Aren't you going to take your exam?" asked Rita in a suddenly business-like tone which, as usual, amazed me. "No, I'm not—see you later!" This "see you later" was uttered in a devil-may-care tone which evoked a picture of careless youth living for the moment. Then there was a click of the receiver and Kirill was no longer at the other end of the line. Rita wept quietly, and I sat in my armchair with my eyes closed, picturing the early morning mist at the railroad station, the telephone booth, chillier than an unheated cellar, the smell of smoke, and the moon, hanging low over the forest. Two figures hurry along on skis. First they follow the path alongside the railroad tracks, then they turn into the forest. A dog greets them from behind a picket fence, and inside the dacha birch logs are burning in the wood stove and it's cozy and warm. . . . Actually, all this is from my own youth—Kirill's girl probably has radiators in her dacha. Yes, all of this once happened to me too. What does he care about his exams! And as for his father, who bloodied his mouth, he probably hasn't given him a second thought!

He no longer *needed* me. That was clear. Well, money, a roof over his head, tickets to jazz concerts, useful contacts—all that went without saying. And a certain agitation when I started having one of my attacks. "Papa, can I get you something? No? . . . Well then, I'm off! There's someone I have to meet on business. You stay there on the couch, don't get up." But what else did he need? One of my friends, a father of my own age, said to me, "You can just be thankful that he didn't respond with a left hook in your gut. My kid once knocked me to the floor." Probably this is all very normal, I'm simply not in a position to judge. When I was Kirill's age, I had neither mother nor father. My mother was sick for a long time and spent months in various sanatoriums, and my father, who was an army engineer, was killed in '39 on the Karelian Isthmus. I was raised by my older sister Natasha, who brought me up as best she could. And perhaps it's because of me that she has remained "a scarecrow." How am I to judge whether a boy needs a father when the boy in question is taller than I am, has a bass voice and a mod haricut; when he can dance for three hours without getting tired, read through a whole English detective story in one day, and walk up to any girl in the street and get her phone number?

That summer, however, it seemed that he still needed a father. "Papa, the head of the department is a man named Mechenov, Alexander Vladimirovich. He's the one who'll be giving us our entrance exam. I know for a fact that he's a friend of your friend Rafik. Do me a favor and. . . ." Both he and his mother know that I don't like this sort of thing—not because I'm so principled that it offends my sense of morality, but because I'm neurotic and don't like putting myself in other people's debt. And who is Rafik? They simply don't understand Rafik's role in my life. They think that if we address each other by the familiar *ty*, drink cognac together at the Hotel National, meet once in a while at Lenin Stadium or at the races (Rafik is a gambler and a sports enthusiast), then that means that we're really friends. Rafik provides me with work. I depend on him. Well, not 100 percent—there are some eight other places that I get work from—but to a large degree, Rafik is a valuable figure in my life, like a queen in chess. It's I who am interested in *him*, not he in *me*.

But this I could never get Rita to understand. Whenever she got caught up in some sort of domestic campaign, she always panicked and did foolish things. And now it seemed to her that if we didn't mobilize Rafik, Kirill would never manage to get into the institute. To tell the truth, I didn't think he would get in even with Rafik's help. For our son was a bit of a blockhead. Despite his height, his deep voice and his surface swagger of independence, he still behaved like some gawky, disorganized little kid. His school compositions were mediocre, his handwriting abominable, and he was weak in math. Except for *Soviet Sports* and *Screen*, he didn't read any newspapers or magazines at all. His knowledge of English? Well, that at least was something. When he was a child we had forced him to join an English language group, and later on he had developed a liking for English detective stories. But even so, all he had was a large vocabulary. When it came to grammar, he was completely in the dark. Moreover, however bold and quick-tongued our son might be at home, he changed completely in the presence of strangers. Unable to utter a word, he would mumble, become flustered, and generally behave like some sort of Mitrofanushka.* How on earth was he going to come through the ordeal of oral entrance exams? At first we heard that there were twelve candidates for each opening, then it turned out to be nine—which was no laughing matter either.

I would have to go to Rafik. No one realized how repugnant this was for me. Rafik was one of those people who couldn't do you a favor just like that, without keeping track of it and without expecting something in return. It wasn't so much a question of "I do one for you, you do one for me," as that morally he blackmailed you, expecting you to pay tribute to his nobility, to feel eternally grateful, etc., etc. In short, you had to keep all of Rafik's good deeds constantly in mind. This was tiresome, but there was no way around it, it was simply one of the rules of the game. And I, being lazy and undisciplined by nature, often broke these rules—that was the problem. Yet no one could understand this, no matter how hard I tried to explain it. To understand, you simply had to know Rafik, that self-satisfied, wizened old man who was at heart a very kind individual. Not long before the problem with Mechenov arose, Rafik had given me a big assignment, a sizeable piece of work on which I subsequently put in a good half year of the most intensive labor. And for that, thank you to my dying day, "thank you very much," as our blockhead would say in English. But the way things worked out, no sooner did I receive this assignment than I immediately disappeared from view. I grabbed up the assignment and crawled into my hole. Well, what about our friendship? And where was my eternal gratitude? And now to suddenly show up with a new request? So I kept putting it off and instead looked around for other possibilities. But nothing turned up, and in the meantime Rita and Kirill kept pressing me. What was most intolerable, of course, was the fact that Kirill was involved in this whole business. I often reproached Rita about this, and in the end, having lost all patience with me, she went ahead and called Rafik on her own and secretly arranged to meet with him.

I remember how she arrived home one evening in June, tensely silent, her face covered with blotches. These allergy blotches always betrayed her excitement, and sure enough, she suddenly announced that she had just seen Rafik, that she had told him the situation, and that he would take care of everything. She had gone with him to the races and had won one and a half rubles.

Apparently this had been one of Rafik's gambling days. He had arranged to meet her at the Dynamo subway station, and they had talked as they made their way to the hippodrome. Once there, she had decided "to give in to his wishes" because he believed in beginner's luck and to stay with him for the races. A very wise step! He had been cool at first, but they had parted friends. First of all, he had actually won some money, and secondly, he had liked her—she was sure of that. Oho, my dear woman, are you sure you haven't had too much to drink? No, she had drunk only water and had eaten some ice cream and two oranges in the snack bar— Rafik's treat. And yet she did actually appear to be drunk. But that was only because everything had worked out so beautifully. What a shame that he was so awful to look at—a real Quasimodo. He had introduced her to several old-timers who had kissed her hand and called her Madame. Mechenov was an old friend of his, they were from the same town, so it was in the bag. . . .

Kirill was exultant: "Mother, you're a genius!" But I felt a certain ambivalence. Of course, it was a good thing that the matter had been taken care of, and perhaps his efforts would be of some help to our blockhead. Still, I couldn't help picturing the expression of Rafik's face when they met and Rita mumbled her first agitated words, her face breaking out in its allergic rash. "He had been cool at first." That was putting it mildly! One had to know Rafik to understand. He would have concluded right away that I had sent her, and most likely he had felt indignant: "What a cad! Why should I forever be doing him favors?" But then she had somehow softened him up. I didn't have any suspicions on that score, nor did I feel the slightest bit of jealousy. Nowadays such youthful feelings come to me rather infrequently, about

as often as the desire to play volleyball, for example—
and apparently the same was true with Rita. Besides, it
was well known that Rafik had no interest in women.
So I attributed this whole episode to whim—just one
more of Rafik's eccentricities. But there had been some
other old-timers who had kissed her hand and called her
Madame. And why had she felt the need to hang around
till the last race?

When all of this was reduced to its simplest terms—
as in a complicated mathematics problem with many
different steps—all that remained was a feeling of awkwardness and, resulting from this, a certain irritation.

I looked at Rita, sitting casually on the sofa, her
legs crossed, a cigarette in her mouth, and her neck still
covered with blotches, and I tried to see her as Rafik
and those old-timers at the hippodrome had seen her.
Rita was one of those women who looked decidedly
younger than her forty years. The forty years were visible, but at the same time it was clear that she looked
younger than forty. She was rather tall, long-legged, and
well-proportioned, though without a good girdle her figure somewhat lost its shape. But this was nothing serious: she still looked *very good*. At one time, some
twenty years ago when I won her away from a certain
young man, a homeopath's son, she was a beauty. It was
because of her that I left my first wife and my son (he's
now a geologist somewhere out here in Central Asia),
and because of her I had a serious quarrel with my
mother, who was against the divorce. A person of infin-
ite kindness, my mother simply had to feel sorry for
somebody, and it always pained her when somebody got
hurt. Later on she became friends with Rita and would
feel sorry for her when she thought that I had offended
her. But all this was years ago. My mother is long gone,
as is the Rita who was so easily offended. Long gone too

my love and our old apartment on Zhitnaya Street, with its communal crush, its cramped sofa, Kirka's cries in the morning, and the feverishly exciting feeling that everything still lay ahead, could still be realized. Rita should not have quit her job, and we should not have gone to the trouble of acquiring this fancy co-op with its sixty-two square meters of living space, not including the storage area.

And now I looked at this woman with her beautiful legs, her beautiful wool dress, and her beautiful, slightly pale face on which there were traces of fading, but at the same time a splendid ripeness—this face on which I could also see traces of a nervous condition and of cholecystitis, of a love of rich food and of yearly sea-bathing, and I said to her calmly, "He liked you? That's bad. That should put you on your guard." And she replied just as calmly, "Very funny!"

We should not have lived together for twenty years. *Also sprach Zarathustra:* that's too long. Twenty years is no joke! In twenty years forests thin out and the soil becomes depleted. Even the best house requires repairs. Turbines stop functioning. And as for the tremendous advances made by science in twenty years—it's awesome to contemplate! Revolutionary discoveries take place in all areas of human knowledge. Whole cities are rebuilt. October Square, which we once lived right next to, had changed its appearance completely. Never mind the fact that new states have arisen in Africa. Twenty years! A time span which can destroy all hopes.

III

I am translating a poem of my friend Mansur, an enormous work of three thousand lines. It's called

123

"Little Golden Bell." Little Bell, as one might be able to guess, is a girl's nickname. Her fellow villagers called her this because of her clear, melodious voice. The poem is going to be published here in Turkmenistan, in Moscow, and in Minsk. Why in Minsk I don't know; that's his business. I'm hurrying with the poem. I need the money and I need to leave this place not later than the tenth of June. Today's heat is temporary, it can diminish or yield to rain. But beginning in June the heat sets in for good, an oppressive heat that tolerates neither a single cloud nor a drop of rain. I do sixty lines a day, which is a lot. I don't wait for inspiration. At eight a.m. I drink last evening's tea, which I pour from a thermos into an Oriental cup, and work at my desk until two. From two to three I eat my main meal in the wretched tearoom next to the post office. Then I continue to work until five or six when I begin to feel pressure at the back of my head and to see spots in front of my eyes. Well, what else can I do? Translating poetry is my profession; it's the only thing I know how to do. I work from somebody else's word-for-word translation. Theoretically I can translate from all of the world's languages this way, except for two which I have some knowledge of—German and English—and to translate from these I don't have the courage or, perhaps, the conscience. I have no need for fame, that's all behind me (not fame, of course, but the need for it).

They say that soon, around the twentieth, the summer restaurant The Plane Tree will open, and this will make life a bit more pleasant. Several days ago, having worked to the stage where there were big black spots before my eyes, I went off to the tearoom. (This tearoom is actually an ordinary tavern where, in addition to vodka, soda water, beer, fortified red wine, hardboiled eggs, onions, sweet buns, and canned fish, they

sometimes have tea and a pilaf containing meat of uncertain origin—camel meat, I'm afraid.) To cheer myself
up, I had two glasses of lousy Ashkhabad vodka. I drank
with pleasure, though also with a certain trepidation.
And the vodka did have a strange effect on me. Not that
it made me drunk (here my previous long abstention
must have played a role), for my head was functioning
clearly and everything seemed normal except for one
thing, as in Kafka, where everything is true to life except for one particular circumstance—Gregor Samsa's
transformation into an insect, for example. What I imagined was that the lousy Ashkhabad vodka standing on
my table was a word-for-word translation which I had to
put into amphibrach tetrameter, and as soon as I did, it
would be transformed into a bottle of *Stolichnaya.* That
day I had turned out more than seventy lines, and later
that night I woke up from an agonizing and familiar
dream—my usual staircase dream. I dreamt I was climbing up an endless flight of stairs, each step harder and
more impossible than the last because I couldn't catch
my breath. And just as it seemed as if the end had come
and I was being asphyxiated, suddenly I woke up. I felt
a pain in my chest and reached out for something to
drink. But my thermos was empty. I had downed all of
my tea last night as a chaser to the vodka. What an
idiot! I should have known that I might need something
to drink in the middle of the night.

I got dressed and went out into the garden. The
moon was out, and it was a beautiful night. I hadn't
seen such a night in a long time. Two plane trees stood
like slabs of rock, surrounded by a cone of pitch-black-
ness. But the acacias, arborvitae, and other smaller
bushes and trees stirred and murmured, their branches
bathed in the silver light of the moon. The air was so
sweet with the scent of their breathing that one felt like

125

drinking it in. After taking a few weak steps, I sat down on a bench and drank in the air. What a night! A perfect night for dying. I thought about the fact that I might die. But there's no such thing as thoughts about death. Thoughts about death are terror. I sat on the bench with my back propped against a warm tree trunk, and my mind jumped from one thing to another: call home, Mansur, he was coming at nine, a car, a cardiogram, about 15 rubles, with a real heart attack the pain is a lot stronger, like an axe in your chest. Oh, what an idiot I was to drink that vodka! Then, when the pain subsided and my breathing became more regular (I even managed to take a couple of deep breaths), I thought about how senseless it would be to die now. After all, there should be some sense to one's life. It should add up to something. Then after that. . . . Now my thoughts were growing calmer.

When the pain goes away, it's easier to think about death. Somewhere far off on the mountain road a car was passing, and in the silence I could hear distinctly each time the driver began to brake on a turn.

No, death didn't frighten me. After all, the vast majority of mankind has already died and only an insignificant portion is still alive. (Now the pain was completely gone. I got up from the bench and started down the pathway. I wanted to get a pitcherful of water from the well, just in case.) It was humiliating, of course. I had accomplished very little. From an outsider's point of view it might not appear that way. I've done this, that, and a number of things. But I myself know how little it has all amounted to. I had planned to do things differently. Though in what way differently? What could I have done differently? I had been sent to the front when I was only a boy, and I was wounded outside of Leningrad. I was sick for a long time, I was treated, and finally recovered. Then as a university student in those gay postwar days, I really seized hold of life. And I married early—out of the same lust for life. From that point on, I went after certain things—those that were easiest—and other things I put off till later, till sometime in the future. And all those things that I'd put off gradually vanished into thin air, like smoke escaping from a chimney. But nobody noticed this except me, and even I didn't think about it very often, only occasionally at night, when I was suffering from insomnia. And now it was too late, there was no more time. And besides that, I no longer had the strength. And another thing: each person gets what he deserves from life. Thus I reflected as I made my way calmly toward Atabaly's back yard, where the well was located.

Some people were talking in the darkness. Drawing near, I saw Atabaly and an ugly, short-legged little man with a large head—Nazar. I had run into this Nazar in the tearoom. He was about as tall as a ten-year-old boy, and as I approached I thought at first that Atabaly was talking with a little boy.

Nazar screamed hoarsely as he tried to break loose from Atabaly's grasp. They were struggling in the moonlight, and Atabaly was chuckling.

"Shame on you!" he said, choking with laughter. "Trying to get in to the women, what a troublemaker!"

I walked over to the well, and bending over, I began to pump the wooden handle. The water didn't come for a long time. I'd been told that this had once been a fine well, but during last year's earthquake the ground had shifted position and partially blocked off the water. Finally it began to flow in a thin stream. Atabaly and Nazar were still quarreling in subdued tones.

"No!" Atabaly was saying. "Go home to bed, troublemaker!"

In the cottage next door a window was flung open and a woman's voice said sternly, "Go home, go on home, Nazarka! Get your shameless face out of here! Oof!" And the window slammed shut again.

During the summer this cottage was occupied by vacationers, but right now its three rooms were given over to the resort's female staff and to several local waitresses.

The dwarf swayed for a moment, moving his large head from side to side like a top-heavy sunflower. Then he turned and walked off without a word.

"He came to see Valya," said Atabaly. "He wants to get married."

"To Valya?"

"Yes. . . ." Atabaly yawned. "Oh my, 1 a.m. . . . What a troublemaker he is, waking everyone up in the middle of the night."

Valya was a tall, plump girl of about twenty-six. She was the staff nurse, and a couple of times I had asked her to take my blood pressure. In the mornings I would see her run, calves flashing in the sunlight, from her cottage to the other end of the garden.

Indicating a waist-high position with my hand, I asked Atabaly, "Would she marry such a man?"

"Oh, don't think anything about his being so small. He's strong. He can take on anybody—you, for example, or me. He'd knock you down right away. And being knocked down by him is like falling off a donkey—you land on your head. From a camel you fall sideways, but from a donkey—headfirst. . . . Yes, he's a real troublemaker, all right. He's a drunkard too, and the women feel sorry for him."

I wandered back to my cottage, leaving Atabaly standing by himself in the depths of the garden. I felt vaguely happy. It was an obscure, nighttime sort of happiness which you can't possibly account for the next morning. Yet here in the middle of the night I suddenly felt a desire to live and a certain joyful exhilaration from the air and the rustling of the trees. It's a good thing, I thought, that dwarfs with big heads drink wine and want to get married, and that women laugh at them, opening their windows into the garden. A good thing too that people come out of their houses at night and converse. I felt no pain anywhere and walked with an easy step. Suddenly I heard a phone ringing on an empty veranda. Who could be calling at such an hour? No one lived in the cottage with the veranda. Some top officials come here in the summertime, and it was they who had had the telephone installed. But it had never rung as long as I had been here.

Normally I would have been asleep at this hour and wouldn't have heard a thing. It was sheer coincidence that I happened to be walking by. But it was just possible that the call was for me. Perhaps Rita was calling. She could have gotten Mansur's number from the Ministry and through him have found out that I was here in Tokhir. It was now ten o'clock in Moscow, still fairly early. And after all, six days had passed since my call! I picked up the receiver. The voice at the other end asked for someone named Sadykov. Hadn't Sadykov arrived yet? It was a woman speaking and her voice trembled.

"I don't know," I replied. "Perhaps he has arrived."

"Probably he hasn't if you don't know about it. Please tell him . . ." and the woman paused to catch her breath, "to call home as soon as he gets there! To call home right away, without fail!"

IV

Rafik had kept his word and done what he could to help. Although actually, who knows? He *said* he had done what he could to help, but this was not the sort of thing that could be verified. The whole business had turned out successfully so he had some basis for taking credit, but for some reason I had the feeling that he hadn't said a word to Mechenov. Kirill said that he had earned his "B" from Mechenov, that he had kept him a whole half hour and given him a rough time. He swore that Mechenov hadn't batted an eye or shown the slightest sign of recognition when he approached the examination table and gave his name. Yet afterwards, whenever we happened to meet, Rafik would ask, "How's my protege doing?" But never mind, the matter was over and done with.

After doing this, there had been Lidia Nikolaevna, an old lady of aristocratic background who had prepared Kirill for his English exam, and then Gartvig appeared on the scene—Gerasim Ivanovich Gartvig, who soon became known as Gera. He was recommended by Larisa as one of the best history tutors in Moscow, and it was she who brought him to us. Kirill had several lessons with him, for which he was paid a very respectable sum—some forty or forty-five rubles. If it weren't for Gartvig. . . . But that was all water over the dam now.

Gartvig was no ordinary individual. There were some things about him I envied, and other things I was deeply contemptuous of and probably even hated. But I did of course give him his due: he knew his subject inside and out, and more to the point, he knew what it was *necessary* to know and did a fine job of coaching Kirill. It turned out, moreover, that he was a friend of the secretary of the admissions committee, a not very likeable gentleman with a sparse, red beard. We subsequently managed to get this secretary out to the dacha of some friends of ours in Snegiri, where he proceeded to get stone drunk and to antagonize absolutely everyone. Our hosts could barely stand him, and finally with great difficulty succeeded in getting him into a car headed back to Moscow. But later on, all of this had its desired effect and Kirill was admitted to the institute. So I thought we had seen the end of Gartvig—*merci et au revoir.* But Gartvig didn't disappear from our lives like the others. On the contrary, he became a dear and close friend, closer than anybody else.

Kirill would say, "Gera and I are going out to the reservoir" or "Gera said it was a lousy film—I'm not going to see it." And Rita would say, "Gera has gotten tickets to Gluck. You're not interested, right?" Gartvig was the sort of person who, when walking down the street and hearing the sound of music in the distance, would automatically stop to listen and then announce, "Aha, there's Comrade Bach!" or "It seems we have Comrade Mozart!" Or something else in the same silly style. On such occasions Rita would blush and turn to me reproachfully, "Why is it that you're so ignorant when it comes to music? That really is your one big failing." Or she might say even more aggressively, "No you really can't be considered a truly cultured person!" Nor have I ever thought of myself as one.

But not at all because I'm not an expert on music.

It's true that I don't understand serious music; it wears me out, whereas I enjoy listening to popular music and all sorts of jazz. And I even whistle these tunes myself. But at the symphony I start to doze or I begin to think about everyday matters, about my job, and all sorts of nonsense. What can I do? It's a shortcoming, a defect, a flaw in my spiritual makeup—but why keep reproaching me for it? Good Lord, a love of music doesn't in itself reveal anything about a person. It doesn't determine his *humanity*. Snakes like music too. There are whole nations that can be called unmusical— the English, for example, and yet no one reproaches them. . . . So there's no need to exaggerate and put on airs. One can love music and still be a cynic.

In such manner I rebuffed Rita a couple of times in the presence of Gartvig, making sure to stress the cynicism idea. For I had realized right away what sort of bird this Gera was. Being an interested party, he would keep quiet or smirk ironically, and only on one occasion did he permit himself to open his mouth, in a seemingly lighthearted and tactful manner but with poisonous enough intent. "You're using the wrong approach with Gennady Sergeevich," he said, turning to Rita. "You shouldn't reproach him for his lack of interest in music, but rather feel compassion—pity him, so to speak." And he went on to tell a mal-apropos anecdote about Socrates and a rude individual who had insulted him on the street. Whereupon I remarked, "I don't believe, Gerasim Ivanovich, that it's customary in polite society to teach a wife how she should behave with her husband!" He laughed and said that he had only been joking. But I didn't want to let it pass as a joke, so I purposely adopted a firm, severe tone and, like it or not, he had to apologize. As he did so, I noticed that he and Rita exchanged glances.

I don't blame Gartvig for establishing a certain control over my wife by taking advantage of her gullibility and idleness and of my own apathy and psychic fatigue —not to mention the fact that for too many weeks out of the year Rita and I were on bad terms with each other. I'm not one of your jealous husbands. And it's possible that nothing even happened between them.

This I don't know and don't care to know. But this isn't
the point. Larisa hinted that something was going on—
which in itself struck me as repugnant, even more repugnant than the thing she was hinting at. A long time ago
Rita and I had tacitly established a certain code of mutual independence. Or more accurately, we had given
our inner consent to the full independence of each of
us. But when your best friend hints at something to
your husband behind your back! I felt sorry for Rita.
But this too is completely beside the point. I blame
Gartvig for bringing into our house—where he found
rather fertile soil, to be sure—his cynicism: his habit of
reevaluating everything, of turning everything upside
down, and of not giving a damn about anything.

I myself have no love for wide-eyed optimists and
have always looked and continue to look at the world
and at people with critical eyes. But the sort of attitude
that Gartvig has—his secret mockery of everyone and
everything—makes me furious. I turn into a rabid con-
servative and feel like taking a big club and pounding it
on that talented head of his. Yes, he's a capable guy, I
know. He's got an advanced degree and a good job
in a research institute. He does some writing, teaches
somewhere—in short, a beautiful set-up. Then why this
cynicism of his? Good Lord, there are so many people
who are not well set up in this life. They try to achieve
something, but can't; they're simply not able to. And
here precisely is where Gartvig's secret lies. He attains
with ease what others spend their whole lives struggling
for, and having once attained it, he can afford to turn
up his nose at his achievement. They say that he was offered the job of assistant director of his institute, but refused it. And how many sick and lonely people there are
around, people suffering from one or another misfortune, people who die at an early age! But he's as healthy

as they come. He's thirty-seven years old, swarthy, and sinewy. He skis cross-country like an Eskimo and cycles along the highway—his favorite sport—like a racer. With his close-cropped hair and small black heard he looks like a Frenchman. (Actually, his mother was a Greek and his father a Russianized German.)

He dresses any which way. Most of the time he appeared at our apartment in some sort of old gym or hiking clothes—in ski pants, faded jackets, and sneakers. Of course, when it came to a Gluck opera, he would get dressed up—but even then in God knows what: some cheap suit hastily purchased in a department store. This aspect of life was of absolutely no interest to him. On several occasions he arrived for his lesson with Kirill unshaven and once he even appeared barefoot. According to Larisa he had been married to two glamorous women. His first wife was a film star and his second was a gypsy dancer from the Moscow gypsy theater, The Romany. He had discarded them both and was now living with a certain lady doctor named Esfir. She was nothing to look at, but was very goodhearted and quite tolerant of all his escapades. He once told me, "Beautiful women don't excite me anymore. Thank God, I've passed that stage." I don't know whether this was mere bravado on his part or a clumsy attempt to assure me that I had nothing to worry about. Naturally I assumed the latter, felt offended, and said rudely, "And did you ever excite beautiful women?" "Sure, lots of times!" That's the sort of braggart he is.

And yet, despite all his bragging he's a most intelligent individual. He knows four languages and reads Latin authors in the original. He specializes in the early Middle Ages, in the history of religion. Thomas Aquinas, Duns Scotus, and so on. From sheer idleness and having nothing better to do, Rita became interested in all this nonsense. And sometimes Scholastic disputes would break out at the supper table. Thus, for example: which was more important—will or reason? Rita was on the side of Thomas Aquinas—for the primacy of reason—and would give us examples from her own life. She considers herself, by the way, *Homo sapiens* to the highest degree. Kirill was on the side of Duns Scotus and defended voluntarism, saying, "If I didn't have an iron will, would I ever have been admitted to the institute?"

I made fun of them, but this had little effect on Rita. She began acquiring, wherever she could, mystical and religious books in tattered, dusty bindings. God only knows where she dug them up. I don't think they sell such rubbish in secondhand bookstores; she must have obtained them from certain individuals directly, on the black market. And now our apartment began to be overrun with bearded and bespectacled youths, book brokers who, along with rare books, also bought and sold certain other items in short supply, such as white diving suits from GUM, for example, on which they made a profit of five rubles. A delightful crowd! A couple of times I threw them out, though Rita would always come to their defense, accusing me of being despotic and stingy. (All these Leontievs and Berdyaevs or, as I called them, White Berdyaevs, cost a good deal of money—money that I couldn't afford, since during the past year and a half my income had for a number of reasons diminished.) But nothing could stop her. She would squeeze out money from her household funds and would swap or sell her own clothes. In short, this was no mere diversion, but a passion and perhaps even a sickness. But none of this was based on genuine feeling: it was all sham and vanity. Of this I was fully convinced, and on one occasion I even told her so.

I was worried about Kirill. He was only a freshman,

and all of this idle chatter bandied about the apartment might confuse him. To tell the truth, I didn't so much worry as *express* my worry to Rita, who replied reasonably enough that Kirill showed even less interest in these books of hers than in his own college textbooks. At this point I raised my voice, "Wonderful! And you, instead of trying to change the situation, instead of trying to drag him away from girls and tape recorders and get him back to his books, you yourself go and get involved in God knows what!" "I'm not doing anything wrong. What I read is my own business, and why are you getting so upset anyway?" I told her that I found the whole business very distasteful. I said that her pseudo-religiosity was so much hypocrisy and deceit, and that the first commandment of any religion—and of Christianity all the more so—was to love thy neighbor. And yet, what did one find with her? Indifference, abandonment of home, bookish vanity. Her husband neglected, and her son left to run wild. It must be menopause, my dear, menopause. And what was needed for that was not Thomas Aquinas but long daily walks and cold rubdowns in the morning.

But our mutual coldness and estrangement had reached a point where even such direct blows had no effect on her. On several occasions I forced myself to read some of these old books, or rather, not to read but skim them, since I was unable to get through a single one of them. They were too abstruse, they really were, and after five pages I would lose track of what the author was trying to say. And after all, I'm not exactly an idiot. More than once, after reading these books, I tried to argue with Rita, to clear the cobwebs from my head. Didn't she see how terribly remote all of this was from us and our real problems and dilemmas! It was beautifully written and perhaps at one time it had moved and perturbed people, perhaps they had had a sense of revelation and had read the prophetic words at the feast of Belshazzar. But in the end, nothing had been revealed, nothing learned, and the reading of such books today was an unnecessary luxury—like owning an Arabian racehorse. What does one do with an Arabian racehorse? Ride it to the corner store to turn in one's empty bottles? Or to the laundry to pick up one's clothes? I don't need all this abstract philosophy, it's absolutely unnecessary, and those who say that they do need it are hypocrites.

I once had the following conversation with Rita: "Well, what did you get out of that book? In what way were you enriched by it?" She had done something particularly irritating that day, and I was just spoiling for a fight. Rita was sitting smoking in her favorite armchair by the standing lamp after having just talked to someone on the phone for a solid hour. Inhaling on her cigarette and gazing at me with unusual attentiveness, she said, "In what way was I enriched by it? Well, if nothing else, I gained a better understanding of your character. Just today I was reading what one author had to say about the eternal feminine in the Russian soul." I burst out laughing. "That's terrific! Well, well, tell me more." And she began spouting all sorts of nonsense about how I was too acquiescent, that I submitted to circumstances and was a "victim of my environment," that in my present work I was merely adapting to the conditions of existence, and that I understood this intellectually but didn't have the strength to rebel against my own way of life. This as a result of the feminine weakness of my character. And also because, thanks to this dualism in my soul, I was lacking in moral self-discipline. At first I listened with a smile, then I got angry.

"And you, my dear woman, are ungrateful," I said.

"I beat my brains out, take on all sorts of assignments that are beneath me, translating one author after another, indiscriminately—and for what? So that you can sit in your chair, smoking your Kents, and say all sorts of nasty things to me? If you have such a highly developed sense of morality, why don't you go and work for our apartment building administration? They need an economist for eighty rubles a month...." "Oh, it seems you begrudge me my crust of bread?" she retorted. I threw up my hands and left the room. Far from our being able to reach any understanding, it was becoming difficult for us even to have a good argument.

On the other hand, when Gartvig was around, she would talk a great deal, laugh, argue, and be full of life. Some crumbs even came my way, since in his presence she would be friendly to me as well. Once she actually called me Genochka, to which I had long become unaccustomed. And now she had a new diversion: excursions by foot, by bicycle, and on skis with Gartvig. I myself had once recommended the idea, and at first they had invited me to join them. I had tagged along a couple of times, but it had been an exhausting ordeal. There was Gartvig, dressed in shorts—even in October the rascal had to flaunt his dark, hairy legs—leaping like a gazelle from one knoll to another. And gasping for breath, Rita would go hurrying after him. As for me, I had no taste for such dashing around. To hell with it—and I left them and myself to the mercy of fate.

Sometimes they went to Zagorsk, sometimes to Suzdal, and sometimes to Svyatye Gory. Ever closer to the monks and to antiquity. Once, somewhere outside of Moscow, they found a little church and became acquainted with the local priest, who let Gartvig climb up into the belfry and ring the bells. They dragged Kirill there, and he too got to ring the bells. This was all foolishness of course, the sort of caprice one associates with *la dolce vita*, and I was not so much upset or annoyed as surprised. For this was the same woman who had once been a trade union activist in the Institute for Municipal Services and Utilities!

No, in this case, of course, there wasn't even a trace of faith in the real sense of the word, but rather a certain spiritual weariness and an excessive amount of time on her hands. Perhaps too, it was even a question of fashion. All these old books, monasteries, and trips to the "Holy Places" in one's Volga had become fashionable, and because of this, banal and commonplace. Earlier everyone had flocked to the Riga beaches, while today they flocked to the monasteries. Oh, the ikonostasis! Oh, what a remarkable old man we ran into in one little village! And the samovars! The ikons! When you visit a pharmacist or some artist who earns his living painting propaganda posters, you inevitably find that they have ikons in their apartments and that they drink their tea from a samovar bought up in some second-hand store for a large sum of money.

All this is noble and good, my friends. You love beauty and are rediscovering our ancient cities, but there's just one thing: what about love of one's neighbor? You haven't forgotten your stooped old grandmother who lives in the village? You haven't deserted your wife at a difficult moment—or conversely, your husband? For after all, that old fellow with the beard who looks out from the ancient ikon hanging in the dining room, above the buffet, commands only one thing: to do good. Well, and what about that, what about goodness?

She should never have stopped working. For if there's no one around you, there's no one for whom you can do good. Nor evil either, for that matter. Still, she shouldn't have quit her job.

Yury Trifonov

But Gartvig—that was another matter. Doing good had no relevance for him! His main attribute, what set him apart from others, was his cool, scrutinizing gaze. In addition to antiquity and the Fathers of the Church he was also interested in contemporary matters and wrote articles on some aspect of sociology. He somehow connected the remote past with today, just how I don't know. He approached religious faith, antiquity, beauty, music, and the people around him all with the same icy zeal and subjected them to the same scrutiny. He did not merely learn about them, but he analyzed them inside and out, to their very core. And where others would hesitate to look, he looked. There was nothing that could embarrass him. This I sensed from the very beginning. He was a genuine intellectual, and it's only these who manage to achieve and create. But don't get too close to such people. Even a woman is only a specimen in their eyes, and goodhearted acquaintances are objects for scrutiny, like some ant or frog.

On several occasions I felt myself being placed in this latter category, and I must say it was not a very pleasant sensation. The two of us were sitting together talking as we waited for Rita. He asked most of the questions, and I answered. His questions were posed in a polite, respectful and, I would say, even searching manner —the manner in which a student might question his professor. Warming to his deferential tone, I replied eagerly and in detail. He wanted to hear about various aspects of my work and about my daily routine: what time did I get up in the morning; what newspapers did I read; did I use a thesaurus; what sort of relationship did I have with my editors and with the authors I was translating? He also asked about what films I liked, about what I did to relax, and where I liked to travel.

Being a simple, straightforward sort of person, I

140

plunged right in with all sorts of explanations and good advice, and only after a while did it suddenly hit me: my God, he's studying me! He's compiling a whole dossier! No, not in the political sense of the word, but in the scientific sense—for his own writings and research. For some pet project. He'd go home and fill up a whole notebook on me. "Such-and-such an individual, forty-eight years old. Class: average intellectual of the late sixties. Genus: literary proletarian. Species: failure—but one who manages to get by. He gets up at eight a.m., reads his newspapers after breakfast, which usually consists of a soft-boiled egg, a slice of bread with cheese, and a large cup of very strong tea. Always likes to drink from one so-called favorite cup—a large vessel that holds a cup and a half and is painted dark red and trimmed with gold. The newspaper articles which interest him the most are those dealing with the works of his literary confreres—both favorable and critical articles. Especially the latter. They perk him up, make him feel like working. . . ."

I told him that he was quizzing me like a doctor his patient. Perhaps I should tell him what sort of stools I had? Or how I fulfilled my husbandly obligations? He replied quite seriously that this would be interesting! Then he remarked that in his conversations with people he did actually try to obtain as much information as possible. What else was there to do? For after all, most conversations were no more than idle chatter—the transmission of rumors and anecdotes and the dragging of mutual acquaintances over the coals. Instead of exchanging ideas we exchange rumors. Naturally he didn't miss the opportunity to show off his erudition, making reference to Socrates, the Peripatetics, and other figures of antiquity, with whom he obviously felt as much at home as a fish in water. And only a little while later did

I realize that he had insulted me. For what he had said, in effect, was that in conversations with me he had no hope of acquiring any *ideas* but only *information*. And never mind what kind of information, if worse came to worst, trivia would do! After all, you can't turn a sow's ear into a silk purse. I recollected how he had once asked me where I'd had my suit made, how much it had cost, and where I had bought the material. And I, idiot that I was, had answered him in the most conscientious fashion. Inherent in his manner was not only disdain for the person he was talking to, but also that main Gartvig trait—a cynical urge to acquire and absorb without giving anything in return. Wanting only to enrich himself, he had no desire, nor did he know how, to share his thoughts and knowledge with people whom he considered inferior and of no use to him.

Unfortunately for me, I put all of this together too late. When I realized that he had insulted me—and was continuing to insult with his silences, his smiles, and his tactful conversations about all sorts of trivia—I wanted to let the rascal have it at the first opportunity, to let him hear the whole truth for once so that he would no longer act so conceited. To tell him that he and I were not like quantities, that our life experiences could not be compared. That the reason I hadn't managed to read so many books or master so many foreign languages was because I was of a different generation: I went to work at an early age, I fought in the war, and I experienced poverty firsthand. So don't take credit where it's not due—the credit belongs to the times in which you live, not to you. You and I took different exams. And in general, damn you, learn to respect people! But the right opportunity to make my speech somehow never came along. Instead the words kept boiling inside me and finally evaporated.

Apparently he himself sensed his inexperience of life. Thus are to be explained his famous flights, which so impressed people who didn't know him very well and which appealed to women especially. At bottom these flights were of an intellectual rather than a romantic nature. The purest rationalism and that same old craving for knowledge. Quite unexpectedly he might leave the institute (take "academic leave") and go off to Odessa, where he would join the crew of a merchant ship and for a long time simply disappear from the lives of his friends and relatives. It's true that this was during his bachelor days, between the gypsy and Esfir. But another summer, when he was already living with Esfir, he wandered around the Ukraine for two months, working in some places as a hay mower, in others as an apple picker or on a road gang. Rita was thrilled by these exploits, which she heard about from Gartvig's friends. "This I can understand, there's a real man for you!" she would say to me. "I can just picture you as a sailor or a field hand. Why, in two days you'd give up the ghost." Of course I would. There's no doubt about it. But then why is it necessary for a man knowing four languages to work in the fields or to load and unload ships? I doubt that the benefit to society is very great. Good Lord, how could one fail to understand? It was simply a matter of self-assertion, of free choice. It wasn't society that needed this, but the individual personality.

Let's say it's self-assertion; that's fine, I agreed. But what lies behind this self-assertion? An inferiority complex. He doesn't have enough experience of life or enough creativity. And when a noncreative person tries to create, he replaces the creative act with anything he can—more often than not, with petty domestic upheavals. And thereby he gains some self-respect. But beyond that? After all, society and those around him neither gain nor lose from these heroic feats. Only poor Esfir suffers and their poor child has to get along without a father. The usual cynicism in a pretty package—turning one's back on everyone but oneself. He wanted to get away from them both and from everyone else for six months, to get away—if only as a sailor, and never mind where—so he simply took off, and that's that.

But Rita would say with a faraway look in her eyes that it wasn't so simple as all that, that one had to make up one's mind to act, one had to dare. And she would look at me with a secret sense of superiority and with a certain pity, as if I were some hopeless case who would never dare to do anything. Other people's foolishness is sometimes dazzlingly beautiful. The absurdity of Gartvig's adventures was perfectly clear to me, but some intellectuals—and especially certain ladies with overly vivid imaginations—went wild over them. Apparently they spoiled him terribly upon his return and gave great dinner parties in his honor! Rita asserted that these flights of his were a form of protest and a sort of challenge to someone or other. What sort of protest? And whom, may I ask, was he challenging? Esfir? Well, perhaps the existing state of affairs at the institute. But, my dear woman, his state of affairs at the institute is excellent. What more could he ask for than to be allowed to disappear for half a year? Oh, you say he was on sick leave, that there's something wrong with his stomach—gastritis or ulcers? So, he was taking advantage of sick leave in order to go off and work as a sailor? A talented young man. He'll go far.

The upshot of such arguments was that I was thought to be unkind, narrow-minded, and somehow unable to rise above my own personal antipathies.

One day that winter Gartvig suddenly appeared at our place in felt boots and a padded jacket and announced that he had gotten a job with a group of lumberjacks and was going off to Kalinin province for a month. They say that these lumberjacks are an interesting breed. It would be good to get a feel for their psychology. And here Rita had an idea. Our maid Nyura was originally from Kalinin province, from the Torzhok district, where her aunt still lived in the village. This aunt was Nyura's only living relative—her mother having died during one of the wartime famines and her father and brother having been killed at the front. And now Rita was asking Gartvig to take Nyura's Aunt Glasha, whom we all knew from her letters, some presents from Moscow: some candy, oranges, and a small transistor radio. Rita was very fond of Nyura. Later on, it turned out that this fondness had its limits, but right now there was no inkling of this. Nyura had been working for us for about ten years. She had come to us when Kirill was in the first grade and she was exceptionally devoted to him. Rita's idea was to get Aunt Glasha to give up one or two of her ikons in exchange for the radio. Rita knew that Aunt Glasha was devout and that she had several ikons which she treasured, having inherited them from her mother, Nyura's grandmother. But if Nyura were to write that she was sick and that the ikons were her only hope, Aunt Glasha might take pity on her and give up the ikons.

Rita wanted very much to hang two or three ikons in the apartment. She had even picked out a spot for them: on the rose-colored wall, next to the large Picasso. Rita felt deprived, not having any. Her friends had already managed to acquire some ikons, and Larisa, who didn't read scholarly books and was not very cultured in general, had simply plundered her country relatives and brought back a whole collection—six ikons, one of which was undoubtedly very old and of the northern school. Gartvig assigned it to the seventeenth century—a real museum piece—and said that one could get a lot of money for it. That lucky Larisa! Everything was always coming her way.

Nyura wrote a letter to her aunt, and they gave it to Gartvig, who returned in January with two ikons. One of them was dated from the early nineteenth century and was quite a find. Rita hung both of them on the rose wall, next to the Picasso. Later on Nyura asked to have the bright, cheap one for herself. She had become ill in fact and thought that the ikon would help. But the older ikon remained hanging in the dining room, and everyone who came to see us would "ooh" and "aah" at its age-darkened surface and say with a knowing air, "Oh, what a magnificent object!"

In the meantime Nyura's illness became serious. I had heard something about this illness before, but didn't know exactly what she was suffering from. Nyura was Rita's department. I only knew that when Nyura or some other woman took care of the apartment, peace was established and I was able to work. Rita hates housework and can't hold out for more than a week without someone to help her. Before Nyura's arrival, when our blockhead was only a sweet little cherub who had to be kept clean, taken out for walks, and otherwise cared for, the maid problem had been most acute, more acute even than the problem of my income. For there was an extended period when my earnings were very irregular and I would have to go off on long assignments in order to bring in more money and to make things easier for the family. I would somehow manage to get by on my own, and it was easier for Rita with one less person around. As it was, we were often down to our last ruble, and it even happened that there wasn't enough money left with which to buy milk for Kirill. And yet despite all this, we always had a maid.

In those days Rita worked at the other end of the city, in Ostankino, and she would be off at seven-thirty in the morning and not return home until late. She simply couldn't get along without a maid, though she didn't get along *with* them either. For some reason she was constantly quarreling with them. Some of them would have worked for us less than three days and already Rita would be groaning, "I can't stand the sight of her! Let her go tomorrow, please...." I understood, of course, that it wasn't easy to get along with these lonely and impoverished old women, these elderly failures, these spiteful shrews. Nor was it any better with the young and foolish ones, who were full of empty hopes (it was, after all, a dying profession), but there was no other way out. And I would tell Rita, "Make more of an effort to hide your irritation. It'll be worse for you without her. You can't manage by yourself. That's already been proved. So, just bite your tongue...." But she was in no mood to listen to logic.

What a procession of colorful characters passed through our home! And what strange personalities our unprotesting Kirka was entrusted to! There was one plump and crimson-faced elderly matron who for some reason was firmly convinced that I might leave Rita for her, only she was the one who couldn't make up her mind. Then there was a woman from Odessa with a long face and mustache who babbled so incoherently that not a single soul could understand her. The husband of the crimson-faced woman was in jail, serving a ten-year sentence for some crime or other, while the Odessa woman had lost all of her relatives during the war. There was one very quiet old woman, a sort of peaceful, gray dove, who in the middle of the night suddenly entered the room where Rita and I were sleeping, and stopping at the threshold, stood there watching us. It was, in fact, just for this moment that she had taken the job. And then there were some unbelievable troublemakers. I felt like typing up a notice and posting it on our door: "Maid constantly in demand here. Inquire within."

One day there appeared a woman with a pale, waxen face who was bundled up like an old country woman. She was uncommunicative and unsmiling, but her eyes shone a clear blue. Her speech was barely audible, and her movements were slow. Nyura was only thirty-two years old, but she looked about forty-five: there was gray in her hair, her face was sunken—she had no teeth left—and she was almost completely deaf. She said proudly of herself, "I'm rotted through and through." She had lost her health and her teeth during the war, during a famine when she and her family had eaten bark to stay alive. Nyura was no less industrious than the others, only slower. On the other hand, she worked quietly, without saying a word. She didn't hear anything and she didn't irritate anyone.

She had never married, and by now, of course, there was no hope of her finding anyone. Who would want such a poor, deaf woman? She did, it's true, have some money, having managed to put away something during her eight years of working in private homes. And as a war invalid she received a monthly pension of some thirty rubles. But in order to keep this precious pension she was constantly having to outwit the authorities. In the domestic workers' employment office where Rita signed a contract with Nyura, they weren't supposed to know about the pension: for if they had known about it, they wouldn't have allowed her to sign the contract.

And she absolutely had to have the contract, since without it she would lose her temporary residence permit. And the permit was necessary because Nyura hoped someday (in ten years, or so the authorities led her to believe) to gain the right to reside permanently in Moscow. In the pension office, on the other hand, they absolutely mustn't find out that Nyura was working as a domestic, since that would have been the end of the pension. So just try to get around that one! But Nyura had long known that no one was going to help her wrest from the authorities what she needed for her survival— there were no such people around: all her old friends and relatives had died, and she could not count on any new ones to appear—and so she got around the authorities herself and promoted her own interests as best she could.

Rita thought of her as cunning and worldly wise. But, my God, what sort of cunning was this! The indelible memory of that long-ago famine that had gobbled up her young life and taken away her mother, sister, and brother, still possessed this woman with all its secret terror. I sometimes observed this at dinnertime, when her hand would reach out terribly slowly, almost reluctantly, for a piece of bread; or when chewing on the meat lying in the serving dish. And smoldering in her eyes would be something of the old terror against which she felt powerless. Some two decades had passed since that famine. Nyura was only eleven years old when she lost her family and would hardly have been able to survive on her own. It was at this point that she had been deceived by her Aunt Shura, the wife of her father's brother. This Aunt Shura had come to Nyura's peasant cottage from the neighboring village, pretending that she wanted to take care of the orphaned girl, but in the end she simply had taken possession of the cottage and forced Nyura out. Nyura wanted to have nothing to do with this aunt and her relatives, although Aunt Shura, shameless woman that she was, kept pestering her with letters—first asking her to send them some sugar, then something else, and constantly complaining about their life back in the village, about how difficult it was to take care of their cow or to find people to mow the hay. These letters with requests from Aunt Shura always brought waves of alarm into our apartment, and Nyura would ask for advice as to what she should do. Rita would reply, "Don't you dare send her anything! Aren't you ashamed of yourself? I won't respect you if you do. That bitch has robbed you of house and home." Nyura would nod her head, "It's true, it's true, Margarita Nikolaevna, she is a bitch. Oh, such a nasty woman!" She would decide not to send her anything nor even reply to her letter. But before two or three days had passed, Rita would notice that Nyura was sewing something into a piece of sacking. "What are you doing, getting a package ready for Aunt Shura?" "Oh well, devil take her!" And suddenly Nyura would break into a smile, covering her toothless mouth with her palm. "At least I live in Moscow and walk along paved streets. But what can she see there in the village, the old fool?"

But her other aunt, her mother's sister Glasha, Nyura loved and was happy to correspond with. Aunt Glasha was a terribly poor old woman who lived as a servant in the home of strangers in the hamlet of Kuvshinovo. She too had been driven from her family cottage, though not by force; it had simply become impossible for her to live there. It was her daughter-in-law Varvara, her son Pyotr's wife, who had made things impossible for her. And only shortly before Gartvig had brought the transistor and other presents to her had Aunt Glasha returned to her native village at Varvara's request after

seven years of working as a servant in Kuvshinovo. A
second son had been born to Varvara and there was no
one to take care of him. Although she was poor and unfortunate, Aunt Glasha had never asked anything of
Nyura, but on the contrary had herself tried as best she
could to cheer Nyura up. Shortly after Gartvig's departure for the Kalinin forests, Nyura had received a letter
from Aunt Glasha in which she had asked permission to
call Nyura "daughter": "I know that you live alone dear
dawter and theres no-one around to treat you nice and
kind like a mother. . . ."

Later on had come letters of thanks for the presents, in which she expressed alarm at Nyura's illness—
the details of this illness having been dictated by Rita—
and expressed regrets regarding the ikons, which she
couldn't quite bear to part with. Her daughter-in-law
Varka kept nagging and tormenting her, while her son
kept quiet and was no comfort at all. So how could she
get along without the ikons? She already regretted having left the people in Kuvshinovo to move back into her
son's home: "Were always fiting and I dont have no
place to put my things where-ever I put them shes always complaning."

Just before New Year's they suffered a terrible misfortune: Aunt Glasha's son Pyotr suddenly died. The
letters in which she informed Nyura of her son's death
remained well-fixed in our minds, since Nyura asked us
many times to read them out loud. Although Nyura was
in fact literate, she had trouble deciphering her aunt's
scrawling hand. Aunt Glasha wrote that her son had
died on the twenty-third of December and had been
buried on the twenty-sixth; that he had never been sick
a day in his life and that it was the vodka, of course,
that was largely to blame. Aunt Glasha's other son, Viktor, had come for a visit, and the two of them had gone

off to the local bar. They'd had too much to drink, and "his heart began feeling bad and he died on the street on the way home the docter says he had scliroses and thats a very dangrous disese so Nyura thats the unhappy things thats been going on here its real sad I cride so much I thought Ide die myself." She went on to curse the daughter-in-law, who had not wanted Viktor and Pyotr to drink vodka at home and had driven them out, as she always did when they were drinking. As a result the evening had come to such a sad end.

Her son's death determined the fate of the ikons. Aunt Glasha didn't want them to fall into her daughter-in-law's hands and she was pretty sure in her own mind that she herself was going to die soon. In a subsequent letter she wrote that she had taken a trip to the camp where the lumberjacks lived, had found Gerasim Ivanovich and given him two ikons, keeping a small one of Gregory the Miracle Worker for herself. Right after her son's funeral, Aunt Glasha went back to live with the people in Kuvshinovo since she couldn't bear to hear Varvara talking about suitors from the very first day after her husband's death. "There you see Nyura such awfull things thats going on here I jest cant get aholt of myself and stop crying I visit his grave every sunday and jest keep crying there til some-one comes and drags me away." And this wicked Varvara, whom her son had always given in to, didn't so much as shed a tear, didn't visit her husband's grave, and was "as happy as a lark."

Why had all of this stuck in my memory—Nyura, who had disappeared for good, her aunt whom we'd never seen, a daughter-in-law, and somebody's death? And yet, all this and many other things equally remote— at least they seemed remote at the time—have in fact contributed to that gross absurdity which is my life. As with a clumsily pitched stack of hay, one dry piece of grass catches onto another, and this second piece is piled onto a third. Everything is coupled and connected; everything hangs, lies, rubs, and rustles, one piece upon another. If a certain Viktor hadn't come to visit his brother, the brother wouldn't have drunk too much and died, Aunt Glasha wouldn't have given up her ikons, Gartvig wouldn't have brought them to us, Nyura wouldn't have started asking for the old ikon in the hospital just at the moment when Kirill's friends were putting pressure on him, and none of the rest would have happened, as a result of which I find myself sitting in this garden in the middle of the night, so far away from my nonexistent home. Undoubtedly no suffering can occur in this world without leaving its mark. But this isn't the point. The point is that Rita should not have quit her job back then, five years ago, for an idle person loses his sense of proportion.

Gartvig returned to Moscow with a bandaged arm, having injured it on site, felling trees. He had a colorful look about him: in place of his small French beard he had grown a full peasant beard and looked like a Russian intellectual of the 1870s. I asked him why he had gotten involved in such nonsense in the first place. He replied that he had wanted to see for himself what tree felling was all about. He had heard a lot about it.

In connection with his bandaged arm, I remarked—and I must confess with the sort of cutting irony that I am quite good at—that he was the embodiment of two different figures, Pechorin and Grushnitsky, and was thus a sort of Grushchorin. "Pechorin and Grushnitsky?" he asked seriously. "That's from Turgenev, isn't it?" I burst out laughing and reminded him that it was from the unforgettable *A Hero of Our Time.** He was embarrassed. Not without a certain malicious pleasure I told Rita of this disgraceful incident that very same day. She couldn't even think of anything to reply, but merely glanced at me with a smile and nodded her head. "That's what comes of burying oneself in all sorts of esoteric trash!" I couldn't help adding. She was silent. At one time she would have taken offense and argued with me over every trifle, but now she had a new method: silence. But this too is completely beside the point.

That winter was a difficult one. I was sick much of the time, and due to a shortage of translation assignments I was earning very little. For some reason Rafik had lost interest in me, and I didn't receive a single payment from him all winter. I would run into him in the club, in the company of some young men whom I scarcely knew—translators of the new breed, types who were quick and efficient and had a wide range of competence. Some of them knew three or four languages, but that didn't change their basic nature—ambitious young go-getters that they were. They had no past to weigh them down with its unrealized aspirations, and they set to work with sharp young claws. Besides that, they were as strong as horses, had normal blood pressure and sound teeth. They could sit up drinking vodka all night and could talk about soccer for hours (what more could Rafik ask for!). In short, they were good at everything. I once happened to run into Rafik in the corridor of the publishing house, and when I greeted him he didn't even bother to reply, but walked right past me, as full of self-importance as some Biblical king. When you're overtaken by a streak of bad luck and are knocked off course, so to speak, who wants anything to do with you! It's your problem—you take care of it.

Actually, nothing so terrible had happened to me. Sickness, professional setbacks, a certain flagging of the spirit—the sort of thing that happens to everyone from time to time. What is needed at such moments is a sense of closeness to those one loves. But Rita was busy with her life, and Kirill with his. He had barely made it through the fall semester (as it was, he had a couple of incompletes) and was starting to talk about taking a leave of absence. Without my knowledge he had even gone to the polyclinic, hoping to get a leave of absence on medical grounds; instead he had gotten a good scolding. He would come to me, begging for money, but I refused to give him any, and he would get angry, taking offense like an adult. Then he would go running to his mother. But Rita didn't have much to give him, and it was at this point that he secretly started asking Nyura for money and she gave it to him.

We didn't know about this for a long time, but later on when we found out by accident, I was furious. "You good-for-nothing, have you sunk so low as to rob a poor woman, taking advantage of the fact that she's devoted to you?" He replied imperturbably that he wasn't robbing anyone, but was only borrowing the money. And he was paying it back on time and even with interest: a bar of chocolate for each ten rubles. This took me completely by surprise. Where was the money coming from to pay back these debts? It turned out that he had been earning money—and pretty good money too—for more than a year, from the time he had started playing the guitar with a rock group called The Titans. I had assumed that all these performances at school dances, parties, and weddings had been for the sake of his playing and in order to meet some new girls. But no! And just how much had he earned, it would be nice to know. Wrinkling his smooth young brow, he conscientiously began adding it up. Approximately 220 rubles. From spring to the beginning of winter.

"And you had the nerve to come to me for one- and three-ruble bills?" "What's so surprising about that? There were times when I was broke. Money doesn't go very far, as you ought to know. Moccasins, trousers, a belt—that's 100 right there. And the blue jacket with the aluminum buttons? And the trip to Leningrad in November—you don't think the thirty rubles Mama gave me covered that?" I absolutely forbade him to borrow any more money from Nyura. I told him that this was almost as bad as being a gigolo, exploiting a woman's love. He was embarrassed, but this didn't prevent his asking me for fifty rubles until February, when some trade union club had promised to pay them. I didn't have any extra money so I gave him five rubles.

But, my God, there's no need to look for any complicated explanations! Everything started coming apart at the seams because we had to cut back on our standard of living. Contemporary marriage is a most fragile institution. The idea of a temporary parting—in order to be able to start afresh, before it's too late—hangs constantly in the air, like some long-cherished dream of taking a trip around the world, for example, or of sailing on the steamship *Victory* from Odessa to Batum. During the whole twenty years that I had lived with Rita, there probably had not been a single week when this thought had not crossed my mind in one form or another. It didn't always come to the surface, but like some intimation it was always there—a hidden source of comfort. When you sit in a packed, stuffy theater, it is pleasant to see the brightly illuminated emergency exit sign above one of the doorways. At any time, you can get up from your seat and head for this sign. You can step outside into the fresh air and, taking advantage of the fact that the evening is just beginning, you can go wherever you please—to a restaurant or to visit a friend. But we rarely leave the theater ahead of time. Only when the play is extraordinarily bad or the air inside unbearably stuffy.

We've paid for our tickets, and besides that it's embarrassing to get up from our seat and make our way toward the aisle, stepping across people's legs and feeling the disapproving glances of the audience. But the realization that we *can* leave at any time is a comforting one, and it should be there, in order to make it easier for us to breathe. They say that everyone, even the completely healthy individual, has the tuberculosis bacillus inside him, but that special conditions are needed for the bacillus to begin to grow and for the disease to take hold. The idea of separation lies hidden inside every one of us like a slumbering bacillus. There's no point in arguing about it, it's a fact. Just look inside yourself.

No, the incident with Nyura could not have been the cause, it was merely the last in a series of chills which precipitated the sickness and its raging fever. One day a woman came to our apartment and said that she wanted to see Anna Fedoseevna—Nyura. She and Nyura shut themselves in the kitchen and had a long talk about something or other. Then the woman came out and told Rita that she was taking Nyura to the hospital for a month, to the psychiatric hospital. Nothing frightening, just a particular form of schizophrenia. It turned out that Nyura had been under observation for a long time, and we hadn't known anything about it.

Without Nyura things began to go badly. All three of us being sloppy by nature, the apartment fell into a state of neglect, and nobody bothered about meals. Rita would continually take to her bed with a hot-water bottle or compress, saying that she could do no more, that she was utterly exhausted. But there was another reason why things went badly without Nyura. In some incomprehensible fashion this deaf, uncommunicative woman managed to keep peace among us. She would come into the room, sit down, and say something trivial but not lacking in sense. And the irritation would vanish, the hurt would pass. She was capable of real devotion, and probably because this was such a genuine feeling, undiluted by any self-interest, it affected us so strongly. Once Rita and I had a serious quarrel and I threatened to walk out on her—to hell with all of you! This was a long time ago, when our feelings still ran high and we took everything to heart. Later on, we made up, and it was all over and forgotten. But suddenly one day I found Nyura crying in the kitchen. What was the matter? "Margarita Nikolaevna said that you're going to leave us. How will she get along by herself?" "Like everybody else, dear Nyura. She'll get a job. She's a perfectly healthy woman, healthier than you." Biting her lips, Nyura shook her head, and not hearing my words, she whispered, "I can always find a job, I'll get by, but what will happen to Margarita Nikolaevna?"

Sometimes in the evening Nyura would come into the living room. She would sit down in a corner and gaze at Rita as she was sewing something, or reading or writing. She would simply gaze at her and smile, without saying a word.

About three years ago, when we were in particularly bad financial straits and Kirill, of course, was no longer a child, we decided to part with Nyura. Well, what else could we do? From one month to the next we were behind in her pay! Nyura calmly heard us out, but that evening once again I saw her crying quietly as she sat on her folding cot in the kitchen. The next day she told us that she was willing to work without pay until things got better and the money began to come in. And now this creature who had held our home together in such strange fashion was gone. The three of us would crawl off in different directions, each to his own room, to his own preoccupations and secrets, to his own

silence, and only she, the protector of the hearth, represented a real home. But then, she too had no one but us.
And for her our motley threesome was the only source
of human warmth, which she reached out for and was
afraid of losing.

Nyura wrote letters from the hospital: "Dear Margarita Nikolaevna Im sending warmist greetings to
you. . . ." She was in a ward with fourteen people, and
everything pleased her: the doctors, the nurses, the
food, her bed, which was the third from the window,
and the window itself, which had a view of the Moscow
River. Sometimes at her request a nurse would call us
from the hospital—Nyura couldn't hear anything over
the telephone—and ask for our news: how was Margarita
Nikolaevna feeling, and had they delivered the sheets
and underwear from the laundry? For some reason she
needed these phone calls; they represented that human
warmth which she could not do without. "Nyura wants
to know if you've remembered to defrost the refrigerator." Rita felt sorry for Nyura and went to visit her several times, taking along some fruit. The doctors said that
Nyura's illness would be difficult to cure, but that it
wouldn't get any worse and it was of no danger to those
around her. They said that she would certainly be able
to do light housework and that she could knit, sew, and
make paper decorations for the New Year's tree, for example. Nyura asked Rita to send her the old ikon to the
hospital, and although Rita was dismayed at having to
part with it, she gave it to Kirill and asked him to take it
to her. For Rita this was undoubtedly a supreme sacrifice, and no one expected it of her. At first she felt
pangs of regret and her conscience wavered, but later on
she was proud of herself and began telling all her friends
that she had given up her most precious possession, the
ornament of her home, to her sick maid. It was a

terrible shame, but what else could she do? There, in the house of suffering, the ikon was needed more than on the rose wall next to the Picasso. And—one has to do good, and not just read about it in wise books. In the course of recounting all this, it was somehow forgotten that the precious item belonged to Nyura.

Gartvig was indignant: "How could you give up such a museum piece? You should have given her the other one, the Palekh ikon. What difference would it make to her?" But it was precisely the old ikon that Nyura had wanted. The reason for this became clear later on, but at the time we were merely surprised at the urgency with which she kept asking us to hurry, hurry, and send her the ikon, as if it were some special medicine on which her recovery depended.

At the beginning of March a doctor called from the hospital, a certain Radda Yulievna, and said that she had some good news for us. Nyura had gotten better and would be able to leave the hospital in time for International Women's Day. The only question was: where would she go? Did we still have a place for her? We hadn't hired anyone to replace her? No, we hadn't hired anyone. Rita was delighted and exclaimed into the receiver, "Of course not, how can you even think such a thing! We can't wait to have her back with us!" Radda Yulievna promised to let us know about the exact date of Nyura's discharge a few days later, around the fifth. As it turned out, she called back the very next day. In the meantime, however, Rita had begun to have second thoughts as to whether the presence of a sick or half-sick person in the house would really make her life any easier. Well, fine, she could do some light house-work—a little cooking and shopping—but still, there was no getting around the fact that she was mentally deficient. There might be complications, and any day she might have to go back to the hospital. . . . This gave all of us pause. Rita discussed the matter with Larisa, and Larisa advised her to wait awhile and not rush into anything. Let them cure her completely and give us some guarantee. As things stood now, they were probably only too happy to discharge her, just to get her off their hands. And when Radda Yulievna called the second time, Rita was foolish enough to express some of her doubts openly. She mentioned the idea of a guarantee as well, which made Radda Yulievna extremely irritated. She said that she had not expected to hear any such talk and was, in fact, astonished by it. Pursuing her previous train of thought with the same foolish openness (she could be terribly clumsy and shortsighted at times), Rita went on to say that she was worried on her own account, that she wouldn't have the strength to take care of a sick person, and that what she wanted, in fact, was to have someone take care of her. At this point Radda Yulievna rudely cut her off and asked to speak to me.

At the other end of the line I heard a sharp voice obviously accustomed to giving orders to subordinates: "You're a professional man—a literary translator, isn't that right? Well then, how can you allow your wife to talk such nonsense—excuse me for saying so. We're not a watch repair shop and we don't give out guarantees. Nyura is completely alone. This is a question of conscience, of your concern for your fellow man. From what Nyura has told me about you I pictured you as completely different people and not—excuse me for saying so—so callous and calculating." "Now just a minute!" I objected. "You don't know either my wife or me, and on the basis of a five-minute phone conversation. . . ." But here, Radda Yulievna cut me off as well. "Excuse me, but I have no time for soul-searching conversations. You think the matter over more carefully and call me back no later than tomorrow evening. I need to know by Saturday." And with that she hung up.

We began to discuss this newly arisen dilemma, arguing about it and, as always, getting irritated and blaming each other. I told Rita that she hadn't taken the right approach with the lady doctor and had ruined everything by turning her against us. For her part Rita accused me of cowardly behavior, of being afraid, as usual, to make a bad impression on others, as a result of which it was she who ended up making the bad impression. Kirill asked, "What's the story, is she going to be with us forever?" I said probably not forever, but for a long time. We were taking a certain responsibility upon ourselves. "Uh-uh!" said Kirill after a pause. "After all, she's not a relative of ours, right?"

We all were thinking the same thing, but Kirill expressed himself honestly, whereas Rita and I continued to rationalize and hide behind words, accusing each other of all the mortal sins and missing the real point. "What sort of people are you?" Rita went on. "Kirill, how can you call Nyura an outsider when she's lived in our home for ten years! Why, she loves you like a son; she brought you up, and now that you're a strapping young man, you say she's no relative of ours. Well, I can tell you, I feel closer to her than to any relative." "Then what's the problem? Take her back!" "Of course, Mama, take her back, take her back. Take care of her, cook her cereal in the morning, buy milk for her." Rita responded that we were mean and lazy, that we didn't help her, that she wore herself out, and now, to add insult to injury, we wanted to saddle her with a sick maid. I just kept repeating one thing, "Excuse me, please, but where is your love for your fellow man? Why have you been reading all these religious books? Here you have a trial sent down from on high, you're required to make a sacrifice, and what do you do? Eh? Turn tail and run? Have we suddenly become atheists? And all this talk about brotherly love is merely some concoction thought up by the priests?" "If I had a different husband and a different son, I would take this woman in without a moment's thought." Yes, yes, of course. But by now it had all been decided. She had already dissociated herself from Nyura by referring to her as "this woman." I replied, "And if I had a different wife, such a question wouldn't even have arisen. My God, how many cases are there in simple uneducated families, where. . . ."

Neither on Thursday nor on Friday did we call Radda Yulievna. Neither Rita called, nor I. We hadn't come to any agreement. Each of us thought the other had called, and we had some justification for thinking this, though we purposely didn't ask about it, so that later on, if necessary, each of us could shift the blame to the other. As usual, in times of crisis, Rita's liver started acting up and she spent the whole day lying in bed with her hot-water bottle and talking with exaggerated anxiety about her medicines and the state of her health. I didn't feel well either—apparently it was my heart. And as I lay on the sofa in the study, swallowing first one sedative, then another, it occurred to me that we did have some justification: we were, after all, sick people. I considered myself less guilty, for I was more seriously ill. There was no comparison between cholecystitis and heart disease. One can live a whole lifetime with cholecystitis, but one dies from heart disease at an early age. So that in all of this betrayal—yes, it was clearly a case of betrayal, if only a small one, and there was no point in trying to deny it—Rita's share of guilt was greater than mine. And in general, she was closer to Nyura than I. What was my relationship with Nyura? I saw her only in the mornings—when she was cleaning the study and I

couldn't wait for her to disappear with her rags and vacuum cleaner—and later on in the day, at dinner. I seldom spoke with her, nor was it easy to carry on a conversation with a deaf woman. But Rita's relationship
with her was another matter.

Late that evening Rita suddenly came into the
study. She was in her bathrobe, her hair was unkempt,
and her face was gray and drawn as it usually was when
her liver was bothering her. She sat down on the edge of
the sofa and looked at me. I could see that she was feeling bad. Either she had come to make up with me or to
complain about something, or perhaps her conscience
was bothering her. But I was feeling bad myself. I
looked at her in silence. "Do you know what I was just
remembering?" she said. "The time we lived in Pod-
leskovo. Kirka was about seven. Do you remember our
cottage there? The porch was so tiny, a typical country
porch, and the hens were always flying up onto it—remember? . . . Nyura was young then, she had just come
to work for us. . . . And that summer I went to the Far
North on a business trip. . . ." I nodded. I also remembered that summer. Rita's father and my mother had
both been alive then. Rita had written us letters from
the North, and all of us, including little Kirka, had eagerly awaited her return. It was a summer filled with anticipation. And finally she had returned in August,
bringing a white puppy with her—a husky, which later
on had mangled our landlady's hens—and a polar-bear
skin, which someone had given her in Murmansk. I tormented myself, trying to guess who had given it to her
and why. The skin hadn't been treated and it soon
rotted. We finally threw it out a couple of years ago. We
never had another August like that one: the tiny little
stream, the Sonia, and the oak forests with mushrooms.
I remember we once took a long walk—about ten

kilometers—to the village of Gorodok, where there was an eighteenth-century bell tower.

"And do you remember," said Rita, "when I became ill that September? We thought it was my appendix, but it turned out that I needed to have an abortion right away. You took me to the district hospital. It was terribly muddy—there had been a lot of rain—and the car couldn't make it up to the hospital entrance, so you and some local peasant carried me the rest of the way." I remembered that too. "Nyura remained alone with Kirka for a whole week," said Rita. "And at that time he too was sick with something or other."

Then she said, "I think that with Nyura's leaving we're losing something forever." "Yes," I replied. I could see that she was about to cry, but she didn't want to show her emotion and left the room.

The next day Nyura suddenly appeared. It was afternoon, and we were just sitting down to dinner. She said that they had let her go out for two hours, to collect her things. She undid her familiar scarf, took off her coat and galoshes, and the felt boots underneath them, stepped into her slippers and sat down to eat with us af if nothing had happened. Enormous satisfaction was written all over her wan face. And she smiled the whole time, gazing at Rita. Once again I saw how slowly her hand reached for the bread basket and how clearly the past was mirrored in her pale blue eyes: love, hunger, war, hopes—all of these mixed together. She felt terribly sorry for Rita. "Oh, Margarita Nikolaevna, how can you get along without someone to help you?" Rita replied that it was very difficult. "Of course," said Nyura. "You need some woman to help you." And the fact that she referred to the unknown person who would take her place so calmly and indifferently as "some woman," meant that she was reconciled to the situation and nothing further needed to be said. She told us about the hospital and about the fact that they had promised to send her to an even better hospital outside the city. This hospital was in the middle of a forest, and one could walk to the nearby railroad station, where there were stands and one could buy a few things. After dinner, Nyura washed the dishes, and then Rita asked her to take out the garbage pail as well. For me this was the last straw. As it happens, there's no refuse chute in our building and we have to carry the garbage out into the courtyard, where there are some large refuse bins. A daily annoyance. Sometimes the garbage was handed to me, and I would carry it out, neatly wrapped in newspaper. In short, no big thing, and I don't know why I suddenly became so furious. But after Nyura had gone out to get a taxi and returned with the driver, who carried her suitcase and two bundles (she was always accumulating all sorts of odds and ends), and after we had said goodbye to her and were left alone, I started shouting, "So you had the nerve to send her away after all! And let her take something out on the way. If only a pail, eh?" "What pail?" asked Rita, and burst into tears.

Suddenly I felt such a burning pain that at first I couldn't decide whether it was my heart or whether I had been stricken by feelings of shame—and despair. I went into the study and locked the door behind me. My own shouts kept reverberating in my mind and I pictured Rita's face as it paled with fright. Two or three hours passed. The apartment was as silent as a tomb. Finally, around six, Kirill knocked at the study door and said in the voice of a prison warden, "Come and have your tea!" I realized that I was forgiven and that the pail and my outburst had been beside the point—the point being that when a betrayal takes place, even a

small one, it is always follwed by feelings of nausea. The
next day at Rita's request we purchased ten blank notice forms at a Moscow Information kiosk, and I sat
down to write in my beautiful hand: "A family of three,
consisting of a husband, wife, and college-age son, is
looking for. . . ."

All of this faded and was soon forgotten. Then one
day I received a phone call. I remember exactly: it was
in the middle of the day, on the fifteenth of March. A
brisk, high-pitched, and as it seemed to me, not very respectful male voice asked for me, Gennady Sergeevich,
and then introduced himself: Investigator So-and-So.
Could I come to see him tomorrow at such-and-such address? I could. Was I free at about—ah, well, let's say
ten-thirty? Yes, that was fine. Well then, it was settled.
I'll see you tomorrow. My office is next to the Synthetics store. The whole conversation lasted no more
than twenty seconds. Somewhat dazed, I put down the
receiver and madly began trying to figure out what this
bad dream was all about. As far as I knew, I had committed no crime. Nonetheless I felt slightly panic-
stricken. Well, perhaps it wasn't quite panic, but some
sort of unbearable nervous anxiety. And the worst part
was that I had no idea what it was all about. Next to the
Synthetics store. It could be absolutely anything! No
one is really insured against anything in this world.

I had never been involved in any criminal investigations, and I decided not to say anything about this to
Rita. Why add her panic to my own? Most distressing
was the fact that I had almost twenty-four hours to
wait. Why hadn't I thought of making the appointment
for today rather than tomorrow? If you wish, I can see
you right now. I'll leave right away. No, tomorrow I'm
busy, I can only see you today, right now. I wouldn't

be able to get any work done today anyway. And why couldn't I have asked what it was all about? I could perfectly well have asked. He would have told me and I wouldn't have had to spend the whole day worrying. On the other hand, he might not have told me. And if he hadn't, I would have been ten times more worried. They do that on purpose, so that you'll be more upset. So that when you come in, your resistance is already down, you're trembling and shaking inside, and then they just touch you with a finger and you crack. But God help me if I knew what I had to crack about. Ah, the Synthetics store—I knew where that was. I once bought something there.

That evening we were supposed to visit my cousin Volodya and his wife Lyalya, who had gotten an apartment on Zhivopisnaya Street in the Khoroshevo-Mnevniki area. For the last month they had been stubbornly insisting that we come to a housewarming. They were rather dull company (one always had to sit through a showing of their home movies, the subject of which was usually their latest hiking or camping expedition), and at first we had declined their invitation under various pretexts. But the day finally arrived when we couldn't put it off any longer without mortally offending them. So we bought a bottle of champagne and two German wall lamps at GUM, loaded Kirill down with them and set off.

Although I went through the motions of shopping, talking, and buying tickets for the subway, the whole time I was thinking only about what was going to happen the next day. And the more I thought about it, the more frightened I became. I soon convinced myself that there were innumerable grounds for my being brought in for questioning. As many as you like! My God, it seemed as if I had committed every possible violation of the Criminal Code.

I could be tried for bribery, if only because I had gone to the races with Rafik a number of times and had paid for his dinner at the restaurant there. On the other hand, there had been instances where he had paid for my dinner. I could also be prosecuted for buying stolen goods. Sometimes I had acquired at almost government prices all sorts of items, such as window glass, wiring, switches, sheet metal, etc., from the workers of our Apartment Management Office. And speculating in foreign goods! When I brought home some sweaters for Rita from my last trip to Austria and they turned out to be too big for her, she sold them to Larisa. And Larisa, who was a real speculator, might have passed them on to someone else at a higher price. And somewhere along the line she might have gotten caught. Beautiful—a face-to-face confrontation with Larisa in the investigator's office! "Are these your sweaters?" "Actually, I. . . ." "Where did you get them? Why didn't you turn them in to a commission store?" And theft? Once when I was abroad, I stole from a hotel a magnificent ashtray which had a picture of the local city hall and the inscription in Latin: *Beati Possidentes.* Even now this ashtray still adorns my desk. Once I happened to steal an encyclopedia volume from the library of a tourist home. I was about to leave the place and I badly needed this volume for the translation I was working on. It's true that when I returned to this same tourist home a year and a half later, I brought the volume with me and inconspicuously put it back on the shelf. Probably murder was the only crime I hadn't. . . . Actually, there had even been murder. A tragic incident six years ago when I was returning from Riga in Arutunian's car. His wife was driving, and on the Minsk Highway we ran over an old man. The poor fellow was dead drunk, and he died in the hospital two hours later. Arutunian's wife was held legally responsible. They managed to save her (she received a year on probation), but actually I too was guilty. I had been in just as great a hurry to get back to Moscow as she. Yes, there was no end of things for which I could be prosecuted. . . .

Such was the mood in which I went to this ridiculous housewarming. Rita divides all of our friends and relatives into "yours" and "mine." She isn't necessarily fond of her own relatives, but she has strong feelings about them. My relatives, on the other hand, she views with indifference and at the same time is quite good at judging their character. She once referred to Volodya and Lyalya as "soldiers of fortune." It was an apt characterization, encompassing as it did their silly passion for travel, their lack of culture, and their absolutely predatory zeal for acquisition. Volodya is a factory engineer, while Lyalya works in a planning and design office. They can't make terribly much between them, and yet they're always buying something new and they always have money. You can even borrow from them for a short period, though it's better not to have to. They're marvelous at economizing, something that's completely unknown in our family—our former family, that is. Rita once nastily observed that Volodya's and Lyalya's preference for spending their vacations on camping trips was also a result of their desire to save money. It was cheaper than staying at some tourist home by the seashore.

Volodya and Lyalya were friendly though somewhat guarded in their relations with us. For some reason or other they thought of us as smart operators, and of course I was even smarter than Rita. It seemed to them that I was making money hand over fist, and once when Rita naively complained about not having any money, they burst out laughing, "Oh, so you don't have any money, eh? Well, what about cashing one of your savings certificates?" And of course our apartment, with its six-ty-two square meters of living space, not including the storage area, had once made a tremendous impression on them. All in all, they were relatives like any other relatives. And knowing them as well as I did, I realized that their stubborn insistence regarding the housewarm-ing had to have something behind it. There must be something they wanted from us. After we had sat around for an hour at the table, munching on delicacies brought up from the nearby Oryol Restaurant, it be-came quite clear what this "something" was.

Volodya's daughter Veronika was just finishing high school, and it was time to think about getting her into college. And just imagine—she wanted to enter the same institute as Kirill. Kirill, it seems, had had some wonderful tutor, someone with connections, who had been a great help—it was a German name, they'd heard that. . . . "Gartvig!" shot out Kirill. Couldn't they mak make use of him too? "Of course," said Rita. "Why not? But I think he's out of town right now. He's always traveling." It wasn't very pleasant to hear about Gartvig —about his connections and how helpful he was—even though it was true. But we hadn't told anyone about him. As it turned out, they had heard about him from a friend of Larisa's who was acquainted with some office associate of Lyalya's. That blabbermouth Larisa seemed to be behind everything! I told them that I didn't think Gartvig was tutoring anymore since he was very busy at the institute. This was true—Gartvig had said so him-self—but Volodya and Lyalya naturally decided that we didn't want them to have Gartvig. Actually, this too was true.

I didn't want them to "have" Gartvig because I was suddenly struck by a terrible suspicion: what if Gartvig, along with his friend, the secretary of the admissions committee—the man who had come out to Snegiri—had just been caught in some admissions scandal? I hardly knew our host in Snegiri. He was one of Rita's friends. Good Lord, how dangerous! I really knew nothing about all of this—it had been arranged without my participation. But with his cynicism Gartvig was capable of anything.

Rita apparently had reasons of her own for not wanting Volodya and Lyalya to "have" Gartvig.

They had guessed correctly. And right there at the table they began trying all the more zealously to wrest Gartvig from us. They demanded that we call and find out whether he was in town or not. And if he hadn't left town, would they be able to count on his help? Rita said that she didn't remember his phone number. I tried to remember it, but without success. Unlike Rita, I never *had* known it by heart. "You want Gera's phone number?" piped up our blockhead. "I remember it!" So we had to call him. Esfir answered and said that Gartvig was at a concert at the Conservatory. They demanded that I call him the next morning, and I promised to do so. Yes, yes, tomorrow morning.

When I thought of the next morning—I would have to leave the apartment at nine-thirty—I felt a tightening sensation in the pit of my stomach, and my legs grew weak. My suspicions regarding Gartvig had taken hold with terrifying strength, and by now I was almost convinced that there was some connection between Gartvig and the investigator. No wonder Gartvig had disappeared the last few weeks and had neither called nor shown his face. And there wasn't a single person I could go to for advice!

Cheered up by the fact that Gartvig was in Moscow —to them the matter seemed as good as settled—Volodya and Lyalya dragged out their movie projector and the white cloth that served as a screen, and the torment began. I didn't take in a thing that was happening on the screen. Whether it was the taiga or the Crimea I really couldn't say. Some people were walking somewhere, then they were eating with spoons from a large pot. This time there was something new: the film was accompanied by a soundtrack which its creators found terribly witty, and, unable to restrain themselves, they would continually burst into laughter. At one point, as Lyalya was flaunting her bare stomach and some sort of indescribable breeches, Volodya's voice proclaimed, "Lyudmila Alexandrovna has taken society by storm with her new outfit from Dior," or words to this effect. Rita heaved a sigh, but Kirill, who was enjoying all this, roared with laughter. Suddenly Rita broke in, "By the way, dear friends, although it's true that Gerasim Ivanovich is an excellent teacher, Kirka got in thanks to his own efforts more than anything else. He studied like mad, he really did."

Volodya and Lyalya replied amicably, "Of course! How else?" I too decided to put in a word, "So don't think that Gartvig is the solution to the problem. And he doesn't have any special connections." "What about his ordinary ones?" Lyalya asked archly. Just at that moment Lyalya appeared on the screen in her bathing suit, standing up to her knees in water and making some sort of dancelike gestures with her arms. Lyalya had strange legs: they weren't rounded above the knee, but somehow broad and flat. Needless to say, she did not look spectacular in a bathing suit. Volodya's voice announced, "The dance of the Dying Swan, performed while wading. . . ." "Actually he doesn't have any connections at all!" I said with sudden animosity. "All this talk about connections is just nonsense!"

Yury Trifonov

After we had left their apartment and were out on the street, Rita said, "Your relatives are really something. The way they dug in with their claws—it was hand over Gartvig or else!" I didn't have the strength to protest. I could have replied, "As far as Gartvig is concerned, that's your department." But Kirill was there, and my thoughts were elsewhere. After all, she didn't know what I knew. Suddenly I felt sorry for her. And I felt sorry for my son too. Just at this moment Kirill gave a piercing whistle and shouted at the top of his lungs, "Hey, cabbie, over here!" As we got into the taxi, it occurred to me that it wasn't at all a bad thing to have a grown son.

That night I hardly slept at all. I finally dozed off around five a.m. and jumped up at eight. One word kept running through my mind all night: "synthetics."

A young man without a jacket and wearing a white linen shirt and a necktie on which there were five Olympic rings asked, "Is this your ikon?" Before me I saw Aung Glasha's old ikon which until recently had hung beside the Picasso. "Yes! That is, actually . . ." and I went on to explain the situation. I was told by the investigator that the ikon had been confiscated from some big profiteer against whom a case was now being drawn up. And this profiteer had bought the ikon from Kirill for 120 rubles. It still wasn't clear whether Kirill would be brought to trial—this would be decided in the course of the investigation—but the case definitely would be publicized, first and foremost in the Komsomol organization of Kirill's institute. I then responded to several questions about Kirill, Nyura, the origin of the ikon, and some friend of Kirill's named Romik, from the Titans group, whom I barely knew. I confirmed that I hadn't known anything about the sale of the ikon and that all of this, in fact, took me completely by surprise.

174

I had assumed that the ikon was in the hospital with Nyura.

A protocol of our meeting was drawn up, and I signed it. I got up to leave and was already at the door when I thought to ask, "And when will you be summoning my son?" I was taken aback by the investigator's reply: "He's already testified. If it's necessary, we'll summon him again." So, last evening when he was roaring with laughter at my cousin's. . . .

My initial reaction upon learning why I had been summoned was a momentary sense of relief. It's not I, not I! Kirill, of course, was also "I," a certain part of this "I," but not a very large part, an immature part. Things were not so terrible, the wound was not a fatal one. But my sense of relief lasted only a moment. For when the whole picture became clear (it all hit me in the course of a second, right there at the investigator's desk, and I was able to fill in the missing details on my own, without any help from the investigator), and when I realized how Kirill had set the whole thing up, how he had persuaded poor, foolish Nyura and had deceived us, how he had dissembled and covered things up, I was suddenly overwhelmed by a feeling that was even more oppressive and more unbearable than fear—a feeling of terrible shame. Because it was, after all, I! I, I myself, and no one else! It was not Kirill, but I who was sitting in front of the investigator's desk and being questioned by this young man who eyed me with cool disdain. Oh, I felt this very distinctly! And if it hadn't been me, my whole being with all my guts, but had merely been a part of myself, a certain Kirill sitting in front of the investigator's desk, I would never have felt that disdain nor experienced that painful sense of shame.

Out on the street, I began rambling aloud, like one delirious. Well, wonderful. Well, splendid. You've gotten

Yury Trifonov

yours, you scum, you good-for-nothing. Yes, let there
be a trial, let them drag you in, you bastard. I haven't
even managed to bring up my only son, pathetic creature, old fool that I am. . . . And I ran all the way home
in order to say something, to ask something—but what?
What was there to ask, what was there to say?
Rita was home. Kirill hadn't yet arrived. Rita knew
everything. He had told her. And what about me—did I
have to learn from the public prosecutor's office what
was going on in my own home? Perhaps I was no longer
a member of the family? If so, please tell me, let me
know. I'll pack my suitcase and leave town.
Rita replied very calmly, "Yes, we decided not to
tell you. We knew you'd fly off the handle, get excited. . . . And in this situation shouting and cursing
won't help. What we need to do is figure out exactly
what's to be done, and how. . . . He behaved abomin-
ably, it's perfectly true, but we've got to rescue him.
We'll have to ask for help from Mechenov, or Rafik, or
Gera—or whomever you please, because if we don't, the
boy will be kicked out of the institute. First he has to
be saved, then we can punish him." No! No! First he has
to be punished! And let him worry about saving himself! She held something out to me in her hand. "Just
calm down, then we'll talk about it. Take this tranquil-
izer." And I noticed in her eyes that same cool, almost
official disdain which I had seen in the investigator. She
went off to her own room, and I locked myself in the
study.
Finally, several hours later, Kirill arrived. I immediately called him into the study. He walked in with
a cigarette in his mouth, sat down on the sofa, and
gazed at me with an insolent smile. Before saying a
word, I grabbed the cigarette from his mouth and tossed
it out the window. "What's that supposed to mean?" he

176

asked. "That's supposed to mean that today I was at. . . ."
"I know! You were at Vasily Vasilievich's." "What Vasily Vasilievich?" "The investigator, Katerinkin." "How
do you know?" "I'm practically an old buddy of his.
He's already called me in four times." "Oh, he has, has
he?" I said sternly. "Four times?" My anger had in fact
spent itself, and unable to muster up any more forceful
emotion, I asked in a voice full of shame and reproach,
"Well, do you at least understand what a scoundrel you
are? Do you?" "Of course, Papa. What's there to understand? I understand." He bowed his head in a show of
despondence. I could see that I was still being made a
fool of. Suddenly he jumped up from his seat, ran up to
the desk, and turned on my small transistor radio. The
announcer was rattling on about something or other,
and Kirill's face lit up with joy. He clapped his hands
and whispered, "Hurrah, hurrah!" I walked up to him,
grabbed the radio from his hands, and turned it off.
"Listen, I'm telling you for the last time and I'm completely serious. You can get out of this mess on your
own! You understand?" "Okay, Papa," he said. "Yes
sir. Just don't get upset." This exasperated me, but at
the same time I couldn't help feeling the absurdity of
the whole situation. "It's not I who should be upset, but
you, you! You should be upset! . . . You stupid character!" "I understand, Papa. And I am upset. But you
shouldn't get upset. Everything will be okay, just don't
think about it. Should I bring you some water?" "Get
out of my sight!" I shouted. He leaped from the study
like a volleyball player, while I remained, lying on the
sofa like some pitiful, crushed insect. And this was the
ultimate proof of the fact that it had been I and not he
who had sat there in front of the investigator's desk.

Later on I acted. What else could I do? Our young
fool was faced with expulsion. Like a chessplayer whose

177

every move is forced, I went running to Rafik and through him was put in touch with Mechenov. Here I was informed: "Your dear son has already been guilty of too many indiscretions. He still hasn't fulfilled his physical education requirements, and during the first semester he cut twenty-two hours of class without any valid excuse." So I was forced to turn to Gartvig, whose friend, the former secretary of the admissions committee, had recently become a big shot in the rector's office. For some reason or other Rita didn't want to call Gartvig. Gartvig was very cold with me but said that he would speak with his friend. He couldn't guarantee that it would do any good, however, since he had, it seemed, lost favor in that quarter. I didn't try to find out what he was referring to. Somebody had already told me that Gartvig was having difficulties at the institute and was perhaps even in danger of losing his job. Well, only time would tell on that score, but I, for one, was not in the least surprised. In any case, Gartvig apparently did call his friend on our behalf and the latter's efforts did help, for Kirill remained in the institute—albeit with a stern reprimand and a warning from the institute Komsomol. I forced him to deliver the 120 rubles to Nyura at the suburban hospital in Murashkovo and to bring back a receipt from her. As for the ikon, it lay gathering dust in the public prosecutor's office, awaiting its allotted hour in court. But this is beside the point. This is completely beside the point! The point is that when all of this was over, a dull depression set in. Rita and I no longer quarreled, we merely exchanged opinions. She once said, "When three egotists live together, nothing good can come of it." "Yes, but each egotist does have a way out," I replied. "He can find a goodhearted person who will forgive him all his faults." "That's such a lengthy business—to start looking for a goodhearted

person. I'm too tired for that. I'm already an old woman."
"Don't worry, you'll still be able to find admirers."
Such was the conversation we had at breakfast one
morning, with Kirill sitting right there, reading the newspaper.

V

Atabaly came to my cottage in the morning with a
jar of milk. I was still in bed, utterly exhausted from my
sleepless night. By all indications my blood pressure had
shot up. Perhaps because there was about to be a change
in the weather—either a cool spell or even worse heat.
Or perhaps I had been working too hard—my brain was
tired, and I needed a break. I asked Atabaly to go and
fetch Valya, the nurse, if she hadn't yet run off to work,
and to have her come and take my blood pressure.

I've just learned something new: Valya is Atabaly's
adopted daughter. In 1945 they took her from an orphanage at the age of three. No one knew who her parents were. In fact, nothing was known about her except
that she was from somewhere in the Ukraine.

Valya came right away. What a goodhearted girl!
And my blood pressure wasn't all that high—140 over
95. This cheered my up, and I even began mumbling
banalities: "Valyushka, your mere presence has a calm-
ing effect. . . ." Although her nurse's smock smelled
slightly of carbolic acid, her hands and face gave off the
fresh scent of her body. Her hands touched my arm as
she rolled up my sleeve and adjusted the blood pressure
cuff, and her face was bent close to mine with an expression of rapt, childlike concentration—as if this were
a game and not a job. It occurred to me that only three
years ago I would not have passed up such an opportunity.

I would have gotten all worked up just from the physical closeness of a young woman and would have pursued her. Now, however, I was possessed by the fear of death.

"You'll have to stay in bed," Valya said sternly.

"A bottom figure of 95—that's a lot."

"What do you mean! For me that's excellent. With a count like that I even feel like chasing after beautiful girls. . . ." I took her hand just as she was getting up from the chair, and she blushed. I held on to her hand, and as she sat down again, my arm involuntarily came to rest on her knees. She could have been my daughter— there were some twenty years between us. She was the same age as my first son.

"Oh, what eyes, " I said. "What lovely blue eyes."

"I'll bring you some medicine this evening," she said, frowning. "What should I bring—reserpine or raunatine?"

"It doesn't matter to me. Just be sure to come."

She got up with the same stern expression and went out across the small terrace into the garden. As she passed by the window of my room, she looked in at me with a smile, and shaking her finger, she said, "Don't you dare get up!"

I stayed in bed for awhile, looking out the open window where the heat of day had begun to penetrate the green of the garden. And I thought about Valya— about how deftly and swiftly she had taken my blood pressure and about how, if only I had had such a creature beside me. . . . What more would I need? Only it was strange that that oaf Nazar had come rushing to see her in the middle of the night. Suddenly my first wife Vera came to mind. She had blue eyes, the same sturdy build as Valya, and her own strong, characteristic scent. She had played handball on a student team. In the beginning everything had been fine, but after we'd been married a couple of months I began to realize that she had no understanding of the most obvious and commonplace matters. It was painful to have to explain every time and I decided to keep silent. And we kept silent all day, all evening, when we went to bed, and when we traveled overnight on the train, in our own private compartment. And our parting was just as peaceful as our two years of marriage—not a single extra word was spoken. We simply had nothing to talk about. After Vera, Rita seemed a veritable Scheherazade. During our first years together Rita and I would talk all night. We discussed our friends, relatives, books, films; we dreamed, and we argued about God knows what. Things were always happening at Rita's office, passions ran high, and Rita would relate everything to me with great dramatic flair. And I was supposed to give advice, pass judgment, sympathize. But the main thing about Rita—with all her strengths and eccentricities—was that she understood what sort of man I was, how I was made, and what had become of me. Even that last day, when we quarreled about the mortgage payment and Rita said that I was just another Professor Serebryakov,* that she had always hoped to find something in me, but there was nothing there, I was just a blank, another Professor Serebryakov —even then I listened and didn't explode because I could feel that there was pain in her words, genuine pain. But after all, Professor Serebryakov was a human being too. Why be so contemptuous of him? He wasn't a gangster or a rapist, he simply wanted to live, like anyone else. He loved a woman, in his own way, to the extent of his capacity, and for years he had worked away at one thing—writing, writing, and more writing. Just as I had done. Yet to reproach a person for not being a Tolstoi or a Spenser simply wasn't fair. But I didn't put any of this into words when she started calling me a Professor Serebryakov, because there was no point in saying anything. I had already reached my decision.

That day I had on the tip of my tongue a silly jingle that I'd made up myself. I like silly jingles such as the following, which happens to be one of my old favorites: "He plays a role in the band, he rolls up rubber bands." Rita was always irritated by such nonsense, calling it a waste of brain power. She didn't understand that for a person who spent his whole life making plays on words, this was a way of limbering up.

That morning we quarreled about the mortgage payment, which I had forgotten to take care of and which had resulted in Rita's being refused some paper she needed from the Apartment Management Office. She had come home in an angry mood, and after her Serebryakov comment I began pacing the floor, mumbling, " 'Tis ill to speak of nooses in the house of a hanged man, 'tis ill to speak of mortgages in the house of a madman!" Hearing this from the next room, Kirill called out gaily, "How did that go? How did that go? Say it again, Papa!" A little while later I told them of my decision. My suitcase was already packed. Apparently they didn't take me seriously, and I myself didn't completely believe my own words. "Aha," Rita remarked caustically but calmly, "so that explains why you didn't pay the mortgage." "No," I replied, equally calmly, "I simply forgot it. The mortgage payments will be made on time in the future." Kirill looked at me with a wry and somewhat condescending smile. Obviously they still didn't believe that I was serious. Nor did I, for that matter. But say goodbye I did. I picked up my suitcase and left the apartment. Out on the street, as was always the case at this hour, there was a line at the taxi stand and I felt chilly, standing there in my raincoat. The temperature was below freezing, as if this were February rather than March. In the taxi on my way to the Warsaw Hotel, where Mansur was staying, I kept mumbling, " 'Tis ill to speak of nooses in the house of a hanged man, 'tis ill to speak of mortgages in the house of a madman. . . ."

Thinking about Valya did somehow comfort me, and suddenly realizing that I wasn't done for yet, not by a long shot, I decided take the day off and give my head a rest. I went out into the garden. The pathway was soft and spongy, strewn with acacia blossoms which stuck to my shoes. The air was humid, which meant that the summer heat was setting in. In the city it might still be over a hundred.

I walked to the rear of the garden, where there was a vineyard, and directly from the vineyard a path hewn in rock which rose up the side of the mountain. It was hot even though I was walking in the shade. Passing under the vaulted branches of some ancient plane trees—they must have been at least 150 years old—I was enveloped in a murky gloom. Nothing grew under these trees, which blocked everything out with their giant strength. I continued along under some tall apple and pear trees and then proceeded in the shade of some acacias and an American maple. Atabaly said that there wouldn't be much fruit this year due to an attack of plant lice. The branches and trunks of the trees and the whitewashed walls of the nearby cottages were all covered with tiny, black midges. These midges were attracted to white. Even my white shirt was covered with black dots, but if I had tried to brush them off they would have left stains. According to Atabaly, the winter had been a warm one, without any snow, and none of these insects had been

Yury Trifonov

killed off.

We were sitting and chatting on a stone bench at the bottom of the path which led up the mountainside. Atabaly told me that Mansur had called and would be arriving today. He had asked him to heat up the bathhouse. And Comrade Mergenov was coming with him.

"Atabaly, how many children do you have?" I asked.

"Oh, a lot. Eleven."

"And how many did you have when you took Valya from the orphanage?"

"Three. That was nothing." He began to laugh. "If we'd had a lot of children then, we wouldn't have taken her."

But from the look on his face, from the way he smiled—his healthy, dazzling-white teeth sparkling through his parched brown lips—I could see that he would have taken her all the same. He began telling me his troubles, complaining of the hard time he and his wife had with the younger children, and with the older ones too. Their four older daughters had gotten married and weren't living with them anymore, but each one of them had her own problems and needed their help. One of them was sick, another wanted to work but her husband wouldn't let her, and the third had an ailing child who was covered with sores which no one knew how to cure. Valya was married to an Ossetian, a bartender in Tokhir, but they couldn't get along. He was wildly jealous and would beat her and even lock her inside the house. Finally they had parted and he had gone off to Bakharden. Upon leaving her, he had wept, saying, "If I stay with you, I'll kill somebody. It's better that I leave." Now all sorts of men were pestering her and asking her to go out with them. But what sort of interest could she have in that? She was a good girl and had been brought up in Turkmen fashion. She didn't look at men. Nazarka had come knocking in the middle of the night, he wanted to marry her and had bought three kilos of candy, but she had said, "Papa, chase that hooligan, that devil, away with your broom!" She loved Misha, the Ossetian. What was to be done if they couldn't get along? . . . Comrade Mansur Geldyevich too, whenever he arrived, was always saying, "Let Valya bring my bed linen!" Well, she would bring it, but that was it and nothing more. Because—no, it wasn't right. But Comrade Mansur Geldyevich would get angry. Why he would ask, should a cultural workers' resort look like some backward village—with the wash and bedding hanging out and children running all over the place? You have too many children, he tells me. It's unpleasant for the guests to have to see all this. They come here to rest, and what do they find but crying children and goats wandering around, just as in the village. But Atabaly can't get along without his goats and cow—how else would he feed his children?

He needed to get back to work, but as always when he ran into me, he would settle down for a long chat, and talk and talk. Usually I would interrupt him with some tentative question, "Well, what do you say, shall we get back to work?" "A-ha!" he would nod readily and smile. "Time for the mules to get back into harness." And we would go our separate ways—he to his hoes and vegetable beds, I to my cottage and desk. But today I had decided to take a break, and I didn't interrupt him. I don't know why people like so much to talk to me. Probably it's because I'm a good listener. They keep on talking, and I nod and think my own thoughts. Right now I was listening to him and thinking, Tolstoi was half right: all happy families are happy in the same way. That's true. But my God, unhappy families too seem to be unhappy in much the same way. And Tolstoi's story itself was such a familiar one, with all the usual characters: husband, lover, mother-in-law. . . . Egoism? That's an insufficiency of love. Most of our unhappiness stems from this one, same cause. Yet can a man who has eleven children be an egoist? It's out of the question! However much he might like to and no matter what his basic character, he simply wouldn't have time.

Atabaly was once again telling me about his cows. He liked to reminisce about them and about the hard time he had keeping them when balding Kel was his boss. That was some five years ago, but he couldn't forget it.

Five years ago, Rita and I had vacationed outside of Odessa. The Arutunians had taken us with them in their car.

"Kel would keep giving orders for our cow to be confiscated, but the police were friends of ours and would warn us in advance, 'We'll be coming tomorrow, so do as you please—drive her off somewhere or slaughter her.' For two months we hid her in a ravine five kilometers up in the mountains, and we brought grass to her, carrying it on our own backs. We could ride one stop on the bus, but from there it was straight up, on foot. But we saved her. Later on Kel disappeared somewhere, praise be to Allah!"

"Really? Well, that's interesting."

Strutting around the beach in his wool trunks with the white belt, Arutunian was saying, "It's an irreversible process. . . ." Rita and Arutunian's wife had gone into Odessa to buy some odds and ends at the flea market.

If I had even four children, if Rita were still working, and if we kept a cow—what a splendid person I

would be! As soon as Mansur arrives I'll have to take
him by the throat. Let him lend me 300 rubles or so,
and later on he can settle with the publishing house.
That man really has no conscience. He knows that I'm
stuck here without a penny. He should send me back to
Moscow and pretend that it doesn't matter to him one
way or the other.

"So Mansur wanted to evict you?"

It was pleasant to hear something negative about
Mansur. He was my friend and was forever helping me
out, but there were times when I hated him. Mansur was
not a leading poet and the local literary people spoke of
him with tongue in cheek, but he was incredibly lucky
and very good at promoting his own interests.

"Mansur Geldyevich came for two days, on a week-
end, and once again he says, 'Let Valya bring my bed
linen!' The next morning he was in a nasty mood. 'You
can smell your kitchen from one end of the resort to the
other,' he says. 'You're going to have to get out of here
once and for all.' But at the district soviet they tell me,
'Yazgul is a hero-mother,* and nobody's going to force
you to move anywhere, so don't worry.' Ha-ha!" he
laughed, his teeth flashing. And now, returning to his
work, he got up and began dragging a bush off somewhere. I realized that his life was exceptionally difficult
—almost ideal in that sense—and that he was a happy
man.

After the heat let up, sometime after four, I went
to the tearoom to have dinner. Little Nazar was standing
on the stone steps by the entrance, speaking arrogantly
to a hunchbacked individual with a black beard and
mustache. The hunchback had an educated but lacklus-
ter look about him, his face resembling that of one of
the Spanish kings. When I emerged from the tearoom a
quarter of an hour later, after a quick meal of pilaf and

Yury Trifonov

tea, Nazar and the hunchback were quarreling and it looked as if there was going to be a fight. Spectators had already gathered, some of them assuming a squatting position in order to be able to look on more comfortably. I was told that the hunchback was a Kurd named Sasha and that he too was always getting into fights. Suddenly Nazar gave Sasha such a hard shove that he fell down. The spectators exclaimed, "Wo-ow!" and I recalled Atabaly's words: "Being knocked down by him is like falling off a donkey—you land on your head." This dwarf Nazar interested me—perhaps because he wanted to marry Valya and to this end had bought three kilos of candy. I took a good look at him. He was wearing a cheap, loose-fitting cotton shirt with some sort of flowered pattern, sateen trousers, dark-red cotton socks, and sandals made of imitation leather. He walked up the steps and assumed his previous position at the entrance to the tearoom. He stood there, gazing down at all of us with blazing eyes.

"What are they fighting about?" I asked one fellow.

"Oh, they're trying to divide up what they haven't got," the fellow said scornfully. "She isn't interested in either of them, and the Kurd told him as much. Well, and so they had a fight."

Nobody noticed as Sasha suddenly reappeared with a knife in his hand and came staggering toward the tearoom porch. Everyone jumped out of his way except Nazar, who stood there motionless, staring at the hunchback. Then he darted through the door and returned a moment later with a huge kitchen knife. Everyone burst out laughing. Puffed up like a cock and with his strong, gnomelike legs spread firmly apart, Nazar stood on the porch, grasping the kitchen knife as if it were a cutlass. Sasha spat and walked off with a wave of his hand. Everyone roared with laughter. In the meantime a car came

188

rattling up to the tearoom and stopped. The car door opened and slammed shut, and I saw my friend Mansur emerging in a white suit and white straw hat.

"Salam! Salam!" said Mansur, as he came up the porch steps, waving his arm in lordly fashion and nodding his greetings to the laughing crowd.

Staring wide-eyed in Mansur's direction, Nazar began to shout, "Comrade Mansur Geldyevich—hurrah!"

Mansur hadn't noticed me, and as I waited for him to come out, I noticed that there was another passenger in the back seat of the car. In a little while Mansur reappeared, carrying a string bag with three bottles of cognac.

"The car's out of gas," he explained to the crowd standing beneath the porch. "So we figured we might as well stop here. . . . Tsk-tsk!" As usual, he didn't laugh, but gave a high-pitched giggle, sputtering through his teeth. And this "tsk-tsk" meant that he was in an excellent mood, that his digestive system was in good order, and that things were going well for him and promised to go even better in the future.

Catching sight of me, he seated me in the car, and we proceeded some 500 meters uphill along the tree-lined street. I hadn't received any telegram, and no one had called. The other passenger was an enormous individual named Mergenov. He was the head of a restaurant and cafeteria trust and a friend of Mansur's. He had come to Tokhir in order to be present at the official opening of The Plane Tree, which was to take place on Sunday. When he got out of the car and stood erect, I saw before me a towering colossus. He couldn't have been less than six feet six. His voluminous stomach was encased in linen trousers which were probably a size fifty, and his gigantic arms were like shovels. Atop this massive body was a rather small head that glistened in

189

the sunlight like a polished brown egg. With its smooth cheeks and large mouth his head looked like that of some monstrous infant. Comrade Mergenov could have played the role of the Idol of the Heathen* in a children's theater. As it turned out, he was a most kind and considerate person. Right after dinner he lay down for a nap and Mansur listened to all twelve chapters (we postponed the rest until evening), since he had to run off to The Rainbow, a resort for ministry officials, where somebody he had to see was vacationing.

I wasn't offended that Mansur didn't have the time to listen to my translation of his own poem—to those endless lines in which were reflected my resourcefulness and invention, my shortwindedness and fatigue. That was in the order of things, and I had gotten used to it. But something else infuriated me. When I asked him on his way out about the money, he replied carelessly, "Listen, let's finish the translation first, then we'll talk about. . . ."

And there was even a hint of annoyance in his voice, as if he were thinking: how tactless, always pestering me for money. But I felt as if I'd been slapped in the face, and I began to shout, "What do you mean— We'll talk about it?! You promised to bring me the money today! God damn you!" I shouted, beside myself with anger. "You must realize the situation I'm in. I've got to send money home to Moscow! I can't put it off any longer, especially not now! Our friendly relationship has spoiled you! You seem to forget that I'm a first-rate translator! Everybody's after me—I have a long waiting list! Do you understand that? . . ."

"Oh I understand, I understand, boss," Mansur nodded, utterly unperturbed. "You're a big shot, I know. . . . Just don't scold us poor camel drivers. . . ."

"Stop clowning!"

190

"Stop yelling. Listen, everything will be taken care of. In the meantime, take this. . . ." He extended his hand with a twenty-five ruble note. We've begun making repairs on our house and don't have any money ourselves. On Monday you and I will go and put on the pressure, we'll take care of everything. . . ."

"No, on Monday you're going to buy me a plane ticket! Damned if I'm going to stay here any longer!"

The twenty-five ruble note went flying onto the floor. He walked out, nodding and winking, and making reassuring gestures with his hands, as if to an invalid. Yet all the while he knew perfectly well that everything would work out just as he wished, and that I wouldn't go anywhere until he had squeezed every last ounce from me. After all, I was stuck. And all of my movements, though seemingly independent, were those of a creature caught in a trap: I could move no farther than the length of my own tail. I picked up the twenty-five ruble note and laid it on the table. Then I lay down on my bed, put a validol tablet under my tongue—my heart was acting up again—and lay there for an hour or so with my eyes closed.

A corner of the sun had crawled into my room. This meant that it was already evening. Behind the partition a bed creaked—Comrade Mergenov had waked up. He breathed mightily, wheezed, and then sighed, "Oh-oh. . . ." There was a heavy stamping of feet, a door slammed, and he left the room. Now, as I lay alone in complete silence, I realized that my unseemly shouting about money hadn't been about money at all. Apparently I had been counting on news from home. I had been counting on hearing from them, and not they from me. But even if it was all over between us, still, this silence was unnatural. For when someone calls you at dawn and tells you that he's sick, even if he's only a former relative and no one you feel close to, still, you have to be completely callous to sit back and make no response for nine days. Though come to think of it, Kirill had once said to me by way of warning, "Okay, but if I were to run away from home, you might have a heart attack. Because I can live without you, but you can't live without me." He had spoken the truth, the rascal. Something must have happened there. To hell with it, I'd call and find out.

I wandered around the room, mumbling, " 'Tis ill to speak of mortgages in the house of a madman, 'tis ill to speak of nooses in. . . ." I was already beginning to feel better because I had come to a decision. Suddenly Valya appeared. I had completely forgotten that she was supposed to bring me some medicine. I sat down on the bed, facing my desk, and she took my blood pressure. It had gone up a bit—to 150 over 100. Aha, so an attack could come any time now. That was what came of getting excited.

"Have you been working today?" Valya asked.

"No, I've been loafing."

"Did you leave the cottage? Have you been out for a walk?"

"Just for a while."

Valya wrinkled her brow and looked at me with fixed concentration, apparently trying to marshal her not very extensive knowledge of hypertension and heart disease. She was no longer wearing her uniform but had on a white, dressy blouse and blue, tight-fitting nylon pants. She must have been pretty hot in these pants, but they did look elegant. I noticed that her hairdo was also different from earlier in the day.

"Are you going out this evening?" I asked. "To the movies?"

"No, I'm going to be home."

She sat with one blue leg crossed over the other, and at the moment I felt no desire to touch her knees or take her hand as I had in the morning. She put the reserpine on the table and put away her stethoscope and blood pressure cuff, but for some reason she didn't leave. I myself wasn't sure whether I wanted her to leave or stay. There didn't seem to be anything to talk about. She didn't say anything and neither did I. Actually, her shy silence was quite appealing. It occurred to me that I wouldn't be able to call home today. The post office closed at five. I'd call tomorrow morning. No long, drawn-out conversation—I'd just find out if they were both all right. And if they were—fine, I'd hang up. All of this was no longer any concern of mine, but still, there were certain proprieties that should be observed.

"Well . . . ," I said after a long silence. "By the way, you know what, Valya? I saw your suitor."

"What suitor?"

"Why, that little fellow—the one who came with the candy in the middle of the night."

"Oh, little Nazar." She burst out laughing, and her face suddenly became animated and looked very sweet. "He's a drunkard—everyone buys him drinks, poor thing, and every day he goes staggering about. And he shouldn't drink. It's bad for his health. He recently broke two ribs, trying to climb through the window into his room. He had forgotten his key. We had to take him to the hospital. He doesn't have any family and he lives alone, just like some poor stray dog. I feel sorry for him, the little fool, and he actually imagined that. . . ."

"What?" I asked with a yawn. I was beginning to have trouble catching my breath, as I always did in the evening, after a hard day's work. But today I hadn't worked at all. "Did he ask you to marry him?"

"Not to marry him, but—well, he wants to protect

me. He told me that if anyone insulted me, I should let him know, and he'd beat the person up. It was too funny for words!"

"Aha!" I simply couldn't manage to fill my lungs with air. "And you . . . you didn't agree to his proposal?"

She remained silent, watching as my lips gasped for air. When I finally calmed down and was able to take a deep breath, she said quietly, "Why should I need such a little devil to protect me? The very idea is ridiculous, don't you think? As far as I'm concerned, I'm quite able to protect myself."

She sat there for a while longer and then left.

Soon afterwards Mansur came bursting in and wanted to drag me off to the neighboring cottage where Comrade Mergenov and the restaurant employees were celebrating the next day's opening of The Plane Tree for the summer season. But why should I be there? Everyone wanted to see me. I was to be brought in dead or alive, right away. Those were Comrade Mergenov's orders. Mansur had obviously been drinking, and slapping me on the shoulder, he shouted, "Your Excellency! Who am I compared to you!" He made a terrible face, squinting his eyes and contorting his mouth. And in order to demonstrate what a nonentity he was, he held up before his nose an invisible mosquito clutched between his two fingers. This was his usual clowning around, and to this too I had become accustomed. Yet for all his quirks, he was a goodhearted fellow—better than most, a lot better! And if I were really in a jam, he would help me out. This I could say for sure, as I had known him a long time.

In the neighboring cottage they were feeling no pain. In addition to Comrade Mergenov there were the restaurant manager and his assistant—two elderly, balding individuals who looked enough alike to be brothers

—and three waitresses who burst into laughter as I walked in. Also present was the husband of one of the waitresses, a captain with the insignia of the signal corps. Leaning in my direction, the captain wheezed into my ear, "Thirteen years I've spent in this dear company. . . ." Apparently I had come in on the tail end of a lengthy meal. Suddenly Nazar arrived and everyone shouted, "Hurrah for Nazar!" Every summer the dwarf worked at The Plane Tree as a doorman and bouncer, and for him these were the happiest months of the year.

"Nazar, go and find Valya! Tell her that Mansur Geldyevich is asking for her, and that there's champagne, and rabbit. . . ."

Nazar ran off, but returned alone. Why doesn't she want to come? What do you mean—she doesn't want to come! Tell her that Mansur Geldyevich has fallen ill, that he's had a heart attack and that she has to help. Whereupon he fell back on the bed so hard that the whole room shook. And waving a towel in front of him, he cried:

"Oh-oh, I'm dying! Call a doctor right away! I need a doctor!"

Comrade Mergenov and the two managers roared with laughter, and the waitresses went on with their singing. I drank one glass of cognac and then, after finishing a second, I stepped outside. It was completely dark. I had no trouble breathing, physically I felt fine. But instead of last night's vague, nighttime euphoria, today I felt nothing—only emptiness. I could just as easily have thrown everything over right here and now and taken off somewhere—perhaps to the North. There, beyond the mountains, were deserts, steppes, forests, and coolness. I was ill. If I had been well, I would have wanted to go on living. I didn't know what to do with myself. I walked back and forth in the garden, then wandered up to the vineyard, and from there took the path past the two Persian huts back to my own cottage. I went into my room and lay down in the bed without bothering to undress. I heard shouts and singing for about twenty minutes, then it grew quiet. Suddenly I heard light, running footsteps under the window, the door opened, and Valya slipped noiselessly into the room. She asked in a whisper:

"May I come in? It's me. . . . You're not sleeping?" She laughed softly, but without any embarrassment. She had the excited air of a conspirator. "May I hide here?"

"Be my guest. Whom are you hiding from?"

"Oh my! Mansur Geldyevich is after me. Tomorrow he'll beg my forgiveness, but tonight he's not himself. And Nazar is threatening to kill him—he's behaving like a fool too. . . ."

Shouts could be heard somewhere in the distance. They were high-pitched and piercingly loud—the sort of shouts one hears during a brawl or fist-fight. We listened carefully, but couldn't make anything out.

"I think that's my father shouting," said Valya. "May I turn off the light? Otherwise they'll see it and come looking for me here."

"You shouldn't be afraid. Well, go ahead and turn it off."

"I'll turn it back on in a few minutes."

She clicked the switch of the table lamp and stars appeared in the window. We had to do something, sitting there in the dark, and so we began talking about one thing and another. She told me about her father and about how three years ago she had first learned of her real mother's existence. She was living in the Ukraine, in the village of Grigorovka in Chernigov province. Valya had gone there for a visit, and her mother had begged

her to stay and live with her. It was a wonderful place—
there was a big river, and they lived well. Her mother's
husband—not her father but her stepfather—was a veterinarian and had his own car, a Pobeda. Her mother
was sick, her legs bothered her, and she could barely
tend to the house and garden. She should have stayed
and helped out, but she didn't have the strength to leave
her family here in Tokhir. Yazgul had cried terribly
upon learning that her real mother had turned up. She
had arrived in Tokhir without letting anyone know and
had sought out Valya in secret. Later on she had sent
her money via poste restante for the trip to Grigorovka.
Undoubtedly she was a good woman. But it just happened that Valya had grown up without her. Your family are those who take care of you. And how much Papa
and Mama Yazgul had done for her! She had finished
high school, and every summer she had attended a
Young Pioneers camp. Next had come her nurse's train-
ing, and later on they had paid for her and Misha's wed-
ding reception for forty-five people at The Plane Tree.
And they had always helped to get her and Misha back
together again. What could one do if it had just worked
out this way? . . .

Then I began telling her about my life. She already
knew quite a bit about me from Atabaly—I having told
him a great deal.

"You're not old yet," said Valya. "What do you
mean—old?"

"Yes, I am, I am old," I said. "And I know it."

"Don't be silly! You'll still have girls falling in love
with you."

"I'm old because. . . . You see, Valya, here's your
father—a gardener; your stepfather's a veterinarian, and
you're a nurse. You all have your place in life, you're

197

settled, established. But all my life I've been struggling, trying to get established. And now I'm old because you get tired of trying, tired of struggling. It's all so ridiculous, you understand?"

It was impossible to understand. But she understood.

I felt her fingers as they found my hand and gently squeezed it. Such a childlike, unassuming squeeze: the sort of approving squeeze that Young Pioneers give to lonely old people when they visit them late in the day, after school.

"You know what?" she said. "You shouldn't feel depressed. Everything's going to work out for you. After all, high blood pressure—that's really not so serious."

"Well actually, I'm not all that depressed."

"Don't be depressed at all! Your son loves you. And your wife loves you. How will they get along without you? After all, you can't run away from people. Here Misha and I have parted, but you know. . . ."

It was a good thing that it was dark. I was embarrassed.

"What?" I asked.

"Where am I going to wander off to, when he's right nearby, in Bakharden? Sooner or later I'll go running to him, don't you think?"

It was a good thing that it was completely dark and she couldn't see anything. She whispered something, and I took her hand and drew her toward me. She sat down on the bed, then threw off her shoes, and finally lay down beside me. She laid her head on my arm, and I embraced her. In the distance someone was shouting, "Va-lya!" Then they shouted something else in Turkmen. She gave a barely audible sob, or perhaps it was a laugh. I held her tighter, and she stroked my head. Such a good, dear, silken creature. Goodness, it seems, has a neck and lips, and can be embraced. And then, barely perceptibly, the bow of the boat hit the sandy shore, and the current started carrying it downstream. I managed to jump out just in time, pressing my body hard against the grassy slope. Straining every muscle, I straightened to a standing position. The iron chain was still in my hand, and turning, I easily dragged the boat to shore. Rita stepped across the middle seat and up onto the bow. I held out my hand and she stepped ashore. I noticed that a storm cloud was approaching from the direction of the forest. It was an ash-gray cloud with a plump body. We had rowed to this cove from a good distance. It was our special spot, and there was no better place for swimming in the whole river, though no one knew this except us. Rita and I had kept our discovery a secret. The water here was clean and warm—always three or four degrees warmer than in the rest of the river. Undoubtedly there was a warm spring here somewhere. Rita had already been forbidden to do much swimming, but when she went into the water, stepping carefully on her long legs, no one would have guessed that she was pregnant. There was a strong wind, and smallish waves kept lashing us as we faced the opposite shore, trying to keep an eye on the storm cloud. Finally we turned our backs to the wind and waves, and as a result just missed the moment when the storm cloud suddenly descended upon us and the whole sky darkened. When the downpour began, the air immediately grew chilly, but the water remained wonderfully warm. Holding hands and laughing hysterically, we began pushing ourselves up from the sandy bottom and jumping out of the warm water into the lashing sheets of rain. Everything around us was hidden by a wall of pounding rain, which was as white and impenetrable as fog. We soon felt cold and decided to stay put in the water. The water was still warm, but the air seemed to disappear and there was nothing to breathe. The water was choking us. It was that same staircase on which I always felt myself suffocating. For some reason I had to keep climbing higher and higher—just one more step, just a little more effort—but there was simply no air.

In Moscow people were still wearing their overcoats. The taxi driver told me that it had been cold and rainy all month; the gardens had been frostbitten, and at the market you had to pay a ruble and a half for a kilogram of new potatoes. I rolled down the window and joyfully breathed in the cold, damp air.

In July Kirill went off with a student work brigade to Novgorod, and at the end of the month Rita and I got vacation vouchers for a beach resort just outside of Riga. We set off for the beach a bit earlier than the date on our vouchers and stayed there in a hotel until the beginning of August, when we moved into the resort. August turned out to be beautiful—sunny and clear, and not too hot. I took long walks every day and, as always, the Baltic climate had a healing effect: I was able to breathe deeply and evenly, my blood pressure went down to normal, and at the end of our stay I got hold of a racket and even played a little tennis.

1971   *Translated by Helen P. Burlingame*

THE LONG GOODBYE

I

   In those days, about eighteen years ago, the spot
where the butcher shop now stands was covered with lilac
bushes. There was a yellow country fence (the area was in
fact full of dachas, and the residents here felt as if they
were living in the countryside), and behind this wooden
fence the lilac bushes clustered. Unable to confine themselves to the limits of the fence, the luxuriant branches
overflowed into the street in a burst of riotous growth.
However much passersby might grab hold of them, pinch
them, pull them or break them, the branches still managed
to preserve their full, rounded contours and every spring
would astonish this dusty, narrow street with their blossoms and fragrance. When the lilacs were in full bloom and
one saw them from a distance, their blossoms clustered
one upon another in patches of white and mauve, they
reminded one of an old city at twilight—a southern, sea-
port city, where the streets are cut into the cliffs and the
houses are stuck one on top of another; a city with monasteries and winding stone steps, where old ladies sit in the
shade, selling small boxes encrusted with seashells.
   But of course this was all a long time ago. Today
in the spot where the lilacs stood, there is an eight-story
apartment building with a butcher shop on the ground
level. At that time, in the days of the lilac bushes, the
people who lived in the small house behind the yellow
wooden fence had to travel a long way for meat—by

streetcar to Vagankovsky Market. Today they would be able to buy their meat much more conveniently. But today, unfortunately, they no longer live there.

Things were pretty miserable when the company first arrived in Saratov. They were lodged in a bad hotel, the heat didn't let up, and no one came to the theater. Everything seemed to go wrong: the actors began getting sick, and Sergei Leonidovich, who couldn't stand either hot weather or bad hotels, took off for Moscow, leaving Smurny in charge. Smurny had joined the theater two years ago and right away had started giving Lyalya the eye. She had rejected his advances without hesitation since it was rumored that he was scheming against Sergei Leonidovich, trying to take his place. This struck Lyalya as despicable and mean, and she couldn't stand mean people. True, she didn't know exactly how he was scheming against Sergei Leonidovich or to what lengths he would be willing to go, but people said that something underhanded was going on, and with some special instinct which she had learned to rely on, Lyalya believed the rumors. Smurny was extremely polite. He had a fair complexion, languid, caressing eyes, and the provincial manner of throwing back the hair from his forehead with a proud, sharp movement of his head. In this connection, Sergei Leonidovich once gave a humorous imitation of a scene he had observed by accident. Smurny had proceeded through the empty lounge at his usual brisk, energetic pace, suddenly stopped and examined himself in the mirror, and then threw back his head with such an air of haughty satisfaction that Sergei Leonidovich was, as he himself admitted, quite taken aback. Sergei Leonidovich's imitations were always killing. He didn't have to say a thing—the personality was rendered in seconds, just by his facial expressions and gestures.

Smurny, of course, was not about to forget that Lyalya had rejected him and soon began getting even with her by giving her a hard time professionally, holding her back in any way he could. At the same time, however, he continued to put out feelers, to see if she might still come around. He had directed two plays on his own when Sergei Leonidovich was sick, and both had been flops. One had dragged on for half a season, the other even less. But this was beside the point. The point was that he hadn't given Lyalya a part in either of them. One of the roles had been perfect for her and everyone in the theater knew it. Nonetheless he somehow managed not to give the part to her. Instead he gave it to one of the promising graduates of their theatrical studio. The whole thing was perfectly obvious, and even Lyalya's girlfriends began saying to her, "Why are you being so stubborn? The man's pride is hurt, give in to him just for the hell of it. After all, you've nothing to lose." But it was as if something had jammed inside of Lyalya. She couldn't even bring herself to sit next to him in the cafeteria, much less "give in" to him.

Something like this had happened once before in her life. The war was just over, Lyalya was eighteen, and a happy group had gathered at Allochka Schlaefer's place on Putnikovsky Lane. Some of the guests had just come back from the front, some from the hospital, and others had recently been evacuated from such faraway places as Kamyshlov and Namangan. Everything was starting up anew: hopes, songs, the youthful urge to live life to its fullest, feelings of love and sympathy for everyone who had returned, long evening strolls through Moscow, and lingering farewells in doorways. Then suddenly there appeared in their midst one young man who was thirty years old, with prematurely gray hair and light eyes as clear as crystal. He didn't ask, he didn't beg, because everyone came to him without his having to ask. He said that he was organizing a theater studio called *The Blue Ark*. Lyalya was dying to get into this studio because she had already decided that life without the theater would have no meaning for her. The studio venture fell through, of course, but she and her friends had believed in it for a long time. At this time Yasha and Lazik were the men in her life. She was torn between them since she felt sorry for both of them. Yasha had come into her life first, in 1943, when he had just been released from the hospital. The rest of his family had perished somewhere outside of Minsk. He was twelve years older than she, an outstanding mathematician, but as awkward and helpless as a child. Lazik was a poet and walked with a limp, having lost one leg at the Leningrad front. He wrote songs and sang beautifully, accompanying himself on the guitar. But the young man with the gray brush-cut and clear eyes was a completely different story: her whole future depended on him. Lyalya didn't know how to behave in his presence. Then came that particular Saturday when some twenty young people had crowded into Allochka's enormous, empty apartment (her parents were off fulfilling some important state function in newly occupied Germany), and all of a sudden he had led her into the hallway and said in a commanding voice that they should go to his place right now so that he could give her the book that he'd promised her a long time ago. Lyalya was unable to utter a single word and began to tremble. And she trembled imperceptibly in the streetcar, all the way to his place, and even had to clench her teeth to prevent them from chattering. It wasn't that she was afraid of anything, she wasn't trembling from fear. What kept pounding through her head was her dream of *The Blue Ark*. Up till now he had never spoken to Lyalya about anything. He had not, it seemed, even noticed her. Nor had there ever been any talk about a book. As soon as they entered his apartment and before the light had been turned on or Lyalya had even taken off her coat, he grabbed her by the shoulders and almost knocked her over as his mouth sought hers in the dark. He kissed her so roughly and possessively that she was stirred to anger and began pushing him away. He wouldn't let go and kept dragging her farther inside. As they struggled in the dark, she punched him in the face, apparently quite hard, because he cried out in pain. At this point she managed to escape.

For two whole days she stayed upstairs in her attic room, telling her parents that she was sick, when in fact she was crying because her life was over, because dreams don't come true, and because people can't be trusted. On the third day she left the house, walked to the Sokol subway station, and bought some ice cream. Ice cream was something new, a prewar delight which was just beginning to reappear, though at high, free-market prices. But this meant that rationing would soon be ended, that former joys were close at hand, and new ones not far off. And now, just from eating this ice cream, she regained her inner calm. As was usually the case, it had come unexpectedly, and from the most trifling of causes. Suddenly she no longer regretted the fact that *The Blue Ark* had fallen through, that she had punched an older man in the face, or that she would never go to Allochka Schlaefer's place again. And remembering and reflecting on what had happened, she discovered something new about herself. It occured to her that the most frightening and unbearable thing in this world is dependence. When you're dependent, that's the end, a blind alley, something you can't get around. After all, when she was riding on the streetcar, trying with all her might to suppress her trembling, she already knew what was going to happen and why

Yury Trifonov

she was going there. She had to make a decision. And right then and there, on the streetcar, she realized: no! She had made a lot of mistakes in her short life, but they had all been mistakes of feeling rather than of calculation. She accidentally ran into this man three years later at the home of one of Grisha's friends, and both he and she pretended that they had never met before.

And Smurny too, who had the same crystal-clear eyes as this first man, appealed to many, especially to younger women, of whom there is always a surplus after a long war. Smurny's influence in the theater grew with every passing month, all the more so since Sergei Leonidovich wasn't well and was often absent for long periods at a time. It was common knowledge that Smurny had separated from his wife, very nobly leaving her their big apartment and taking with him only a set of underwear and a typewriter (query: what did he need with the typewriter?). It was also known that he lived alone in a modest, one-room apartment near Krasnye Vorota. He was thirty-eight—an ideal age for a man—and it was clear to everyone that before very long he would have everything he wanted, all of life's blessings. Lyalya, in the meantime, languished in second-rate roles and seemed to be stuck there. After her initial rebuffs Smurny had soon stopped looking in her direction, and when he took over for Sergei Leonidovich in Saratov, he put her in the worst room on the ground floor, together with the makeup woman.

In Saratov they were performing a play staged by Sergei Leonidovich that spring, in which Lyalya had only a walk-on role—two appearances onstage and some twenty-five words. It was a boring production, not through any fault of Sergei Leonidovich, but because of the play itself—some sort of dull fare about forest conservation. They had staged it because of its theme.

The newspapers praised it, but theater attendance had been poor. The Saratov papers were especially enthusiastic about the play because its author—a new and relatively unknown playwright—was a native son. Actually, the playwright lived in Moscow, but he had spent his childhood and youth in Saratov. And now that the company was here on tour, he had returned to his native city and was staying with his mother and his mentally retarded young daughter. And on a hot July day—a Monday, when there were no performances—he had invited all the actors connected with the play to come to his home for supper.

The day got off to a bad start. That morning Smurny ran into Lyalya in the hotel corridor and without even saying good morning—which seemed strange, since he was normally very polite—he asked her to come to his hotel room for a talk.

"Just for five minutes!" he said, thrusting the open fingers of one hand somewhat foolishly before Lyalya's face.

Smurny's room—the best in the hotel—was classified as "family deluxe." It had curtains of raspberry-colored velour, and a cloth of the same material covered the oval table in the center of the room, on which there stood a carafe of water. There was an alcove, also draped with raspberry-colored velour, and in its depths something loomed large and white. At the moment, the room stank of cigarette butts and inexpensive eau de cologne. Lyalya took a seat by the oval table as Smurny disappeared into the alcove, only to reappear seconds later with a piece of paper in his hand.

"Take a look at this. It arrived yesterday from Moscow. It was forwarded from the Ministry to our Moscow address, and they forwarded it to me here."

Lyalya saw several sheets of paper covered with

writing and was horrified to recognize a familiar hand. It was a letter from her mother!

Here it was, the very worst—the thing Lyalya had always been most afraid of: her mother out to get justice. Good Lord, how many times had she told her, beseeched her, gotten down on her knees and begged her not to interfere, not to write any letters of complaint. But letter writing was her mother's favorite occupation. At one time she used to write to the principal of Lyalya's school, demanding that her letters be discussed at the parents' council meeting. She had also written letters to the District Office of Education. Then, later on, when Lyalya wasn't accepted into drama school, she had written to the Ministry. Even at home, when she was angry at someone, she would use letters as a means of clarification. And quite often Lyalya would wake up to find two or three sheets of paper lying on her table. Sometimes there would be even more—a whole school notebook covered with large, run-together sentences without any punctuation: "Liudmila you should know that when you borrow something from someone you should return it without waiting to be asked that's very inconsiderate you took my black fur shawl. . . ."

Stifling a groan, Lyalya took the handwritten sheets obviously torn from her father's big ledger and began quickly reading through them, jumping from one line to the next. She didn't have the strength to read slowly, pausing over every word. "As the mother of a young actress, I am writing to . . . Even in her school dramatics club, which was directed by a distinguished actor . . . She's already been a member of the theater for six years . . . Is it possible that our young actors and actresses are supposed to . . . How long is this tyranny of directors going to . . ."

"Well, what can I say, Herman Vladimirovich?"
Lyalya threw down the sheets of paper and gave a
despairing glance at Smurny who was leaning over the
table and looking down at her with a stiff smile on his
face. "This was written by my mother. You must
realize that I can't be responsible for what she does—
especially since she's a sick woman."

"A sick woman? You'd never guess it from her
letter. It's quite coherent, and she makes serious accu-
sations, though of course they're unsubstantiated and
only so much slander. But the letter is cleverly written
and she makes certain insinuations between the lines.
A sick person wouldn't be capable of that."

"What do you mean, between the lines?"

"Well, right here!" he said, pointing with his finger.
"Here's a juicy spot."

Lyalya read the line which she had skipped in her
first reading: ". . . she did not respond to his advances,
and so he took his revenge. In both of the plays which
he directed, she was not . . ." Oh-oh! Why did she have
to bring that up? My God, why, why that? And now
Lyalya couldn't bring herself to look up at Smurny. As
the seconds passed, she moved her lips, pretending that
she was having trouble deciphering her mother's handwriting.

Smurny waited patiently, then finally said, "Well?
I'd like to hear what . . . "

"Well, what can I say?"

Lyalya looked up at him. He wasn't smiling. His
eyes were leaden and stern, and his lips were pursed.

"What can you say? You can tell me the meaning
of all this rambling! What revenge? What's this nonsense all about?"

"I don't know, Herman Vladimirovich, I really
don't. . . ."

And suddenly, unable to restrain herself, she burst out laughing. It was all such pathetic nonsense. Did she really have to spell it out for him? And that face of his —crimson and trembling with rage. Granted, her mother had behaved foolishly, but what she had written was the truth, after all. He knew that it was the truth, and yet there he was, gazing at her with dull eyes and demanding—my God, what was it he wanted from her?—that she, Lyalya, should feel shame for her mother, that she should die of shame, so that he in some small way could be compensated for the unpleasantness he had experienced, receiving such a letter forwarded from the Ministry. But now it no longer mattered what she did, so why should she feel shame for her mother? Why be ashamed of an unhappy woman who tormented herself and was unable to sleep at night because of her daughter's problems, a woman who tried as best she could to . . . Yes, and after all, the point was—the real point was that she had written the truth! Everything she had written was true, from start to finish.

And now, completely calm, Lyalya began to explain all this to Smurny. Her mother was, of course, no diplomat, she had acted foolishly—and for this she would get a good scolding—but she was right in some of the things she said. Right in what? What are you talking about? Well, about that, about that. You know perfectly well what I'm talking about! You seem to be terribly sure of yourself! It's just that I have nothing to lose. No, my dear, you have plenty to lose. You don't frighten me, Herman Vladimirovich. Even a job with the Moscow Variety Theater or on the radio would be better than working here, under your wing. Don't think it's going to be so easy to find a job, especially for someone like you without any professional degree. Don't worry, I'll always be able to earn my 650 a month,* and even more. Well, fine, I'm not really interested in your personal plans. But as for this concoction of your mother's, we're going to send this on to Sergei Leonidovich today and see how he swallows it. The higher-ups demand an answer. Well, it's all the same to me, do as you please. Well then, the matter is settled. Goodbye. All the best. And by the way, Herman Vladimirovich, you really should air out your room. There's some sort of bad smell here.

Lyalya ran from Smurny's room out onto the street. She wandered around the square for a while, mechanically getting into line for something or other. Then she returned to the hotel, went to her room, and lay down. Her heart was pounding, and all of the just and nasty things that she had left unsaid came rushing to mind. And why should Milyutina, who was completely new in the theater? . . . —and so forth and so on. But she wasn't going to harbor any ill will against Zhenka Milyutina—poor thing, with a child to bring up all on her own. But what a beast that Smurny was: "without any professional degree!" This was the second time he had shoved that in her face. One could have a degree and still be a fool. There were plenty of examples of that around! One is born an actor, it's not something that can be taught, idiot! She had been accepted into the company at the personal request of Sergei Leonidovich, and he certainly knew a lot more than someone like Smurny. But that wasn't what bothered her. What bothered her was the shame she felt for her mother. No, not for her mother but for herself. She felt unbearable shame for herself. That much he had succeeded in doing: he had made her burn with shame. And to tell the truth, that was what she felt like doing now. She would simply stretch out, grit her teeth, close her eyes, and lie there motionless, burning with shame.

213

Oh, to disintegrate and disappear. For her, life in the theater would become a nightmare. Sergei Leonidovich would bawl her out, and the actors would laugh and make nasty jokes at her expense when they found out, which they were sure to do, Smurny would see to that. And eventually she would leave the company. But that was impossible, she didn't have anywhere to go. If only Grisha had made some progress with his career, she might be able to risk it. . . . But as things were now—how could she? Where was she going to earn her 650 a month? And as always after she had received a slap in the face (she had received a good many such slaps in her life, and each year they became more painful), after the hurt and silent despair, after the hasty and confused considerations as to what to do next and how to protest, suddenly she would be overtaken by doubts. And these doubts were the worst of all—the thing that nearly killed her. What if they're right? What if I really have no talent? And they all see it, they all realize it. Sergei Leonidovich takes pity on me because of our old friendship, but Smurny has no reason to.

Depressed by such frightening thoughts, Lyalya lay for a long time without moving in the empty room. The makeup woman had gone off somewhere, so there was no one with whom to share her thoughts. Suddenly a cry from the corridor delivered her from her gloomy paralysis: "Telepneva, you have a phone call!" It was Monday. And her mother always called on Mondays when there were no performances.

It was a good connection and her mother's voice was as clear as a bell: "Lyalya, darling! How are you? What's new?"

The telephone was in the hotel lobby, and there were all sorts of people milling about. Pasha Kornilovich and Makeev crossed the lobby with shopping bags in their hands, probably headed for the outdoor market. As he passed by, Pasha slapped Lyalya's behind, ruffling her skirt in the process. That wretch, he was always slapping her! And now, despite the fact that she was upset and already deep in conversation, Lyalya put her hand over the receiver and shouted, "Come back here and straighten it, come back and straighten it this minute!"

Pasha obediently ran back and straightened her skirt. She didn't want her admirers to lose interest, not now.

Here in public she obviously couldn't tell her mother what was seething inside her, so she asked instead about her father's health. Her mother reported that he was feeling well and was continuing to make efforts to save his garden, though there was no progress as yet. Grisha was staying on Bashilov Street and a few days ago had brought them some vegetables at her request. The potatoes, of course, had been a mistake. They were small and expensive—right now young potatoes cost 3.5 rubles a kilogram everywhere—and he had made a foolish purchase. He'd set off early in the day and had paid 4 rubles for them.

This talk about potatoes put Lyalya slightly on edge, for there was a hint here of her mother's usual dissatisfaction with her son-in-law. And now with a certain irritation she interrupted her mother, saying that the price of potatoes didn't interest her; what did interest her was Grisha's work—had he received an answer from the film studio? Her mother seemed to be waiting for just such a question, since she now replied in an aggressively complaining tone, "You ought to know by now that your Grisha never tells us anything about his work!"

Normally Lyalya wouldn't have paid any attention

to such a remark, considering it merely normal. But on this occasion, when she could barely keep from screaming at her mother, she simply could not keep quiet and replied in an equally aggressive tone, "But you could at least express an interest, couldn't you? You know how important this is for us."

"I don't like to interfere in other people's business."

"Oh yes, you do!" Lyalya burst out. "You do so!"

And no longer able to restrain herself, she blurted it all out: how she had asked her a hundred times not to do this, had begged her, reasoned with her, and now to have it happen here—how stubborn and mean did she have to be? Now there'd be a scandal. Well, okay, there was no point in discussing it, what was done couldn't be undone, but things had turned out very badly.

Her mother, not understanding, sputtered at the other end of the line, "What is it? Speak more clearly!"

"I'm talking about your verses!"

"What verses?"

"The ones you like to jot down and send off in every direction!"

"Good heavens, why that was . . . when was that? Four months ago."

The conversation was pointless, and Lyalya said in a weak voice, "Well okay, Mother, good-bye." And she hung up the receiver.

The elderly actress Almazova was on her way to the boiler for some hot water for tea. But she had loitered in the lobby with her ears pricked up, and when Lyalya hung up the receiver, she was briefly aware of the old woman's avid glance. Either she had overheard Lyalya's conversation and guessed what it was all about, or else Smurny had already begun to spread rumors. In any case, that evening when they were visiting the playwright, one of the other actresses whispered anxiously in Lyalya's ear, "Is it true what they're saying about your having written in some sort of complaint against our directors?"

Lyalya's mood was such that it would have been better not to have gone to this supper at all. She had hesitated, but then had decided that anything was better than staying alone in her room. That would be just too depressing. And it was a free meal, after all. She'd be able to drink a little wine and improve her mood. But in this large room where they were packed together like sardines, she found it distressing to see Smurny's smug face before her at the head of the table. It was irritating to watch him throw back the hair from his eyes—his eyes now carefully avoiding hers—and to listen to the silly toasts, jokes, and mutual eggings on. Equally revolting was the way in which the actors—especially Pashka Kornilovich and Makeev in their usual vulgar fashion, and Smurny too, though somewhat more subtly—teased the poor author, actually ridiculing him. The author didn't understand their jokes, or at least not all of them, and would make feeble attempts to joke back. His elderly mother, who was intimidated by the group, would either sigh or mumble words of thanks. The guests kept roaring with laughter at their own jokes, all of which seemed to turn on the subject of food.

"Hey Pash, the cabbage pie's gone bad, don't you think?"

"No, I don't your excellency. But the mushrooms, I dare say, are not quite right."

"What do you mean, not quite right? Why didn't you speak up sooner? I've already tossed down two platefuls of them!"

"A mushroom in the stomach is not a permanent

guest, your excellency. An autopsy will show that. . . ."

Such was the style of their repartee, which the actors obviously found amusing. And laughing themselves to tears, they sat there drinking, munching, and gulping. Suddenly someone jumped up and exclaimed fervently, "Dear Nikolai Demianovich! Thank you for every line that you've written! Thank you for your very existence!"

They applauded and shouted "hurrah." Poor Smolyanov sat there embarrassed, his face drained of color, just as it had been that spring, at the time of the play's premiere. Not knowing whether to thank them or to respond with a joke, he merely smiled and nodded mutely.

"Nikolai Demianovich!" shouted Makeev. "You've completely talked our heads off! You don't give anybody else a chance to open his mouth!"

Once again they roared with laughter and Smolyanov nodded and smiled.

Lyalya found all of this very distasteful. She didn't like it when people made jokes at others' expense. Well, so what if it was a weak play and he was no Shakespeare? Perhaps he was a good man. He had invited them with an open heart and he had squandered some 3,000 rubles on them. And they had all come, after all, they hadn't declined. Smurny had come too, even though Lyalya herself had once heard him abusing Smolyanov in the director's office, calling his play sycophantic. (Lyalya hadn't known the meaning of the word *sycophantic* and had had to check on it afterwards.) And Bob Mironovich was here, hovering around the meat pies and vodka, even though he had openly spoken out against Smolyanov's play at meetings of the theater council, had quarreled with the executive director over the matter, and had tried to persuade

Sergei Leonidovich to reject the play. All of them, all of these secret critics and scoffers were here. They had all come running for free drinks and a free meal. Ah, the unfortunate lot of the actor! Eat, drink, and be merry. My God, what a revolting spectacle! One felt sorry for them, poor things, and at the same time one couldn't help laughing at them. They were like children. They played, made lots of noise, amused themselves over trifles, and at the same time they could be cruel and destructive—just like children.

And now, not wanting to be outdone by the others, the pathetic little actor Ivan Vasilievich Yeroshkin suddenly stood up and added, "Dear author, allow me to raise my glass and express the hope that you will honor us many, many times in the future with your splendid . . . (pause) cabbage pies!" This was followed by shouts of "hurrah" and "bravo." Unable to look at the author's tormented face any longer, Lyalya went into the next room and began to help Smolyanov's mother, Yevdokia Nilovna, prepare the table for tea and dessert.

The poor old lady was wearing herself out. Lyalya had been drawn to her the moment she saw her, because she was like her grandmother—just as bustling and eager to please. Her grandmother had died two years ago in Izmailov, where she had continued to live in grandfather's old house.

"Oh, don't put out the pies," Lyalya whispered to the old lady. "The cookies will be enough!"

"I shouldn't put them out?" the old lady asked apprehensively.

"Oh, don't worry about the guests. They'll get along without them." She felt sorry for all the trouble Yevdokia Nilovna was going to. In only half an hour they had polished off two dishes of meat pilaf and an enormous plate of meat pies.

A little later Lyalya made her way up the creaking staircase to the second floor. The old lady was taking her up to meet Smolyanov's retarded young daughter. And now Lyalya was surprised once again. At home in Moscow she had just such a small attic room, in which she had spent her childhood and youth and where she now lived with Grisha. Smolyanov's daughter was thirteen years old. She was plump and well developed, with a full bosom like that of a grown girl, but her face was sheeplike and she gazed at them with an empty, mindless look. It was obvious that Yevdokia Nilovna loved her Galochka. She immediately spoke to her in a soft, gentle voice and began straightening her socks, fastening the buckle on her shoe. All the while the young girl continued to rock back and forth in her swing as she played with her rubber ball fastened to a piece of elastic. After straightening her granddaughter's clothes, Yevdokia Nilovna gave her a piece of pie on a plate and a cup of tea. Galochka didn't want the tea and pushed it away with her hand, but she ate the pie. She refused to let go of her ball as she ate, and kept bouncing it on the floor.

"And I was wondering who that was, banging upstairs," said Lyalya.

"Bouncedy-bounce," said the old lady affectionately. "That's our Galochka going bouncedy-bouncedy-bounce. . . . " Then she whispered in Lyalya's ear, "She keeps bouncing like this all day long. It's sad, terribly sad. . . . "

Downstairs, in the front room, they had begun to sing. Someone was starting to do a Russian dance, and the others were making a lot of noise as they moved the furniture. Lyalya feld a sudden, strong desire to go home, to see her father and Grisha! To go out into the garden. And now she remembered that at home they would sometimes sing and dance like this. Some of her Moscow relatives would get together— Uncle Kolya, Aunt Zhenya with the children and Uncle Misha. At other times her father's relatives would descend on them from the Urals. Someone would strike up a song, and later on, when Lyalya tired of it all, she would run upstairs to her room and start reading a book. And downstairs the noise and dancing would continue.

The little girl kept throwing her ball, not looking at Lyalya and apparently not noticing her presence at all. The old lady informed her in a whisper that Galochka was the daughter of Nikolai Demianovich's first wife, who had died. She had grieved terribly over her daughter, whereas Marta, his second wife, was a self-centered woman who didn't even want to meet Galochka or to see her, Yevdokia Nilovna. She had no intention of coming here for a visit, nor did she ever write to them. She even forbade Nikolai Demianovich to visit them. Send them money, she would say, and nothing more. And what did he send? To tell the truth, it wasn't a very large sum—400 rubles a month. And it was only when he and Marta had been quarreling that he would come and visit them—every once in a great while. Mama, he would say, she's not at all the right woman for me, she's unstable and unpredictable, but I do love her, and she helps me in my work.

Lyalya listened to the old lady, sympathized with her, and as she looked at the dull, sheeplike face of the girl, it occurred to her: "There's some sort of misfortune in everyone's life. He's a playwright, after all, a successful one. . . . " And the very thought that everyone had some such misfortune and that there were even worse ones than this, made her own troubles

221

seem lighter and more bearable.

An hour later Smurny put in a call for their special bus and the guests began making preparations to leave. Ivan Vasilievich Yeroshkin, who had succeeded in behaving outrageously, had to be dragged out by the heels, and it was midnight when they finally departed. Lyalya felt sorry for the old lady, however, and stayed behind to help with the dishes. The bus driver promised to return for her in half an hour, but for some reason he never showed up.

Clad in a T-shirt and pyjama bottoms, Smolyanov would hum as he passed from room to room, dragging furniture along the floor, putting it back in place, and bringing the dirty dishes out to the kitchen. Every now and then he would approach the sideboard and take a nip of vodka. Lyalya thought that he must be about ready to collapse, but he kept going, gazing at her with kindly blue eyes through his round-framed spectacles and smiling deferentially, like a waiter. He was obviously happy that the guests had left and that it was all over with.

Lyalya kept hoping that he would drop in his tracks and begin to snore, as one expects of a man who has had too much to drink and as had always been the case with her father and with Uncle Misha and Uncle Kolya. And with Grisha too, who would sometimes fall asleep and start snoring at the table, even when they had guests. But apparently the playwright was made of stronger stuff. He had an athlete's broad back, and tattooed above the elbow of his left arm was a mermaid and two names. When Lyalya caught sight of the mermaid, she began to feel uneasy. It occurred to her that right here and now in the middle of the night, in this house where there was no one but an old woman and a retarded child, this playwright might turn out to be no playwright at all, but merely a normal male who in his drunken state might try something. But Smolyanov apparently wasn't thinking of trying anything. Nor did he even seem to realize that a young woman was spending the night in his house—for, after all, where was she to go at 2 a.m.? Suddenly he took her hand, pecked at it with moist lips—just as he had done onstage back then, on the day of the premiere— and mumbled in a low, tearful voice, "Forgive me, my dear . . . don't be angry with me, okay?"

"I'm not at all angry with you, Nikolai Demiano-vich," said Lyalya, though at the same time carefully removing her hand just to be on the safe side.

"I'm nobody important, nobody worth mentioning —I know my own worth," muttered Smolyanov. "I'm nobody like your . . . but damn it all, what sort of man am I? . . . But all of them are nobodies too. . . . Only, please don't be mad at me, okay? My dear, kind . . ." and once again he tried to peck at her hand.

Lyalya began to feel nervous and called out loudly, "Yevdokia Nilovna!"

Smolyanov slumped over the table and suddenly began to cry. Then he took off his glasses and began wiping his eyes with the palm of his hand.

Since she had no place to go, Lyalya lay down on the sofa, covering herself with her coat. But she was upset and felt so terribly awkward about the whole situation that she couldn't fall asleep. Somehow she felt herself guilty for all of this—for Pashka and all the others who had played the fool. Why on earth did they have to insult this man? Such a strong, broad-shoul-dered, broad-chested man, not at all old, though he did already have a bald spot. . . . And why was he crying, why should he be unhappy? After all, he must be wealthy. No, wealth doesn't make you happy. Something else was needed for happiness, something essential.

Yury Trifonov

And at this thought a vague feeling of happiness, a feeling of her own good fortune, came over Lyalya. For it seemed to her that she possessed that mysterious something which was necessary for happiness. She couldn't quite explain what it was, but she knew for certain that she had it. And the reason she knew this was that when other people were unhappy, she always felt sorry and wanted to make things easier for them— to share something with them. And the fact that she always felt this desire to share with others meant, of course, that she had something to share. Sometimes she thought that this desire arose from the fact that she had no children. But probing deeper, she realized that having children would not lessen her desire to share with others this essential something that was necessary for happiness. For her own children would merely be an extension of herself.

And growing all the more anxious, Lyalya asked the playwright if he wouldn't like her to make some strong coffee. He said he would, and Lyalya went out to the kitchen, emerging a few minutes later with a cup for each of them. After the coffee—by now it was two-thirty—neither of them felt like sleeping. Smolyanov had sobered up and began telling her about his life—how difficult it was and how difficult he found it to write. He had no friends—people didn't trust him, and things hadn't worked out in his personal life. He had come to Moscow four years ago, having worked in the provinces until then. He had been a newspaper reporter at the front during the war, and before that, in the thirties, an Arctic explorer, spending his winters in Dikson. He had served as a frontier guard and as a police detective, and had also worked in various physical education depart-ments, having previously trained as a boxer. At the Kalach railroad station he had once shot and killed a bandit with his own hand. And now this was already his third play—the other two had been performed in the provinces—but he was lacking in education; he'd had to do everything on his own, by sheer grit. And that past winter he'd had such a tough time getting *Distant Forests* accepted in Moscow that his strength had almost given out. They'd wanted to throttle him—they'd already prepared the noose—but things hadn't worked out according to their expectations. He knew now what vile people there were in this world—and in her beloved theater too, oh yes! And suddenly he burst out laughing: so, you don't want anything to do with my cabbage pies, eh? Well, never mind, my friends. Someday you'll beg for them, someday you'll come crawling on your knees for them. Dear Nikolai Demianovich, please give us one of your cabbage pies! Lyalya listened with avid interest and was suddenly struck by the thought: he's probably right, that's probably just what will happen. In the meantime they were throwing his lack of education in his face, using this against him. She could just picture them all coming after him, bearing down on him with a noose and he, this rugged specimen, letting them have it with a right hook.

It was growing light and the roosters had already begun to crow. Smolyanov and Lyalya went out into the yard and descended along a path through some underbrush where they caught the fusty scent of nettles. Then they passed by an old cemetery whose crosses drooped at various angles, and finally came out onto a bluff above the Volga. Here they sat down on a log.

"My entire youth is bound up with this dear old log," said Smolyanov. "And why didn't they use it for firewood during the war. . . . Of course there weren't any men around. . . ."

225

Lyalya was hunched up and shivering from the cold, and he put his arm around her. The river was covered with whitecaps, and only at its outer edges did one see dark expanses of water. Hulking next to the shore was the black form of a barge, and on the shore itself were some other black forms—probably skiffs. Down on the sand, in the midst of these dark shapes, someone had lighted a campfire. Smolyanov told her that this was a gathering place for various criminal types and that the area was unsafe. And if they were to venture down there right now, somebody might knife them—just like that, for no good reason. He told her something about this gang and reminisced about some of the bandits he had known. He was interesting to listen to, and Lyalya didn't feel the slightest bit afraid—only cold.

As they made their way back, his arm still around her, he suddenly stopped and awkwardly pressed her to him, trying to keep her warm. And thus they stood. It was, in fact, incredibly cold—hard to believe that it could be so hot during the day. He began to warm her by rubbing his palms up and down her back and sides, and as he did so, he kept muttering to himself and humming. He stroked her slowly and firmly, ever more firmly, and the longer this lasted and the more she felt his strength, the more for some strange reason she felt sorry for him.

After returning to the house, they drank some vodka in order to warm up, and then went upstairs. They stole into a small, dark room where the blinds were still lowered and which smelled of dogs and male habitation. Here they continued to converse in a whisper so as not to wake up his daughter, who was sleeping in the next room.

As he went on in a hurt voice, muttering

incomprehensibly, threatening someone, Lyalya could not help but feel ashamed of her fellow actors. And feeling that she had to make excuses for them and at the same time wanting to comfort him—after all, they had insulted him for no good reason, simply for being nice to them—she did her best to make him understand. There was no need to get angry with them. They were naive and goodhearted, terribly goodhearted. And what splendid friends and colleagues they were, ready to share their last crumb with you. It was just that they sometimes said dumb, stupid things, just to be witty. So forget about them. She, Lyalya, always forgave them because—well, because they had a hard life. Just try to get by on 700 rubles a month. And Ivan Vasilievich—Yeroshkin—had a family of five. He had to love the theater a great deal—for its own sake, not for money. And even she, Lyalya, had enemies—people who were out to get her, trying to hold her back—but still they couldn't spoil her enthusiasm for the theater. And for the sake of this enthusiasm and perhaps even for the happiness which she felt in the theater—however fleeting this happiness might be—she had to be patient and to forgive because . . . well, why should one do otherwise? . . . And by now he was comforted, and he nodded, "Yes, yes, I understand you. . . . "

And then came Lyalya's untimate demonstration of kindness and pity. Much later that morning, as she pried open her eyes and had trouble remembering where she was, she heard a knocking sound. And it suddenly came to her: it was Smolyanov's retarded daughter, bouncing her ball in the next room.

II

A month and a half later Lyalya returned to Moscow from the Crimea, where she had gone on vacation after the tour. On almost her first day back she ran into Smolyanov, who told her that he was working on a new play. He had submitted the first act to Sergei Leonidovich, and the latter had apparently approved it.

Lyalya knew that she always looked her best after the Crimea. Almost everyone looks more attractive after a summer vacation, but with Lyalya this was especially the case. As her close friend Mashka would declare, she looked disgustingly attractive—and this because she would lie fearlessly in the sun until her skin turned black, her light hair faded to the color of straw, and her blue eyes shone all the more brightly in her tanned face. And she would spend hours in the water, swimming as tirelessly and as far out as the best of them. Then in the evenings there would be volleyball and tennis. And although she wasn't necessarily a first-class player, still she played as hard as she could, just for the pure joy of running, jumping, laughing, and exerting herself to the point of exhaustion. And she never permitted herself any summer affairs—that wasn't for her, and no good ever came of them anyway. As a result, when she returned, she was always full of energy and full of longing for her husband, her girl friends, the theater, and simply for her own, familiar street running past the church and the vegetable store.

Smolyanov gave Lyalya a long, lingering look and smiled. In his smile there was something joyful, masculine, and uninhibited—something which Lyalya always

loved to feel, since this feeling meant that all was well
and everything was just as it should be. At such moments of inner rejoicing even her voice would change.
And it was with this changed voice that she greeted
Smolyanov, offering him her hand and noticing how her
voice took on a slightly affected, sing-song quality:
"Well, Nikolai Demianovich, so you've got something
for us. That's great, really wonderful!"

As she said this, she was amazed to think that there
had been a night when she had felt so terribly sorry for
this man with his dull face—good Lord, whatever for?
There was something doughy and sodden about Smolyanov's face.

He was mumbling incomprehensibly, in his usual
fashion, and rubbing her hand. Lyalya said lightly,
"Nikolai Demianovich, I'll see you soon! So long for
now!" And with this she was off. But a second later
she stopped, and glancing back, she said, "I'm very
glad you're back here at the theater with us again!"

A few days later it was as if every trace of the
Crimea had vanished. Or perhaps it was simply that
Moscow had overwhelmed her with its rain, chill, and
feverish tempo—not to mention her father's illness,
Sergei Leonidovich's anger, her agitation in connection
with the new fall production, and her endless running
from one store to another in search of some rubber-
soled shoes for the wet weather.

As Lyalya had expected, she was given no part
at all in the theater's fall production. But in December
Smolyanov submitted his new play *Ignat Timofeevich*
and started coming frequently to the theater—first for
readings, then for discussions, then for revisions, and
finally for the selection of roles. Initially Lyalya was
promised nothing, then she was given a small, insignificant role, and finally a good one—as one of the heroines.

She hadn't asked for anything; rather it was the play-wright himself who thought to bring the matter up with Sergei Leonidovich. Smurny protested at a meeting of the theater council, but Nikolai Demianovich said firmly, "This is the way it's going to be!"–and Smurny shut up.

Although the role of Yevdokia, Ignat Timofeevich's wife and the principal of the seven-year village ele-mentary school, was not a particularly enviable one–it was terribly overdone, with all sorts of jealousy, suffer-ings, and didactic conversations–still, Lyalya hoped to impress everyone, to show what she could do by "turn-ing a carp into a suckling pig," as Sergei Leonidovich would say. She put heart and soul into the part and re-vealed such nuances and depth of character in her heroine that the author himself was astounded.

"Well, well! It never occurred to me that . . . "

Whatever such know-it-alls as Bob Mironovich, Nika Gerasimov, or even her own Grisha might say about Smolyanov–some out of snobbism, others, sad to say, out of envy at his success–nonetheless, his name began to be mentioned more and more frequently and favorably in the newspapers. *Distant Forests* was already playing in forty theaters, and there was in fact something solid and appealing in this provincial play-wright, some sort of clumsy ability to win over his audience and to get to the heart of the matter, to make his point, with swift, bearlike strides.

By now Smolyanov was coming to the theater every day ot sit in on rehearsals. Sometimes he and Lyalya would slip off from the others after rehearsal and go to a restaurant together, usually to the tenth-floor dining room of the Hotel Moscow, where he knew the headwaiter. From there they would drive to the empty apartment of one of Smolyanov's friends

who had gone off to China and left Smolyanov his key.
On one occasion they drove to the outskirts of town
and visited a shoe store where the manager was a friend
of Smolyanov's. Here they managed to buy the rubber-
soled shoes which Lyalya had been hunting for ever
since fall. All she had to do was open her mouth, and
suddenly there they were, just what she wanted! Lyalya
was amazed. Why, here he was, a relative newcomer to
Moscow and already he knew all the ins and outs of
the city and had a flock of acquaintances. And it wasn't
that he was terribly sociable, he was even somewhat
morose—not at all one of your lively, outgoing types.
So he must have some special talent. There are such
people: in their own quiet way they succeed in everything they do. Their business affairs go well, they're
never short of money, and women—foolish creatures—
seem to be attracted to them like bees to honey. It's a
talent—the most precious talent of all!—to be able to set
up one's life, to furnish it, so to speak, as one would
furnish an apartment. If only Grisha had even a little
of this talent.

And so it was that which in Saratov had been a
chance occurrence, a compassionate gesture, an early
morning chimera—had it really happened at all?—became
now, toward the end of the winter, a normal part of
her life, something which it seemed she simply could
not do without.

In March, when the play was about to have its
premiere, Lyalya noticed that Smurny had begun to
smile at her and would be the first to nod respectful
greeting from a distance. And by now all the unpleasantness of winter—the cold and the slush—had been
forgotten, and it seemed to her that it had been warm
and sunny all along and, more to the point, that it
would always be this way. In the depths of her heart

she had long feared, had even resigned herself to the fact, that she would never have the chance to make good. But now, suddenly something was happening that she had been dreaming of for years, almost without hope. Sergei Leonidovich had begun working with her alone, and the makeup woman—hypocrite that she was—had started addressing her respectfully as Liudmila Petrovna. There was even one occasion when the executive director's car was sent to pick her up and take her to the radio station where she along with the executive director and Sergei Leonidovich were to discuss their work on the new play. All these and other equally happy circumstances occurred at the end of the winter of 1952, when Lyalya had just turned twenty-five. She got used to these changes very quickly, perhaps even instantaneously, and it seemed that things would stay this way and perhaps be even better in the future.

What had brought about this sudden change in her life remained for Lyalya a mystery, nor did she give it much thought. Perhaps the winds in the sky had shifted direction. Perhaps hurricanes had spent themselves thousands of miles away. Her deceased grandmother used to love to quote the saying: "Everything comes at its appointed hour." And now Lyalya's hour had come—and why not? She had waited so patiently and persistently. Her mother, of course, thought that this change for the better had come about thanks to her own recent letter of complaint. Perhaps this was true. Or perhaps it was Nikolai Demianovich's influence. Or more likely, it was Sergei Leonidovich himself. Ever since the time of her drama school entrance exams, which she had failed, he had always been nice to her, almost too nice. Then he had gotten used to her, even tired of her, and now it was as if he had suddenly taken a fresh look and had been astonished: "My dear colleagues, what on earth are we doing to Liudmila Telepneva?" As she learned later, he had once said of her, "Well, she's got appeal, a great deal of appeal, but does she have anything more than that?" Yes, but after all, if one appeals to people, that's already half the battle. You don't find this sort of appeal just lying around on the street. "The ability to appeal to others is a God-given talent," Ksenofont Fyodorovich, the set designer who had conveyed Sergei Leonidovich's words to her, used to say. "You have to cherish and foster it, and not turn up your nose at it." Ksenofont Fyodorovich was a wonderful person, and Lyalya had loved him like a father. He had died, poor thing, of a heart attack. He had drunk a lot.

But all the same, it was her grandmother who was wiser than anyone else: "Everything comes at its appointed hour."

The curtain closed, and the actors rushed offstage. But Lyalya didn't manage to catch up with the others, and when the curtain opened again, she was caught in a loud wave of applause. Finding herself alone on stage, she couldn't make up her mind whether to take a bow on her own or to wait for the others. Someone grabbed her by the hand, and squeezing her fingers painfully, dragged her to the footlights. She bowed and saw out of the corner of her eye that it was Makeev. Smiling at the audience, he whispered spitefully, "Well, go on and bow! They're applauding you!"

Then it happened again. Pushing and crowding one another the actors hurried offstage, but Lyalya for some reason was left behind, and the wave of applause caught her alone. Someone threw a bouquet. Then the actors stopped bowing, and then forming an

uneven line, they too began applauding   Everyone
turned toward the right wing of the stage, where Sergei
Leonidovich was emerging with that pale, weary, and
somewhat jaded expression which he usually wore by
the end of rehearsals. Looking at Sergei Leonidovich,
Lyalya was barely able to hold back her tears. She
wanted to embrace him and tell him what a wonderful
person he was. Suddenly he took her by the hand and
led her forward. They stood alone before the auditorium, which by now was half empty. Those who remained roared their approval as they surged and pressed
toward the stage with even more enthusiasm than before.

"Thank you, Sergei Leonidovich," said Lyalya,
"thank you. . . . "

"Face the audience, the audience!" he mumbled
without looking at her.

Then Nikolai Demianovich appeared onstage in a
handsome, light-colored suit, sporting a white handkerchief in his pocket. He was wearing a new pair of
glasses with thick, black, American-type frames, and
these glasses changed his appearance completely. Somehow he seemed a changed man. No longer did he bend
low, like a waiter, in making his bows; his face was
no longer covered with a deathly pallor, nor did it
glisten with sweat. He held himself erect and bowed in
proper fashion, merely lowering his head as if he were
nodding in agreement with someone, "Yes, yes."
After bowing to the audience, he walked up to Sergei
Leonidovich, embraced him and kissed him. Lyalya
noticed how Sergei Leonidovich flushed crimson as he
spontaneously embraced Nikolai Demianovich and said
something in his ear. After this, Nikolai Demianovich
walked up to Lyalya, kissed her hand, and whispered,
"Tonight we're going to have to celebrate."

Before Lyalya had a chance to reply, he had

walked off and begun shaking hands with the actors and kissing the hands of the actresses. When the applause finally died down and faded away, they all descended the narrow staircase to the dressing rooms. Everyone was talking at once, laughing loudly and congratulating one another. Sergei Leonidovich continued to hold Lyalya's arm.

"Seven encores! Seven!" shouted Lemberg, the stage manager. She was standing at the bottom of the stairs, indicating the number seven with the outstretched fingers of her hands. "It's a success, Sergei Leonidovich!"

"Yes, well, we'll see," the director nodded. "But I must say, Ada Maksimovna, you were in an awful hurry with that curtain. You overdid it, just as they would in the provinces."

"But you asked me to yourself, SergeiLeonidovich!"

"You have to use your common sense. When you see that the play's a success, there's no need to hurry with the curtain. They'll clap without that. Just use your common sense. Well, never mind, it's not important; Congratulations, you've done a good job." And smiling wearily, he shook Lemberg's hand. "Oh, make a note that the clouds should be removed from the third act. They don't accomplish anything and just look messy."

Sergei Leonidovich walked on, and Lemberg embraced Lyalya from behind, taking her by the shoulders and kissing her on the cheek. "Congratulations, Lyalya dear! Oh, sorry, I've smeared your cheek. Well, never mind, you'll be taking your makeup off anyway. Everything was marvelous, wonderful—there's only one little spot in the last act. When Makeev is approaching the porch and you turn. . . "

Lemberg rattled on excitedly, moving her large,

painted mouth, but Lyalya took in very little of what she was saying.

"Thanks, Adochka, thanks a lot," she nodded and smiled, almost in a trance. Then she too kissed Lemberg on the cheek. As she did so, it suddenly struck her that only a month ago—or even yesterday!—she would not have dared to address her familiarly as Adochka, much less to kiss her. And now this had happened so simply and naturally, and Lemberg herself seemed to be glad that Lyalya had kissed her. Everything around her continued to change, and Lyalya could feel that she herself was changing. That was how it should be. There was nothing strange about it, nor any reason to be surprised. Everything that surrounded her and was connected with her was changing, changing inexorably with each passing second, and people seemed to sense this, just as birds sense a change in the weather.

After removing her makeup and changing her clothes, Lyalya went into the backstage room where Sergei Leonidovich stood surrounded by a group of actors. He was commenting on a particular scene, demonstrating how it should be played and where the mistake lay. And from the humorous, animated way in which he was acting out the scene, it was obvious that he was in an excellent mood. Not only was he savoring the success of the evening's premiere, but someone must have already forecast the play's bright future. The actors sensed this and roared with delight as they watched his demonstration. Smurny was there too, with a feigned expression of joy frozen on his smiling face. As Lyalya approached, he turned and said, "Tremendous, really tremendous, Liudmila Petrovna! My sincere congratulations!"

From the expression of his eyes it was clear that his congratulations were anything but sincere. Nor was Zhenka Milyutina sincere when she kissed Lyalya and said that it was high time for the younger actresses to unite and put an end to the old women's reign of terror. Earlier, when things had been going well for Zhenka and it was Lyalya who was out of favor, she had not made any such proposals. But none of this bothered Lyalya at the moment. She wanted to forget about the bad times—to be kind and generous. And now, reading in Smurny's eyes a deeply concealed, animal-like terror, she even felt something akin to sympathy for her former enemy. And she replied cheerfully, "Thank you, Herman Vladimirovich, thank you!"

At this point Nikolai Demianovich entered the room and announced something about a banquet at the Grand Hotel, presumably on Monday. Lyalya wasn't listening very carefully; she was more concerned with what was going to happen next. Grisha was waiting downstairs and she would have to introduce him to Nikolai Demianovich. Nikolai Demianovich now approached her and said softly but calmly, as if there were no one else around, "I'll wait for you downstairs, outside the executive director's office. I'll have two friends with me."

And with this he disappeared.

Lyalya returned to her dressing room, packed her things in her small suitcase, gathered up her flowers. Before leaving the room, however, she sat down for a moment in front of the mirror. She felt uneasy, her present happiness clouded by feelings of apprehension at the horribly awkward situation that was about to develop. Grisha hadn't been at all eager to attend the premiere, nor did he like coming to the theater in general. He was painfully proud, and people offended him here. But she had persuaded him to. Her mother, who wasn't able to leave Lyalya's father, had also tried to persuade him, though in her own fashion: "Go ahead, you go! Someone has to be there to meet Lyalya and escort her home."

Her relatives were attending in droves—Uncle Kolya with all of his family, her mother's youngest sister Veronika, and Aunt Zhenya and Uncle Misha with Lyalya's two cousins, Mayka and Borka. Mayka was an ardent theater fan and would be sure to be there. Valentina Abramovna, Uncle Misha's sister, also wanted to come, and Aunt Toma planned to make a special trip in from Aleksandrov. Her mother had gotten them all so worked up that Lyalya had even quarreled with her. Was it really necessary to organize this Telepnev march on the theater?! Actually, it would be more accurate to call it a Fomichev march, since all of them were her mother's relatives. And if anyone from her father's side were to come, it would only be Slavik, Uncle Fedya's son.

In any case, they had all been told in no uncertain terms that there was to be no waiting around in the lounge to greet her, no bouquets, no hurrahs or family demonstrations. At the end of the third act—collect your coats, boots, and off you go! I'll see you at home, at 32 Chetvyortaya Pochtovaya Street. Only Borka, an avid photographer, was to be permitted to take one or two pictures of her in the lounge, when it was all over with. And only Grisha was to meet her and escort her home. But Grisha, as Lyalya knew full well, was the one person who had come here without any enthusiasm and probably without even any bouquet. Well, never mind that; it wasn't really important. One could forgive his morose state of mind. At times she felt terribly sorry for him and would lie in bed at night, racking her brains, wondering what was to be done and how she could help him. And right now it seemed to her that if she hadn't dragged him to the theater tonight, he would have been even more depressed, sitting at home in his beloved library. Everything would have been all right if Nikolai Demianovich hadn't suggested that they go out somewhere after the performance. Apparently he was alone, without his wife. They must have quarreled again. What a horrible woman—to pick a fight with him on this particular day! She managed to spoil all his special occasions. Oh, how nice it would be to go somewhere —to the Aragvi, for instance—and have a good meal and something to drink, a nice, dry red wine. At the very thought Lyalya could feel a gnawing in her stomach and the taste of *satsivi* on her tongue. But Grisha . . . Yet what if the three of them were to go out together? And really—what would be so strange about that?

Lyalya looked at herself in the mirror. Her face was pale except for a slight rosy hue at her temples, and the light-colored German lipstick she was wearing gave her lips a moist and somehow very fresh, girlish luster. Everyone said that Lyalya had a beautiful mouth, and she knew it for a fact. And now she looked at her mouth with satisfaction. She was taking her time. Let the other actors disperse; there was no need to hurry. It would be easier to meet Nikolai Demianovich in an almost completely empty lounge and then introduce him to Grisha somewhere by the cloakroom in the front lobby. And let her relatives disappear. Mayka was especially dangerous with her untimely comments, as was Uncle Kolya's wife Lipa, Olimpiada Afanasievna, the universally acknowledged fool in the family. And of course there was no way of avoiding a certain awkwardness between Grisha and Nikolai Demianovich. Perhaps Grisha already sensed something, though most likely he didn't—he was so caught up in his own misfortunes.

Yury Trifonov

There had, of course, been that awkward incident with
the shirt she had bought as a birthday present for
Nikolai Demianovich. She had kept the shirt in their
bureau and Grisha had accidentally discovered it. He
had been surprised and had asked about it. The neck
was forty-five centimeters and obviously too big for
him; he wore a forty-one. So she had had to lie, saying
that she had picked out the shirt as a collective gift for
one of their colleagues, a nice man named Tamarkin,
who was a cellist in the theater orchestra. She was
ashamed of herself, but what else could she do? If she
had told him the truth, she would have dealt a monstrous blow to his pride. This would have been in-
humanly cruel, especially now, in his present state of
mind. And besides, "the truth" in this case would not
really have been the truth, but only a partial truth.
For what had gone on between Lyalya and Smolyanov
could not be called a love affair in the usual sense of
the word; nor could it be called by any other precise
term. Lyalya didn't know what to call it. She hadn't
asked or expected anything of him, nor had there been
any of the inflamed passion, the burning desire to see
him and know what he was doing every day, every
hour, which she had experienced in the past with others.
Weeks could go by without her seeing Smolyanov and
she would not suffer from the fact that he didn't call
her at the theater or come looking for her. But when
she did see him, it always felt good. And she always
felt sorry for him for one reason or another. She knew
that he needed sympathy, for he could not expect any
from his egotistical wife, his retarded daughter, or even
from his old mother in far-off Saratov. Much less
could he expect any sympathy from his theatrical
friends or the theater-going public. He used to tell
Lyalya, in fact, "You're the only one who even half

understands me."

To leave Grisha for him! Perhaps he would even have liked her to, but the question had never come up and Lyalya would never have agreed to it—she would have felt even worse about leaving Grisha. And the fact that they weren't even officially married was quite beside the point. For her whole life—her school days, her youth, the war and its famines, her hopes, and her unborn children—all were bound up with Grisha! And to leave him now, just when things were beginning to look up for her . . .

Lyalya's throat suddenly constricted as she pictured what would happen to Grisha if she were to abandon him. No, never! Right now it was raining—she could hear the water gushing down the iron drain-pipe—and Grisha was undoubtedly out on the street somewhere. He wouldn't think of waiting for her inside the theater of even under the theater marquee, but would be standing somewhere off at a distance, huddled against a wall. That was the way he was. He was full of complexes and overly sensitive about everything. And now Lyalya began to hurry, snatching up her small suitcase, the flowers, and turning out the light as she hastily left the room.

As she proceeded quickly down the corridor, almost at a run, she overheard the fragment of a conversation:

"Did you notice how she detached herself from the rest of us and remained onstage by herself? Just like some provincial prima donna."

"Good Lord, what do you expect? In this theater that's the only way you can gain any recognition. . . ."

For a second she was tempted to go back and see who it was. But never mind. She would have to put up with that sort of thing now—it was starting already.

But such was the inevitable order of things and just as it should be.

The lights had been turned down in the lounge, and the audience had almost completely dispersed. Thank God there were no familiar faces. Suddenly there was a blinding flash from the left—it was Borka who had jumped forward and clicked his camera at almost point blank range. Lyalya hadn't even glanced in his direction. At the other end of the lounge Nikolai Demianovich was talking with two strange men, and right beside him stood the theater's executive director, Roman Vasilievich, and the business manager, Bravin. Lyalya walked past them, nodding modestly as she wished them all the best. The men replied gaily, one interrupting the other. They seemed to be a bit high already from the cognac they had drunk. The executive director flashed a smile with his gold-filled teeth and the business manager shouted, "Lyudochka, be so kind as to join us for tea! To celebrate the premiere!" Nikolai Demianovich said to her, "Liudmila Petrovna, can I give you a lift? I have a car at my disposal."

Rebrov, of course, had missed the performance. To attend one of Smolyanov's plays—that was asking too much! Since eleven o'clock that morning he had been ensconced in Scholars Reading Room no. 3 of the Lenin Library and had been reading about Ivan Gavrilovich Pryzhov. The day before, he had ordered everything he could find in the card catalogue: *The Russian Archives* for the year 1866; *A History of the Tavern* and *Beggars in Holy Rus;* articles in *The Voice, The Moscow Gazette,* and *The Saint Petersburg Gazette;* Altman's book; a collection of articles and letters from the year 1834; *Bygone Years,* and a great deal more. It was splendid reading material for several days. As for why he needed Pryzhov, Rebrov himself didn't know. Why *did* he need him?! This habit of sitting in the library and devouring old books, newspapers, and journals had become so irresistible that it was like a passion for cards or drugs. Rebrov had stumbled onto Pryzhov at the time he had been researching Nechaev.* Actually he had first come upon his name a year ago when he had been reading some old journals right here, in Scholars Reading Room No. 3. There was no point at all to this reading; it was simply a narcotic which he couldn't do without. If fact, there were days when he didn't even bother to eat, but would simply visit the smokers' lounge. Yet what he needed to do was to get something down on paper, to write some sort of sketch from which he could work out a film scenario. For Rebrov simply could not get Ivan Gavrilovich Pryzhov off his mind. And this despite the fact that he was a completely useless character long forgotten by everyone, an unsuccessful rebel, a historian, a drunkard and a parasite, and at the same time a man of great nobility of character, a chronicler of Russian everyday life and customs, who had lived 100 years ago. Could it be that all this preoccupation with Pryzhov was merely a reflection of his own insatiable curiosity or worse, of his own laziness? This was a question which Rebrov had asked himself more than once.

By six that evening he had managed to fill up some twenty pages of a notebook—my God, what on earth for?!—with various facts and ideas drawn from Ivan Gavrilovich's life and writings. Then, as spots were already dancing before his eyes, he left the library and set off to have supper in the cafe of the Hotel National. Here he settled in his favorite seat by the window and ordered a schnitzel and a helping of dry mashed potatoes which they knew how to prepare properly only here at the National. All evening he nursed his cold schnitzel along with several cups of coffee. He also had two glasses of brandy, to which he was treated by acquaintances who stopped off at his table to talk. Rebrov himself was broke. That morning, in fact, he'd had to take a 10-ruble note from Lyalya.

In the National everything followed a set pattern: people shared tables, got acquainted, and left; others came bearing messages, reporting on the events of the day, cracking jokes; some tried to intimidate, others got indignant, some lent money and made deals, others got drunk and created a scene. After six o'clock people began arriving from the races, telling about their winnings and any new swindles that had been unearthed. At nine, as always, the artist Rysev appeared, a man who was rumored to be an informer and whom you had to be careful with. Between nine and ten, actors began showing up—those who didn't have appear on-stage during the last acts. "They say it's a real flop at the Maly. . . ." "Was Myshchikov really fired?" "Listen, do you know this one? A rabbi comes to a prostitute and . . ." "For that little item you'd have to go to Riga!" "Hey, look at that pretty girl sitting with our friend!" "What's going on: Lyalya has a premiere, and he's carousing here? Why aren't you there, in the director's box, scoundrel?"

Not wanting to enter into any explanations, Rebrov gave a lazy, contemptuous wave of his hand. His contempt was directed both at the content of the question and at the individual who had asked it. Was one supposed to give an accounting of every sot in the tavern? And the words *scoundrel* and *Lyalya* jarred on him—that excessive familiarity which one always found among actors. He was still under the spell of

Ivan Gavrilovich, and talking with these drunkards, he thought of him. The tavern syndrome, it seemed, had remained unchanged over the years: the same yearning for company and for forgetfulness. It was not for nothing that Pryzhov had burned the last two volumes of his *A History of the Tavern,* fearing that the government would increase its surveillance and begin harassing these miserable establishments. No one at the National, of course, had any idea of what was passing through Rebrov's mind.

At about ten o'clock, when Rebrov was just getting ready to leave (it didn't take more than fifteen minutes by trolley bus to get to the theater), Shakhov appeared. He was on the run as usual and asked Rebrov hastily how his work was going. His manner was businesslike, like that of some inspector, and as he asked the question, he cast an eagle-eyed glance over the neighboring tables, not wanting to waste a moment. Rebrov replied that there was nothing new to report and added a la Pryzhov, "I'm dying, but one leg is still kicking."

"Well then, I'll tell you what, dear fellow," said Shakhov, now catching sight of someone in the far corner of the room, "you call me in about five days, or I'll call you. Maybe we can come up with something. We'll do a bit of kicking together. . . . "

Out on the street it was cold and raining hard. People were already leaving the theater, but only a few at a time—those who were dashing off before the play was over. Not wishing to run into any actors or any of the familiar pests who usually attended on opening night, Rebrov did not come and stand under the marquee. Above all, he wished to avoid running into any of Lyalya's relatives. It wasn't that he disliked these people, most of whom were from Irina Ignatievna's side of the family, but he tried to keep his distance from them. Perhaps some of them were fine people, perfectly decent, but in each one of them he seemed to detect something of his mother-in-law. He pressed against the side of the building in order to protect himself from the rain and at the same time to keep an eye on those who were emerging. And why—for heaven's sake why!— couldn't he have stood by the entrance, greeted acquaintances with a smile, shaken hands with Lyalya's relatives, and jokingly responded to their greetings? "What have we here—a nervous husband?" "Well, what can you do? *C'est la vie!*" Or even better, why couldn't he have waited with a bouquet of flowers in the downstairs lounge, rushed forward to greet her in front of everyone, and hugged and kissed her to the approving murmur of the crowd?

But all of this was completely impossible. The thing which Rebrov feared most in this world was to make a fool of himself. This trait, characteristic of those who are proud and reserved by nature, created a lot of difficulties in his life. These difficulties had begun a long time ago, as far back as grade school. He and Lyalya had been in the same class and he had always liked her. He had felt some sort of painful, mute attraction to her, though he didn't know why—whether it was her braids, her voice, her early developing feminine figure or the boldness with which she had sung the role of Nelly in their school performance of *Till Eulenspiegel.* He couldn't tell her his feelings; he couldn't even bear to look in her direction. And as a result, he suffered. Once he had run out into the schoolyard with some of his friends after class and Lyalya had asked him whether he was on his way home. Instead of shouting back, "Sure, let's go!"—he had almost choked and muttered, "Well, no, I'm staying here. . . . " If only the other kids hadn't been around! But they were keeping an eagle-eye

on both of them, and Lyalya walked off. She didn't
ask him again, and thus it continued for a whole year
—the two of them sometimes walking off in the same
direction, but never together.

Then, when they were both in the ninth grade,
there was an evening movie in the dark auditorium in
some club on Tverskaya-Yamskaya Street. On the
screen people were dashing about on horseback, and
foes of the Revolution were being rounded up and shot.
But Rebrov and Lyalya, who were sitting in the last
row, didn't understand a thing that was going on. His
left hand and Lyalya's right had joined together in the
dark and were caressing and fondling each other, squeezing until it hurt. All this went on for an hour and a
half. Neither of them said a word and their faces
remained turned toward the screen. When the lights
were turned on, they got up and headed for the door,
still not looking at each other nor saying a single word.
When they were out on the street, Lyalya suddenly
burst out laughing and said that he was very funny.
Wounded to the quick, he mumbled, "You're funny
too!"

Yes, yes, it was his old fear of making a fool of
himself. But there were to be worse moments than
this. Simply to say "I love you" struck him as ridicu-
lously absurd, a breach of good form, and as a result
he maintained a dumb silence which was even more
absurd. Actually, it was she who first suggested that
they get married—in the winter of '47. By this time
their relationship had long been consummated. But
he still couldn't bring himself to ask her, for what if
she should suddenly refuse? What was he to do then
—hurl himself in the path of an oncoming train? And
there had always been other men in her life: the one

with the limp; the one who had helped her to get into the theater; then some Yasha or other and a certain Valery, a childhood friend and the son of one of his mother-in-law's best friends. His mother-in-law had long dreamed of Lyalya's marrying this Valery and even now she apparently still clung to this wild hope.

Yet Grisha had always loved her the whole thirteen years they had known each other. Not a single day had gone by that he hadn't thought about her. Whenever she went off on tour or on vacation to the South—she liked to go on vacation by herself, and such was already the established rule—he didn't know what to do with himself. He would wander about, numb with longing and unable either to work or to go out and have a good time. His friends would introduce him to girls in an attempt to distract him, but it was precisely when Lyalya was traveling and the ideal time was presumably at hand that he lost all interest in such distractions. Now if she had been in Moscow and everything were as it should be, then he would have had nothing against it. Though even in such cases it was more a question of talk than of action. "Wouldn't it be nice to—break loose, right here and now. . . ," he would say to a friend over a cup of coffee, glancing at some sallow-complexioned young coed in the library cafeteria. But, good Lord, in all of those years there had been only two or three times when he had actually "broken loose." Was that any "big deal" for a young man? It was really nothing at all. Contributing to his fidelity was a superstition or, more accurately, a sort of secret terror which he did not admit even to himself: that if he allowed something to happen, then she too would allow something to happen. And the suspicion that this something had already happened tormented him more than anything else in his life. For she was terribly

openhearted and thought nothing of kissing a man
or responding casually to his advances. This did not
mean, of course, that she would go all the way, but she
would go *part* of the way without a moment's hesitation. And it was not a question in this case of that
familiarity one usually associates with actors or of
environment, but simply of her own character—of that
damned kindness of hers. There had been an incident
a long time ago, before the war—that is, just before the
German invasion in June of '41. After one of their
school exams the two of them had gone swimming at
Shchukinsky Beach. Before the war there hadn't been
any beach there, but only a very high and steep sandy
bluff. It was the very beginning of summer, and of
course the water had been cold. They had taken two or
three dips and were lying on the sand when suddenly
three young fellows appeared from nowhere and began
flirting with Lyalya. At the same time they began to
heckle Rebrov and eventually drew him into a fight. As
always in such situations he put up with the heckling for
a long time, grew increasingly tense, and then, as if
exploding, furiously went at them with his fists. They
started hammering away at him too and would probably
have beaten him to a pulp if Lyalya hadn't rushed up to
defend him, shouting, "Stop it! What are you doing?
What do you want from us?!" And then suddenly
adding, "Well, if you want me to, I'll kiss each one of
you." And in fact, she did kiss all three of them, one
after another. And as they stood there, too stunned
to protest, she took Rebrov by the hand and led him
away. She took him home with her on the streetcar.
Her parents were horrified at what had happened and
bathed his wounds with some sort of lotion. Then they
fed him and had him spend the night on the veranda
of their small house. Lyalya came to him in the middle

of the night, but nothing happened except for the car-
resses which were an impetuous manifestation of her
pity. Nor did Rebrov feel any need to prove his man-
hood—he had proved it with every inch of his proud,
battered body. There was only one thought which
tormented him, making it difficult to fall asleep. And
the next morning, as the birds were singing and the sunlight filtered through the leaves, this same thought
woke him with its sharp, nagging aches: how could she
have kissed them, all three of them, and so easily? And
later, when he asked her about it: good Lord, she had
simply wanted to save him. And she had saved him,
she had! But what if in order to save him she had had
to do something worse? With all three of them? After a
moment's pause she answered firmly: if she had to, in
order to save him, she could have done it. He groaned
and fell back on the couch, biting his lip until it bled.
What made him feel such despair was not the fact that
she could have done it, but the fact that she had responded so easily, so firmly, without hesitation.

Three years later, after being tossed around by the
war—after service at the front, after being wounded and
evacuated to a Siberian hospital—he had actually run
into Lyalya at somebody's house near Sretensky Gate.
He saw her sitting next to the lame poet whose claim to
fame was that he wrote songs for the blind and the disabled. He was a frail, pitiful creature, an alcoholic, and
Rebrov was told that Lyalya looked after this Lazik—
such was the lame man's name—like a nurse and was
terribly devoted to him. And when the poet was discarded—with difficulty, to be sure—and had been
crossed off her list with thick, black indelible ink, still
for Rebrov this was not the end of it. For in his own
mind he saw peering through this thick, black ink not
only Lazik but also the three young fellows on the shore

and some other scoundrel who had tried to rape Lyalya, as well as many unknown figures whose existence he could not be sure of, but could merely guess at. And he was unable to rid his mind of any of these figures for good.

Different periods brought different anxieties. Later on there was Makeev, then Sergei Leonidovich himself, about whom she always spoke with a certain breathlessness, as if he were some sort of divine being. More recently he had been troubled by the new director Smurny, even though Lyalya hated him—which should, of course, have put his mind at ease. But with Lyalya's softheartedness Rebrov knew that the strongest hatred could easily transform itself into feelings of pity or even sympathy, so here he would have to keep his eyes and ears open. Nor was it easy to put up with Valery and his mother, whom his mother-in-law was always inviting over for dinner. Sometimes there were playwrights who provoked his suspicions, especially such successful ones as Fedka Arnoldov, with his dark eyes and jet-black hair which were quite to Lyalya's taste. Smolyanov might also represent a certain danger. But it was a certain actor named Kornilovich who irritated him more than anyone else. Under the guise of camaraderie this Pashka was terribly familiar with Lyalya, and even in Rebrov's presence he would tell her dirty jokes, address her by the familiar form, put his arm around her, and take her hand. And for this reason Rebrov did not like to be around Lyalya's actor friends. And what was he supposed to talk to them about? Not only did he find them boring, but he also felt tense in their company and was continually having to suppress his jealousy, which in turn led to all sorts of nasty and degrading behavior on his part. And herein lay his problem, for however tormented he felt, he did not want anyone to know his true feelings. He would rather have died from a fit of grief than rush off to the city where she was on tour or to the resort town where she had flown off on vacation with her girlfriend. Nor did he ever call her when she was out of town. Rather it was her mother who would call and afterwards report to him everything Lyalya had said. And as he greedily took in her every word, he would take on a calmly subdued and even absentminded expression which his mother-in-law secretly resented. For she assumed that if he didn't feel much excited at hearing about Lyalya, this meant he didn't love her very much. And this only helped to confirm what she suspected already. But whenever Lyalya returned—oh, happiest of days!—from the very first minutes, as they were leaving the railroad station or the airport, he would try as subtly as possible to ferret out any changes which might have occurred during her absence, and even the slightest change in her habits, voice, health, or attitude toward him would be subjected to his intense scrutiny. The very first night upon her return she would secretly be put to the test, and heaven forbid that her lovemaking reveal any new experience. Lyalya, of course, never had any inkling of Rebrov's suspicions. And probably because of these suspicions, he did not find it easy to come here to the theater, to smile and converse with these people. When the company had come back from Saratov that previous summer and Rebrov had gone to the railroad station to meet her, Kornilovich had spoken up in an intentionally loud, jesting voice, "Well, Lyalechka, shall we confess everything to Grisha? Shall we? Let's tell him!" The actors had roared with laughter and Grisha had done his best to smile, but inside he felt torn apart: who could be sure, perhaps something had actually gone on between them?

252

There was another reason why he didn't like to come to the theater. People humiliated Lyalya there and he wasn't able to defend her, for they humiliated him as well. He had submitted two plays to the theater —one a young people's play about the construction of a university, the other a sort of fable for children about the Korean war—and both had been rejected. True, Rebrov's own attitude toward these plays was ambivalent. On the one hand, he didn't take them very seriously. He saw their weak points, their obvious contrivance, but wasn't very upset by it because in his own mind these plays were something secondary and unimportant. On the other hand, however, they were very important—more important than anything else from the financial point of view—for his future depended on them. And quite apart from that, it was insulting to have them rejected. Were they really so bad, or indeed any worse than anyone else's plays— any worse, for instance, than the sort of rubbish turned out by Smolyanov?

By now the audience was streaming out of the theater in droves. The rain was coming down harder, and those who passed by were talking about taxis or the subway or about how they had to stop off at the bakery. No one spoke of the performance. "Well, naturally! Just as one would expect," thought Rebrov without the slightest bit of surprise. He had never met Smolyanov, had never seen or read his plays, but for some reason he was convinced that he was a scheming nonentity and that his plays were absolute rubbish.

All of a sudden he noticed the theater's chief literary consultant Boris Mironovich Marevin, or Bob, as he was called in the theater. This Marevin had held on to Rebrov's plays for four months, the swine, and only recently had sent a message through Lyalya that they weren't suitable. He couldn't even find time to invite him to his office to discuss them. Nor did he write him any official letter of rejection. Well, why stand on ceremony?   You're one of our own people, Lyalechka's husband, not really an author. But when Berg or Fedka Arnoldov submitted one of their plays, he probably devoured it in one night and called them up the next morning at the crack of dawn: "Listen, you should be shot for depriving me of my sleep, I simply couldn't tear myself away from it. . . ."

Out here on the street he looked completely different from that intimidating Marevin before whom authors trembled when ushered into his office with its inkstand of green marble decorated with bronze. And especially in the rain he seemed rather pitiful— a homely, ill-proportioned little man in a beret, with a briefcase at his side, and wearing a coat which was no better than Rebrov's. As he came running out into the rain, his body bent and thin, little legs twitching like a mosquito's, he glanced from side to side, and catching sight of Rebrov, he bowed. Rebrov responded with a haughty nod. At this point a strong, wet gust of wind hit Marevin full force and swept him toward the wall of the building. Having been brought involuntarily to Rebrov's side, he had to greet him and say a few words.

"Are you waiting for Lyalya? This was a big day for her. My congratulations to you too. . . . "

Not wishing to discuss Lyalya with him, Rebrov asked, "Well, and what about the play—was it a tremendous success? Did the audience applaud madly?"

"Are you crazy?!" whispered Marevin. "It's the usual sort of crap. Well, all the best. . . . "

And with that he was off, running along with little hopping steps. Suddenly it occurred to Rebrov that one

could write an excellent play about Ivan Gavrilovich.
His life had all the necessary ingredients—drama, death,
picturesque shabbiness, a woman's devotion, and all the
torments of an impoverished literary man who was
willing to sell his manuscripts for a glass of vodka. But
how would one handle the murder? For of course he
hadn't wanted to kill Ivanov;* he had refused, pleaded,
said that he was old and blind, but the others had said,
"We'll take you to him." And apparently all they had
to do was fill him up with vodka. And therein lies the
whole horror of his situation. Dostoevsky created a
brilliant caricature of the incident in *The Possessed*, but
if one were to tell his story simply, just as it was . . . But
why should one? And who would want to hear it?

Makeev emerged from the theater entrance in an
elegant coat with a fur collar. He was wrapped up to
his nose in a white scarf, his hands were in his pockets,
and someone behind him was carrying his small suitcase. Makeev's young female admirers had been waiting
under the marquee and now started squealing in unison,
"Makeev's a darling—rah! rah! rah!" Then a large crowd
came pushing through the door. In the center of this
group was Lyalya with an enormous bouquet of flowers
which she held cradled in one arm like a baby. Some
woman kissed Lyalya on the cheek, and shouting and
waving their hats in farewell, the group quickly dispersed. Rebrov moved out from the wall into the rain
and took a few steps toward the entrance. But Lyalya
was still talking with someone, and recognizing Smolyanov, Rebrov stiffened and stopped dead in his tracks,
telling himself that he wouldn't take another step in
Lyalya's direction. Let her come up to him. Talking all
the while, Lyalya and Smolyanov gradually came
closer. Lyalya had caught sight of him, but was so
engrossed in her conversation that she hadn't nodded

255

Yury Trifonov

or smiled in his direction, nor made any sort of gesture that would indicate that she had seen him at all. Apparently they hadn't even noticed the rain. "Damn it all, why does she have to drag him along?" thought Rebrov, beginning to feel upset. Lyalya and Smolyanov came up to him, stopping a few feet away. And without even looking at him, Lyalya handed him her bouquet.

"What's this for?" asked Rebrov, taking the bouquet. "Is this supposed to be a present or something?"

"Grisha, please hold it," said Lyalya, now looking at him for the first time. She had a slightly dazed expression on her face, and her eyes were sparkling. "Oh, sorry, Grishenka! You two don't know each other. This is Nikolai Demianovich Smolyanov. And this is Grigory Fyodorovich Rebrov. Grisha, Nikolai Demianovich is suggesting that we go somewhere to celebrate. . . . "

Smolyanov touched his hat and shook Rebrov's hand. He had a surprisingly strong handshake.

"My congratulations to you on this—er, special occasion. . . , " mumbled Rebrov, sensing something nasty and hypocritical in his own voice. But then he immediately found justification for his words: after all, the poor fellow could hardly be blamed for the fact that he had no talent; and it was a premiere for him.

Smolyanov apparently hadn't caught what he said, since he didn't thank him or bow even slightly in response to his congratulations. Instead he began babbling some nonsense of his own:

"It's a strange thing, Grigory Fyodorovich. I wasn't acting or running around; I was sitting in a box seat and watching. And yet, you know, my back aches as if I'd been carrying potato sacks. Watching one's own play is really hard work! I'd even recommend that they give playwrights milk free of charge, just as they do workers in high-risk occupations. . . ."

At this point two men approached, and Smolyanov introduced them. One of them was from the central theater administration, and the other a friend of Smolyanov's from Saratov, who was now working in Moscow. This individual said goodbye, but the man from the theater administration offered them a lift in his Pobeda. Just as they were getting into the car, five or six of Lyalya's relatives suddenly appeared from out of nowhere. Led by her loud and foolish Aunt Lipa, the whole kit and caboodle pounced on Lyalya, overwhelming her with kisses, flowers, and shrieks. A light bulb flashed indicating that someone had managed to capture this moment of confusion on film. Finally Lyalya broke loose and escaped into the back seat of the car. Rebrov, whom, thank God, no one had noticed, climbed in behind her, and Smolyanov squeezed in last, slamming the door behind him. The car was so crammed full of flowers that they could barely move. For some reason or other Lyalya was laughing hysterically. Where were they headed? It was decided that they would try the new Hotel Sovietskaya on Leningrad Boulevard. The restaurant was supposed to have gypsy singers.

III

Before the Revolution the little house in which the Telepnevs lived had been the dacha of some minor factory or government official who had not had the stamina to settle in a real suburban dacha—one of those riverfront porperties in Kuskovo or on Lociny Island. Because he had to come into Moscow every day to work, the main factor in his choice of a dacha had apparently been its proximity to the city. The Revolution had swept out all of the dacha owners, both the wealthy and those of modest means, and had populated their living rooms, porches and small, second-floor bedrooms with former soldiers and peasants—all working class people who had come streaming into the capital to escape the famines in their own regions. Thus it was that in 1922 the demobilized Red soldier Pyotr Telepnev settled here in this little house which at that time was still located beyond the city limits. Originally from a lower class family in the city of Yekaterinburg,* he was a master boiler maker by trade and a gardener by avocation. He completed his secondary education in a factory school, working first as a foreman and later on advancing to the position of shift engineer in a large new factory which had sprung up not far from his home, on the old Khodynskoe Field.

But more than his factory, more than his precious boilers, and perhaps more than his wife and his daughter, Pyotr Telepnev loved his garden, which he had cultivated over three decades. His dahlias were particularly magnificent and were known all over Moscow. Other flower growers called them "Telepnev dahlias," or sometimes simply "Telepnevs," since everyone knew which flowers were being discussed. And he had other flowers in his garden: tulips, asters, chrysanthemums, gillyflowers, and some splendid irises for which he was also famous. Finally there were lilacs—eighteen bushes of them—which grew luxuriantly along the entire length of the fence. For some reason, however, Pyotr Alexandrovich was less jealous and protective of his lilacs than of his many other flowers. He would transplant them from one place to anther, allow others to cut off branches, and would himself give them away right and left—all the more so since he had relatives all over Moscow.

During the war the garden had almost perished.

He could hardly worry about flowers when his family
was half starving and barely keeping alive; when his
daughter had neither dresses nor shoes and even in the
month of May had to run around in felt winter boots;
and when his wife was suffering from an ulcer and had
to be hospitalized for weeks at a time. Yet somehow
they managed to live through it all and to save the
garden as well. It was Pyotr Alexandrovich who saved
it—by hours stolen during the day and during the
night from the normal routine of his life and by his
faith that someday, when the world came to its senses,
people would ask, "What is it that seems to be missing?
Wasn't there something that used to stand in the middle
of the table?" And in fact, people did start asking
for flowers once again, and Lorkh potatoes* and early
radishes gradually began to go out of style. That is,
although they had not yielded their position in people's
vegetable gardens, they no longer functioned as powerful landlords, so to speak, but were more like temporary
residents whom one puts up with out of necessity, because of their good income and because one has little
hope of getting rid of them in the immediate future.
But just at this point a new danger suddenly loomed
on the horizon. Two years after the war was over they
began lining all of the nearby streets with new buildings
of stone and concrete. And now Pyotr Alexandrovich's
lilacs and forty-eight varieties of *Dahlia variabilis* were
threatened with the evil of demolition. It didn't matter
about the house—it was only a pile of wood anyway,
and they'd be given an even better apartment to take
its place—but as for the garden, it seemed doomed to
destruction.

Pyotr Alexandrovich set to work, drawing up
various papers and documents. He collected signatures
from important people who had at one time or another

been the recipients of his lilacs, and he wrote petitions to the district soviet, the district housing administration, the Moscow soviet, the Moscow housing administration, and to the city's chief architect—and all with the same request: that this garden, which was one of a kind and would be bequeathed to the State after his death, be preserved in its entirety; and that its owner, Pyotr Alexandrovich, be given an apartment in the nearest apartment building so that he could continue to care for the garden and carry on his investigations, which were of universally acknowledged scientific significance.

This had been going on for three years. Pyotr Alexandrovich kept writing, calling, hanging around reception rooms, knocking on every door. But still the concrete came closer. The whole street had already been built up from the church to the Tarakanovka, and already this dirty little stream was strewn with rubble. The soil was already there with which to fill it in, the small park right next to it had been dug up, and the trolley bus was already operating once again. Lyalya had already appeared in three plays but was still dissatisfied and wanted to quit; she and her poor, unlucky Grigory had already separated a number of times and managed to get back together again; and their only child, a daughter named Varenka, had been born and died right away from meningitis. But still the fate of the garden remained undecided.

The district engineer told him, "Your house is in block eight. Right now we're winding up with the two blocks beyond the Tarakanovka, then it'll be your turn. If the Moscow soviet hasn't come to a decision by that time, you can expect a tractor at your doorstep."

To add to his troubles, two of Pyotr Alexandrovich's neighbors who lived in wooden houses just like his own began scribbling letters of petition and gathering signatures. But they, by contrast, were trying to speed up the demolition process and abused Pyotr Alexandrovich in every way they could. The policeman Kurtov gave him a particularly hard time. They had once gotten along well, had drunk vodka and gone fishing together, and their daughters, Lyalka and Margaritka, had been classmates and friends. But now, as a result of all this hullabaloo they did nothing but quarrel.

Pyotr Alexandrovich's face had dulled and his shoulders had become stooped from all this agitation and running around. One September day he had gone out into the garden to cut some white and yellow *Dahlia imperialis* which he planned to present to retired Colonel Dudarev who had just turned sixty. The dahlias were exceptionally beautiful that fall—good enough to put on exhibit in Geneva—and the *imperialis* were some fourteen feet high. But now it suddenly occured to him that next year at this time neither he nor the *imperialis* would be here. Instead there would be a foundation pit with lime spattered all over the place and female laborers carting bricks in wheelbarrows. And at this very instant something pierced his heart like a sharp instrument and knocked him to the ground. He lay there on a bed of irises, fully conscious but terrified; the pain kept boring into him and he couldn't move a muscle. He called out in a weak voice, "Irina! Irina!" Irina Ignatievna didn't hear him, but Kadidka, smart dog, started barking by the fence, and a little later his wife came out and found him. For the next two months Pyotr Alexandrovich remained at home in bed, and for the first twenty days he was ordered to lie flat on his back without moving his head or shifting from side to side. Gradually he got better, was able to be up on his feet again, and in January he was sent to a sanatorium for six weeks. He returned home seemingly recovered, but only outwardly so. He looked well enough, but was not really his old self.

Such was Pyotr Alexandrovich's not very satisfactory condition at the time of Lyalya's premiere and great public triumph. Naturally he was happy for his daughter and especially for his wife, who had blossomed out and even managed to forget about her ulcer, so proud was she of her daughter's success. Nevertheless, Pyotr Alexandrovich continued to be tormented by thoughts of his garden.

In the meantime he had had several new ideas. What if a letter were to come from the theater—from the whole collective? People's actor so-and-so; honored actress such-and-such. And get the artistic director involved too. . . . "Having learned of the barbarous destruction of this haven of horticultural development that is about to take place in the Leningrad District. . . ." Lyalya had promised to speak to the theater's business manager, Comrade Bravin. He was, she said, a very knowledgeable and helpful individual whom people were always turning to with their problems. He would write letters for them, go to court, and help them in their efforts to obtain divorces and larger apartments. But somehow Lyalya never managed to speak to him. She needed to be alone with him in order to explain everything in detail, but in the theater everyone was always in a hurry or crowding around and there simply wasn't a quiet moment. But she had promised that the matter would be taken care of. "Perhaps," she said, "I should invite him home for a glass of vodka. That he wouldn't refuse."

Pyotr Alexandrovich's second idea was to have some sort of satirical sketch appear in the newspapers. For this he would have to lean on Grigory. He did, after all, know a lot of newspaper people and was himself

good at writing. Pyotr Alexandrovich had a talk with
him, and Grigory promised to help, but as usual you had
to remind him at least ten times before he'd even begin
to move. And it wasn't so easy to remind him, you had
to choose just the right moment. He was often in a bad
mood, secretly annoyed with Irina Ignatievna or quarreling with Lyalya. And sometimes, for no discernible reason, he would even be annoyed with Pyotr Alexandrovich himself. At other times, Lyalya would warn him,
"Go easy on Grisha today, he's having a hard time working. He's very upset." But then, when did he ever have
an *easy* time working? For the last few years he's had
nothing but hard times and bad moods.

The right moment to remind and prod him would,
in Pyotr Alexandrovich's opinion, be on Monday, when
he and Lyalya returned from the banquet—if, of course,
it was not after midnight. Pyotr Alexandrovich had observed that when Grigory drank, which was not very often (he didn't have the money to buy liquor himself,
and nowadays people didn't very often buy drinks for
you), he became talkative and outgoing and wasn't even
stingy. In general, Pyotr Alexandrovich considered his
son-in-law a stingy person—not so much with money as
with other things. Whenever you asked him for some
small thing, like a razor blade, a shaving brush, or a scarf
to put on when you ran out on an errand, he would give
it to you only after a while and with seeming reluctance.
And when you asked for a book, Zhukovsky, say, or
Anatole France, from his personal library on Bashilov
Street—his library was quite extensive and very carefully
chosen—he would promise, "Okay, Pyotr Alexandrovich, I'll bring it tomorrow." And then, when tomorrow
rolled around, "Oh, I forgot! The next time I'm there,
I'll definitely pick it up." He had shilly-shallied for two
months with Zhukovsky and finally told him that he

263

had made a point of looking for it just the day before, but hadn't been able to find it; it must have disappeared somewhere. He was stingy—what more could one say? On the other hand, of course, his life hadn't been easy. He'd been struggling for so many years now, and with nothing to show for it. No one would take his plays, nor his film scenarios either. And he wrote pretty well, splendidly in fact. He had a lot of talent—as much as the others, at any rate. He had let him read his novella about the Siberian uprising—tremendous! It was written in a clean, crisp style and was well researched. Apparently he didn't have the right connections. In the literary field you couldn't get anywhere without them. You could beat your brains out for a hundred years, and all for nothing, you wouldn't get anywhere. . . .

Pyotr Alexandrovich fell asleep before Grigory and Lyalya got home that evening, and had an oppressive dream. A tractor was slowly advancing into his garden, cracking and breaking down the wooden fence and trampling the flower beds, first the dahlias, then the pale-rose phlox in full autumn bloom, and finally the irises and the gillyflowers—everything trampled to bits. And now Mitka Kurtov, who was sitting behind the wheel of the tractor, shouted spitefully, "That's enough! We've won!" Pyotr Alexandrovich woke up with a stabbing pain in his heart. He called out to Irina, but in vain. There was a lot of noise, and people were talking in the next room. He could hear Lyalya's loud, happy laughter. It was half past one.

Suddenly Irina Ignatievna came running in and asked in alarm, "Father! Are you awake?"

"Where were you, old woman? It's going on two, time for decent people to be . . ." he mumbled angrily, still under the spell of his nightmare. Then his voice trailed off, "How long is this celebrating going to keep up? . . . Give me my heart medicine and something to wash it down with." When he felt this terrible pressure in his chest and was overcome by the frightening feeling that death might be close at hand, everything else seemed silly and unimportant: his wife's joy, Lyalya's successes and failures—everything, absolutely everything. And only one thing mattered—his garden. "Tell Grigory I want to see him."

"Petrasha, they have a guest out there, they're drinking tea," whispered Irina Ignatievna, bending close to her husband's face and for some reason smiling foolishly in the dark. "The playwright's here, the one whose play Lyalya's in. . . ."

"So what! What the hell do I care about him. Go get Grigory right away. Tell him it's urgent!"

A little while later Grigory came in, pushing the door wide open and swaying somewhat as he cautiously sat down on the chair next to the couch. A strong smell of wine permeated the room.

"Grisha, what I want to discuss with you. . . ." began Pyotr Alexandrovich, trying to adopt a strictly businesslike tone. He explained that they couldn't afford to lose a single day, a single hour. As far as the newspaper sketch was concerned, he must start in right away, the next morning. He should write it up, make phone calls wherever necessary, and deliver it in person. It was a crying shame, sabotage of the highest order, and anyone who heard about it would find it hard to believe that this sort of thing could still happen in the thirty-fifth year of Soviet rule.

Grigory sat with lowered head, his elbows resting on his knees, and nodded despondently, "Yes . . . yes . . . yes. . . ." Then suddenly he raised his head and asked, "But Pyotr Sanych, why haven't you congratulated me?"

"What should I congratulate you for?"

"For the premiere of my common-law wife Lyud-mila Petrovna Telepnova."

"Well, why not? Of course. My congratulations!"

"You certainly should congratulate me," he said, shaking an admonishing finger. "Everyone's been congratulating me, and I've been thanking them right back. Why, just now in the Sovietskaya everyone was shaking my hand and saying, 'We congratulate you, dear man.' Or else they'd say, 'We sincerely congratulate you, dear man.' And I would thank them right back. Thanks, thank you very much. One has to thank people! Mankind is perishing from a lack of gratitude—gratitude in the highest sense of the word, gratitude with a capital 'G'...."

Standing in the doorway behind her son-in-law's back, Irina Ignatievna was making signs to her husband: kick him out, he's drunk—can't you see? From her jerky movements and foolish smile—in the middle of the night she'd taken it into her head, the idiot, to serve them tea —he could see that she was pretty far gone herself.

"Well, okay, you can go now . . ." he said in a weak voice. "We'll talk tomorrow. My congratulations."

"Thank you, thank you. I'm genuinely touched by your words . . ." whispered Grigory, shuffling his feet and bowing low, like some court jester. Whenever he got drunk, he would always whisper this way and play the buffoon.

Irina Ignatievna turned out the hall light. Half a minute later Grigory turned it on again, pushed his way back into the room, and whispered, "By the way, the playwright's going to spend the night here—since it's so late. He says he's been quarreling with his wife and doesn't want to go home."

"Well then, let him stay here," said Pyotr Alexandrovich. "We've got enough room. Is that Comrade

Smolyanov?"
"Yes. Comrade Smolyanov. And I must say he's a
most enigmatic figure. Certain facts and the most trivial
observations lead me to believe that . . ." he leaned over
and whispered, "he hasn't even read Dostoevsky!"
"Really?" exclaimed Pyotr Alexandrovich, pretending to be shocked.
"Really, he hasn't. I swear he hasn't! Tss-tss-tss. . . ."
Grisha giggled, waving his arms above the supine Pyotr
Alexandrovich. "And I don't think he really knows his
Tolstoi either. . . . By the way, in *The Possessed* Dostoevsky expresses the idea that to be happy, a man needs
equal portions of good fortune and bad. That's very pro-
found, Pyotr Sanych! You see, Ivan Gavrilovich Pryzhov. . . . Didn't I tell you about him? Well, never mind.
He was a retired collegiate assessor.* There's a whole
story connected with him. But never mind that. The
point is that this Pryzhov had an incredibly rough life—
one misfortune after another—and yet despite all this,
Pyotr Sanych, he was happy. How could he be happy,
you wonder. Well, his wife, you see, Olga Grigorievna
Martos . . . a really selfless woman. . . . Well, she wore
herself out with him in Moscow—he never had a penny,
was a continual failure and a terrible drunkard, an incur-
able one—and then, later on, she followed him to Siberia. . . . Yes, such is the mess he made of his life. . . ."
Swaying slightly, Grigory wiped his tear-stained cheeks
with the palm of his hand. He remained standing there
for a whole minute without saying a word. Then he tip-
toed out of the room.
     The next day Lyalya brought the playwright, Com-
rade Smolyanov, in to meet her father. While Pyotr
Alexandrovich and Nikolai Demianovich were talking,
Lyalya and her mother prepared breakfast. With them
was Aunt Toma, who had made a special trip in from

Alexandrov on Saturday to attend Lyalya's premiere. Grigory, in the meantime, had run out to get a bottle of vodka—for the morning after—at the nearest store, which happened to be right next to the church (they referred to it as the "church store") and a mere run through the park.

The playwright proved to be a nice, good-natured fellow, though at the moment he was suffering from a terrible headache and couldn't wait for the vodka to arrive. It turned out that he was a great fishing enthusiast, and near his home outside of Saratov he kept a motorboat and tackle. Every summer he would flee from the unbearable noise and commotion of Moscow and take refuge there for a month or six weeks. Sometimes, he said, they caught sturgeon weighing up to forty pounds. His father, who way back when, in the year one, had been a fish merchant and had owned two Astrakhan longboats, used to tell how in his day they would catch sturgeon weighing close to 200 pounds. Gradually the conversation was brought around to the subject of gardens, and Pyotr Alexandrovich poured out to the playwright all his accumulated pain and anguish. Nikolai Demianovich promised to help. He would discuss the matter with someone; and if, he added, there had been a telephone here in the apartment, he would have called up right away and straightened the matter out.

Pyotr Alexandrovich was overjoyed. He summoned his wife and demanded that their guest be taken outside and given a tour of the garden. His heart began to pound: could the playwright really be going to help him? He was, after all, an important man. If he wanted to, he could do it! Having ordered his wife to bring the folders with all his papers, he laid them out on the blanket—all his notes, letters, telegrams, and petitions.

"And, here's Struzhaninov, a doctor of sciences...."

He's a prominent man too, and here he writes, 'Having been outraged to learn that. . . .' "

At this point Grigory returned with the bottle of vodka and they say down to breakfast. But just as Lyalechka was about to take up her guitar, there was a sudden knocking at the window and three people entered: their neighbor, Kurtov, who was dressed in his police uniform—that of a first lieutenant; another neighbor, Bespalov, who was retired; and Auntie Roza Khalidova, the school janitress. Irina Ignatievna had once been on excellent terms with Auntie Roza. She used to come in and do their laundry, run errands at the market, and sometimes even help Pyotr Alexandrovich sell his flowers. Irina Ignatievna had felt sorry for her and would occasionally give her something extra for the children—she had four of them, and her husband had been killed during the war. But during the past year, as luck would have it, she and Irina Ignatievna had had a falling out.

Once again the commotion began. Auntie Roza jabbered away in her thin voice, not making any sense whatsoever, and the retired Bespalov grumbled and shook his fists. Lyalya tried to reason with them and put an end to this scandalous outburst—how embarrassing in front of a guest!—but this only spurred them on, and they began waving some sort of document from the district architect. Pyotr Alexandrovich knew this man— a worthless sort, who would sign anything you put in front of him.

He lay back on the couch and didn't say a word. He was listening to the pounding of his heart. There was no feeling in his hands, and he began to feel faint as waves of numbness spread slowly through his whole body.

Irina Ignatievna suddenly cried out, "What are you doing, you scoundrels! There's a sick man lying here—

can't you see? Swine!"

"Why shout and call people names?" thought Pyotr Alexandrovich almost indifferently. "That sort of thing isn't necessary, it doesn't do any good. . . ."

Mitka Kurtov was droning something about the district social security office. "His pension will be taken away . . . they've been profiteering on their flowers. . . ."

"You're a fool, Mitka," uttered Pyotr Alexandrovich so softly that probably no one heard him.

Nikolai Demianovich suddenly grew crimson, his cheeks began to quiver, and his fist came crashing down on the table: "All of you are to get out of this room immediately! Out, out, out! Right away, this minute! And as for your behavior, Comrade First Lieutenant," he siad, thrusting a finger at the stupefied Kurtov, 'I'm going to have a talk with Ivan Grigorievich about you! What's your precinct? Are you in the Leningrad District?"

They were herded out of the room, but the noise could still be heard through the wall. Irina Ignatievna sat down next to the couch, covered her face, and burst into tears: "What a horrible day, Lyalechka, those scoundrels. . . . Petrasha, but what if they—oh, the hell with them! Your life is more important. . . ."

Pyotr Alexandrovich didn't say a word. He was listening to the inner workings of his body, and he didn't like the sound of things. His whole insides had become tremulous and fragile, and he didn't want to talk or move because whatever it was that was pressing down on him might bring an end to this temporary fragility. And in fact, it was happening already—the pain was beginning. The playwright came back into the room and said, "We'll bring them to their senses! And don't be upset, they were just talking nonsense!" Out in the yard Grisha was shouting in a high-pitched voice. The pain,

The Long Goodbye

which was fierce enough without that, grew worse with each passing second. He was hardly able to utter the words, "Maybe you should call the doctor. . . ."

IV

That summer was Leningrad—the first time Lyalya had ever been there. With Nikolai Demianovich she went on excursions and spent evenings at the Astoria Hotel, where there was a real jazz band—from somewhere in China—and dancing, with anyone you felt like, until the place closed down. Her heart was torn with pity for both the man she was with and the one she had left behind. Nikolai Demianovich was hard to get along with, he drank heavily and sometimes the doctor had to be called in the middle of the night. And Grisha, she knew, shed tears at night and was forever running off to his room on Bashilov Street. For him she bought a leather coat in a special second-hand store on Nevsky Avenue.

In the theater everything had changed. *Ignat Timofeevich* had been nominated for an award, and the new season began with a promotion and raise in salary for Lyalya. Nikolai Demianovich bought himself a car and moved into a new apartment. The canvas bag lying on his trunk in the entryway bulged with letters, many of which came from soldiers. After Lyalya's portrait appeared on a magazine cover, Smurny started playing up to her and she sensed a secret, malicious jealousy on the part of her girlfriends, some of whom simply disappeared, unable to come to terms with her success. In the meantime, her poor father was languishing in Botkin Hospital. He'd been sent there again at the end of the fall, after his third heart attack.

Once again it was December, and once again there

was snow. But this December was completely different from all the others. Lyalya had gone to the hospital to visit her father, bringing with her some tangerines and the new book *Moonstone*, which everyone was trying to get a copy of. During her long visit she also managed to slip fifty rubles to the elderly nurse to make sure that she took good care of her father. And now, emerging from the hospital yard, she made her way slowly along the darkening side street which lay wrapped in a frosty mist. People kept passing her by—people with string shopping bags and bundles, all running toward the nearest streetcar stop—but she walked along without hurrying. A car was waiting for her. And for some reason it was right here outside the hospital, in a moment of fatigue and grief for her father, that Lyalya suddenly experienced for the first time the comforting and unaccustomed sensation of being a wealthy woman.

All these people ahead of her, equally weighed down with the misfortunes of their dear ones, went hurrying about their business, as endless and dreary as the hospital fence. Yet she walked along slowly, breathing in deeply, calmly, and sadly, as befitted a woman of wealth. This sensation was a complex one, on many levels, and had little to do with the amount of money in her pocket—money was one thing she did not have, it disappeared so quickly. Rather, her sense of well-being was reflected in other things: in the fact, for example, that in cold weather she was warm. In this luxurious merino lamb coat with its fresh, lovely fragrance, she had no fear of the cold weather—perhaps for the first time in her life. It was also reflected in the peace of mind she felt with regard to that which is most important in life and without which one has no sort of life at all. For now no one would dare to say anything bad about her or even to think it. She had proved herself beyond all doubt, as could easily be seen by the crest-fallen faces of the other actresses whenever she walked into the rehearsal room or whenever she . . . but one could go on forever, the examples were endless. Her sense of well-being also arose from the fact that men liked her, that she was a favorite, and that they suffered because of her. And it arose from the fact that she could buy certain things which before had seemed inaccessible —a Chinese tea service, for example—and that she could go out in the evening, drink red wine, and order her favorite dishes, such as chicken *tabaka* and *suluguni* cheese. And finally, it arose from the fact that she was meeting all sorts of new and exciting people.

After the first premiere there had followed a second, then a radio performance, then an invitation to the Moscow Film Studio, then reviews, articles, a portrait, another raise in salary, the promise of a new apartment, invitations to appear at a conference, at a reception, and her nomination for an award. And at the fur store on Sretenka Street, as they were hunting for a fur cap for Grisha, the store manager, an elderly lady with glasses and with allergy blotches on her chin, had suddenly blushed and asked, "Excuse me, but aren't you from the Drama Theater? Is your name Telepneva?"

The cap had been brought out from the back of the store and wrapped in newspaper so as not to upset those who had been waiting in line in front of them. As they emerged from the store with their purchase, Grisha had muttered with a laugh, "Damned if you're not becoming a celebrity! It's almost awkward to be out in public with you, Madame."

Yes, it was awkward, very awkward. Lyalya could sense how he shriveled up inside whenever he was prodded by reminders of her fame. He was happy for her of course, secretly rejoiced, and had even cried on one

occasion—someone had seen him wiping his eyes at a
concert where she had been singing Evdokia's songs
from *Ivan Timofeevich*. (These songs had become popular and she often sang them at concerts, sometimes
even traveling to other cities for performances.) But inside something seemed to be eating away at Grisha,
something which he could not control. After all, his
own career hadn't moved forward at all, not the slightest bit. This was a new cause of suffering which, how-
every much she felt herself to be a "wealthy woman,"
stood in the way of her achieving genuine happiness and
perhaps even bliss. And she was not really very far from
a state of bliss. But now this suffering, which was someone else's and yet at the same time so close to her, got
in the way. Her mother's nervous irritability, loss of
weight, and daily anxiety over her father also got in the
way, as did her father himself, whose fate was still unknown. One day it would seem that he was going to
pull through, the next day they would expect the worst.

Nikolai Demianovich opened the car door from the
inside, and gathering up the folds of her merino lamb,
Lyalya jumped nimbly into the back seat. In the past
she had watched from a distance as ladies gathered up
the folds of their expensive furs with casual grace before
disappearing into the depths of an automobile. And now
here she was, herself a similar object of envy to the
women passing by.

As the driver started off, Smolyanov asked about
her father. They sped past the Belorussky railroad station and Mayakovsky Square, then turned left onto Sad-
ovaya Street.

"Where are we going?" Lyalya asked.

"We're going to Alexander Vasilievich's. He's invited us for supper."

Alexander Vasilievich Agabekov, a friend of Nikolai

Demianovich's, lived near the Kursky railroad station. What exactly he did for a living Lyalya didn't know, but he had some sort of important position. Lyalya had never visited his apartment before, nor did she feel like going there now. On this particular evening she would have preferred to stay home. She was worried and depressed about Grisha. Undoubtedly he was moping about somewhere, feeling bitter. He might be at the library, or at a friend's, or at home, restlessly pacing back and forth, awaiting her return. But what was she to do? How was she to help him? He was, after all, a good man and a capable one. A wonderful man! A man of rare qualities and a genuine intellectual. He had learned Polish on his own in order to be able to read Polish newspapers. Actually, he was good at everything—he drew very well and he loved music. But he never seemed to have any luck. And as a result, time was passing and he wasn't getting anywhere.

Nikolai Demianovich listened somewhat unsympathetically.

"He has no roots in the soil, that's his trouble," he suddenly remarked. And Lyalya remembered that he had expressed this sentiment once before, using the exact same words: "roots" and "soil."

That summer they had had some sort of evening get-together with the public on the open-air stage at Gorky Park and had acted out scenes from Smolyanov's play. Smolyanov himself had taken part, and for some reason Grisha had been there too. Afterwards the three of them along with Sergei Leonidovich and one of the actors had gone to the Poplavka Restaurant for something to eat. An argument had arisen—something philosophical—Grisha had gotten annoyed and said something sarcastic, and at this point Smolyanov had made his comment about Grisha's having no roots in the soil.

Naturally, this was very indiscreet on his part, and he had no right to say it. Grisha had flared up and started shouting, "What soil are you talking about? The chernozem? The podzol? Fertilized soil? My soil is that of historical experience—everything that Russia has lived and suffered through!" And then for some reason he had begun telling about his family background: how one of his grandmothers had been a Polish political exile: how his great-grandfather had been a serf and his grandfather had been implicated in some student disorders and banished to Siberia; how his other grandmother had taught music in Petersburg; how her father had been born into the soldier class and how Grigory's own father had taken part in both the First World War and the Russian Civil War although he was by nature a peaceful man who had been a statistician before the Revolution and afterwards an economist. And all of this taken together, Grisha had shouted excitedly, was the soil of historical experience, the experience of Russia itself—so you can go to hell with your screwed-up notions. It had been an unpleasant scene, almost a genuine quarrel. Sergei Leonidovich had tried to calm him down by saying that Nikolai Demianovich had probably been referring to his lack of experience, the fact that he was young and had little experience of life. But Smolyanov had kept muttering with drunken persistence, "No, I definitely meant that he has no roots in the soil, that's exactly what I meant. . . ." Grisha had said something nasty in return, but just at that moment something unexpected had occurred. A vicious fight had broken out at the next table and the police had come rushing to the scene. And by the time they left the restaurant they were no longer talking about "roots" and "soil."

"What do roots and soil have to do with it?" asked Lyalya. "The man needs help."

Nikolai Demianovich was silent for a moment.

"Well, what if he were to get a full-time job somewhere? It wouldn't be easy, of course, but I could try...."

"No! You know yourself that he's very proud and sensitive...."

"But we could find him a good job."

"No, Kolya, what he needs is help in getting established in his literary career. If you could just give him a hand, open a few doors for him—he'd go the rest of the way on his own. If you could just put in a good word...."

Lyalya's voice trembled slightly. She had never made a direct request like this to him before, and if he had done things for her in the past, it had been on his own initiative. But now, for the first time, she was asking. And right away she felt uncomfortable because she could sense his reluctance. And yet he was a kind and goodhearted man. Lyalya knew that he had helped many people—people from his native Saratov, young people, poor people, or people who had had bad luck. She also knew that he couldn't bring himself to leave his wife even though he didn't love her and was continually having to put up with her foolishness and bad temper. No, he couldn't leave her; she was mentally unbalanced and he felt sorry for her.

But Grisha's case was different. Lyalya sensed that here she would meet with resistance and she decided to meet it head on, unpleasant as this might be. Undoubtedly he hadn't forgotten that outburst in the Poplavka, but he had never once said a word about it to Lyalya. Only on one occasion had he observed rather timidly, "I just don't understand how you can live with such an adolescent." Lyalya had taken offense. No, that she wouldn't tolerate! Grisha was no adolescent but a real man in the best sense of the word. "And how can you

277

live with that hysterical wife of yours?" But he managed to justify himself by saying, "Marta isn't a'hysterical
wife'—she's a sick woman. And I don't have any feeling
left for her except, perhaps, a feeling of obligation and a
fear of inflicting a fatal blow. But as for you, you'll
never break away from your Grisha." That was true.
Why should she deny it? Grisha was Grisha, and that
was all there was to it. Somewhere in Chekhov there was
the line: "A wife is a wife." And the strange part of it
was that Grisha was not even her "wife," that is, not her
husband. They were not officially married, and he still
kept his own room on Bashilov Street, which he would
regularly flee to after the two of them had quarreled or
on days when he felt particularly depressed. He didn't
support her, as a husband was supposed to, he didn't
pay for her clothes, and yet, nonetheless—she didn't understand why, it was impossible to explain!—she didn't
have the strength to drive him from her heart. He had
become an integral part of her; she was bound to him
even by the ills of his childhood—his measles, scarlet fever, lisping, rashes, sweating spells. . . .

Nikolai Demianovich laid his hand on Lyalya's and
said, "Okay, we'll think about it. . . ."

Agabekov's other guests had already arrived. They
were seated at the table in the living room in a formal,
stagelike manner. The room itself must have been well
over 100 feet long—Lyalya had never even seen such a
large room—and above the table was a magnificent chandelier. The meal was already well under way, and there
was a great deal of food of the choicest variety. One
could tell immediately that it was not homemade but
had been brought up from some restaurant.

As soon as he could do so unobtrusively, Nikolai
Demianovich whispered in Lyalya's ear, "I forgot to tell

you, it's his father's birthday today."

The little old gentleman was seated at the head of the table. He had unusually bright and rosy cheeks, almost like those of a mannequin, and was dressed in a black Circassian coat.

The toasts and speechmaking had already begun. One lady suddenly and enthusiastically raised a toast to "the lady who is here with us this evening and such a splendid representative of. . . ." The men gazed at her in delight and exclaimed, "To you, Liudmila Petrovna! Bottoms up! Everybody drink to Liudmila Petrovna!"

Someone shouted, "I'm warning you, anyone who doesn't empty his glass for Liudmila Petrovna. . . ."

In their excitement and eagerness to clink glasses one sensed a certain joyful admiration and perhaps even devotion. Although Lyalya realized that this was the usual sort of nonsense brought on by alcohol and that most of these people probably hadn't even heard her name, much less seen her on stage, still, she found it pleasant—extremely pleasant. A guitar appeared, and Lyalya was asked to sing. She was reluctant at first, but gave in after they pleaded with her and after Nikolai Demianovich, squeezing her knee under the table, softly entreated, "Please don't refuse." After a while, when she had already finished her second glass of wine, she he herself was in the mood and enjoyed singing "Up in the Firmament, among the Glimmering Stars," along with some gypsy songs and "Raising the Dust along the Street," which her mother had taught her and which had been one of her favorites ever since childhood. As she sang, Alexander Vasilievich kept staring at her with unblinking eyes. It was a strange look, directed straight at her mouth, and because of this—because he did not look at her eyes but only at her mouth—she felt uncomfortable. There was something cold and lifeless in the gaze of this man with his small mustache and high, prominent forehead. His gaze grew glassier and glassier, even terrifying for a moment, but finally his eyelids fluttered and the glassiness disappeared. The Georgian guests went on to sing some of their own songs in their characteristic manner, which was really quite beautiful, and Lyalya tried to accompany them on the guitar. Then one of the guests suddenly jumped up and, clapping his hands, began to sing in a strong Georgian accent:

We'll drink, drink, and have a good time! . . .

The others joined in, singing and clapping, and dragged Lyalya with them as they moved into the other room. Already somewhat lightheaded, she felt like being silly and, for that matter, playing along as the belle of the ball. She plunked herself down on the floor with her guitar, and seated there on a bearskin, she began to sing with feeling and so loudly that she drowned out the music coming from the radio-gramophone:

Bold Khas-Bulat
Poor is your mountain hut. . . .

And why was she suddenly in such a gay mood? Because they used to sing "Khas-Bulat" at home. Her father would sing bass, and Uncle Misha, Aunt Zhenya's husband, would strain to sing tenor. Yet half an hour later, when they returned to the large room with the chandelier, Lyalya felt a sudden stabbing pain, like that of a sore rib that has accidentally shifted position. It was the thought of Grisha flashing through her mind. By now there were only men sitting at the table in the large room. They were arguing, and Nikolai Demianovich

wasn't among them. Lyalya was told that he had gone
off in the car to pick up a friend and would soon be
back. Lyalya remained in the room, listening to their
conversation—something about the American president
and about Germany and Yugoslavia—but none of this
interested her, and she was utterly bored.

Two hours later, Alexander Vasilievich and Lyalya
were sitting at a small table in his study. There were
three candles lighted in the gilded wall bracket over-
head. They both felt warm from the heat of the radiators and from the wine they had drunk, and Alexander
Vasilievich had loosened his tie and unfastened the top
button of his white shirt. They were talking about
music. In her childhood, Lyalya had attended music
school for three years. She was found to have absolute
pitch and a good voice, but her parents would have had
to buy a piano and her father could somehow never
raise the money since he spent every extra penny on his
garden. It was only just before the war that they finally
managed to buy one, but in 1943, when they didn't
have enough to eat, they sold it. True, her mother did
buy her a guitar by way of compensation. Alexander
Vasilievich said that he loved Italian songs and opera
and that he had a lot of German recordings of Caruso,
Gigli, and Toti Dal Monte. Lyalya's eyes lit up; she was
dying to listen to them. They went into the other room
and sat down on the sofa. The guests had all left by this
time, and there were just the two of them. The records
were so beautiful that Lyalya forgot about everything—
about the fact that she was expected at home, that Nikolai Demianovich had disappeared somewhere, and that
Alexander Vasilievich hadn't really appealed to her earlier in the evening. She had suspected him of being a
Don Juan—a type that she absolutely detested. Not that
she had any real evidence of this; she just sensed it

instinctively, and in the most foolish details: his trim, little mustache and his overly delicate treatment of her, as if he were taking pains not to lay so much as a finger on her.

As one a.m. drew near, Lyalya became extremely agitated: "Where can Nikolai Demianovich be? What if there's been an accident?"

"Kolya will be back soon," Alexander Vasilievich firmly reassured her. "He'll definitely be back."

"But in the meantime I'm keeping you up."

"Oh, don't worry about me. I never sleep at night, that's when I get my work done. And if I yawn, that's my heart acting up. I just have to take something for it." He took a small glass receptacle from his pocket and shook several tiny, red capsules into the palm of his hand.

"Can I bring you some water?"

"Please do, if it's not too much trouble."

She ran into the kitchen and turned on the light. It was an enormous room—more like a public cafeteria than anything else—and from behind a cloth partition she could hear someone snoring. She poured some water from the cold teakettle into a cup and returned to the other room. Alexander Vasilievich was lying on the sofa with his eyes half closed. His face, which had been flushed from wine just a short time before, had gone pale and his cheeks were sunken. None of this boded well.

After swallowing the water, Alexander Vasilievich took Lyalya's hand. "Don't go away, Liudmila Petrovna."

"I'm not going anywhere," said Lyalya, at the same time thinking to herself: "Where would I go? It's after one—too late for the subway. There's something wrong with him, and Grisha's expecting me. . . ."

"Sit closer, right next to me. That's it. Here, please. . . ." He didn't let go of her hand, but continued to hold it tightly. It was as if he were afraid to let her go, as a sick man might cling to a nurse. But for some reason Lyalya felt no pity for him. Suddenly the phone rang in the living room. It was Nikolai Demianovich, reporting in a weak voice—she could barely hear him through the static of a pay phone—that they had gotten stuck in the Zamoskvorechie section of town. They had landed in a ditch, and there were no cars around. No one would be able to get them out until morning.

"Please forgive me, and spend the night there, at Alexander Vasilievich's. I'll pick you up in the morning. Only behave yourself, you hear? Behave yourself!"

"Are you all right?" she cried in alarm.

"Yes, yes, I'm all right. Please forgive me!"

She couldn't understand why he should ask her to forgive him.

"Nikolai Demianovich won't be coming," said Lyalya, returning to the room where Alexander Vasilievich was still lying on the sofa. "I'm going to be off, Alexander Vasilievich. Maybe I'll still be able to catch a trolley-bus. Goodbye. Oh, where did I put my handbag?"

It suddenly swept over her: she had to leave right away, she mustn't stay a second longer. That was the way it was sometimes—she wouldn't know why, but all of a sudden there would be no power in the world that could hold her back. Her host tried to dissuade her and even jumped up from the sofa with unexpected vitality. Where was she going? What had happened? He refused to give her back her handbag. No, no, she definitely had to go. But it was almost two a.m! Never mind, she'd find a taxi. But what about calling her family? No, no. No, no, no! No, that was impossible, completely out of the question. He'd keep her handbag as a souvenir.

Yury Trifonov

Excuse me, but I'm leaving, I'm on my way, thank you very much. But why the big hurry? What on earth is the matter?

He looked at her with a certain haughtiness mixed with incredulity.

"What did Smolyanov say to you?"

"He said that I should behave myself. What do you think he meant by that?"

"He meant . . . I think that. . . ." He seized her hand and pulled her toward him. "He's an idiot! What do you need him for, anyway?"

And right then and there she was struck by the chilling realization. It always happened that way with her: at first a feeling or intuition, then the realization. For the first second she couldn't believe it herself, but then—yes, perhaps that call had not been the result of any accident. For if there really had been an accident, why would he have felt the need to apologize? A person who is drunk isn't capable of dissembling. He had given himself away involutarily by asking her forgiveness.

"There's a lot we need to talk about. We didn't have a chance to. . . ." This man with his high forehead and somewhat pompous look was speaking very sternly now and tightly gripping Lyalya's hands. She tore them loose, though not with all her strength, since he did have some sort of heart condition and she was afraid. He started talking about the Academic Theater and about how he was going to have her transferred there and appointed to a permanent position, with a promotion and a raise in salary, and how he would arrange for any concerts she wanted to give or any trips she wanted to take. And if she refused, she should realize that a woman with such lips. . . . Well, that did it! No one had ever gotten anything from her using that technique. Suddenly she asked disarmingly, "Tell me, is Nikolai Demianovich terribly afraid of you?"

"What? He certainly is!"

Lyalya burst out laughing. Easy, easy does it. You should take it easy and not tire yourself out this way. It's bad for your heart. And now she felt both sadness and contempt for Nikolai Demianovich, that petty liar who had suddenly been transformed in her own mind into a pitiful nonentity. As for herself, she vowed never to say another word to him or even glance in his direction.

She flew through the snowstorm along the enormous and now empty Sadovoe Ring. Where was she headed? After running a long way she suddenly realized that she was going in the wrong direction. The subway was closed and she needed to head in toward the center of town—toward the inner ring of boulevards and Masha's place on Clear Ponds Boulevard. Half an hour later and by now thoroughly exhausted, she finally reached the inner ring. Here it was as quiet and deserted as a forest: no tramps, no policeman, only the benches in their thick, snowy armor. And now, wandering along one of the boulevards with tears running down her face, she thought to herself: "Lord, what a fool I've been! What have I been doing with my life? . . . And Grisha, my own beloved Grisha. . . ."

V

Rebrov managed to earn a little money by answering letters for two editorial offices and by writing radio scripts. Besides this, he sometimes published short historical sketches in popular magazines. All this brought in next to nothing but it was at least a way of staying afloat. At best he would earn about 1,000 rubles a month; sometimes 700, sometimes 300, and at other times, nothing at all—a big, fat zero. Now that Lyalya was earning good money and all sorts of unexpected bonuses kept flowing in, things should have been easier for him. But instead, this improvement in their financial situation only made him feel all the more frustrated and depressed. Before when they hadn't had money, well, that was all there was to it. He was no aristocrat, he could get along with a simple cup of coffee when he went out in the evening. Nowadays Lyalya might hand him a thirty- or even a 100-ruble note. Still, he hated being in the position of having to ask. Then there was his mother-in-law, who only made matters worse. It seemed to her that he was forcing Lyalya to run around and make extra money from concerts and other special appearances—or in other words, that he was exploiting her. Irina Ignatievna did not come out and say this in so many words, but she let her feelings be known, and Rebrov was very much aware of them. Moreover he sometimes came across her epistles to her daughter— Lyalya would carelessly leave them lying around—and there were times when he felt that he was beginning to hate his mother-in-law. In the evenings she would complain to Lyalya directly, "He came into the kitchen and didn't even say hello. . . . Three times I've asked him to chop up some firewood. . . ." All this was irksome and impossible to put up with, and he was dying to escape to his room on Bashilov Street. But Lyalya begged him to stay, since otherwise she would have had to go with him. This was what had usually happened in the past, but right now she didn't feel that she could run off and leave her mother alone. So she begged and pleaded with him, but never had the courage to take her mother firmly in hand.

He kept silent, put up with it, and every day he would sneak off to the library early in the morning and return home as late as possible.

On this particular day, as luck would have it, he had come home early and rather upset. For in one of the editorial offices where for three years now he had regularly been assigned to answer correspondence, he was suddenly told that the new editor-in-chief had been looking through the list of part-time employees and that his future there was in jeopardy. Why? Why should it be? One of his acquaintances in the office shrugged his shoulders in embarrassment: "I don't really know anything about this. I suppose the situation will be clarified before long." And a female acquaintance remarked ironically, "It seems you're not so hard up anymore. Your wife is doing very well, isn't she? And there are people whose only source of income is these letters."

He should have stood his ground, complained, and appealed to their sympathy, since the matter did not seem to have been definitely decided. But his old fear came to the fore—wouldn't he have looked foolish and pathetic in the role of supplicant?—and he gave in. Of course, there were people who were more deserving, he couldn't deny that. Everything they said was true. Nevertheless, this was terribly unpleasant news. But rather than let his feelings show, he even joked with them, told a humorous anecdote, and walked off with proud composure. His income had been reduced by one third. He didn't want to see or talk to anyone, he only wanted to go home, to Lyalka. Only she could make him feel better by telling him something silly and reassuring.

Lyalya was to have visited her father in the hospital at six and to have arrived home at about seven, since there was no performance that day. But she didn't come home at seven, or at eight, or at ten. Her mother began to get worked up, which, as usual in her case, took the form of all sorts of pointless flailing around. First she wanted to run off to the subway station, when she thought of calling the hospital from a public pay phone, and finally she was simply going to head out there on her own. It was only with difficulty that Rebrov dissuaded her. Did she want to upset Lyalya's father—how foolish that would be!

Tamara Ignatievna, Lyalya's Aunt Toma from Alexandrov, had already been living in the house for several days now, having come to give his mother-in-law a hand with the housework. She was a tall, quiet old lady with a very unhappy fate: all her immediate family, her husband and children, had been scattered and killed during the war. Although she was registered as a permanent resident of Alexandrov, 100 kilometers away, she usually spent a good part of the year in Moscow, living with her sisters Zhenya and Veronika, with her brother Kolya in Izmailov, or less frequently here, with her sister Irina. She was a private seamstress, and not a very good one, having learned to sew in order to support herself. In connection with her work she often had to live for weeks at a time in the homes of complete strangers. His mother-in-law didn't really like her sister, and in fact, Lyalka and her father treated Tamara more kindly than did Irina Ignatievna, who seldom invited her sister to visit. Her most common excuse was that she was afraid of being fined for having an overnight guest who was not officially registered in Moscow. And considering the fact that their neighbor, police lieutenant Kurtov, had it in for Pyotr Alexandrovich, such a fine could easily come about.

But the heart of the matter lay elsewhere—in an old woman's foolish jealousy whose underlying causes reached back some quarter of a century. Yet when

Pyotr Alexandrovich had gone off to the hospital for the second time, Irina Ignatievna had herself written to Aunt Toma, asking her to come and stay with her. And all of her pent-up anxieties and frustrations—her fear for her husband's life, her irritation with her son-in-law, her apprehensions about her daughter, the pain from her ulcer—all of this had been unleashed on quiet, lanky Aunt Toma. And she had been patient and long-suffering, she had forgiven her sister and tried to calm her. Right now too, she was trying to pacify her, or at the very least to dissuade her from setting off for the hosptial. But for this her only thanks was the cruel retort, "You've been without a husband or children for so long, you can't possibly understand how I feel."

As it got close to eleven, Rebrov himself began to get nervous. He ran out to the pay phone to call Lyalya's girlfriend Masha, who acted as their telephone go-between—Lyalya sometimes leaving messages with Masha for him. Masha was at home—but no, no one had called. Perhaps—yes, most likely a concert had come up. It seemed that they had been planning to give some sort of concert in Krasnogorsk.

"How come you didn't go with them?" asked Rebrov suspiciously, though he already felt somewhat relieved.

"It wasn't our theater's concert, it was the group from the Moscow Variety Theater," Masha explained. "But I don't know for sure. It's just a guess."

When Rebrov told his mother-in-law about the concert, she seemed somewhat reassured and the three of them sat down for a late evening snack. But Lyalya didn't appear either at twelve or at one. The Moscow Variety Theater usually traveled by bus when making outside appearances, and on the way back the bus would drop Lyalya off right at her door. Nonetheless, at half past twelve his mother-in-law grabbed her fur coat, put on her scarf, and ran off to the Sokol subway station in order to meet her. Whom did she think she was going to meet? Rebrov tried to explain to her that this was absurd, a complete waste of energy. Irina Ignatievna was already in such a dsitraught state, however, that logical argument had no effect on her.

"Of course it's not very pleasant to be out walking the streets late at night. It would be much pleasanter to be sitting inside, where it's nice and warm," she muttered.

"Well, I could go instead, I'd be happy to. Only what's the sense?"

"Sense, sense! Everything has to make sense for you. You just can't seem to understand that when a person is terribly upset—I just can't sit here doing nothing. . . ."

From the yard Kandidka gave a thin, joyous yelp. Irina Ignatievna must by untying her and taking her with her, which meant that he, Rebrov, didn't have to worry: Kandidka would tear any would-be assailants to pieces. But there was something offensive in this whole scene—in this senseless running off, just to make a point. For it wasn't to meet Lyalya that she had gone running off to the subway—not even she herself had any hope of that. She had gone in order to insult and reproach him, and so that her sister might see how horrible and unfeeling he was, staying at home while an old woman went out alone in the middle of the night. But he for his part couldn't bring himself to perform some senseless act just for the sake of proving her wrong.

Tamara Ignatievna came quietly out of Pyotr Alexandrovich's room. There was a guilty look on her face. She shuffled about in her felt boots for a while, then she said, "I wanted to go with her, but she chased me off. . . . She's angry with me because I stood up for you. Well, what does she think—that I don't have any right to express my opinion? I say exactly what I think. . . ."

Rebrov was sitting at the table, smoking. Continuing to shuffle about, the lanky old lady droned on in a plaintive voice, "I'm not a sponger or a beggar of some sort. I have my own house. And I have hundreds of friends in Moscow. There's Natalya Alexeevna Mikhnacheva, for example, a general's wife—how many times has she begged me to come and live with her, she's even sent two telegrams. But why did I come here? Because I felt sorry for Irina. She's going crazy without Pyotr—she's lost her bearings and is a nervous wreck. As I know only too well. She hasn't been through what some of us have been through. . . . And I felt sorry for Lyalka and wanted to help. . . . But why should I have to listen to her telling me that I don't know how to do this or that I don't understand that? Or that I'm always playing up to you? As if I were playing up to you! Well, if that isn't a foolish idea! Why on earth should I play up to you? Are you going to give me a pension or feed me chocolates?"

"Your sister likes to humiliate people," said Rebrov.

"It's true, Grisha, it's true! She likes very much to humiliate people. You're absolutely right. Even when we were still students at the gymnasium, she was like that. She once made our youngest sister Veronika eat chalk before she would show her some letter that Veronika was begging to see. . . . No, Irina was not the kindest member of our family. . . . And yet she's turned out to be the happiest! All the rest of us have suffered some family disaster—or at least something has gone wrong in our personal lives. Zhenka's Mikhail Abramovich is her

second husband—her first died before the war. Veronika
doesn't have any husband at all—or rather, she had one,
but he was a drunkard and she kicked him out. Then
there's my own case, which speaks for itself. And even
in Kolya's case—there's nothing good you can say about
his marriage. Olimpiada is so greedy and materialistic.
She actually shortened our mother's life. No, none of us
is happy, only Irina—and now, as you see, life's misfortunes have caught up with her as well. But as for what I
said in your behalf, it was nothing special. I merely told
her that I always sympathized with you because you're
all alone in this world. You have no father or mother or
sisters or brothers—no one at all. Isn't that true?"

"Yes," said Rebrov, "but you don't have to feel
sorry for me."

"Grisha, it's not a question of feeling sorry for
you. I was simply pointing out that she should be more
understanding. I reminded her that she has Lyalka,
Petya, us, and all sorts of relatives—enough to fill a
whole village—but whom do you have—no one at all."

"You really don't have to sympathize with me. I'm
not interested in that."

"And she tells me that I'm playing up to you. Or
that being alone is not a reason for praising someone.
And she points out that I'm alone too. Well, I gave up
trying to talk to her—never mind, I thought, life hasn't
taught you anything yet, but you'll soon learn. Yes...."

She sat down at the table, under the lamp, which
immediately illuminated her large nose and heavily lined
face. It was the face of a useless old woman, but at the
same time it was strangely reminiscent of the weather-
beaten face of a sailor. It bore the traces of time, the
many places she had been, and the many sufferings she
had known. Suddenly, turning to Grigory, she said
gently and even entreatingly, "Still, please don't be angry

with her, all right? You have no idea how beautiful she used to be, and how many men proposed to her that year, in 1923! She was simply spectacular. She was, after all, a ballerina. She studied with Polyakov in his studio on Bronnaya Street, and the whole family would turn out to see her perform. Polyakov invited her to join him when he emigrated to Riga. But she didn't go. She felt sorry for Mother. Father had just died and Kolya was having a hard time. . . . Petya had already appeared on the scene by that time, but no one had any idea what was going to develop there. . . . No, it was only because of Mother, only because of Mother. . . . I say that she's been happy. But what sort of happiness has she had—squatting in the soil and manure, planting potatoes, sawing and chopping wood like some peasant? We've all kept telling her over the years that she and Petya should sell this house, the garden, and buy a small, convenient apartment in the center of town, where they could start living like other civilized people. After all, what does one need with a house and garden in Moscow? But no, Petya couldn't do that. He couldn't live without his garden. And here you have to give her credit: she's always been devoted to her family. For after all, her youth, all of her hopes, and whatever talent she had—and she did have quite a bit—all of it has gone into tending this house and garden. There's her happiness for you, Grisha, and what has she got to look forward to now? Heaven forbid that anything should happen to Pyotr Alexandrovich! She wouldn't survive it. . . . Oh, how silly and naive she can be. If I were to tell you. . . ."

As Tamara Ignatievna mumbled on, Rebrov strained his ears for the sound of a dog or of voices, but he heard nothing. It occurred to him that the human face, when seen through a magnifying glass, must be repulsive, with all its pores, little hairs, and surface irregularities. But that's exactly what we do in life, we see everything through a magnifying glass. Every minute, every second, is magnified a thousandfold. And yet, one should always look at the years, the whole...then there wouldn't be any hatred. It would be impossible to hate a woman who had given birth to that other woman who was his very life. It would be impossible because they were, after all, one whole, one continuum. They were like a tree and its branches. You couldn't separate the pain of the one from the other. She had wanted to be a ballerina and instead led a poor, kitchen-garden sort of life. And so? And so one shouldn't hate her. A person doesn't notice when he gradually changes into something else....

Irina Ignatievna returned after an hour and burst into tears as soon as she learned that Lyalya hadn't arrived. Rebrov himself began imagining various accidents, assaults, catastrophes. There wasn't any possibility of his sleeping, of course, but to remain in the same room with his sobbing mother-in-law was beyond his strength. He went upstairs to his and Lyalya's room and tried to read, but was unable to concentrate. So he lay down on the bed, smoked, and felt miserable. Sometimes he would be overcome by drowsiness, and the next few minutes would pass in a sort of delirium. Then he would suddenly jump up and reach for a cigarette. At some point or other Irina Ignatievna appeared at the door. Her face was swollen and wisps of matted hair protruded from under her kerchief.

"All this extra money be damned! All the money in the world isn't worth an evening like this! Why do you send her out to earn extra money for you? You should be ashamed of yourself!"

Rebrov felt a choking sensation in his throat. *"Who* sends her out to earn extra money?"

"You! Don't you have any conscience?" And her tearful eyes expressed not spite but a genuine belief in what she was saying and genuine despair as she confronted him, the villain.

"No one sends her out to earn money! It's you who...I...," he began shouting, gasping for breath. "You are the one who's destroying our life together! You, not me! You! You!"

"But you, you send her out to earn extra money...."

"Don't lie! You've already destroyed our family—yes, yes! You forbid Lyalya to marry me! You force her to have abortions!"

"But you're not a real husband to her, so why should she have children by you?"

"Yes, I am a real husband to her, but you're not a real mother, because you make her life miserable, simply miserable!"

This was followed by another fit of sobbing and a scream through her tears, "Don't you dare say such things to me! I love my daughter more than life itself!" And after blowing her nose and wiping her mouth with tidy precision she added, "You're no husband, you're nothing but a pitiful failure, and my daughter is unhappy with you."

He ran downstairs, grabbed his coat and fur cap, pulled on his felt boots, and ran out into the snowy yard. As he circled around in the dark, he was oppressed by a nasty sort of feeling—a fear of himself, of what he might have done in that moment of hatred, almost of insanity. How had it happened? Why, just a short while before, he had been thinking about the old woman quite calmly. He was going out of his mind and turning into a nasty, spiteful person. He had to do something. Perhaps he should apologize to her? No, that wasn't it—he had to do something about *himself!* Sometime after two and completely numb from the subfreezing temperature, he came back into the house, went upstairs, and collapsed on his bed.

Lyalya arrived in the morning, her cheeks rosy from the cold. She kissed Rebrov passionately, with a certain greedy impatience, while simultaneously expressing concern for her mother.

"My God, you haven't slept at all! Oh, my poor dears! Aunt Tomochka, and you didn't sleep either? How awful of me, what I've put you all through...."

"Lyalya," her mother asked tearfully, "why do you wear yourself out with these concerts?"

"I wasn't at a concert at all. I stupidly got stuck at a certain person's place, Smolyanov promised to come and pick me up, but his car broke down and I ended up going to Masha's on foot at 2 a.m. The whole thing was a nightmare...."

"Oh, Lyalechka...."

Her mother sighed, but one could tell that she was immediately relieved upon hearing Smolyanov's name and the reference to a "certain person's place." Rebrov could guess what she was dreaming of.

But now he was overwhelmed by a new anxiety: where *had* she been? Had somebody been forcing his attentions on her? Here was Smolyanov cropping up again. Yet despite his anxiety he was happy over the fact that she had been so genuinely upset at his suffering and had kissed him passionately and without embarrassment in front of her mother and aunt.

Lyalya sensed the tension between her mother and husband right away, and after she and Rebrov had gone upstairs to their room, she asked him if everything was all right at home. He replied that everything was the same as usual.

"Grisha, I'm begging you—please!" Lyalya whispered urgently. "Be as gentle as you can with Mother. She going out of her mind on account of Papa...."

"Okay," said Rebrov.

Lyalya threw off her dress and heels, put on a bathrobe, and lay down. The frosty glow had disappeared from her face and as she lay there with her eyes closed, she looked pale, her cheeks sunken with fatigue.

"Well, where were you actually? Before Masha's?"

"Oh, Grisha, it's a very dull story. I was at somebody's apartment, they were celebrating some old man's birthday...I'll tell you about it later. Right now I want to take a nap."

"Did some cad try to proposition you?"

"Of course...and not only one! All sorts of people were trying to proposition me...." She turned over on her side, with her face to the wall. "Please wake me in an hour. I'm being picked up at eleven-thirty. And please put the blanket over me. Thanks, Grishenka."

Rebrov left the room. In the hall he ran into his mother-in-law and said to her quite unexpectedly even for himself, "I shouted some foolish things yesterday, Irina Ignatievna. Please don't pay any attention...."

"Yes, yes, I understand. We were both upset. It's that naughty girl in there who's to blame. Grisha, would you please run out and get some milk?" On her face there was a sweet, pleading smile, as if the previous evening had never happened. "She's coughing and I want to give her something hot to drink."

Rebrov ran off to the store with a light heart and returned with two bottles of milk. Then he went upstairs to his "study."

Next to his and Lyalya's room was a tiny little room, a mere cubbyhole with a slanted ceiling and sloping walls formed by the eaves. A table and chair were all

that would fit into this "study," but there was a small
window and one could work here. Rebrov began laying
out his folders and thick notebooks. The notebook
which he now took in hand had on its cover the words:
"Outline for pl. on P. W.," which meant "Outline for a
play on the People's Will movement."* He had been
working on this play for the past few weeks, actually
almost a month, ever since he had become interested in
Nikolai Vasilievich Kletochnikov, a People's Will agent
who had operated within the Third Section.* He had first
learned about Kletochnikov four years ago when the
Academy of Sciences published a new edition of Morozov's* memoirs. Later on he had read about him in other
books, such as Figner's* *Records of a Life's Work.* But the
idea of writing a play about Kletochnikov had come to
him only recently and, as was usually the case, it had
come all of a sudden. He had begun working on it with
great enthusiasm—with the same sort of enthusiasm that
he had begun his novella about the Decembrists, then
about the uprising of the exiled Poles in Siberia, then
about Ivan Pryzhov, and finally about the poet Mikhai-
lov. All of this unfinished muddle lay heaped in draft
notebooks inside innumerable folders, awaiting the right
moment for completion. A day would suddenly come,
however, when he would be forced to ask himself what
all of this was for. The question would present itself
timidly at first, only slightly cooling his ardor, but promising to return full force later on, with predictably
chilling effect. And when this happened, his creative
impulses would become stalled, he would feel fed up
and depressed, and his mind would turn to the more
urgent matter of earning a living.

He took out a thin stack of paper from the folder.
On the top page, along with several handwritten para-
graphs there were ink drawings of faces with sideburns,

of swords, and of horses. Rebrov loved to draw horses, though this was not out of any particular love for horses. Actually, these shaggy monstrosities were not really drawings at all, but the offspring of his nervous tension. They would come to life on their own, spontaneously, the moment he plunged deep into thought.

A large quantity of ugly horses on a crossed-out page was a bad sign—it meant that a period of creative paralysis was close at hand. Well, he knew what the problem was. And it was his own fault! Three days ago he had talked about Kletochnikov to one of his magazine acquaintances. After hearing him out, his acquaintance had said that no, probably no one would be interested. Rebrov had guessed as much himself, but still, it would have been better not to ask. Poor Nikolai Vasilievich Kletochnikov, this police section chief who had quietly died from a hunger strike in the Alekseev salient of the Peter and Paul Fortress after a quiet, short, and heroic life—what could he hope for now, seventy years later? He had been incurably ill, doomed to death. And doomed to oblivion. There was absolutely no future for a play based on his life, even a fool could see that. So Rebrov had come to a decision. Maybe he should go off somewhere, to a different city, heaven knows where. But Lyalya wouldn't be willing to go with him, not now when things were going so well for her.

With his customary dexterity—the product of his despair—Rebrov kept fashioning horses at lightning speed, one after another, one after another....

Two years ago he had been offered a job in Barnaul, with the local newspaper, and Lyalya had applied for a job with the Barnaul Theater. They had been just on the point of leaving when at the last moment his mother-in-law had managed by superhuman efforts—tears and demagoguery—to spoil their plans. But his mother-in-law was beside the point. The one thing she was afraid of, of course, was that Rebrov and Lyalya would become firmly united forever. And Barnaul would have meant precisely that—forever! For Rebrov the move would have involved a tremendous sacrifice— the loss of Scholars' Reading Room No. 3, old books and antiquarian bookstores, and the popular magazines in which his historical vignettes were published (could he send them in by mail? probably not, and besides where would he get his material?)—but nonetheless, he was prepared to make this sacrifice. Temporarily, of course. He was even eager to do so, in order to break with the past and start afresh. After all, one lives a long time.

Yes, his mother-in-law had protested with all her strength, but Lyalya was not the most exemplary daughter and she had often acted against her mother's wishes before—she had left music school against her mother's wishes, she had had an affair with that lame poet and had run off and lived with him against her mother's wishes, and now for the last five years she had been living with him, Rebrov, against her mother's wishes. What this meant was that she herself couldn't make up her mind about moving to Barnaul and being with him forever. He had to go through some sort of trial period in order to show what he could do and to provide her with a guarantee. His mother-in-law spoke about this openly, while Lyalya thought the same thing—he was convinced of it—only subconsciously, without even being aware of it herself.

But if one were to probe deeper, to the very heart of things, then probably even Lyalya was beside the point. The crux of the matter lay in himself. He could not say either to himself or to her that it was forever. Not because he didn't love her enough, but because he loved her too much. His love constricted him and weighed him down. It was as if he were in an overloaded boat which was about to capsize and he was afraid of falling into the open sea. Yes, he first had to prove to himself what he could do and to provide himself with a guarantee. And Lyalya sensed this too: "Grisha, now that we don't have to worry about where the next penny is coming from, you can sit calmly and work...."

At breakfast Lyalya hastily told about her visit to her father and about how he might be able to come home by the beginning of February. Then she said something about the theater, about Smurny's intrigues, and about the conflict that had arisen between Sergei Leonidovich and Smolyanov because Sergei Leonidovich didn't want to stage his new play. Bob agreed with him, but the executive director was insisting that they go ahead with it. Bob was in danger of being fired, and Smurny was already playing up to Smolyanov. Irina Ignatievna was eager to know more, but Rebrov kept silent. He didn't like to discuss theater matters with Lyalya in his mother-in-law's presence. Suddenly, however, he blurted out in spite of himself:

"And he's right in not wanting to stage it! He's finally come to his senses."

"Why is he right?"

"Well, because his plays are no good. No one needs that sort of...."

"Grisha, you're wrong, and excuse my saying this, but I think you're a bit envious. Some of Smolyanov's plays are quite good, and the public likes him."

"The public likes him! As if that were any criterion! Well, just put two fools on stage and let them start punching each other in the face, and naturally the public will.... But what really gets me is your saying that I envy him. What do I have to envy? His money perhaps?

In that case I might as well envy our neighbor, that young shoemaker Arkashka."

"You know, Grisha," said Aunt Toma, now entering the conversation for the first time, "I don't agree with you. I liked that play of his that Lyalya was in. I laughed a great deal."

"Don't distract her with idle conversation, or she won't manage to eat her breakfast," his mother-in-law said sternly.

Rebrov burst out laughing. "Well, the three of you really surprise me! Don't tell me you take all this business seriously? His so-called success—all this uproar and publicity?"

For some reason he had gotten stirred up and said more than he should have. His mother-in-law immediately asked, "And you don't think he is a success?"

"You know, Grisha, Smolyanov is kinder than you are. You speak about him so spitefully, and yet he wants to help."

"I'm not being spiteful at all. And who's this he wants to help?"

"I was talking to him yesterday. About you."

"What about me?" He looked at her in astonishment. She began to blush. Lyalya rarely blushed, and if she did, it meant that she had good cause. "Well, what could you be discussing with him about me?"

"Well, it was stupid of me. He's not very reliable, and I shouldn't have...."

"But what was it you were discussing?"

"Well, about how he might be able to help you. With your work...."

"That's really ridiculous!" he muttered. "How could he possibly help me?" And with an impatient wave of his hand he got up and left the room. He was infuriated by her lack of tact—talking about this in front of her mother! Besides, he wanted to question her right away, this minute, about Smolyanov, so that he could either dismiss or confirm the suspicions which already rankled like a wound. But of course he could not speak of such things in front of the two old ladies, so he waited impatiently for her in their room. Finally, Lyalya came running upstairs—the car from the theater had already arrived and was parked out front by the gate. As she hastily began collecting her things and throwing them into her little suitcase, he asked her how the conversation with Smolyanov had happened to come up. Lyalya said something in reply. Suddenly he seized her by the shoulders, and looking her straight in the eye, he gasped in despair, "You're having an affair with him!"

For a second she gazed at him in bewilderment, then once again she began to blush. "Of course, what do you expect! After all, he's our playwright and we all depend on him. No, Grishenka, it turns out that he's a stupid man. And as you know, stupid people don't exist for me. Well, I'm off! See you later!"

Watching from upstairs, Rebrov caught a glimpse of her merino lamb coat as it flashed against the white background of the garden, amidst the bare trees. Nothing had been settled. Of course she had been joking about Smolyanov. It was inconceivable that she was having an affair with him. She knew that he wouldn't be able to live with that.

An hour later he set off by streetcar to Bashilov Street. He needed to pick up some books which he was planning to sell, having torn them from his heart long ago and already adjusted himself to their absence. Upon arrival, he was told by his neighbor Kanunov that someone from the housing administration had come around, asking to see his employment certificate. And he had better come up with it in a hurry, or his residence permit would be cancelled and he would be forced to leave Moscow. This neighbor was not a very nice man. He had seized his own one-room apartment right after the war, and rather highhandedly, under the guise of being a disabled veteran. The room had previously belonged to some good people, Rebrov's original neighbors, but when the war came to an end, they were still stuck in some evacuation camp and thus were in no position to prevent Kanunov from settling into one of their two rooms. Once he was there, parasite that he was, neither boiling water nor kerosene could flush him out.

He repeated the business about the certificate three times, barging into Rebrov's room to do so.

"The man said, Grigory Fyodorovich, that if you didn't present it by the first, they'd inform the police."

"Okay, okay, I'll present it."

"And you'd better make sure you do, since I'm now the official housing representative for our section of the building."

"How nice...." And having to exert a certain amount of force—since his neighbor refused to back away—Rebrov pushed against the door and closed it.

A minute later there came a knock and Kanunov's voice, now much harsher and more demanding, "And please seal up that window! You live somewhere else, nobody knows where, and you make the rest of us freeze. So please, seal up that window right away."

"Go to hell," Rebrov muttered inaudibly. Right now all he felt was irritation and fatigue. Nor was there any point in starting an argument without someone like Kanunov. He was supposed to produce a certificate? Okay, he'd do it. Without wasting any time he began rummaging through his bookcase and shelves, looking for the books that he wanted to sell. He came across some old school notebooks, some albums with clumsy, schoolboy drawings, and then he stumbled upon his Polish grammar and an *Italian Self-Taught* book—good Lord, how many worthy undertakings! His books were in a chaotic state, and it took him an hour and a half to set aside enough volumes to bring in the amount of money he needed—some 120 rubles. In the meantime he enjoyed poking his nose into these dusty notebooks and other old things, immersing himself in this aimless reading and forgetting about everything else. Finally, having stuffed his briefcase to overflowing, he left the building—this building which at one time had been dear to him, his only home, but which later on, after his parents' and brother's deaths and the beginning of his new life with Lyalya, no longer seemed habitable, more like a barn than a place to live.

The editorial office that had given him his certificate for the housing administration over the last two years just happened to be the one that had crossed him off their list of part-time employees the day before. He would have to find some alternative, and quickly too! Kanunov would follow through with his promise. Apparently he wanted his, Rebrov's, room for himself. Well, it was understandable; he had a family, they were overcrowded, and when he could see that the room next door was empty for months at a time, it struck him as unfair. At the housing administration they had perhaps forgotten about the certificate—he had presented one last year—but Kanunov would remind them. What did he do there at that meat-packing plant of his, anyway? Was he a foreman, engineer, rate-fixer—damned if Rebrov knew! At any rate, he made sausage. Before you could bat an eye, he would slap you into the machine and you'd come flying out the other end as a roll of

Yury Trifonov

Favorite Choice, wrapped in cellophane and neatly
sealed at each end. If the film studio would take his
scenario or some theater would accept his play—even
for use at some future date and with revisions, but just
as long as there was a contract—then the certificate
would be in the bag. But in the meantime he was an
absolute zero, a purveyor of air. At the brick factory
they always needed unskilled workers and they'd give
him a certificate. After all, he wasn't even the husband
of a well-known actress. Kanunov had sensed something, and it was not for nothing that he had asked him
several times, "Well, why don't you register yourself at
your wife's place? And aren't you a member of some
sort of professional union?"

It was all very clear: Kanunov had swung into action. Last time he had very politely tried to find out
Lyalya's address under the pretext of wanting to forward Rebrov's mail, so that it wouldn't lie around and
perhaps get lost. But Rebrov had sensed some kind of
danger and not given him the address. Never mind, it
was all right if his letters lay around. Otherwise this
character might show up at Lyalya's some day and announce, "We've come about your certificate, Grigory
Fyodorovich."

Rebrov glanced around involuntarily, but the street
was deserted. The wind was sweeping the snow along
the narrow little sidewalk.

Down the street from the Moscow Art Theater, in
Bookstore No. 14, where he happened to know the
stock manager, he received ninety rubles for his books.
From here he went straight to the editorial office on
Gogol Boulevard where they sometimes published his
"Historical Curiosities" and "Forgotten Facts." Here he
was told that they couldn't give him a certificate be-
cause he wasn't on their official staff list. There was

absolutely no point in going on to the other editorial office, since he had worked for them—answering letters—only sporadically.

He wandered on to the Hotel National. And the first person he ran into in the hotel cafe was Shakhov. "A-ha!" said Shakhov with would-be amicability. "Well, young fellow, how are things going? Sit down and have a shot of brandy. You look about as cheerful as a frozen fish."

"Everything's going fine with me," said Rebrov, taking a seat and pouring some brandy from Shakhov's decanter into a wine glass. He was putting up a brave front since he had already decided to order 200 grams of vodka right away. "Listen, you had something in mind for me, remember?"

"What? Oh yes, I remember. But I forget what it was," Shakhov burst out laughing, at the same time giving Rebrov a wink. His purplish-red cheeks, puffy from the brandy he had drunk, shook with laughter, and his eyes had a seemingly drunken look, though at the same time there was something piercing and attentive in their gaze. "We'll discuss it right now. You just have a good meal. Order the carp. It's tremendous today...."

His proposal was the following: there was a certain person who could help him. He would have to submit everything he had, show him both the scenario and the play, and then this individual would tell him what, where, when, and how much. He was an extremely important person with a great deal of experience. What would this be—some sort of co-authorship? Why should it necessarily be that right away? But who knows—time will tell. It's not out of the question. Yes, it is out of the question! God damn it! Who *is* this extremely important person, anyway? Sh-sh, don't get so upset, especially with that carp in your mouth. It has too many bones.

"As the saying goes, it's ours to propose, yours to dispose...."

With his red and always moist little eyes he looked like an old setter suffering from conjunctivitis. He was close to seventy, but everyone addressed him familiarly as Kostya. In his day, it seems, he had even had something to do with *The Stock Market Gazette.* Or he might have been working seventy years ago, or a hundred or more, for that matter. Perhaps he'd had something to do with Kraevsky's *Voice* or Katkov's *Moscow Gazette* in the last century.... But my dear Kostya, this is sheer effrontery, unspeakable effrontery—it simply won't do! Why do you say that, I'd like to know? And exactly what opinion do you have of yourself, young fellow? Well, okay, order yourself another 200 grams and we'll forget about this whole conversation. But just in case you need me, I'll be here on Tuesday after six. What's going on in the theater these days? And how do things stand with Sergei Leonidovich? I hear that he's having problems—some sort of conflict with the executive director.

It was about 3 p.m. when Rebrov left the cafe and set off for the theater. He hadn't been there in a long time—he always hated going there. But now his back was against the wall, and he felt he had to make one last effort to be heard. After all, Marevin never had given him a proper answer regarding his plays, nor had he even discussed them with him. And both manuscripts were still there. Besides, he wanted to see Lyalya and question her right away. Whatever she told him would decide his fate.

He slipped through the empty lobby, tossed his coat on a hook in the cloakroom, and headed straight for the small, smoke-filled office of the theater's chief literary consultant.

Marevin sat slouched on the office sofa, with one short little leg tucked under him and the other hanging loose. Beside him was a lean, skittle-shaped lady who sat decorously erect on the edge of the sofa. They were talking in subdued tones, and Marevin was fingering his worry beads. He always had them with him, as if he were some orthodox Muslim. He glanced up at Rebrov with a tired look, at the same time showing some surprise.

"Excuse me, Grisha, but it seems to me that we did discuss the matter. Didn't we? I think you're mistaken about...."

"Nothing of the kind! It was through Lyalya that...."

"Yes, we did discuss it, we did. It's just slipped your mind. You were asking me over the phone about 'A Many-Storied Building'—or whatever the exact title is—and I conveyed Sergei Leonidovich's opinion...."

"And where's my official, written reply?"

"I don't understand, Grigory Fyodorovich...." The look of displeasure in Marevin's black eyes grew more intense. There were bags under his eyes, like dark sores, as if he had been drinking too much. And this pygmy, this pathetic creature with his ulcer, here in this theater he was God and Tsar!

"What is it you want from us? An official discussion? We wanted to spare you.... What would you gain from it? Our actors and the members of the theater council are rude, tactless people. They might say something unpleasant—and there you'd be, so discouraged that you wouldn't be able to get back to work for six months. It was in your own interest.... But as for an official reply, that I'll be happy to give you—right this minute if you wish."

It seemed that Marevin was mocking him. But probably only on professional grounds. Apparently he considered him a third-rate writer. His head was throbbing with pain, as if someone had twisted a towel around his skull and were drawing it tighter and tighter. Oh, to hell with it! And suddenly, in an unrecognizable, vulgarly aggressive tone—the sort of tone one would expect from a third-rate writer—Rebrov said, "Boris Mironovich, I'd like to have a certificate to the effect that I'm your author and am working on a play for the theater. I've got to have it...."

The phone rang. The pygmy lowered his little legs from the sofa and got up to answer it.

"....for the housing administration," Rebrov finished his sentence.

While Marevin was muttering into the phone, the lady bent her lean torso in Rebrov's direction and whispered, "Did you know that Boris Mironovich has suffered a terrible blow. His wife has just died. And now he's completely alone. He has no children, nor any close relatives...."

Marevin continued to mutter into the phone, "My resignation, yes, yes, on Monday, and please have all my papers in order, yes, yes, yes, it's vitally important...."

"What did she die of?" asked Rebrov, now with genuine interest.

"She'd been sick for a very long time," the lady replied with a sorrowful and deferential nod. Tremendous respect for Boris Mironovich was written all over her face.

Marevin was trying to grasp what certificate Rebrov was talking about. Once he understood, he advised Rebrov to have Liudmila Petrovna discuss the matter with the executive director. He probably wouldn't refuse her. He, Marevin, could talk to Roman Vasilievich himself, but there wouldn't be any point in that now that he was leaving the theater. Roman Vasilievich wouldn't do anything for him—in fact, just the opposite —but if Liudmila asked, perhaps he'd do it. She was in his good graces at the moment. As Marevin returned to the sofa and began rubbing his worry beads, Rebrov shuddered at the thought of losing the one person in the world one felt close to and of being left *completely* alone. Scrutinizing Marevin's small, wan face—he could see now that it was wan—he realized that this man was in a bad way. He wasn't the type who'd be able to live completely alone. Nor would prim ladies like the one sitting here on the sofa be able to save him. Suddenly Rebrov was struck by the frightening thought: "Bob is going to die soon! Without the theater...."

"And perhaps you should drop in on Sergei Leonidovich," said Marevin. "Discuss the matter with him. Go and see him, go and see him right now. I happen to know that he's in his office."

Rebrov felt like telling him: never mind. Never mind all this business about plays and certificates. It's all nonsense anyway, and not worth discussing. It really is nonsense. He'd get around this situation somehow, and life would go on. After all, one lives a long time. And what they should be discussing was something else: death and loneliness. But that was the one thing which it was impossible to discuss. So he merely shook Marevin's hand, gazed into his eyes—there was a defenselessness about them, but at the same time a certain haughtiness—and having hesitated while squeezing his hand, he walked out of his office without saying anything at all.

Why, he asked himself, should he bother to see Sergei Leonidovich now? After all, everything was perfectly clear and there was nothing to be gained by it. But at the moment—as was often the case with him—he was acting from inertia and didn't have the strength to do otherwise. The artistic director knew Rebrov fairly well as Lyalya's husband, but they had never sat down and had a serious conversation. Everything had been casual and in passing—chitchat over dinner or a few words exchanged at the railroad station, in the cafeteria, or in the cloakroom.... And now, to Rebrov's utter astonishment, this stout, gray-haired individual suddenly began telling him all his troubles and innermost thoughts. No sooner had Rebrov said something to him about the certificate than Sergei Leonidovich declared that he was mad at the whole world, that he was in an extremely negative, misanthropic mood, that mankind had not acquitted itself honorably, that hypocrisy would be our downfall—and more in the same vein. He paced furiously back and forth as he spoke, while Rebrov remained standing by the window, his back pressed against the high windowsill.

It seemed that a meeting of the theater council had adjourned just half an hour ago and the old man had lashed out at all of them—at the executive director and his assistant, and at the assistant artistic director! The previous night, while suffering from insomnia, he had suddenly realized that the only possible way to save the situation was to tell people the truth to their faces. Of course someone would go and tell Smolyanov right away what he'd said about him, since it was Smolyanov who had sparked the whole controversy in the first place, when Boris Mironovich had tried to block his third play.... And as for that third play of his, that, you understand, was a subject in itself. Its action jumped back and forth between Chicago, Belgrade, and the Volga-Don Canal....

"And why is it that I'm telling you all this? Probably because your Liudmila was the only council member who tried—even timidly—to help me save Bob."

He gave Rebrov a long, searching look, then his voice suddenly changed and he went on in a dry, unfriendly tone, "Well, now let's talk about you. But I've warned you—I'm feeling merciless today. Is that all right? Can you take it? Well then, when I read your plays and those of other young playwrights—including Smolyanov—I can't help wondering why it is that people make things so difficult for themselves. Why do they write about things which they have only the vaguest notion of? After all, each one of us has something which lies close to our heart and can move us to tears, just as Chekhov had his Uncle Vanyas and his Doctor Astrovs and Gorky, let's assume, had his petty bourgeois—his Bulychyovs and Dostigaevs. But you—whom do you have? What do you have? Here you've written a play about the Korean War, and yet you don't know Korea, you haven't had the slightest exposure to the war there, and in general you've probably never been farther east than the Kazan Railroad Station, eh what? Am I right?"

"The play isn't meant to be completely railistic... it's more a fairytale," mumbled Rebrov, unable to hold back a smile, which probably made him look all the more foolish. "Or perhaps even a parable...."

"A parable! Listen, it's very presumptuous to say: I've written a parable! Parables are written by peoples, not by authors. Now, regarding your other play, the one about the construction of a university. Just be patient and listen to what I have to say—this is just one of those days. Well, my dear young friend, for God's sake have the sense to start off by writing about normal-size houses—about workers barracks or the cozy little rooms with flowered wallpaper where our Pyotr Ivanoviches and Maria Ivanovnas live. Later on you can tackle your university skyscraper with its forty-five stories! Take

313

Yury Trifonov

Smolyanov, for instance, a man not lacking in ability. Some time ago he submitted his first, straightforward little play about forest conservation. It had something fresh about it, something true to life.... He didn't know much about writing, but he was trying to do something worthwhile.... I hestiated, but the others managed to convince me that his theme was an important one that needed to be dramatized, so I went ahead and produced it. But now in this new play of his he introduces elements of myth and even some sort of theory of mythology...."

Rebrov was unable to concentrate sufficiently to take in everything Sergei Leonidovich was saying. It was something about Smolyanov, something incredibly long and complicated, and expressed with a great deal of emotion. But after all, all of this was trivia, a lot of silly details. Why did he have to go on about it for so long, and with such heat? Well, one thing was clear: Smolyanov had managed to cause him a great deal of trouble. He was feeling lonely and hurt, and there was no one to complain to, no one to pour out his feelings to. Apparently he had come to some sort of decision and it frightened him. A few other fragmentary sentences managed to reach Rebrov's consciousness: "Herman Vladimirovich, that master of hypocrisy, is dying to become artistic director.... While previously, you remember.... They were both my productions—but it was my own fault, all my own fault. I was the one who gave birth to this golem...."

"But Sergei Leonidovich," said Rebrov, "what's your answer to my question? What am I to do?" As in Marevin's office he felt once again that vulgar compulsion to hammer away at the same point. Well, what else could he do? He had come here as a supplicant, so he might as well behave accordingly. "If I could just have a certificate."

"A certificate? What sort of certificate?" the artistic director asked in surprised. "Oh, the certificate you were telling me about. Well, you should speak to the business office about that."

He turned on the desk lamp and began moving the papers on his desk. In an instant his face had turned into that of a tired, crotchety old man. Suddenly Rebrov sat down on the armchair near the lamp and said, "Listen, could you spare me ten minutes? I want to tell you about something. No, it has nothing to do with those two plays of mine. They don't count. And please understand that I don't resent any of the things you said about them...."

"Well, just don't waste my time. I've already given you seven minutes."

They remained in his office for two and a half hours. Rebrov told him about Nikolai Vasilievich Kletochnikov—about everything that had been burning inside him for the past few months but which a few days before had begun to cool and turn to ice. Now he found himself getting fired up again: after all, Nikolai Vasilievich's life was an example of how one should live, not worrying about the eternal questions and not thinking about death or immortality. It wasn't even clear whether he had been a genuine revolutionary—that is, whether he had been fully aware of the goals and purposes of the revolution. This ailing, bespectacled, mousy-looking provincial official had appeared unexpectedly, from out of the blue, and offered his help to the revolution. No one knew him and there were doubts, hesitation—after all, there was nothing heroic about him! Neither Alexander's steel-like muscles, nor Sergei's pistols and daggers, nor Lev's erudition, nor Nikolai's Carbonarist romanticism. He had nothing,

nothing at all. He was an instrument. He carried out the
will of others, which some called the people's will. He
planted himself in the gendarmerie, penetrated its armor and infiltrated into its very core, into the heart
and entrails of the Third Section. And from here he was
able to help, save, and kill. In so doing he was also carrying out the demands of his own conscience. And that
was all. It is almost impossible to explain his actions, for
conscience is a nebulous concept, almost as nebulous as
the fourth dimension. Just try to explain the concept of
a fourth dimension—nothing will come of it, and you'll
start stammering and groping for words. Yet nonetheless, conscience is a tremendous force. Of course, at certain times it grows stronger, at other times weaker, de-
pending on—who knows, perhaps on certain explosions
of solar matter. At his hearing he made all sorts of absurd statements, slandering himself by pretending that
the revolutionaries had paid him for the information he
had given them. He had to give the authorities some sort
of explanation, and what was he to tell them? Well, of
course, he was sick, suffering from consumption, and
would not have lasted more than two or three years.
But sickness only intensifies that which is in a person
to begin with, and in this case what was intensified was
conscience.

When he played cards with his fat landlady, a police informer, trying to please her so that through her
he would be able to get a job in the desired institution...

Sergei Leonidovich was listening with all the eagerness and enthusiasm of a child. There definitely was, in
fact, something childlike about this stout old man. And
every once in a while, as Rebrov proceeded with his
story, Sergei Leonidovich would spontaneously interject
a few words on the subject of "worldly hypocrisy."
Finally he said, "It's amazing how many splendid and

forgotten people have lived on this earth. And this really was only a short time ago! My father was a contemporary of your Nikolai Vasilievich, and also a resident of Petersburg...." And struck by Rebrov's story, he went on to make some comments of his own. Rebrov was almost touched. It seemed that this was the first time that the artistic director had ever heard the name of Nikolai Morozov, much less than of Lev Tikhomirov.*

"How funny it is: for you 1880 means Kletochnikov, the Third Section, bombs, assassination attempts on the Tsar, while for me it's Ostrovsky, *The Female Captives* at the Maly, Yermolova in the role of Yevlalia, Sadovsky, Muzil. . . .* Yes, yes! Lord, how terribly interrelated everything is! When you think of it, the history of a country is like a many-stranded cable, and when you rip off one of the strands.... No, you can't look at things this way! Historical truth is interaction through time, everything taken together: Kletochnikov, Muzil.... Oh, if one could only depict on the stage this flow of time which carries along everything and everyone! But today I announced that if Boris Mironovich goes, I'm going too. So the management will have to decide. Usually this office is packed after council meetings; there's a lot of noise and joking around. But today they all hurried off, I had surprised and upset them...."

When Rebrov left the theater, it was twilight and the street lights were already on. He was completely worn out from his long conversation with Sergei Leonidovich, and yet for some reason he felt happy—which was really absurd, since he hadn't accomplished a thing, not a single thing. In this strangely happy frame of mind he wandered from Pushkin Square to Trubnaya Square and from there down Neglinnaya Street and up Pushkin Street, back toward Pushkin Square. By now, however, his happy mood had faded and he was beginning to feel depressed. It was not so much because one more day had been wasted—he hadn't even managed to get to the library—but because it suddenly occurred to him that he himself, like the old man, Sergei Leonidovich, had no desire to go home. The thought saddened him, and when a few minutes later he happened to run into an old friend, Tolya Shchyokin, by the entrance to the health food cafeteria, he already felt utterly depressed. Rebrov had studied with Shchyokin at the institute and was always running into him on the street. His friend had been disabled during the war and received a pension from the government. He had no family and led an incredibly frugal existence. He didn't drink, he didn't smoke, he ate in public cafeterias, and he always wore the same thin coat with the same checked scarf.

For some reason, whenever they ran into each other, Shchyokin would smile condescendingly at Rebrov and adopt a patronizing air. Yet Rebrov always enjoyed running into him. The very sight of this individual who had given up all attempts to get ahead in life was enough to improve one's mood. Usually they talked about women. Rebrov would ask whether Shchyokin had gotten married. Shchyokin would roar with laughter, "Are you kidding? Never!" There was always a ruddy glow on his cheeks, and his gold-filled teeth would sparkle. His girl friends were sales clerks, waitresses, dishwashers, shoe-repair and dry-cleaning attendants with whom he would spend a few scheduled hours each week. He would invite them up to his modest room, treat them to a modest supper and a bottle of wine—or sometimes simply to tea and sausage—and rejoice at his modest catch. But about the "catches" themselves they spoke only briefly as a rule, on the run. On this occasion Rebrov was too tired and depressed to feel like jesting, and with a sullen look at Shchyokin he asked from sheer force of habit, "Well how are things—have you gotten married yet?"

"Never! Not on your life!" replied Shchyokin, laughing heartily and giving Rebrov a friendly, if somewhat patronizing, slap on the shoulder. He was almost at the head of the cafeteria line—there being only three old ladies in front of him. Behind him stood some twenty people. Apparently they had been standing there a long time. They were frozen, and now, noticing Rebrov entering the line ahead of them, they became angrily alert. Rebrov was in fact hungry. He had had lunch around twelve and it was now after six.

"I hear that your wife's doing very well for herself," said Shchyokin. "Are you planning to buy a car?"

"Who told you about Lyalya?"

"Ah, all Moscow is talking about her..."

"Citizen, the line begins back here!" came a rasping voice from behind.

Shchyokin announced in a booming voice that Rebrov had been standing in line in front of him. The line swayed slightly forward, and someone shouted, "We didn't see him!" The atmosphere became charged and tense, but Rebrov didn't turn around. And when the door opened, he managed under false pretenses—as friend and protector of the disabled—to wedge himself inside behind the three old ladies. Over soup and a casserole Rebrov told Shchyokin his problems. He realized that he needed to confide in someone, and Shchyokin was a good listener. He would nod, inject some trite but sympathetic remark, and smile condescendingly.

Suddenly he said, "The trouble with you, old man, is that you've got too much pride! That's why you keep writing all these plays and stories...."

"What are you getting at?" Rebrov asked in

surprise.

"Your vanity has gotten the better of you. You're making all these efforts for nothing. As for me, I'm content to teach literature at night school, six hours a week. And how enjoyable it is: Fonvizin, Pushkin, Derzhavin. . . .* 'I'm a king—I'm a slave, I'm a worm, I am God!' If you want, I'll get you a job there. You can teach history. And they'll give you the certificate you need."

Rebrov shook his head. "No thanks. At least not for the time being."

"Well, okay, keep trying a little longer. But as I say, you're making all these efforts for nothing. Shall we have another helping of the fruit-juice dessert?"

Rebrov was too despondent to answer.

There was a certain naive but deadly accuracy in what his honest, well-meaning, and not very bright friend (for some reason Rebrov was convinced that Shchyokin was not very bright) had expressed so openly. Here it was, *truth* staring him in the face. And the specific criticisms of his plays made by Sergei Leonidovich were really quite beside the point. And actually, wouldn't it be better to take the easy way out? History courses at the night school. Six hours a week. A certificate, a job, a means of support. Shchyokin was hobbling toward him with two glasses of the dessert, and saying something about the brunette behind the counter, whose name was Rita and who came from a good family. "I could give you her phone number. Shall I give it to you?" But Rebrov was so buried in thought that although he heard the question, he didn't reply.

When they came out into the street, Shchyokin said, "Don't take it all so hard. Twenty years from now everything will be reversed. You and that director, Sergei Leonidovich, will have changed places—that I promise you." He began to laugh. "And I'll be the only one who's stayed in the same spot."

"Twenty years from now! Who needs that? I'll be an old man by then, almost as old as he...."

"That's just my point: you'll have changed places. And he'll no longer exist—almost in the same way that you don't exist now. Ha-ha."

"Thanks a lot, you've really cheered me up."

"Just don't be depressed, old man! Give me a call. And don't forget about the night school. There's also an opening for a club director in the First of May District. I could get you the job. You won't perish!"

And the playboy of the health-food cafeteria set moved on down Pushkin Street toward the subway. Rebrov set off in the opposite direction. Shchyokin's last words, seemingly so well-meant, had utterly disheartened him. It was hard to believe that he had spoken without malicious intent. "But of course he's right, the scoundrel—I don't exist...."

He wandered around for a long time, pondering the matter.

If he were suddenly to give up the ghost, who would mourn for his death? Who would even stop and take notice? Lyalya would mourn for him. She wouldn't have anyone else to feel sorry for. But in three months she would be introduced to some consumptive—a physicist and lover of symphonic music—or to some other splendid man—a surveyor and hard drinker. It wouldn't matter who or what he was—Irina Ignatievna would be happy all the same and would be sure to discover his good qualities. And one thing you could say about a consumptive or a hard drinker: they *did* exist.

Snow was beginning to fall, but it was still too early to go home. And now, drawn toward the inner ring of boulevards, he proceeded down Trubnaya Street and then over toward Sretensky Gate. He knew what was drawing him: their old house on Sretensky Boulevard. The "A" streetcar was making its slow ascent of the hill. The passengers with their winter-pale faces could be seen swaying back and forth inside its cozy, heated interior. Barely quickening his pace, Rebrov caught up to the streetcar and jumped on. Suddenly he remembered a similar moment which had occurred long ago. It had been winter, snow had been falling, and the trees stood skeleton-like on the ascending boulevard. And right here, in this very spot, where the dark brick wall of the ancient fortress rose on the right, he had jumped onto the streetcar, hitching a ride. Holding his school satchel in his left hand, he had walked briskly and precisely, trying to get in rhythm with the streetcar wheels. Then a valiant jump and—there he was, with his feet on the step and his right hand on the door rail. Thus it had been every day until that March, when one icy afternoon his foot had landed in empty space, his satchel had fallen, and some strong hand had grabbed him by the collar and dragged him onto the streetcar. At Sretensky Gate, which was the goal of his short, stolen ride—it was only one stop away!—he heard a shout and saw the figure of a man waving his arms as he came running downhill from Trubnaya Street. It was his father, and he was carrying the satchel which Rebrov had been planning to run back for. He came running up to him, white-faced and breathing heavily, and without saying a word, gave him such a slap in the face that Rebrov landed hard on the sidewalk. No sooner had he gotten up on his feet than his father hit him again, proclaiming in a frightening, hate-filled voice, "I saw you, you rascal, trying to sneak a ride!" And for a long time afterwards his father secretly kept an eye on him. Just like a real spy he would take cover behind a house on Rozhdestvensky Boulevard, waiting to see if Rebrov

would try to hitch a ride on the streetcar on his way
home from school. The trouble was that his father had
nothing better to do. He was no longer working by that
time and had become peevish and irritable, often picking quarrels with Rebrov's mother. But she felt sorry
for him, and whenever Rebrov would complain to her
that his father was spying on him and that the other
kids had noticed and were teasing him about it, she
would tell him not to pay any attention. "Let him do as
he pleases," his mother would say. "After all, he is suffering and there's nothing we can do to help him." Rebrov couldn't understand why his father, who was an
economist, couldn't find another job and stop suffering.
He was unaware that his father was already ill. At the
end of the summer he was taken to the hospital, never
to return. Rebrov's mother would go there to visit him,
but she never took Rebrov or his brother Volodka with
her. Once she returned from a visit in a cheerful mood,
saying that their father had recognized her. He had been
sitting up in bed, piecing together a quilt out of scraps,
and when she entered the ward, he had suddenly looked
up at her and said in his usual querulous tone, "Vera, we
have a lot of old scraps of cloth at home. Why didn't
you bring me any?" His mother had been so flustered
and overjoyed that she couldn't think of anything to
say, and she burst into tears. Later on, when the war
broke out, the hospital was evacuated to Kirov Province. Rebrov's father died of pneumonia at the beginning of 1942, but Rebrov didn't learn of his death until
two years later. His mother probably found out right
away, since she was in correspondence with the hospital.
She was living in Kuznetsk, where her plant had been
evacuated. Before her own death from a heart attack in
1943, she had written to Rebrov expressing her anxiety
over the fact that she had had no news from his brother

Volodka in almost a year. When Rebrov returned to
Moscow toward the end of the year, after his stay in the
military hospital, he began making inquiries. He wrote
to every place he could think of, but the answer was
always the same: we have no information on this individual. Later on, by putting two and two together—the
historical facts plus certain information supplied in
Volodka's last letters—Rebrov concluded that his brother's unit must have been trapped in the Nazi encircle-
ment of Kharkov in the summer of '42.

There it was, the two-storied house with its stone
columns and chipped lion faces. The best years of his
life—up to the sixth grade—had been spent here, on the
second floor, third and fourth windows from the right.
When his father had had to stop working, he couldn't
bear living here any more—he suffered from insomnia
and said that the street noise kept him from falling
asleep—and they had moved to quiet Bashilov Street,
which was almost in the suburbs. How Rebrov had protested at the time! How he hated having to leave his
school, his playmates, the boulevard, the Clear Ponds
skating rink, and the stamp shop on Kuznetsky Bridge
Street where he and his friends would run after school
and where, in the covered passageway next to the shop,
vicious fights would take place! On one occasion his
mother had given him six rubles to buy the French
colonial series, and no sooner had he happily emerged
from the shop than someone pushed him into the passageway. Three boys began twisting his arm and trying
to grab his newly acquired stamps. He fought back desperately and finally managed to break loose. He went
running off down the street, and only when he had
reached the subway did he notice that the whole front
of his new spring coat was hanging in shreds. It had been
slashed with a razor. But his pride in having fought them

off and having saved his precious stamps far outweighed his minor annoyance. After all, what was a mere coat?...

The snow was coming down harder now, covering everything in sight: the snack bar, from whose slamming doors warm air would escape, the sidewalk, the people trudging along it, their caps, their faces, and his own memories—memories of himself as a little boy in a black sheepskin coat, which was first too long and then too short. Four people have lived behind those windows on the second floor, and Rebrov was the only one of them who remained. And here he was, standing and looking into his prewar past.... Where had they disappeared to? They were neither here nor there—nowhere. This was the way it had turned out. He was their only representative on earth, where the snow was now falling and the trolley buses crawled along with their headlights turned on....

Later that evening Lyalya asked, "Why did you show up drunk today?"

"Where did I show up drunk?"

"Bob told me. He said that you came in completely smashed and started demanding a discussion of your plays—and that you wanted some sort of certificate. But you do know, don't you, that Bob is going through a terribly rough time?"

Rebrov waved his hand. Yes, he knew, but he didn't have the strength to discuss it. All he said was, "You can thank Smolyanov for that!"

They got into bed and Rebrov told her that he had walked to his old house on the boulevard today. Rebrov's prewar life always intrigued Lyalya, and she loved to ask him about his father and about the times when he was very little—before the seventh grade, when the two of them had first met. And now she lay very still beside him and listened. He was telling her how a long time ago, around 1939, his father had bought two children's wicker chairs and attached them to the rear of his and their mother's bicycles. On Sundays the four of them would go riding together, with Rebrov and Volodya seated in their chairs in the rear. Somewhere there was a photograph of this; he'd have to find it. Lyalya's hand touched his hair and forehead in the dark and began to caress him. He took her hand and pressed it to his lips. He told her that someone had offered him a job today—to teach history in a night school for adults. He could also get a job as director of some club in the First of May District. Lyalya caressed his face without saying a word, and he went on to mention still another proposal. He could bring his two plays to a certain individual who had connections and would be able to help him. He'd probably have to make this person a co-author, but that would be better than standing still and getting nowhere as he was now. Still, he hated to do it.

"And you don't have to," Lyalya whispered and began kissing him. "You don't have to, my sweet. You don't have to, my love. Don't think about any of these things. Everything's going to turn out all right for us. We'll get that certificate and you'll be able to work undisturbed. You're going to get everything that's coming to you. After all, you're talented, so please, don't give up. Who was the idiot who offered you the club director job?"

He lay perfectly still. He was listening, drinking in her every word—her sweet, whispered murmurings which enveloped him like some ethereal mist.

"You know what I think?" she whispered. "That I'm...you understand?"

"Really?"

"Yes, I think I am.... And this time I want to have it."

His heart was pounding, and all his strength seemed
to return. Joy and fear, both mixed together. Equal portions of good fortune and bad—yes, that was all that one
needed in life. And this warm, beloved being beside
him was the only proof he needed of the fact: I exist.

And at that moment, as often happens in dreams,
he was struck by a truth which seemed age-old and self-
evident: it was not *cogito ergo sum,* but *amo ergo sum.*
And that was all one needed to know. Why was it that
people didn't guess this? Why did they refuse to realize
it? After all, it was terribly obvious. "And I exist too!
I exist in spite of you all," he thought with a fierce and
angry tenderness, not feeling anything but the taste of
love on his lips and a great surge of strength.

At about eleven the next morning two men arrived
from the telephone service center and began checking to
see from what point they could hook up a telephone
line to the house. No one had requested them and everyone thought they must have come by mistake, but the
workers showed them their order slip, which indicated
the name L. P. Telepneva and bore the signature of the
head of the service center. At this point Lyalya realized
what had happened and said, "Oh, I know what this is!"
She was obviously embarrassed, however, and didn't
seem very happy about it. When Rebrov demanded an
explanation, Lyalya told him that the theater management had been trying for a long time to get her a phone,
since it was inconvenient for them to have to send a car
around every time they wanted to relay some message.
But nothing had come of their efforts—there was no
underground cable nearby, and it was expensive to hook
up a special above-ground line. Now it must be that
Smolyanov had interceded with the telephone people.
He had connections there too.

"What a wonderful surprise, Lyalechka!" Irina Ignatievna exclaimed joyfully. "Please thank Nikolai Demianovich for us and tell him how grateful we are. And you can tell him he's a wonderful man, an absolute dear..."

"Mama, I don't like getting favors from people."

"Don't be silly, Lyalya! And how can you talk about getting favors when all of our friends and relatives have had phones for ages! Why, you'd think we were living in some backward village...."

There was something in all of this sudden fuss, in Lyalya's discomfort and her mother's excessive rejoicing, that put Rebrov on his guard. Though damn it all, a telephone—that really was something! He had never had a phone in his life before, not in their Sretensky Boulevard apartment nor on Bashilov Street. Still, there was something strange in Lyalya's embarrassment over the matter—as if she were stumbling on a perfectly even surface.

The car from the theater arrived shortly afterwards and Lyalya left in it. Within an hour his mother-in-law had managed to call Uncle Kolya, Aunt Zhenya, Uncle Misha, and all the remaining horde of relatives in order to report their new telephone number and the latest news regarding Pyotr Alexandrovich, who was to be released from the hospital in another week.

Two days later, as Rebrov was returning from the subway station and had almost reached the Telepnevs' yellow fence, he saw something that took him completely by surprise. The policeman Kurtov and his own Bashilov Street neighbor Kanunov were standing and conversing by Kurtov's gate. Kanunov, who was dressed in a long, black coat and stood with his back half turned away from Rebrov, pretended that he hadn't seen him. Rebrov likewise pretended that he hadn't recognized

Kanunov, though he had walked right past him and they had almost touched shoulders.

It was a nasty experience, and so unexpected that it left Rebrov feeling weak in the knees. Nor could there be anything pleasant about discovering that someone was trying to dig out the ground from beneath him. Here he was, just leading a normal life, going about his business, while this someone was snooping around, thrusting his nose where it didn't belong. "Well, I'm in for it now!" thought Rebrov. And as he reached his own gate, he involuntarily burst out laughing. Glancing back, he saw that the policeman and Kanunov were watching him.

VI

Smolyanov's lucky star, which had risen sharply over the last four years, suddenly slowed in its course. Actually, nothing so terrible had happened in his professional life, there had been no catastrophes, but he had lost momentum—which might be taken as a bad sign. And however much Nikolai Demianovich tried to persuade himself that even the best soccer team—the Red Army team, for example—occasionally loses points and that it's impossible not to make some mistakes or to suffer some losses, still he lacked the wisdom and self-restraint to wait things out. Instead of proceeding coolly forward, without reacting to the groans and insults from the sidelines, he let himself be provoked and ended up behaving in scandalous fashion. Somewhere on the theater stairs, right out in public, he began answering Sergei Leonidovich's shouts and rude remarks in kind. He shook his finger and threatened him, and he called the former literary consultant Marevin a two-faced hypocrite, and, like a fool, completely exposed himself. His nerves simply gave out on him—which was perhaps understandable since that January he had been beset by one misfortune after another. In Saratov his mother had suffered a paralytic stroke and lost the use of her legs and her powers of speech. Now he didn't know what to do with his little girl or where he was going to place her. For the time being he had hired an old lady to look after her, one of his mother's neighbors. Ten days later his wife Marta had pulled a stunt of her own and had tried to jump out of the window of their new, sixth-floor apartment. His sister-in-law Frosya had seen what she was up to and had pulled her down from the windowsill. This was the second such attempt, the first having been in October, in their old apartment. Naturally he had to report his wife's attempted suicide, and she was taken off to the Kashchenko psychiatric hospital. He didn't tell a soul about his troubles, especially anyone in the theater. What would be the point? No one was going to feel sorry for him, and they might even try to make things worse for him.

As a result of all this Nikolai Demianovich was in the worst possible mood, and to add insult to injury, Liudmila had been avoiding him for the last two weeks. Whenever they ran into each other in the theater, she would return his "hello" with a cold nod and walk right past him. There were moments when he thought about starting things up between them again, but well, to hell with her and her hurt feelings! He didn't know for sure, but he could guess the reason for her resentment. Apparently she had decided that he had tried to set her up with Alexander Vasilievich. It was true that Alexander Vasilievich had requested this, even demanded it, and there had been no way that he could refuse. But if only she knew, the little fool, how he had suffered because of her, what nightmares he had lived through in his imagination, and how he had counted on her independence of character, which had so often irritated him in the past. He hadn't slept a wink that whole night and had been tormented by fantasies and hallucinations. One moment he had imagined that Alexander Vasilievich was yelling at him and pounding his fists on the table, looking right through him as he knew how to do. Then at another moment he had pictured Liudmila together with Alexander Vasilievich in some insufferable pose and sticking her tongue out at him, Nikolai Demianovich. Yet despite all this he had believed with all his heart, with his very bones and marrow, that no, no, a hundred times no, not for anything in this world! He was almost one hundred percent sure and would have bet a thousand rubles to one that Alexander Vasilievich wouldn't get a thing from her. My God, no, not on your life! Not in this case. And when Alexander Vasilievich had telephoned him the next morning, his deep bass voice had sounded angry as the devil—so angry, in fact, that it was impossible to understand what he was saying. Nikolai Demianovich had jumped for joy right then and there by the phone. "Oh, dear, you poor man! Heartburn, you say, and shortness of breath—well, I *am* sorry," he mumbled sympathetically, while at the same time making comic faces at himself in the mirror.

He had gotten used to Liudmila, had become attached to her—there was no denying it. And so quickly too! True, she wore him out, irritated him with her hurt feelings, and sometimes alienated him with her foolish Grishenka and with her whims and arbitrariness. What a fuss she had made about Marevin! And how foolishly she went on defending the old man! Sometimes she drove him to the point where he felt like breaking with her for good. After all, did she think that she was the only desirable woman around? There were others even more desirable, and as a matter of fact he had endless opportunities—all he had to do was beckon. Yet although he had been introduced to all sorts of women and had taken them here and there—to his dacha, or to Khimki, or to visit friends—still, after an hour or so he would feel bored and depressed. For these new acquaintances were empty and shallow; all they wanted was fun and good times. And he had known more than enough of such people. His own life had been difficult, and he was not the easiest man to get along with. It was not every woman who could understand him.

But Liudmila did understand him. Altogether she was extraordinary: she never asked him for anything, never abused him, and never took any money from him. He had offered her some two or three times, but she had flatly refused it, telling him that he ought to be ashamed of himself. This pleased him, not because he would have begrudged the money, but because she was such a wonderful woman and—she loved him. His total expenditures had amounted to 380 rubles—for the rubber-soled shoes that he had bought her a long time ago. Well, of course there had been their evenings out, but these went without saying.

Nikolai Demianovich tried to be patient, to wait things out. But he grew tired of waiting, and one day when he didn't have the strength to wait any longer, he stopped her in the corridor, and taking her hand, he said, "You know, Liudmila, something terrible has happened."

She looked up at him. "What is it?"

"My mother's had a stroke. She's in the hospital, and I don't know what I'm going to do with Galka...."

Whether out of concern or out of pity, Liudmila's

eyes gleamed with their old, familiar kindness. "You should bring Galochka here to Moscow. It'll be the end of your mother if she starts worrying about..."

"Things are bad here in Moscow too. Marta has...."

He gave her a brief account of all that had happened. Things seemed to be pressing in on him from every side. There was a fullscale war going on at the theater, and that swine Marevin had turned both actors and critics against him—thank God they had at least gotten rid of him! At home he was barely keeping his head above water. And those whom he felt close to were turning away from him, not giving any comfort or assistance.

"I feel sorry for Marta, terribly sorry for her. She's only thirty-eight, not even middle-aged, and yet her central nervous system is utterly shattered. She's going to have to undergo treatment for at least a year, and no one knows what the results will be. It's terribly sad. And she was such an excellent teacher—she taught gymnastics in an elementary school. What happens is that she has periods of insane raving, and it seems that she's obsessed by certain ideas. It was terrible, the way she used to behave with Frosya—screaming and attacking her with her fists—well, you already know about that. And now it turns out that she's been mentally ill all along, and there's nothing one can do about it. It's just so sad...."

As Nikolai Demianovich quietly droned on, he noticed that Lyalya's dear face grew pale and her eyes filled with tears. Suddenly it occurred to her to ask, "Is there anything I can do to help?"

He nodded. "Come home with me right now!"

But then he stopped to consider. Frosya might disapprove and the plates would start flying. Oh well, to hell with her. He could send her off somewhere—to

333

his dacha in Tarasovka. Ah, but the dacha would have to be heated—it hadn't been heated in months.

"Where's the nearest phone? I'll just make a call and then we'll leave."

"No...we won't."

They had left the corridor and were standing next to the window on the broad staircase landing. One could see the courtyard below with its patches of muddy ground and trampled snow. The executive director's car was parked by the entrance to the car repair shop with its hood up. Next to the brick wall between the theater and the building next door hulked some stage sets completely covered with snow.

"I must remember to stop off at the repair shop and have my battery checked," thought Nikolai Demianovich.

"It's all over between us, Nikolai Demianovich," he heard Lyalya's voice. "I've made up my mind."

"Why?"

"Just because...."

A door slammed below, and someone started heavily up the stairs, wheezing and panting. Liudmila broke off in midsentence. The old man, one of the theater's retired actors, greeted them, and Liudmila returned his greeting. Then, when he had passed through the door leading into the corridor, she repeated more firmly:

"Just because!"

"Couldn't you have found a better time?"

"I didn't know about your misfortunes."

"But you know now."

"Yes, and I do sympathize...." She stopped for a moment. "But that doesn't change anything."

Her eyes were distant and cold. "I thought you were...but you see, you're not what I thought you were! I'm used to weak men.... I thought at first that you needed me too...."

"And what is it you see in weak men?"

"At least they don't do despicable things, they don't go around hurting people."

"You don't think so? Of course they do!"

"No, they don't have it in them."

"You're wrong! You don't know what you're talking about, you're simply talking nonsense," he muttered, feeling an unpleasant agitation, a sort of feverish chill, pass through his body. "Well, and what have I done, for example, to hurt anybody? Whom have I killed or strangled?"

"You'd be up to killing or strangling anybody, if the situation required it. You've already strangled Bob, and now it's Sergei Leonidovich's turn—I can see what you're...."

"Well, what of it? You see correctly. But my role in all of this is really beside the point. His day is past, do you understand? He's made a mess of things, he's not up to the job—he's fallen hopelessly behind."

Lyalya burst out laughing. "Behind whom? Behind you, I suppose."

"Behind the *times,* my dear!"

"Oh, my God..." she continued to laugh.

Suddenly he realized that the feverish chill that had gripped him was fear—fear because the end had come. He could see it.

"Well, if that's the way you feel, why did you play along in the first place?"

"I didn't realize, Nikolai Demianovich, I really didn't. I'm just a stupid female—what more can I say? If I'm guilty, then punish me. Grisha's not a strong person; actually, he's a rather weak person, and without me he'd never make it.... Still, he would never do anything despicable...."

335

"You're wrong, completely wrong, you're just talking nonsense," he repeated in a barely audible, birdlike voice, not having the strength to speak any louder. "Your Grisha is an ordinary man, just like me. Do you think he doesn't know what's been going on between us? Of course he knows, but he puts up with it."

"He doesn't know."

"He does so, he knows perfectly well, only he has more brains than character."

"He doesn't know."

"He does so, he knows perfectly well, only he has more brains than character."

"He doesn't know!" Lyalya suddenly shouted, her eyes flashing so angrily that Nikolai Demianovich recoiled.

"You're wrong," he whispered despairingly, then watched as she nodded, made a parting gesture with her hand, turned, and walked away.

Two days later Kostka Shakhov brought this very same Grisha to Nikolai Demianovich's apartment. As Grisha began showing him his precious scribblings in their frayed, string-wrapped folders, he seemed terribly tense and kept repeating in the wrong places, "You see, the point here is that...." Nikolai Demianovich looked at him with a certain sad amazement and thought: "What *is* it she sees in him? And how did all this come about?" Grisha had a scared, dumbfounded look on his face and started babbling incomprehensibly about some sort of certificate for the housing administration. Kostka in the meantime was thoroughly enjoying himself as he sat at the small magazine table, impudently downing one brandy after another in anticipation of his commission. Nikolai Demianovich had asked Kostka to keep Grisha in the dark as long as possible, not letting him

know to whom he was being taken until today, when
Kostka had arranged to meet him at the subway stop
nearest to Nikolai Demianovich's apartment. And even
when Kostka had told him their destination, Grisha
had not protested or cried out in indignation, "Ah, so
that's the story!" Nor had he gone running back into
the subway. No, he had come along as nice as you
please, and now here he was, sitting decorously on the
sofa with his legs crossed, a cigarette in his mouth, and
looking for all the world like a worthy, honorable man.
Was it possible that he hadn't guessed? Good God, no!
He knew, the dog. Of course he knew. Liudmila had
told Nikolai Demianovich how Grisha had stumbled
upon the shirt which she had bought for his, Nikolai
Demianovich's, brithday and which she had left in their
bureau. Grisha had asked her about it at the time, and
she extricated herself by saying that it was a collective
gift for one of the musicians in the theater orchestra.
Nikolai Demianovich had put on this shirt today and
purposely let it be seen from under his lounging robe.
And Grisha must have noticed the shirt right away,
though he didn't say a word or even ask about it; instead he merely stared at it. In the meantime they had
discussed everything there was to discuss, including the
critics and the theater's artistic director, who should
have retired long ago and allowed someone else to take
over. But of course Sergei Leonidovich didn't want to
retire and was kicking and thrashing in protest. And in
this connection Nikolai Demianovich suggested that
something ought to be done about the situation: someone ought to get up at a meeting and tell about the disgraceful things that were going on and about how young
authors were being held back: "You could even bring up
the matter yourself, Grigory Fyodorovich."
    All the while Grisha's eyes had remained glued on

the shirt. He was obviously beside himself, and finally
when he could stand it no longer, he asked, "Tell me,
Nikolai Demianovich, where did you buy that shirt?"

"Oh, this one? Liudmila Petrovna gave it to me."

"Ah!" said Grisha.

And that was all. Apparently it was true that weak
men never made a fuss. They didn't punch you in the
face or even cry out, "Wha-at?! What's going on here?!"
And in fact, the two men parted on peaceful terms, with
the understanding that Nikolai Demianovich would
look over the manuscripts, think about them, and let
him know in three or four days.

"You have a phone now, I know, I know," he said
with a benignly superior smile and an amiable wave of
the hand as he accompanied Grisha to the door.

He read through the compositions in the worn
folders that very day and consulted with various people
about them. Then Kostka gave them to Levka and Alinka to read. Nikolai Demianovich always listened to
what Lev's wife Alinka had to say. She was a smart
woman—with a degree in sciences. Alinka said that the
stuff wasn't badly written, but that it could have been
put together with a lot more imagination. If one just
shifted things around a bit and served it up in a different
way, they might just have something. But there was no
reason for both names to appear on the title page. Anyone would be happy, of course, to be a co-author with
Smolyanov, but Rebrov—who was he? How would you
package him? "You'd package him," thought Smolyanov and even burst out laughing, "together with his
wife. He and his wife come in one package!" Well, it's
just a joke, nothing to get upset about. Don't worry, my
dear, we're going to help you, but not because of your
beautiful eyes and not because of what was, but because
of what *still is to be.* And here Nikolai Demianovich

was overtaken by a compelling image: imagine a small bird suddenly flying onto your porch on a summer evening. If you shut the porch door and all the windows, the bird will beat its wings against the glass— flap! flap! flap!—until it finally becomes so exhausted that it falls to the floor and you're able to pick it up in the palm of your hand.

Nikolai Demianovich pictured the whole scene very clearly, and his mouth even went dry as it usually did whenever he thought about a woman. About five days later, having settled some other business matters, he called Liudmila's number and asked to speak to Grigory Fyodorovich. A woman's voice replied that Grigory Fyodorovich didn't live there anymore.

VII

Lying on his wooden upper berth, Rebrov had been tormenting himself for the past three days, endlessly turning everything over in his own mind. On a sheet of paper he had written the words: hill—hall— hole—mole—mope—dope—dupe.... This saving diversion had been handed to him by the man in the opposite berth, a certain Modest Petrovich, as soon as they had left the outskirts of Moscow behind them and plunged into the deep snow and dark picket fences of country dachas. Whenever Rebrov put down his piece of paper and stopped mumbling "loop—lop—loss—moss," his gaze would fix on the ceiling or slip down to the dull whiteness that lay beyond the window (it was the beginning of March, but winter and its snowdrifts still reigned supreme) and he would hear the voices and see the faces which he was tearing himself away from forever, as he flew off into the unknown. Pyotr Alexandrovich

Yury Trifonov

would smile with his withered, yellowed lips, "You know best, Grisha. Do as you think best...."

The old man was indifferent to everything. Even the garden, which had once been his whole life, no longer excited him. For days at a time he would sit in his chair by the window, listening to the radio, or dozing, or reading *The Light*. And frozen on his face would be a smile of indifference to everything that was unrelated to his sickness—that is, to death. He spoke only about the state of his health, about his medicines, his doctors and nurses. One of the nurses was good with the needle and spoke to him in a pleasant manner; the other was rather morose and inserted the needle painfully, not always finding the vein on the first try. He hated this woman and called her "the jabber." "How a man's whole personality can change!" Rebrov had reflected in amazement, not yet knowing that *his own garden,* which had once been his whole life too, would soon be abandoned—and abandoned forever.

"My advice, Grisha, is not to pay any attention. Just forget about it, forget about it! Oh, my God...." The old man gave several faint gasps—not out of any onrush of feeling for Rebrov, but because he was overtaken once again by thoughts of his illness. "You don't know women...they're made differently from us. Irina, for example, can never understand that when she opens the door to the kitchen...." Suddenly he went on to ask in a whisper, "But why did you go to see Smolyanov?"

"What difference does that make?" Rebrov exclaimed with irritation. "I felt I had to, so I went."

Of course his going there had been a stupid move. No, actually, a cowardly one. He had suddenly been overwhelmed by fear and desperation—a feeling that he had to do something right away, had to earn a lot of money so that they could start their family and have a

340

place of their own. No, that wasn't it; probably the main reason for his going there had been some sort of base, masochistic urge to satisfy his curiosity, to subject himself to a particularly humiliating experience. For after all, he had long since guessed that Smolyanov was the "certain person" Shakhov had in mind, the "certain person" who would be able to help him.

For two whole days after this nauseating visit Rebrov had not asked Lyalya for any explanation. He had not wanted to believe any of Smolyanov's insinuations or to get to the bottom of them. For what would the point be? This wasn't the sort of thing that could be proved. The fact that she had given him the shirt as a present and that he had smiled insolently when telling about it didn't necessarily mean a thing, especially since he was such an insolent brute to begin with. Three days after their meeting, however, the situation changed. That morning Rebrov accidentally came across one of Irina Ignatievna's epistles to Lyalya on the floor of their attic room. Rebrov had gotten used to these compositions written on the pages of school notebooks and sometimes placed in an envelope, sometimes not. The fact was that his mother-in-law became a graphomaniac whenever she quarreled with her daughter. And Lyalya, with her usual negligence, would leave her mother's epistles lying all over the place—so that you couldn't help but pick them up and start reading them. Obviously something had happened between the two women— they hardly spoke to each other—but Rebrov hadn't asked what it was all about. One thing he knew: it had begun with them, but it would end up involving him. For Lyalya couldn't endure long quarrels with her mother. Still, he shouldn't have picked up that letter. He should have said the hell with it!

Characteristically, the letter was written in the

most avant-garde prose, like something from Dos Passos,
without periods or commas: "You're a fool a real fool
life doesn't seem to have taught you anything you're
a complete idiot why do you need this? Just remember
I'm not going to take care of it so don't count on me I
don't have the strength it's enough for me to try to get
your father back on his feet you work like a mule for
him running around all over the place now with a baby
in addition you'll be completely tied down you'll get
old very soon you'll be a wreck like Aunt Zhenya's
Mayka she's completely lost her looks her children have
worn her out and yet you have talent but you're such a
fool you're willing to waste it children don't bring joy
only grief and disappointment there's a lot you don't
understand you're as naive as a child he exploits you
like nobody's business he sits around the National
eating and drinking at your expense while you're out
working like a horse if he were a real husband to you I
wouldn't be so upset Nikolai Demianovich was courting
you but you've rejected him—and for what? If you
don't call in Alexei Ivanovich I won't have anything to
do with you you two can do as you please just don't
count on your father and me you can start paying half
of the ground rent and house taxes and your share of
the utilities the telephone will be your expense we don't
need it you can eat out I refuse to cook for you And I
want the 240 rubles back that I lent you for the fur
coat...."

In all this semidelirious rambling Rebrov was
struck by one sentence: "Nikolai Demianovich was
courting you but you've rejected him." That evening
he could stand it no longer and asked Lyalya, "Well,
what's the story, are you going to call in Alexei Ivanovich or not?"

Alexei Ivanovich was an elderly gynecologist who

had once been Irina Ignatievna's doctor and who had performed two abortions on Lyalya in the past. Rebrov could see that Lyalya was tense and worn out from her mother's hostility—this being the fourth day that her mother had given her the silent treatment. The situation would have resolved itself somehow, so he should have kept his mouth shut—but he lost his self-control. One word provoked another, and this seemed to be all that was needed for the volcano to erupt. Lyalya and her mother started accusing each other, and her mother, as always, proved to be the stronger of the two. Lyalya burst into tears and suddenly began to feel faint. They gave her some medicine, and her mother, now thoroughly frightened, began babbling as she sprinkled Lyalya's face with cold water, "Dear child, I won't leave you." An awkward silence followed, and after a while the two women went off to their separate rooms. Rebrov was left alone with Pyotr Alexandrovich, who had stood there throughout, leaning on his cane and not saying a word.

"Grisha, I want to tell you something," the old man suddenly began as he slowly walked up to Rebrov. "It's all the same to me.... You'll be taking off tomorrow and I'll be dead the day after tomorrow. So it doesn't make any difference to me. But fifteen, maybe sixteen years ago there was this Valentin...." He glanced around and then went on in a whisper, "Valentin Ivanovich Skobov. He was foreman of the forge in our factory —a good man. A very good man, quite impressive in fact. We used to go fishing together, visit each other, do this and that together. And suddenly I sense that there's some sort of hanky-panky going on between him and Irina—the woman was pining away, falling in love, you understand...."

Rebrov smiled, "If...."

"Well, maybe it wasn't love, I don't know. Who knows what it was, call it anything you like. But the point is that there came a moment when I thought I'd leave her. I'd definitely leave her. I'd take little Lyalya with me and simply leave town...."

"Well, what happened?"

"Nothing happened. I was just being foolish, don't you see? Such foolishness doesn't last, whereas life goes on for a long time."

"No," said Rebrov. "This is a different situation. I'd be happy to...but I can't. I can't because...." And without finishing his sentence, he gestured despairingly and ran off upstairs.

He left the next day. And leaving, he realized that this was not at all like the other times when he had rushed off with hurt feelings to Bashilov Street. It was a sunny winter day and the sky was clear, bright blue. The old man sat with a smile on his face, looking out the window at the blinding snow. He bit his lips and said, "Do as you think best, Grisha..."

Three nights later Lyalya arrived with her suitcases —to move in with him. She had broken off with her mother for good. Couldn't he forgive her and trust her? After all, how could he treat a person this way—without pity or compassion? He was dying to understand and to forgive her. But still—how had it happened? Crying and repentant, Lyalya told him something so shameful, so base that he couldn't bear to listen. Yes, yes, she said, somewhere deep inside and perhaps only half-consciously she had probably wanted to further her career. Rebrov felt like shouting, "My God, how can you slander yourself this way? That couldn't have been the reason!" It could, it could so. She refused to yield on this point. He hoped that she would, but no, that was the way it was. And this truth, this whole, *naked truth* was wilder than the wildest, most naked passion. And now he began pressing her, wearing her down and forcing her to tell him everything: about this man and that, about all of her old loves. And when she had told him everything down to the last detail, including this last, pathetic truth, it was as if they both had gone mad. Looking back on it, he could see that that night had been the end. But they hadn't realized it at the time, imagining only that this was an opportunity to begin anew.

The next day, however, when Lyalya went off to the theater and Rebrov was left alone in his room, he felt so empty and depressed that it occurred to him that perhaps he should just drop her a note in the mailbox and take off for some faraway place. A little later the same day, Shakhov arrived and said that Smolyanov had long been expecting him. Rebrov replied that he wasn't interested. Then one evening a few days later, Smolyanov himself appeared, bringing with him Rebrov's folders, a bottle of brandy, and a cake for Lyalya: "If the mountain doesn't come to Mohammed...."

He reported that he had found Rebrov a job at the theater as chief literary counsultant in place of Marevin. He had reached an agreement with the executive director and with the central theater administration as well. Lyalya was in a performance that evening, and Rebrov felt ashamed of his cramped, messy room, of Kanunov's crying children who could be heard from the other side of the wall, and of his own slovenly appearance—dressed as he was in slippers and an old pair of pyjamas. He vaguely sensed that what he ought to do at this moment was either to punch Smolyanov in the face or else go to the director's office and accept the job. He was deterred from the former by the thought that the man had, after all, come with good intentions and was trying to help him. So why should he suddenly start punching him in the face? He did refuse the brandy, however. Of course there was still the problem of the certificate, since Kanunov kept pressing the matter, but he felt a certain strange lack of urgency in all of this, as if it were happening in a dream. And even his feelings of shame seemed to be part of this dream, as did his sense of surprise.

"Why hasn't Lyalya said anything about this?"

"She doesn't know about it. So far I've discussed the matter only with the executive director and with Herman Vladimirovich.... Herman Vladimirovich, as you may already know, is probably going to be the new artistic director.... Sergei Leonidovich was taken off to the hospital yesterday. He's had a heart attack, apparently a very serious one. But then, what can you expect? He's been pushing himself too hard.... The salary is 1,500 a month; you won't have to be at the theater until one, and there'll be some days when you won't have to come in at all...."

For the past several days Rebrov had had the distinct feeling that something inside him had changed irrevocably. This change had taken place back then, just before his departure, and was of such magnitude that it seemed to him that he had become an altogether different person, with a different blood type and a different chemical makeup. And this different person—this new self—had the right to behave differently from his old self, just as his old self did not have to be held responsible for the acts of his new self. In response to Smolyanov's job offer Rebrov said that he would have to discuss the matter with Lyalya.

"What's there to discuss?" laughed Smolyanov.

But he never did have a chance to discuss it with her. Lyalya fell ill that very day and stayed in bed at her mother's where he subsequently went to visit her. Two

days later they sent for him by telegram and when he
arrived he was told that Alexei Ivanovich had come and
gone and that everything had been taken care of. Lyalya
was still weak and confined to her bed, but there was a
bright, happy, and as it seemed to Rebrov, guilty look
in her eyes. The old Rebrov felt like rushing to her and
pressing his forehead to her white hand, for the happiness which shone in her moist eyes was that of suffering
overcome. But the new Rebrov said in a calm voice,
"How do you feel? I'm glad that it's all over with."

His mother-in-law smiled at him in conciliatory
fashion and whispered, "Just don't upset her now, all
right? And Grishenka, would you please run to the market and buy her some fruit?"

"She'll be in her power forever—until one of them
dies," Rebrov thought to himself. An hour later, when
he returned from the market, Lyalya was asleep, and
Rebrov went back to Bashilov Street.

The following day, Friday, Shakhov came to see
him. They went out to a restaurant for dinner and from
there hailed a cab to take them to the theater. They had
drunk so much that Rebrov's legs would barely move,
but his mind was working clearly. There's nothing
worse, he thought, than a long goodbye. At Mayakovsky Square he ordered the driver to stop. Then he
opened the door and put Shakhov out on the sidewalk.
He was experiencing a fantastic sensation of lightness—
something both delightful and absurd. If he hadn't been
afraid of making a fool of himself, he would have taken
off from the ground and winged his way above the
buildings. The train was leaving at 9 p.m. Right now
Lyalya was probably wandering around her room in
her bathrobe, having an evening snack, and here he
was flying off without saying goodbye, soaring through
the winter sky above the rooftops, vanishing without

347

Yury Trifonov

a trace.

Modest Petrovich swung his gray, wool-clad feet
over the edge of the berth, and dangling them above the
man sleeping below, he asked, "So, Grigory, my boy,
have you just finished college?"

"No, dear fellow. I'm almost thirty, thank God,"
said Rebrov. "I've just finished life."

"Ah, so that's it...."

Modest Petrovich burst out laughing. Outside the
window the sky had already turned a deep, bluish black,
and someone switched on the lights. One life had
finished and the other was just beginning. Actually,
every man, including even this prospecting geologist
Modest Petrovich, lives not one but several lives. He dies
and is born anew; he is present at his own funeral and
watches his own rebirth as once again life slowly starts
up with all its new hopes. After one's death one can
look back on one's past life, and this is what Rebrov
was doing now, as the train carried him eastward
through the ever deeper snows and harsher frosts.

On the morning of the fifth day there was a loud
commotion in the corridor outside their compartment.
In a strange voice which boded no good, a woman was
wailing loudly, "Oh-oh-oh-oh!" Their compartment
door burst open and a red, crumpled, jellylike face
thrust itself forward and gasped, "He died...at 5 a.m...."
Rebrov stepped out into the corridor. In one of the
compartments sobs could be heard, while in another the
door was wide open and people were playing cards. One
individual was running along the corridor with an enormous Chinese thermos in his hand, pushing his way
through the rapidly assembling crowd. Rebrov returned
to the compartment and climbed up onto his berth.

Unable to fight back the tears, he turned toward the wall, and with his face buried in his pillowcase, now dampened by his tears, he thought about the life which he had led so far and wondered what it had all added up to.

"But the real question," he muttered through clenched teeth, "is will I have another one...."

A week later Rebrov witnessed the following scene from the window of his hotel room on Great Siberia Street, where he was awaiting a visit from the local Party leader. A fight had started on the pavement below. One man had stabbed two others in the stomach and taken to his heels. Several bystanders had run after him, knocked him down, and were now starting to beat him. Three people had grabbed him initially: a worker in white, flour-covered overalls (he had been unloading flour sacks from a truck on the corner), a soldier who happened to be passing by, and a woman. By the time Rebrov managed to run downstairs, however, a crowd had already gathered around the assailant. One of the men he had stabbed was lying on the pavement, groaning, while the other was still reeling on his two feet, half doubled over, and clutching his stomach. Several people kept raising the assailant up to a sitting position and then bashing his head down on the pavement. They were trying to finish him off in a hurry, before the police arrived. Five minutes later a police car came rolling up. The crowd made way, and the assailant remained lying on the pavement, his face lifeless and as black and grimy as the sole of a shoe. It was clear that justice had already been done. The two policemen picked him up, and holding him under the arms, began dragging him to the open rear door of the police car. Suddenly, however, the assailant straightened his cap, pulled it tighter on his small, childlike head, and climbed into the car on his own two feet.

Rebrov went back into the hotel and up to the second floor. How easy it is to kill a man, he thought. And how impossibly difficult. The Party leader Balashov arrived soon afterwards. He was a native of Tomsk and a nice fellow. By now the pavement below was deserted and all that remained was a powdering of white in the spot where they had been unloading the flour sacks from the truck. Balashov was informing him of the latest employment opportunities. There were office jobs available in the city through the middle of April, then from the twentieth it would be off to the taiga for five months. And on his way back from the taiga, Rebrov decided, he would be able to stop off in Petrovsk-Zabaikalsky, formerly the site of the Petrovsky Ironworks, where Ivan Pryzhov had died in exile, yet managed to keep "one leg kicking" up to the very end. Rebrov wanted to see what the place looked like and what changes had been wrought by the passage of time.

Lyalya sometimes took a trolley-bus to a quick-service dry cleaners on Karbyshev Boulevard, and as she rode past the eight-story building with the butcher shop on the first floor, she would suddenly recall something from her old life of eighteen years before: Grisha, the theater, the old director Sergei Leonidovich, the scent of lilacs in the springtime, or their dog Kandidka, clanking her chain along the fence. And whenever she thought of these things, her heart would momentarily and painfully contract, and she would feel a strange mixture of joy and sadness that all of this had once been part of her life. Sometimes, however, she would ride past the building with the butcher shop without feeling a thing—so preoccupied was she with her present cares and concerns. And of these she had more than enough. There was her husband and her eighth-grade son to think of, and all sorts of complications at work: the Director of the House of Culture would load her down with all sorts of extra tasks because she was as strong as a horse and would take everything on herself. Then there were her local trade-union committee obligations and, in addition, her activities with the physical education group at Dynamo Stadium, where she jogged on Saturdays with other middle-aged colonels' wives. Lyalya's husband was a military man, a university graduate, who taught at the Officers' Academy. Her father, her mother, Aunt Toma, Uncle Kolya, and even the unhappy Mayka, who was five years younger than Lyalya, had died during the past eighteen years. Her old theater friends had all disappeared, nor did she feel like seeing any of them. She had fought a long legal battle when they fired her. She fought desperately and had even developed asthma in the process, but all to no avail: she had been forced to give in. And now she had a new circle of friends—military people, engineers, and automobile enthusiasts. Vsevolod himself was crazy about cars, and every summer they and their friends would take off in two or three cars for the Crimea, or the Carpathians, or the Baltic. But as for her old theater friends, she only felt uncomfortable whenever she happened to run into them.

Once she bumped into her old friend Masha in line for pillows at GUM. How Mashka had changed! Not only had her face aged, but she had become affected and a bit spiteful. For some reason Masha began telling her about Smolyanov. As if she, Lyalya, were interested in hearing about him. Actually, she had trouble remembering what he looked like—whether he was fat or thin, and whether or not he wore glasses. Apparently he was hard up now and suffered from poor health. He was no longer writing plays and had to live off the income he got from renting his dacha to summer people. Well, so what—who cared? She really wasn't interested in hearing all this.

"And your Rebrov is having an affair with the daughter of one of my girl friends."

"Really?"

Though she assumed a look of indifference, Lyalya listened with interest as Masha began telling her about Rebrov. The girl in question had acted in one of his pictures, and the two of them had traveled together to some film festival in Argentina or Brazil—or one of those countries—and some common acquaintance had traveled with them.... But here Masha's account was broken off, for by now the two women had reached the counter and were quickly swallowed up in the surging crowd. Nor did Lyalya make any effort to find her friend after completing her purchase. Actually, she already knew from others that Rebrov was doing well— that he was earning good money from his movie scripts, that he lived in the southwest section of town, also had a car, and apparently had already been married twice. Such was the extent of her knowledge. And she was happy for him. After all, she had always had good feelings about him. There was one thing she didn't know, however, and which she wondered about. Did he often think about his life, evaluate it from every angle as he used to do—this had been one of his favorite pastimes, especially when he was traveling—and did it seem to him now that those years when he was poor and discouraged, when he envied, hated, suffered, and lived almost like a beggar were actually the best years of his life, since to be happy one needs equal portions of....

In the meantime Moscow was spreading out

farther and farther, beyond the circumferential highway, across fields and ravines. It was throwing up
building after building, stone mountains with a million
lighted windows; it was laying bare the ancient soil,
traversing it with giant concrete pipes, strewing the land
with foundation pits, laying asphalt, building up, tearing
down, destroying without a trace. And every morning
the subway platforms and bus stops would be swarming
with people, more and more of them crowded together
with each passing year. Lyalya would wonder in amazement: "Where have they all come from? Either there are
an awful lot of newcomers or else everyone's children
have suddenly grown up."

1971   *Translated by Helen P. Burlingame*